Luke Owen Pike

A Constitutional History of the House of Lords

Luke Owen Pike

A Constitutional History of the House of Lords

ISBN/EAN: 9783337338060

Printed in Europe, USA, Canada, Australia, Japan

Cover: Foto ©Andreas Hilbeck / pixelio.de

More available books at **www.hansebooks.com**

A

CONSTITUTIONAL HISTORY

OF THE

HOUSE OF LORDS

FROM ORIGINAL SOURCES

BY

LUKE OWEN PIKE, M.A.

OF LINCOLN'S INN, BARRISTER-AT-LAW, ASSISTANT KEEPER OF THE PUBLIC RECORDS, EDITOR OF THE
'YEAR BOOKS' PUBLISHED UNDER THE DIRECTION OF THE MASTER OF THE ROLLS
AUTHOR OF 'A HISTORY OF CRIME IN ENGLAND,' ETC.

London

MACMILLAN AND CO.

AND NEW YORK

1894

PREFACE

THOUGH there are many Constitutional Histories of England and Histories of Parliament, there has, it is believed, hitherto been no Constitutional History of the House of Lords. The reader in search of information could only extract it laboriously from disconnected passages in works of great length, or find it shaped as ammunition for the purposes of party warfare in political treatises. The scope of the present work is different from that held in view by such well-known historians as Hallam, May, Gneist, or Bishop Stubbs, or in the polemical essays of Prynne or Freeman. The materials used, though, to some extent, necessarily the same as those upon which they relied, have been largely drawn from other sources, and have been wrought to other ends. Statements of fact are consequently often inconsistent with those made in preceding works on the Constitution, but the original authorities on which they rest have been indicated. It has, therefore, been thought needless to point out the variations, except in some very remarkable instances.

One example may, perhaps, suffice to show that the reasons for differing from previous authors of repute could not always be set forth with a due regard for space, and may at the same time serve to illustrate the principles of original research on which the book has been written.

It was stated by Blackstone, nearly a century and a half ago, that the whole Act for the Uniformity of Common Prayer was passed 'with the dissent *of all the Bishops*' and that the words 'Lords Spiritual' were, for that reason omitted throughout. The statement has been repeated again and again in successive editions of his Commentaries, and in the latest editions of Commentaries founded upon his. Hallam also has asserted in his *Constitutional History* that 'all the Bishops' protested against the Bill.

Blackstone and his followers give as their authority Gibson's *Codex Juris Ecclesiastici*. Gibson, however, says not that the whole Act, but only that a portion of it, was passed by the 'Lords and Commons' without any use of the word 'Spiritual,' 'because all the Bishops *present* dissented,' and he cites D'Ewes's *Journals* in support of his proposition. In the edition of the Statutes entitled the 'Statutes of the Realm,' it is again said that a portion of the Act was passed without the assent of the Lords Spiritual, and again upon the authority of D'Ewes's *Journals*.

Upon reference to the passage cited it is found that D'Ewes does not speak either of all the Bishops, or even of all the Bishops who were present, as dissenting either from the whole or from any portion of the Bill, but mentions only the Archbishop of York and eight Bishops.

Hallam's authorities are the *Parliamentary History* and Strype's *Annals*. The *Parliamentary*

History affords no warrant for the assertion ; Strype's *Annals* show only the names of the dissenting Archbishop and eight dissenting Bishops, though they are in one passage described as 'all the Prelates.'

D'Ewes, who professes to have obtained his information from the original Journals of the House of Lords, alleges that the Bill was read a third time on the 28th of April, 1559. When, however, the printed Journals of the House of Lords are consulted it is seen that there is no record of any sitting between April 22 and May 1. So far, therefore, as printed documents are concerned, there is absolutely no authority for a very important statement which has passed unquestioned during some five generations. The statement is, however, not improbable in itself, and the question naturally arose whether it could be established by any Journals of the House of Lords which have, for any reason, not been printed.

Mr. E. Fairfax Taylor, of the Judicial Office of the House of Lords, whose very able Calendar of documents of the House is in course of publication, for the Historical MSS. Commission, has most kindly instituted a search, and I cannot too warmly express my thanks for the courtesy he has shown and the pains he has taken. He has succeeded in tracing the MS. Journal for the year 1559, which has served as the basis of the printed Journal. As in the latter, so in the former, the days between April 22 and May 1 are missing. The pages, however, are in due order of succession, and there is no reason to suppose that the MS. ever contained anything which has not been printed.

It is not known that the original Journals of the

period are in existence elsewhere. In the library of
the Inner Temple there are some copies of so-called
Journals of the House of Lords which I have in-
spected, and in which the missing days are included.
They do not, however, give the names of the Lords
who were present. They show that the Bill was
read a third time on April 28, and that the nine
prelates dissented, but nothing more. They are
evidently taken from the document with which
D'Ewes and Strype were acquainted, which must
have been merely a short note or abstract, and not
a true Journal of the House in the ordinary sense
of the term. D'Ewes, indeed, complains, in one
passage, of the carelessness shown by the Clerk
of the Parliaments, and it seems more than probable
that no complete Journal was ever drawn up. In
that case it would be impossible to prove the asser-
tions made by Blackstone, Gibson, and Hallam,
which have, in any case, been made on insufficient
authority.

The omission of the words 'Spiritual Lords'
from any particular Act, or portion of an Act, in the
reign of Elizabeth, affords no safe ground for an
argument that they all dissented. It was at that
time a common practice to omit all mention not
only of the Lords Spiritual, but also of all the
Estates of the Realm from individual Acts or
Chapters of a Statute, a not unusual form being
'by the authority of this present Parliament.'
There was, however, a general heading to the
Roll of Parliament, upon which all the Acts of
a Session were enrolled; and the heading to the
roll of 1559 is to the effect that the Act for
the Uniformity of Common Prayer was passed,

like the rest, 'with the common assent of all the Lords, as well Spiritual, as Temporal, and of the Commons.'

Having arrived at these curious and somewhat contradictory facts, I had to decide whether the mode in which the Act was passed should be mentioned in support of a portion of the text (p. 327), in which the relation of the Spiritual Lords to legislative power is considered. I came to the conclusion that (except the general heading of the Parliament Roll) there was not sufficient evidence on which to base any definite statement. The heading, however, might be a mere form implying no more than the consent of a majority of the House of Lords. The number of the Bishops present, and their action, could be authoritatively ascertained only from the original Journal of the House; and the condition in which the Journal is found is of itself sufficient to suggest the necessity of the utmost caution.

I hope, therefore, I may venture to ask those who find some familiar statement omitted, or meet with a statement which they did not expect, to believe that the cause is not in every case inadvertence.

The publication of this book at a time when there is some political agitation in reference to the House of Lords is an accident. The work has been written without any political intention, and, to the best of my belief, without any political bias. I trace back the first idea of it to a question which a learned friend asked me, long ago, as to the mode of trying John Fisher, sometime Bishop of Rochester. In the course of the twelve years during which I have been Editor of the *Year Books*, many points relating to the peerage have forced themselves upon my attention. I have found Bishops and Abbots commonly described as Peers of the Realm, and, for that and other reasons I have had to consider the status of Peers in general, their original position in the constitution, and the changes which it has undergone.

In excluding politics I have been compelled to exclude many matters of controversy. It could, I think, serve no good purpose to mention all the Bills which have been accepted in the House of Commons and rejected by the House of Lords, or which have been first brought into the House of Lords and have been sent thence to the House of Commons. I could not presume to say that either House had acted rightly or wrongly. In each case one party might hold one opinion, another party another opinion. To set down a bare catalogue of measures would be both wearisome and useless. I have even refrained from giving an account of the one Act which has acquired the special title of 'The Lords' Act'—that which was passed in 1758, for the relief of imprisoned debtors, and which, as its name imports, had its origin in the House of Lords. I have departed from the general rule only in cases in which the constitution of the House of Lords itself was affected, or appeared to be threatened with change.

For similar reasons I have noticed the increase of the peerage since the accession of George III in general terms only, and without reference to the . real or supposed motives of particular Ministers, in which, perhaps, one party might see the highest political virtue, another the lowest political depravity.

The orthography of early names is of no great importance in relation to the subject of the book. I need only say that I prefer Rollo to Rolf, Canute to Cnut, Ethelred to Æthelred, for two very simple reasons. I know that classical English writers have written the words as I have written them, and I do not know that there was any settled and invariable spelling when Rollo, Canute, and the Ethelreds lived. It is possible that 'Ælfred' may be good *Englisc*, but I think it can hardly be denied that 'Alfred' is good English.

Since the manuscript of the work left my hands, many events have happened which it has been impossible to notice in the text. A new ' Peers Disabilities Removal Bill' has been introduced into the House of Commons, but has not proceeded further. Important questions have arisen out of the death of Lord Coleridge, and the subsequent acceptance of the office of Steward of the Chiltern Hundreds by his eldest son and heir; but the evidence laid before the Committee of the House of Commons on the mode of vacating seats has not yet been officially published. There have been some remarkable discussions in the House of Lords on a Finance Bill; and a Report of the Judicial Committee of the Privy Council made in 1886, in relation to the Legislative Assembly of Queensland and Money Bills, has been brought into singular prominence during the arguments.

Some of these matters belong, perhaps, quite as much to the domain of modern politics as to history. None of them appear, thus far, to call for any modification of the following pages. That which has occurred in the past cannot be undone by the re-assertion of old or the development of new opinions or principles in the future:

τὸ γὰρ
φανθὲν τίς ἂν δύναιτ᾽ ἀγέννητον ποιεῖν;

I can only hope that the imperfections which may be noticed in my story, as I have told it down to the beginning of the present year, may be excused. The number of widely different subjects which it has been necessary to investigate must have given many opportunities for those errors which it is the innate human tendency to commit; but if revision after revision of the text, and verification after verification of the references are of any avail, the statements of fact should, at any rate, be in the main, correct.

AUGUST 27. 1894.

CONTENTS

CHAPTER I.

THE PRE-NORMAN PERIOD.

CHAPTER II.

THE IDEAS OF NOBILITY AND SUCCESSION BROUGHT BY THE CONQUEROR FROM FRANCE, AND THEIR SOURCES.

CHAPTER III.

Effects of the Conquest from William I to Henry I: the 'Witan' and Baronage mainly Foreigners.

CHAPTER IV.

The King's Court or Curia Regis: 'Parliament': Councils and their Subdivisions.

CONTENTS   XV

CHAPTER V.

EARLDOMS AS OFFICES: GROWTH OF HEREDITARY EARLDOMS: EARLDOMS BY TENURE, AND DUKEDOMS.

CHAPTER VI.

EARLY BARONIES: TENURE.

b

CHAPTER VII.

BARONY BY PATENT: BARONY BY WRIT: PRECEDENCE: ABEYANCE.

CHAPTER VIII.

THE DOCTRINE OF BLOOD.

CHAPTER IX.

THE POSITION OF THE SPIRITUAL LORDS.

CHAPTER X.

Judgement by Peers to the Reign of Richard II:
End of 'Appeals' in Parliament:
Beginning of Impeachments.

CHAPTER XI.

TRIAL BY PEERS FROM THE REIGN OF HENRY IV: COURT
OF THE LORD HIGH STEWARD: TRIAL OF SPIRITUAL
LORDS: TRIAL OF PEERESSES: IMPEACHMENTS.

CHAPTER XII.

Rights and Privileges in general of the House of Lords, and of its Members : Disabilities.

CHAPTER XIII.

THE JUDICATURE OF THE HOUSE OF LORDS IN GENERAL.

CHAPTER XIV.

Legislative Power.

CHAPTER XV.

CHANGES IN THE COMPONENT PARTS OF THE HOUSE OF LORDS.

PART I.

THE FEUDAL PERIOD: DISAPPEARANCE OF THE ABBOTS: THE POSITION OF THE CHANCELLOR: ABOLITION OF FEUDAL TENURES: COMMENCEMENT OF A NEW SYSTEM: PEERAGES AS REWARDS FOR POLITICAL SERVICE.

CHAPTER XV.

CHANGES IN THE COMPONENT PARTS OF THE HOUSE OF LORDS.

PART II.

INTRODUCTION OF THE PRINCIPLE OF REPRESENTATION AMONG PEERS: THE UNION WITH SCOTLAND: ATTEMPTS TO LIMIT THE PEERAGE: THE UNION WITH IRELAND.

CHAPTER XV.

CHANGES IN THE COMPONENT PARTS OF THE

HOUSE OF LORDS.

PART III.

RAPID INCREASE IN THE NUMBER OF PEERS: MODERN AT-
TEMPTS TO EXCLUDE THE BISHOPS: PEERAGES FOR
LIFE: CONCLUSION.

CONSTITUTIONAL HISTORY

OF

THE HOUSE OF LORDS

CHAPTER I.

THE PRE-NORMAN PERIOD.

IN tracing the history of the House of Lords, as consisting of two estates of the Realm—of the Lords Spiritual and the Lords Temporal—it is unnecessary to consider in very minute detail the events which preceded the Norman Conquest. There are, however, without doubt, some broad and well-marked features of earlier periods which can be recognized as persisting through the modifications caused by the lapse of time and the mutability of human affairs, and which, therefore, cannot be dismissed as absolutely irrelevant.

The titles of honour of the Temporal Lords are derived, in the first instance, from titles associated with some kind of service to the State or to the Sovereign—military service, or administrative service, or judicial service, or some combination of the three. This statement applies equally to Duke, Marquess, Count (or Earl), Viscount, and Baron. *The origin of temporal titles of honour.*

Comes, Comte, or Count may, perhaps, be regarded as the earliest of these titles. Even during the Roman occupation there were in Britain two *Comites*—one the *Roman Counts and Dukes in the*

B

CHAP. I.

Western Empire, and in Roman Britain.

Comes Saxonici Littoris per Britanniam, the other the *Comes Britanniarum*. The former, the Count of the Saxon Shore, had a military jurisdiction, which extended from Brancaster, in Norfolk, past Caistor and Yarmouth, round the Isle of Thanet (with garrisons at Reculver and Richborough) to Dover, and thence to Shoreham, with probably intermediate stations at Lymne, Hastings, and Pevensey. His power may possibly have extended further westward, but, as four out of his nine fortresses were almost certainly in Kent, it is clear that his chief strength was concentrated there. His nine castles are delineated in his ensign in the *Notitia Utriusque Imperii*[1]. The *Comes Britanniae*, or *Britanniarum*, had a much wider, if not a supreme military jurisdiction in Britain His ensign was one large fortress on an island somewhat in the shape of Great Britain ; and it is distinctly stated that he had under his disposition the *Provincia Britanniae*[2].

The signification of *Comes* or Count.

At different periods of Roman history the word *Comes* had different significations, but the only three which it is necessary to bear in mind are that of an officer having military authority, that of an officer having administrative jurisdiction, and that of the companion of the Sovereign. At the time of the compilation of the *Notitia* there appear to have been six *Comites rei militaris*[3] in the Western Empire, of whom two were the Counts in Britain already mentioned. There were many more in the Eastern Empire; and both in the Code of Theodosius and in the Code of Justinian there are divisions relating to these Counts for military affairs, and to the Counts who govern provinces[4].

The jurisdiction of the *Dux* or Duke.

The title which seems to be next, if not equal in antiquity, is that of Duke, which is also of Roman origin. There was during the Roman occupation of Britain a *Dux*

---

[1] *Notitia Occidentis,* cap. xxv, ed. Böcking, vol. ii. p. 80*, and Notes, p. 580* et seq.

[2] *Ib.,* cap. xxvi, ed. Böcking, ii. 82*.

[3] *Ib.,* cap. i, ed. Böcking, ii. 4*.

[4] *Comites qui provincias regunt,* Cod. Theod. lib. vi. tit. 14 and 17 ; Cod. Justin. lib. xii. tit. 12 and 14.

Britanniarum. His ensign, like that of the Count of the CHAP. I.
Saxon Shore, was an island with castles upon it, but he had
fourteen, while the Count had only nine. He had fourteen
prefects under his command, in addition to those holding
fortified posts along the line of the wall of Severus[1].
He was, like the Counts, a military officer, and his chief
duty was apparently to guard the northern frontier. He
was the only Duke in Britain; but there were eleven others
in other parts of the Western Empire[2].

Little or nothing is known from contemporary evidence Gap in the
of the events which happened in Britain for some genera- Britain
tions after the Romans finally abandoned the island. In after the
that part of it which was subsequently called England the of the
Roman language seems to have been effaced by Teutonic Romans.
forms of speech as effectually as the language of Gaul had
in an earlier age been supplanted by the Roman language
itself. The Christian religion, which must also have pene-
trated into Britain during the Roman occupation, was, so
far as is known, destroyed in the same district by the
invading Angles, Saxons, Frisians, and Jutes, who conquered
the land. The fate of the previous inhabitants must always
remain uncertain. It has been the theme of endless con-
jectures, of which probably the best are those founded on
the analogy of other countries, where Teutonic tribes came
into contact with Roman civilization.

Roman Britain, however, differed in one very important Differences
point from those continental provinces of the Roman the condi-
Empire which were overrun by Teutonic invaders. Being tion of
farther from Rome it was farther from the influence of the that of
Roman Church. The Christian religion in Britain appears Roman
at a very early date to have differed in some points from on the
the Roman doctrines, and, having less support, fell an easier Continent
prey to the invaders. The course of history was consequently
somewhat different. The language and the religion naturally perished together from similar causes.

[1] *Notitia Occidentis,* cap. xxxviii, ed. Böcking, ii. 112*.
[2] *Ib.,* cap. i.

CHAP. I.   An interval of more than a century and a half passed

Augus-   between the departure of the Roman legions and the arrival
tine's   of the Roman missionaries under Augustine, by whose means
mission :
Bishops   the inhabitants of the country which had been Roman Britain
and   again became Christians.   This was a very important epoch,
Abbots.
            not only in church history, but also in constitutional history,
            because bishops and abbots were to play a very important
            part in the moots, councils, and parliaments of a future age.
            Bishop and Abbot, like Count and Duke, were Roman
            words, but Roman only by adoption from other tongues.
            Bishop, the Latin *Episcopus*, came from the Greek 'Επίσκοπος,
            an overseer.   The word has gone through many changes in
            many languages, but both the English Bishop, and the
            French *Évêque*, though they have not a single letter in
            common, can be traced historically to the common ancestor,
            the Episcopus.   Abbot is said to be derived originally from
            the Syriac and Chaldee *Abba*, a father, but the word became
            thoroughly Romanized in the form *Abbas*, from which it
            has grown into modern European languages.

No firmly   When Christianity was at length firmly established in
established
kingdom of England, the Bishops and Abbots, but at first more par-
England   ticularly the Bishops, began to be leading men in the State.
before the
Conquest.   The sees, however, differed from those of later times.   It is,
            indeed of importance to remember that before the con-
            quest of England by William the Conqueror there had
            not practically been any firmly established kingdom of
            England.   The petty principalities into which we find it
            divided when it first appears in history had never lost their
            distinctive names, and had never been firmly united under
            one dynasty.   The first king of England was Athelstane,
            rather than Egbert; and he died only a hundred and
            twenty-six years before the battle of Hastings.   His English
            successors had but an unquiet time for half a century, when
            the invasions of the Danes ended in the recognition of Canute
            as king in 1016 ; and England remained under the sway of
            the Danes until the time of Edward the Confessor, who, if
            of English blood, was hardly English in his sympathies.
            The early bishoprics represented the successive conver-

sions of the petty chieftains who held sway in different
parts of England, and of their subjects. Canterbury and
Rochester represented the conversion of Kent; London
the conversion of the East Saxons and Middle Saxons;
York the conversion of Northumbria; Dorchester in Oxford-
shire the conversion of Wessex; Lichfield (at one time
made an Archbishopric) the conversion of Mercia; Dunwich
(afterwards Elmham, and Thetford, and still later Norwich),
the conversion of East Anglia; and Selsey (afterwards
Chichester) the conversion of Sussex.

New sees were subsequently created, and some re-
distributions of dioceses were effected, but originally each
little king of the Heptarchy, or Octarchy, had a Bishop,
who was the head of the Church in his little kingdom,
and who was his adviser in all religious affairs. From
a superior knowledge of letters the bishop also acquired
an influence which extended beyond his spiritual authority;
and, though somewhat changed in relative value, the
authority and the influence remained when England was
nominally united under one government.

Where once there had been petty kings or princes, there
were in later generations Earls, owing some sort of allegiance
to the King of England. Where there had been one Bishop
or Archbishop, there were bishops in greater number.
Still, there always remained a practice that the Bishop
should be the associate of the Earl, though his relative
importance diminished, as the Earls continued to be few
and the Bishops became many. At the Shire Moot, or
County Court, the Earl was supposed to be present with
the Bishop; but a single Earl must have sat in many Shire
Moots, while the Bishop had a seat in one only, or, at any
rate, in fewer than the Earl.

These lay and ecclesiastical magnates not only sat to
administer such law as was known in those times, in their
respective districts, but were summoned as *Witan* or wise
men to advise the King of England. Abbots also, or
some of them, at times formed part of the King's Council,
as well as other persons, of whom a greater or less number

CHAP. I. appear to have attended, or to have been summoned to attend, according to circumstances or to the particular object in view at the particular moment.

The titles of Lord and Earl : Lords and lordless men.   The origin of the two titles of Lord (*Hlaford*) and Earl (*Eorl*) is lost in the obscurities of an unlettered age, and the two words have become the playthings of rival philologists. Of the Saxon or 'Englisc' lords little is known with certainty except that which may be learned from the Saxon laws. Every man was supposed to have a lord[1] : and a lordless man was in evil plight[2]. Lords, too, might have over-lords, and the over-lord of all was the king. From one point of view the lord stood in a personal relation of superiority to those who were his men or vassals. From another point of view he was a land-holder who exacted services from his undertenants or his slaves. But there is nothing to show that every person who might be called lord was entitled or summoned to sit among the Witan; and it seems to be as a term of respect that the expression endured after the Conquest rather than as a term implying any right to legislate or to be the King's Counsellor.

Ealdorman or Alderman and Earl.   Earls, however, were in a different position, and it may be necessary to say a few words as to their early functions and status. Before the time of Canute the various divisions or shires appear to have been under the lay jurisdiction of an officer called *Ealdorman* or Alderman. whose authority was both military and civil. He appears to have been responsible for the military array of his particular shire, and to have sat with the Bishop in the Shire Moot for various legal and administrative purposes. His title is almost the exact equivalent in signification of the French *Seigneur*, each implying, in the first instance, seniority, and then, derivatively, respect and authority. While, however, the

---

[1] *Ancient Laws and Institutes of England.* There are abundant illustrations from the time of Wihtred (about 700 A. D.) downwards.

[2] He might be slain as a thief. Laws of King Athelstane I. *Ancient Laws and Institutes*, p. 85.

French *Seigneur* became a term implying chiefly lordship over land, the Alderman, though no doubt usually a land-owner, was, as Alderman, only an officer having certain duties and responsibilities. As land-owner the English equivalent of the French *Seigneur* was Lord.

The Alderman's title does not appear to have been strictly hereditary, though it may often have remained in the same family. The lands which an Alderman held he might have held by inheritance, but he was not necessarily land-owner over the whole of his shire, and consequently his honours did not necessarily descend with his lands. When he attested a charter in the Latin language he often called himself Duke, or rather *Dux*, the word being used perhaps as the equivalent of *Heretoga*, or military leader[1], more probably in imitation of Roman fashions. He was not, however, a Duke in the modern sense, possessing hereditary dignity without official responsibility. It was essential that he should be capable of service in the field, and if at his death he left only an infant son, that son would be wholly incapable of performing his duties either in the field or in the Shire Moot.

The territorial jurisdiction of the Alderman extended sometimes over a large district, sometimes over a com-paratively small district. It is not known with certainty when the country was first divided into 'shires'; it is hardly certain that any Alderman ever presided over a shire of exactly the same extent as one of those which are seen to be in existence in Domesday Book. He seems more frequently to have had the command over a territory representing one of the earlier kingdoms, as, for instance, Northumbria, Mercia, or East Anglia. The point is, however, of but little importance, because the title practically disappeared with the Danish supremacy under Canute. From that time forward the officer who exercised a similar jurisdiction was called *Eorl*, the modern Earl.

Marginal notes: Chap. I. — Alderman and *Dux* or Duke. — Territorial jurisdiction of Alderman or Earl.

---

[1] See, for instance, Kemble's *Codex Diplomaticus*, charter No. 219, and see *The Saxons in England*, ii. 129, note.

CHAP. I.   His authority also was not usually restricted to a single shire, as the shires are set forth in Domesday Book. In some parts of the country it seems to have been of variable extent, in others more nearly uniform from one generation to another. Sometimes one Earldom appears to have been more or less subordinate to another, and at other times to have been in no such subordination. Sometimes the Earldom passes from father to son, as if hereditary; sometimes, though not from father to son, yet from one member of a house to another member of the same house.

Earldoms before the Conquest not strictly hereditary.   There has been some evidence produced to the effect that. before the Norman Conquest, the Aldermanship or Earldom of Chester passed from father to son for seven successive generations[1]; but if so, the case was quite exceptional. The Earldom of Northumbria affords perhaps another illustration of the office or dignity being frequently in the hands of members of the same family. It does not, however, show an absolutely continuous hereditary descent, and it did not always pass as an undivided Earldom[2].

Absence of settled principles in England before the Conquest.   An Earldom, being a military, judicial, and administrative office, was necessarily subject to the inevitable rule that it must be in the hands of some person capable of executing it. The throne itself was not strictly hereditary, much less the official rank of an Earl. Moreover, the country had, since the departure of the Romans, never been in a condition sufficiently settled or even sufficiently civilized to render men familiar with the idea of definite principles

[1] The pedigree which is not, perhaps, to be taken otherwise than *cum grano salis* is appended to a MS. of Florence of Worcester cited by Dugdale, *Mon. Angl.* iii. 192, as belonging to the Archbishop of Armagh. I am indebted for the reference to Sir Francis Palgrave's *Rise and Progress of the English Commonwealth*, Part 2 (Proofs and Illustrations), p. ccxci.

[2] The genealogist may be interested by the comparison of the pedigree given by Florence of Worcester (English Hist. Soc.), ii. 251–2, with that given by Simeon of Durham (Rolls Series), ii. 197–9 and 382–4. Not only does one differ from the other, but neither agrees with the statement in the A. S. Chronicle, *anno* 1016, as to Eric the Dane having then become Earl.

remaining fixed from generation to generation. After the
Conquest there was some clamour for 'the laws of Edward
the Confessor,' but not for laws rendered venerable by
a higher antiquity. The six centuries which had elapsed
since the last of the Roman legions left the island, had not
sufficed for a reconstruction of the warring elements within
it, or even greatly changed the external conditions. The
country had never been free from intestine strife, and never
secure against the attacks of invaders from the Cimbric
Chersonese and its neighbourhood. A strong hand, a stern
discipline, and a genius for organization were required to
convert England into a homogeneous whole. They came
not from within, but from without. Harold's deficient
and comparatively ill-trained levies were as little able to
resist the French chivalry, under William of Normandy, as
any king reigning, or seeming to reign, in England, had
been able to mould his subjects into a well-governed
nation.

CHAPTER II.

CHAP. II.

Necessity of considering the ideas brought from France.

A S it was necessary to give some slight account of the position of the Bishops, the Abbots, the Earls, and the Lords whom William the Conqueror found when he made himself master of England, so also it is necessary to give some account of the organization and the ideas of nobility which he brought with him from Normandy. This can hardly be rendered intelligible without casting a retrospective glance at a far more remote period, and bringing to mind once again the Counts and Dukes (the *Comites* and *Duces*) of the Roman Empire.

Roman *Comites* and French Counts; the Counts and the *Missi*.

After the successful invasion of Gaul by Clovis in the year 486, and the establishment of his kingdom, the conquered territory was divided into districts which were placed under the government of Counts. Thus the old Roman term was preserved and applied to the divisions of the Frankish kingdom. It was for many centuries afterwards associated with a territorial jurisdiction in France, though the country passed through innumerable vicissitudes. The jurisdiction was not only military but civil, and in the time of Charlemagne there was an organization which very much resembles in principle, though not in the intervals of time, that of the County Court in relation to the Eyre in England in the thirteenth and fourteenth centuries. Charlemagne's

Missi, or Justices specially delegated, were four times
a year to hold pleas with the several Counts in some
convenient place, while each Count was in the intervening
time to hold his own pleas and was himself to do justice[1].

The title of Duke also became early associated in France
with territorial jurisdiction, and there seems, indeed, to
have been in some cases but little distinction between
a Duke and a Count, though in others the area of the
Count's authority was far more limited. The French *Duc*
derived his designation etymologically from the Roman
Dux, and there is every reason to believe historically also,
though he at length impressed upon it a more permanent
character than that of the Roman *Dux* in a Roman
Province.

It has, indeed, been suggested that the titles of Count
and Duke are historically of Teutonic, and not of Roman
origin, though no one has yet been bold enough to deny
that the words can be clearly traced downwards from
the times of the Roman Empire. The tribes which overran Romanized Gaul, as well as the tribes which overran
Romanized Britain, had, in their own dialects, a word which
was nearly the equivalent of the Roman *Dux* in its original
sense of the leader of an army. This took various forms,
Heretog, Hertog, Heertog, Heretoga, Heretocha, or, in High
German, *Herzog*. It does not appear, however, that before
any contact of Teutonic peoples with the Romans, the term
implied any territorial jurisdiction. Every fighting tribe
or nation must, of course, have had a leader of its forces,
but only a great and long established Empire like that
of Rome could, in the first instance, have given the
leaders of its forces a clearly defined territoral jurisdiction
passed on from one leader to his successor. A Duke of
the Frankish Empire or Kingdom had more in common with a Roman *Dux*, such as the *Dux Mauritaniae
Caesariensis*, the *Dux Pannoniae Secundae*, the *Dux Belgicae*

Marginal notes: Roman *Duces* and French *Ducs*. The German *Comites* of Tacitus; the German *Heretogs*, or leaders of armies.

---

[1] *Caroli Magni Capitularia*, ed. Pertz, *Capitulare Aquisgranense*
(A. D. 812), § 8 (vol. i. p. 174).

CHAP. II. *Secundae*, the *Dux Germaniae Primae*, or the *Dux Britan-niarum*[1] whose head-quarters were at York, than with a general of forces destined for the invasion of the lands of a neighbouring tribe or of the Roman Empire itself.

There are some often quoted passages in the *Germania* of Tacitus from which it has been argued that the continental title of Count is of purely Teutonic origin. The words of Tacitus, if they could be rightly interpreted to support this remarkable proposition, could with equal propriety be adduced to prove that the worship of Mercury was learned from the Germans (who offered human sacrifices to that god) as well as the worship of Hercules and Mars, to whom the Germans sacrificed animals[2]. According to this author, who nowhere states the sources of his information, the German tribes or nations had kings who were chosen by reason of noble birth, and *Duces* or leaders who were chosen for their valour. These kings had not absolute power ; and the leaders were popular in proportion to the distinction of their services in the field[3]. There were councils of two kinds, those in which the *principes* or chiefs took part, and those in which the whole tribe was present. In the former, matters of smaller moment were settled ; matters of greater importance were decided in the latter, though discussed in the former. The chiefs or *principes* were elected in council and their function was to administer justice in different districts. 'A hundred *Comites*, from among the people, attend upon each, at once constituting his council and lending him authority.' A very young man of princely rank might, without degradation, be one of the *Comites* of another chief[4], and there were various degrees of *Comites* regulated according to the pleasure of the chief whom they followed.

[1] *Notitia Utriusque Imperii*, cap. v, ed. Böcking, vol. ii. p. 23*.

[2] Tac. *Germ.*, cap. 9. Caesar's description is entirely at variance with that of Tacitus. According to him the Germans had no gods but the Sun, the Moon, and Vulcan or Fire, and had never heard of any others. Caesar, *Comm. de Bell. Gall.* vi. 21.

[3] Tac. *Germ.*, cap. 7.

[4] *Ib.*, caps. 11-13.

On these passages which are in themselves very obscure, has been built the theory that the mediaeval Counts are the representatives of the *Comites* or 'Companions' who attended the German *Principes*. There is however, not the slightest evidence to show that any one of these companions ever had any territorial jurisdiction whatever. It was the *Princeps*, whatever he may have been, who had jurisdiction. His *Comites* or companions were young men, or men of martial prowess, and not sage elders. In epigrammatic language Tacitus says 'the *Principes* fight for victory, the *Comites* for the *Princeps*[1].'

Attempts have been made to show a connexion between the High German *Graf* (the modern High German equivalent of the French *Comte*) and the English or rather '*Englisc*' *Gerefa* (*Reeve*), and to make both equivalents of the dignity to which Tacitus gives the name *Comes*. It is not by any means certain that there is any affinity between *Gerefa* and *Graf*, and it appears highly improbable that the word *Graf*, which is always associated with the name of a place, can in any way be traced back to the *Comes* or companion of a German *Princeps*. The most remarkable effort in this direction was made by the distinguished philologist Grimm[2], who derived *Gerefa* from *Rôf* a roof, suggesting apparently that *Gerefa* and *Graf* meánt a companion in the sense of a person who shared the same roof, just as *Gefährte* means a person who travels with another, or is his travelling companion. The derivation, it is true, was put forward only interrogatively; but in all its vagaries philology probably never wandered further astray than in this conjecture. The last thing of which, according to Tacitus, one of the ancient German *Comites*, as the Roman called them, would have thought, was a roof. Not only were his dominant ideas those of glory in the field, but he and his fellow-countrymen had no knowledge of the use of mortar or tiles[3].

Gerefa and *Graf*; Grimm's etymology untenable.

---

[1] Tac. *Germ.*, cap. 14.
[2] *Deutsche Grammatik*, ii. 737, 'Rôf (Tectum) daher Geréfa (Socius, Comes)?'
[3] Tac. *Germ.*, cap. 16.

The slender, vague, and contradictory notices in the works of Caesar and Tacitus cannot be supplemented by any German writings of the same period, or of any period within some hundreds of years afterwards. There is no German literature of any kind whatever of earlier date than the translation of portions of the Bible into Gothic by Ulfilas near the end of the fourth century; and this, of course, throws not the least light upon German manners and customs. It tells us, indeed, that German literature began when Germany had felt the influence of the Roman Empire, and through the Roman Empire, of Christianity.

The first real glimpse which can be obtained of Teutonic laws presents itself to us after the Teutonic tribes had settled in portions of the Roman Empire, and then, so far as the continent is concerned, they have, for the most part, arrayed themselves in the Latin language. As might have been expected *a priori*, these laws of kindred tribes, settled in different portions of the same empire, have much in common, though differing in many of their details There is a family likeness between the laws of the Visigoths in Spain, those of the Lombards in Italy, and those of the Burgundians, and those of the Franks, whether Ripuarian or Salic, in Gaul.

While, however, there is only similarity in laws there is absolute identity in titles and terms of respect, and they are, without exception, of Roman origin. As in France, so in Spain and Italy, the two Roman titles of *Dux* and *Comes* were perpetuated, with an uninterrupted succession, from the time of the Roman Empire into times when the imperial ideas of government and of society had given place to ideas wholly different and even utterly opposed. The *Duque* and the *Conde* in Spain survived the Vandals, the Visigoths, and the Moors. The *Duca*, the *Doge*, and the *Conte*—titles which had had their origin in Italy itself —were preserved in Italy through successive generations. They were different, it is true, from the Roman *Duces* and *Comites*, but different only as a descendant differs from an ancestor.

Concurrently with the titles of Count and Duke there Chap. II.
must have continued in Gaul, Italy, and Spain another The
Roman term of great significance—that of *Senior*, used French
originally in the sense of an elder, afterwards in the sense *Seigneur* : Seigneur
of one entitled to respect—the French *Seigneur*, the Italian and Lord of Parlia-
Signor, the Spanish *Señor*. Like many other words it ment.
probably existed in conversational Latin, or the Latin of
the lower classes, and asserted itself when the Empire had
fallen on evil days, when literature had decayed, and when
the colloquial speech of the inferior population alone remained to perpetuate the imperial language. It probably
descended from a very remote period when the Senate
consisted of a Council of Elders, and when one of the
qualifications for the rank of Senator was that of being
a Senior [1].

Whatever the origin of the word, however, it is of importance in the sense which it acquired in France, of lord,
or person having seignory in the legal sense of the term.
It came to be used in Law French in England, sometimes
in this sense, and sometimes also in the sense of a Lord of
Parliament.

In Spain, Italy, and Gaul, the barbarian invaders very Adoption
soon adopted, not only the language and the titles which of the Roman
they found existing in the conquered lands, but the religion religion
also. They came as heathens, they remained as Christians. by the barbarian
While however they adopted the titles and the faith which invaders.
they found in the conquered lands, the form of government
was necessarily modified by new conditions. The new

---

[1] It is curious to find in Livy the *Patres Conscripti* or Senators
divided into *Seniores* and *Juniores*, the greater respect being for the
Seniores :—'consulibus et senioribus patrum,' Liv. ii. 30; '*Consulares
ac Seniores,*' Livy iii. 41. It has been suggested that *Dominus*, lord,
was replaced by the Latin *Senior* only as a translation of the
German *Elder*.—Professor Max Müller's *Lectures on the Science of
Language*, i. 229. This theory is noted; but it would be a very
remarkable coincidence if all the tribes which invaded France, Italy,
and Spain, always used the word elder, as the only word expressing
lordship, and if all the inhabitants of all those countries translated
it by the same Latin word.

CHAP. II. comers did not rule, as Rome had ruled, by an organization having their ancient home for its centre. When Romans conquered a province they conquered it for Rome; when the barbarians conquered a province they conquered it for themselves, made it their habitation, and severed themselves from their mother country for ever.

Power acquired by the Bishops and Abbots. The outcome was everywhere very similar and very remarkable. The Church acquired an extraordinary power over the invaders, or, at any rate, the descendants of the invaders who had come in without any knowledge of the Christian religion. It is said that in their native wilds the Teutonic chieftains never had absolute power. They certainly had not when they settled in foreign lands and accepted a foreign faith. They had always, perhaps, been controlled by a council of some kind ; they may possibly have taken advice of some of their pagan priests in their northern homes ; but until they reached their new settlements their acts and their counsels were never influenced by a hierarchy which, in spite of occasional bursts of heresy, acknowledged the Roman Pontiff as its head. They imposed a yoke on those who had once been subjects of the Roman emperors, and themselves accepted the guidance of Bishops who represented a spiritual instead of a temporal Roman Empire.

The power of the Bishops, supplemented by that of the Abbots, varied in different kingdoms or dukedoms, and at different times, but the prelates everywhere succeeded in obtaining a place in the councils of the sovereign, and in the deliberative assemblies of the nation—in France no less than elsewhere. The barons or lay tenants-in-chief also had their place in these councils and assemblies, but it appears to have been usual to give the prelates precedence, as they are commonly mentioned first when any council or assembly is noticed.

Dukes and Counts, Bishops and Abbots, through- It thus appears that, wherever there was a Teutonic settlement in a portion of the Western Empire, the form of government and the social condition differed alike from those of imperial Rome and from those which, according

to Tacitus, existed in ancient Germany. In names or titles, CHAP. II.
however, the old Roman influence prevailed. Dukes and out the
Counts, Bishops and Abbots were borne above the deluge Teutonic settlements
of foreign invasion; and although Barons, and at a later in the
period Marquesses were added to their ranks, a majority Western Empire.
of Roman appellations has always been maintained on the
continent.

Some four hundred years after the Western Empire had Parallel between
perished, Rollo the Northman fell upon a province of the oc-
France, very much as the Franks and other tribes had cupation of Neustria
fallen upon Roman Gaul. Then occurred a very curious by the
repetition of history. The Normans who overran and Northmen and of
settled in Neustria accepted the language, the religion, and portions of
even the political institutions of the French, just as the the Roman Empire by
Franks and other tribes had a few centuries before accepted earlier invaders.
the language and the religion of the Romans. Normans
became French Counts and afterwards Dukes, like other
French Counts and Dukes with a territorial jurisdiction.
It might indeed almost be said that they became more
French than the French themselves, and gave increased
vitality to the feudal system which they adopted.

Though less than two centuries elapsed between the The Normans
descent of Rollo the Northman upon Neustria in 876, and accept the
the battle of Hastings in 1066, the interval sufficed not only religion and
to efface the differences between the inhabitants of Normandy language
and the inhabitants of the rest of France, but even to of France.
render the inhabitants of Normandy proud of the title of
Frenchmen. They called themselves not Normans, but
Frenchmen, and it was as Frenchmen that they distinguished themselves from the English whom they had
overcome and in whose land they had settled. In most
of our records [1], when occasion arises to draw a distinction

[1] The *Dialogus de Scaccario*, lib. i. cap. 10, may perhaps be cited as
an exception. The *Francigenae* are there called *Normanni*; but the
Dialogus, though appearing in the Red Book and in the Black Book
of the Exchequer, is not a record of legal proceedings. It is merely
a treatise which has been bound up with other matter relating to the
Exchequer. The term used in rolls and charters is *Francigenae*;

CHAP. II. between the two populations, the English are described as *Angli* or *Angligenae*, the invaders from Normandy and their descendants as *Franci* or *Francigenae*.

The hereditary principle in France: succession of the Counts and Dukes of Normandy. The ideas which William the Conqueror brought with him were, therefore, the ideas of Frenchmen. The feudal system had reached maturity in France, and William himself held his Duchy of Normandy as a fief of the French crown. The principle of hereditary succession appears to have been now accepted in relation to the kingdom of France itself, to the great French fiefs, of which the Duchy of Normandy was one, and to the lands held of the greater feudatories by subinfeudation. Hugh Capet had transmitted the crown of France to his son, to his grandson, and to his great grandson, Philip I ; and it was destined to be transmitted to his descendants for many generations afterwards. In the County, or, as it afterwards became, the Duchy of Normandy, the principle had been recognized without interruption from the time of Rollo. Rollo, on his abdication, was succeeded by his son William, and William, who left no legitimate issue, by his natural son (though a minor) Richard I. Richard II (though also a minor) succeeded his father Richard I, and was, in turn succeeded by his eldest son Richard III. On the death of Richard III, apparently without issue, he was succeeded by his brother Robert, who left no legitimate offspring. Robert's natural son, William II, however, was, like Richard I, recognized as the heir, though a minor only some nine years of age.

Contrast between the principles accepted in Normandy and those accepted in England. In Normandy, it will be observed, the succession from father to son was maintained in the most adverse circumstances, the omission of the marriage ceremony by the parents not being regarded as an objection to the child when the child was duly recognized by the father. William the Second of Normandy was William the Conqueror—William the First of England. According to our later law he would

the latter term is more correct in every way, as the Conqueror's followers were not all from Normandy.

have been styled 'no man's son' (*nullius filius*).   He,
however, represented, in his own person, according to the
manners and customs of the age, two principles which had
been consistently followed since the time of his ancestor
Rollo—the principle of hereditary succession, and the
principle that the rights of a minor were not to be set
aside.

The principles which were observed in the case of the
Norman Counts and Dukes who held of the King of
France, were without doubt observed in the case of the
vassals who held of the Duke of Normandy.   In both
cases they may have had to undergo the strain of an
ambitious and turbulent nobility always ready for war and
always seeking self-aggrandizement.   In France they bore
the strain and survived ; in England they never completely
asserted themselves before the time of the Conquest.   Of
the two previous kings of England one (Edward the Confessor) was not the direct heir to the throne, and the other
(Harold) had no title but that of election.

CHAPTER III.

CHAP. III.

The Conqueror assumes the part of rightful sovereign, recognizing the privileges of his English subjects.

THE Conqueror, though he had no sort of hereditary right to the throne, had, as was alleged, the expressed wish of Edward the Confessor that he should succeed, and had, after the battle of Hastings, the assent of the majority of the people. He took the coronation oath which appears to have been usually taken by English kings. He assumed at first the position of lawful successor to Edward, of a victorious and rightful sovereign who had delivered his country from the usurper Harold. Except those who had borne arms against him, he did not immediately dispossess the English landholders of their lands. Though he regarded Stigand, the English Archbishop of Canterbury, with disfavour, he did not immediately dispossess the English bishops of their bishoprics. He accepted his consecration at the hands of Aldred, the English Archbishop of York, sent his greeting to the Londoners in their own language, confirmed their privileges and those of other townsmen, and even extended the hand of friendship to Edgar the Atheling, who, if the principles of hereditary succession had been followed in England as they were in Normandy, would now have been King.

Delusive character of the as-

Partly for these reasons, and partly because there is a fashion in history, as in most mundane affairs, there has

of late years been a tendency to minimize the effects of the Conquest. The natives of England continued to speak of Earls after the Conquest as they had spoken of Earls before. They spoke of William meeting his *Witan* just as they had spoken of Edward the Confessor and of earlier kings. There were still Sheriffs in the shires, and Moots still assembled in them. *Saç* and *soc*, *tol* and *team*, *infangenetheof* and *utfangenetheof*, and many other words of sound as sweet to native ears were still applied to native customs not yet extinct. How then did the Conquest change the government of England?

At first sight the answer to this question might seem to be that no change of great importance was effected. And if mere words were regarded, instead of the facts underlying them, the same answer might be given even after closer inspection. Any person, however, writing the *Englisc* language of the day could only express himself as that tongue permitted him. According to his education there was but one word to convey all that was signified by the Latin *Dux*, *Comes*, or *Princeps*, by the French *Duc* or *Comte*, and that word was *Eorl*. According to his ideas the persons who constituted the council of a sovereign or quasi-sovereign were *Witan*, and any assembly of such persons was a *Witenagemot*. William himself, regarded as Duke of Normandy, or rather of the Normans, was *Eorl*[1], and whenever he held a council it was necessarily a *Witenagemot* or Council of *Witan*. When a French follower of the Conqueror became possessed of an English lordship he became possessed of all its incidents. It was nothing to him that the natives called them by the accustomed names, for which he had the most profound contempt. He took his privileges and his profits, his *sac* and his *soc*, his *tol* and his *team*, his *infangenetheof*, and his *utfangenetheof*. The greater the privilege and the greater the profit, by whatsoever names they might be called, the better he was pleased.

---

[1] A. S. Chron. A.D. 1052. See also A.D. 1031, 'Robert Eorl of Normandi,' and A.D. 1087, where William's eldest son Robert is 'Eorl on Normandi.' A foreign Count is always 'Eorl' in the Chronicle.

CHAP. III. The natives, whose master he had become, may have called him lord, as they had previously called the native lord who had been ousted. He did not so style himself. He was their *Seigneur*, his right was seignory, and as seignory it was known ever afterwards in the laws of the country.

If William was elected King in a Witen-agemot, it was not a Witenage-mot of Englishmen alone. The *Witan* assembled after the Conquest[1], but they were never again the *Witan* which had assembled before. The *Englisc* words *Witan* and *Witenagemot* conceal a revolution under identity of expression. From the very moment of William's coronation there was a change which became greater and greater during his reign and those immediately succeeding. His title, if not that of the sword, or of the bequest of Edward the Confessor, was elective; but his election was not in an English *Witenagemot*. The French invaders were present as well as the English *Witan*, and though the Archbishop of York asked the English whether they would have William for their king, the Bishop of Coutances put the same question to the French[2]. His election was an election by both, but, so far as the English were concerned, practically under compulsion. The Council of the Conqueror was never wholly English, and in the time of his son Henry I the process of denationalization was almost complete.

Gradual substitution of foreign for native dignitaries both lay and ecclesiastical. Nothing, perhaps, reveals more clearly than contemporary charters the policy of the Conqueror and the yoke under which the English were being passed. They show by their attestations the persons by whom he was surrounded, and who constituted his Council. He would have been more than human had he not more trusted those who had supported him in his enterprise, and to whom he owed his success, than those whom he had vanquished, and who would have expelled him as an usurper had they only had the power. Before he had been fifteen years upon the throne he had abandoned all pretence of recognizing native laymen as his councillors, and he had made great progress

---

[1] A. S. Chron. A. D. 1085, and even A. D. 1100.
[2] Gul. Pict., *Gesta Guillelmi Ducis*, pp. 205-6.

in placing the highest dignities of the English Church in the hands of foreigners. Lanfranc, the Archbishop of Canterbury, was an Italian from Milan; Thomas, the Archbishop of York, was a Frenchman from Normandy, and other English sees had also foreign occupants. The Abbeys and Priories alone appear for some time to have retained native English Heads.

By a reflected light, as it were, the word 'Parliament' may be carried back to the reign of the Conqueror—to the year 1081, though it does not seem to have come into use for some time afterwards. An assembly which was then held is described in a law report of the reign of Edward III[1] as a Parliament. It was not, nor was it represented as being a Parliament in the modern sense, but it was that kind of Parliament to which the term has for centuries been applied when reference was made to the judicial functions of the House of Lords.

On May 31, in the fifteenth year of the Conqueror's reign, was decided a very important cause arising out of a dispute between the Abbot of Bury St. Edmund's and Arfastus or Herfastus, Bishop of Thetford, to the effect that the Bishop could not exercise the rights of Ordinary over the Abbot. The judgement was then embodied in the form of a charter with a recital of the proceedings[2], the names of various persons being appended as those of witnesses.

The persons who were present in the 'Parliament' are described in the later law report as 'the Archbishop of Canterbury, and all the other Bishops of the land, Earls, and

---

[1] Year Book, 21 Ed. III, fo. 60 (No. 7).

[2] The instrument has been printed several times. It appears in the editions of Dugdale's *Monasticon Anglicanum*, and in the recently published *Memorials of St. Edmund's Abbey* (Rolls Series) vol. i. pp. 347–50. The charter itself was, in the form of attestation, not unlike those immediately preceding the Conquest, and there is one (of the year 1021) to the same Abbey which is very similar, though no Chancellor there appears. It is the recital of the judicial proceedings and judgement by 'Parliament' (as the assembly is styled in the Year Book) which gives importance to the Conqueror's charter to the Abbey of Bury. The proceedings are described in the *Memorials*, i. 65–67.

CHAP. III. Barons,' though they were not described precisely in those
Bishops, words in the charter itself. In one part of the charter they
Abbots, appear as the Archbishops of Canterbury and York, Odo
Earls, and
other (the King's half-brother), Bishop of Bayeux and Earl of Kent,
Principes several other Bishops. the King's son Robert and 'other
of the
Realm, or *principes* of our realm (*regni nostri*).' In another part they
Proceres. are mentioned as 'Archbishops, Bishops, Earls, and other
our faithful knights (*aliorumque militum nobis fidelium*).'
The King himself impressed the sign of the cross upon the
charter in token of confirmation. The witnesses were the
Queen, Matilda, the Archbishops of Canterbury and York,
Odo, Bishop of Bayeux, and the Bishop of Coutances, the
Bishops of London, Winchester, Worcester, Lindisfarn (or
Holy Island), 'Bath,' Exeter. Chester, Thetford (party in
the cause), Rochester, Salisbury, and Hereford, and the
King's three sons, Robert. William, and Henry. All of
these added some word of agreement, consent, or approbation. The Chancellor, Maurice, added that he had read
the document and sealed it. The following witnessed the
instrument without further remark : the King's chaplain,
the Abbots of St. Augustine's (Canterbury), Chertsey,
Westminster, Glastonbury, Evesham, Ramsey, and Peter-
borough (who for the most part bore English names) ; Roger,
Earl of Montgomery ; Hugh, Earl of Chester ; Alan, Earl
of the East Angles ; Aubrey, Earl of the Northumbrians ;
Robert de Beaumont, and Hugh de Montfort. Richard,
son of Earl Gilbert, added the word *consignavi*, and following him, without comment, are his brother Baldwin, Henry
de Ferrers, Hugh de Grentmesnil, and Walter Giffard.

It is not certain that the whole of these witnesses were
present in the Council or ' Parliament ; ' but all those who
were present were regarded as being either Prelates or
Principes (who were also knights) ; and these *Principes* were,
in the time of Edward III, understood to be Earls and
Barons. The Conqueror in his charter describes himself as
King of the English and *Princeps Normannorum*. He was
a *Princeps* in relation to the crown of France. The lay
members of his Council, perhaps the whole of the members

(for that is a question of construction), were *Principes* of his CHAP. III.
Realm, and, although the expression 'Peers of the Realm'
had not yet come into use in England, it is not difficult to
see how the Principes of the realm of one reign became
the Peers of the realm of another. In the writ[1] which
followed the judgement and was addressed to Roger
Bigod as Sheriff, the assembly is described as having
consisted of the 'Archbishops and Bishops, Abbots and
Earls, and other my *Proceres*.' In later times, and down
even to the present day, the Latin equivalent for the House
of Lords has been *Domus Procerum*.

Though the Council or 'Parliament' which heard and Foreigners
determined the cause may have included persons whose were now
of the
names do not appear as witnesses to the charter, and though nobility of
England,
it is possible that some of the witnesses to the charter may and de-
not actually have sat in the Council or 'Parliament,' there scribed as
Witan.
is no reason to suppose that the two classes were very
widely different. One of the most remarkable facts to be
observed in the list of persons is that some are identical
with those who attended William's Council in Normandy
before the final decision was taken to risk the invasion of
England. Both Odo, Bishop of Bayeux (and now Earl of
Kent), and Roger, Earl or Count (*Comes*) of Montgomery,
had given their advice in favour of the undertaking, and
Walter Giffard was, if not the same person, a son of the
Walter Giffard who was present on that occasion[2]. These
and others had now become English nobles, as possessing
English lands, and were among the *Witan* of the King of
England, as they had been and still were among the
Council of the Duke of Normandy. Thus the first assembly
in England to which the word 'Parliament' has been
applied by any legal authority, was an assembly resembling
the House of Lords in its constitution, but consisting largely
of foreigners.

[1] Printed in *Memorials of St. Edmund's Abbey* (Rolls Series), vol. i.
p. 350.
[2] Gul. Pict., *Gesta Guillelmi Ducis*, p. 197; Wace, *Roman De Rou*
(ed. Pluquet), 11124-11130.

CHAP. III.

The
Witan,
baronage,
or Parlia-
ment,
chiefly
foreigners
in the
reign of
Henry I.

When all the Earls and greater Barons, and most of the Bishops were foreigners, the Abbeys and Priories could not long retain native Heads. Many vacancies had occurred during or before the reign of Henry I, and had not been filled up; but when that King was about to embark for Normandy in the year 1114 he bethought him of making good the omission. It is expressly stated that what he did was done by the advice of his Bishops and *Principes*. The Bishops and *Principes*, not being of English extraction, did not wish men of English extraction to be advanced to high places. All the new Abbots were foreigners, not one of English birth. If any man was an Englishman, piteously complains the chronicler of the day, no merit could aid him to be considered worthy of any honour. If any man was a foreigner, he was straightway thought worthy of the highest honours of all [1].

Thus the King's Council, his *Witan*, his baronage, and, according to the ideas of a somewhat later time, his Parliament, had almost wholly ceased to be English. He had advisers of the same class as Ethelred II, but advisers who were in a different position with regard to the lower population. They were the foreign advisers of a foreign king ruling a subject people, the ruler and the ruled speaking different languages, and having no sympathies in common.

The upper classes by degrees adapted themselves to the situation. They learned to speak French, intermarried with their rulers, had their children baptized with names imported from France, and at last became indistinguishable from the French themselves. This fusion among the higher ranks is said to have been complete towards the end of the reign of Henry II, though it had not affected the serfs, villeins, or unfree people, who retained their native language [2]. In their case the difference of race did not cease to be recognized until the reign of Edward III, when the 'Presentment of Englishry,' the last badge of subjection, was abolished [3]:

[1] Eadmer, *Hist. Nov. in Angl.* (Rolls Series), p. 224.
[2] *Dialogus de Scaccario*, lib. i. cap. 10.
[3] 14 Ed. III, stat. 1. cap. 4.

CHAPTER IV.

TO the *Curia Regis*[1] (or King's Court) may be traced
a great part of our early constitution. The expression,
however, was used in various senses, and the institution developed in various directions. The King was, in the early
days after the Conquest, as well as before it, in the habit
of holding his Court (in *Englisc* his *hired*) at different places
and times, though usually the times were coincident with
the three great festivals of the Church. The Court was an
assemblage of the principal persons of the realm, lay and
ecclesiastical—of the Earls and Barons, of the Bishops and
Abbots, and of the great officers of state. Its meeting was
the opportunity for them to pay respect to the Sovereign,
as at a modern Court, though many kinds of business were
also transacted. It is often indistinguishable from the *Commune Concilium*, or the '*Englisc*' Witenagemot, at which
advice might be taken, and aids granted. It was moreover
a Court in the legal sense of a Court of Justice[2].

CHAP. IV.

The Curia Regis or King's Court: Royal Court, and Court of Justice.

[1]. With regard to judicature it is not unusual to find *Aula Regis*, or
Aula Regia, used by modern writers as a synonym for *Curia Regis*.
The *Aula* was at most but a small part of the *Curia Regis*, in any of
its senses, and had relation to the household of the King. There are
still extant *Placita Aulae* of various reigns. The proceedings were
before the Steward and Marshal of the Household.

[2] In the *Reports from the Lords Committees, touching the Dignity
of a Peer of the Realm*, vol. i. p. 20, it is suggested that 'the Supreme

CHAP. IV.   In the latter sense it was a Supreme Court, having within itself the powers of a court of first instance, of a court to which causes could be removed from courts below, and of a court of error or appeal. It had, in an inchoate form, all the functions subsequently divided between the Court of Common Pleas, the Court of King's Bench, the Privy Council, the Exchequer Chamber, and the House of Lords. The Court of Exchequer seems to have been distinguished in very early times from the King's Court as a whole, because when not mentioned simply as the Exchequer, it is described as the King's Court at the Exchequer[1]. The Chief Justiciary, however, sat there as well as in other courts. The time at which the division of jurisdiction (apart from that of the Exchequer) began is not easily to be fixed with precision. It can, however, be shown to have begun much earlier than the date usually assigned—than the granting of *Magna Charta* by King John.

Cases heard in the King's Court or 'Parliament.' William I to Henry I.   We have already seen how the King's Court, or *Curia Regis*, was exercising judicial functions in the reign of the Conqueror, and how the lawyers of the reign of Edward III were unable to distinguish it from a Parliament. In the year 1096, William II and all his *Optimates*, or *Witan*, were at Salisbury, where Geoffrey Bainard accused William de Eu of conspiring against the King. The fact was decided by battle, and the King passed sentence against the offender[2]. Rufus also held his Court for the first time in the new Hall at Westminster in 1099[3]. In the reign of Henry I it is found that the Earls and Barons of all England assembled at Salisbury in the year 1116, and there heard the cause

Court of Justice denominated *Curia Regis* ' was the King's ' Select Council '—a small body chosen by the King, and consisting, in the main, of the judges and great officers of State. Sufficient evidence will be adduced in the following pages to show that the original *Curia Regis* was not so limited, and that the real fountain of justice was the *Commune Concilium Regni*, which afterwards became ' the King in his Council in his Parliament.'

[1] *Curia Regis ad Scaccarium.*
[2] A. S. Chron., A. D. 1096. Hoveden (Rolls Series), vol. i. p. 151.
[3] A. S. Chron., A. D. 1099.

between the Archbishop of Canterbury and the Archbishop CHAP. IV.
elect of York[1]. In the year 1123 the King held a Court,
Council, or, as the native writer calls it, *gewitene mot*, at
Gloucester in which was elected an Archbishop of Canterbury (William de Corbeuil), though apparently there were
many dissentients, including Earls and Barons. In the
year 1124 King Henry I was in Normandy, but in his
absence a *gewitene mot* was held under Ralph Basset
(presumably Chief Justiciary), at which sentence was passed
on a great number of thieves, of whom forty-four were
hanged and six mutilated[2].

Up to this point it is, perhaps, equally difficult to prove Judicial
and to disprove that there was any division of jurisdiction, functions of
except in so far as Justices in Eyre or Justices Itinerant *Regis* in the
may have carried a delegated authority into the shires. reign of
Legal or constitutional reforms were hardly possible during indications
the disturbed reign of Stephen. In the time of Henry II, of division.
however, it may be considered certain that the whole of the
functions of the *Curia Regis* were not discharged by one
undivided Court. Still there are instances in this, as indeed
in subsequent reigns, in which the King's Court is seen to
be constituted as the full King's Court had been continuously
since the Conquest. A famous meeting at Clarendon in the
year 1164, at which the Earls and Barons were present, and
from which Becket, Archbishop of Canterbury, withdrew, is
distinctly called the *Court*[3]. In the same or following year
King Henry II assembled a *Great Council* at Northampton,
but the Archbishop sent to the King a message that he would
not come to the *Court* except under special conditions.
On the morrow of the meeting, however, he came to the
King's *Court*, in his chapel, and was then required by the
King to answer charges made against him. In the end the
Barons of the King's *Court* (*Curiae Regis*) adjudged him to
be in the King's mercy[4].

[1] Hoveden (Rolls Series), vol. i. p. 170.
[2] A. S. Chron., A. D. 1123 and 1124.
[3] '*Recessit Archiepiscopus a Curia*,' Hoveden (Rolls Series), vol. i.
p. 222.   [4] Hoveden (Rolls Series), vol. i. pp. 224-225.

CHAP. IV.   During all or a portion of this time, however, there is
Delegation some reason to believe that delegates from the King's Court
from the were sent into the shires, partly, perhaps, in aid of the local
King's jurisdictions, partly, perhaps, to check them. In France, if
Court;
early origin not in England, a similar practice had existed since the time
of the
Justices in of Charlemagne, and, if it was unknown in England before the
Eyre. Conquest, it could hardly have failed to be introduced soon
afterwards. As there are no judicial records earlier than
the reign of Richard I, and no Exchequer records between
Domesday Book and the Great Roll of the Exchequer of
31 Henry I, the point must always remain in some obscurity.
There are, however, in the Great Roll of Henry I some
indications of the Eyres, which are known to have been
definitely established in the reign of Henry II. It is there
apparent that one of the persons who holds pleas (G. de
Clinton)[1] travels over no less than twelve counties. The
names of others appear in as many as six counties. So also
in the time of Henry II, before the famous Assize of Northampton in 1176, there are entries in the Great Rolls of the
Exchequer which it is difficult to explain otherwise than
by the assumption that Justices were sent from the King's
Court into the counties, as *Missi*, Justices Itinerant, Justices
Errant, or Justices in Eyre. Numerous instances have been
collected which appear to show the existence of these *Missi*,
or Justices in Eyre, in the twelfth, thirteenth, and fourteenth
years of the reign[2]. In the sixteenth year (1170) some
'Barons in Eyre'[3] were sent (*Missi*) into the several
counties to make enquiry as to the conduct of Sheriffs.
Among them were an Earl and two Abbots[4].

---

[1] He appears to have acted as Chief Justice under some Commission,
as the pleas are sometimes described as *Placita G. de Clintona*, sometimes (e.g. in the part of the roll relating to Yorkshire) as *Placita G.
de Clintona et Sociis ejus.*

[2] The *Great Rolls of the Exchequer*, under the heads of the
several counties in the years mentioned. The passages are cited
in the notes to Madox's *History of the Exchequer*, cap. iii. § 10,
ad fin.

[3] *Barones Errantes.*

[4] Gervase of Canterbury (Rolls Series), A. D. 1170. The instructions

In the year 1176, we are told, the kingdom was divided CHAP. IV.
into six parts, to each of which were to be sent three The
Justices, or eighteen in all. This, indeed, is the date eighteen
commonly assigned to the creation of Justices in Eyre, Eyre, and
though it is clear that there were *Missi* long before. On six Circuits
this occasion, however, if not on previous occasions, the 1176.
appointment was in very solemn form, the King holding
a 'Great Council' touching the laws or statutes of his
realm, at which were present the Archbishops, Bishops,
Earls, and Barons of the Realm, and the decision was taken
by common counsel of them all [1].

In the absence of contemporary judicial records, it is The Eyre
impossible to form a sound opinion as to the conduct of of 1176
these eighteen Justices. The Eyre, so far as the Crown five
part of its jurisdiction was concerned, was always unpopular, appointed
and complaints appear to have been made before the year to hear the
1178. In that year Henry II, having returned from abroad, the people
'made enquiry touching the Justices whom he had ap- in 1178.
pointed in England, and whether they had treated the
people of the realm well and with moderation. He learned
that the realm and the people had suffered grievances
through the great multitude of Justices, they being eighteen
in number. Then, by advice of the *Sapientes* (*Witan*)
of his realm, he chose five only, two ecclesiastics and three
laymen, and these were all of his private household. And
he ordained that these five should do right, and should
not depart from the King's Court, but should remain there
to hear all the claims or plaints of the people. Nevertheless,
if any question should come before them which could not
be brought to an end by them, it was to be presented to
the King's hearing and determined as should please him
and the *Sapientiores* (*Witan* or wise men) of the realm' [2].

Thus the particular Eyres of the year 1176 were brought

to enquire are printed also from Rawl. C. 641, in Bishop Stubbs's
Select Charters, p. 148.
[1] Bened. Abb. (Rolls Series), vol. i. p. 107; Hoveden (Rolls Series),
vol. ii. pp. 87–8.
[2] Bened. Abb. (Rolls Series), vol. i. p. 207. A portion of this

CHAP. IV.

The Court of Common Pleas (with a jurisdiction dele-, gated from the *Curia Regis*) now practically in existence.

to an end, to be succeeded from time to time by new Eyres under new Commissions. It will be observed that the five Justices of the King's Court appointed at this time are not said to have any authority in Crown matters. They are only to hear the claims or plaints of parties, and not even to determine the plaints if any special questions should arise. Here, to all appearance, the Court of Common Pleas comes into being. It is, at any rate, in being here. The disputes between party and party are to be brought not before the King and his Witan, or Common Council, in the first instance, but before his Justices. Through the Court of the Eyre the public had already become familiar with the idea of a delegated jurisdiction, away from the King's Court, in pleas both civil and criminal. By the appointment of Justices to sit in the King's Court and hear causes between plaintiff and defendant, or between demandant and tenant, they became familiar with another though similar kind of delegation.

But still moveable with the King's Court.

The Justices in Eyre were sent partly, it is true, for Crown purposes, but partly in aid of the local jurisdiction for civil causes. It would obviously be inconvenient for the King and all his Court of Archbishops, Bishops, Earls, and Barons to hear every small cause which might commence in the *Curia Regis* or be removed into it from local courts. Consequently, when there were no Eyres in Commission, it was a very natural idea that causes which were not

passage has been frequently used with the object of proving a totally different argument, which it in no way warrants. Mr. (afterwards Sir Thomas) Hardy in his Introduction to the Close Rolls, p. xxv, says 'the Court of Judicature which sat in the *Curia Regis* or the King's Court is also presumed to have been instituted by the same Prince [Henry II] in consequence of complaints made to him of the partiality of the *Justiciae* resiant in his Court, the number of whom he reduced from eighteen to five, and enacted 'quod illi quinque,' &c., as above. *Resiant* is a technical word not exactly applicable to Justices in Eyre. It is strange that neither Mr. Hardy, nor the many writers on the *Curia Regis* who have copied him, should have perceived that the eighteen Justices were the Justices in Eyre, and that no other eighteen are mentioned by Benedictus Abbas.

of exceptional importance should be heard by persons CHAP. IV.
deputed for the purpose. There is not the slightest indication in the words used, that these deputies or Justices
were to remain in any fixed spot. They were to remain in
the King's Court and not depart from it. As the King's
Court was moveable so also must they have been, but they
were not to move independently, as Justices in Eyre. This
was, no doubt, a great inconvenience, and finds its place in
that part of King John's *Magna Charta* which provides
that Common Pleas are not to follow the King's Court.
The Justices, however, who were not to move except with
the King's Court, were, there can be little doubt, those who
were soon after called 'the Justices of the Lord the King of
his Bench'—'the Bench' meaning invariably not, as might
be supposed by laymen rather than lawyers, the King's
Bench, but the Common Bench or Court of Common
Pleas.

About the time of the appointment of the Justices in
Eyre by Henry II in 1176, and even a little earlier, it
becomes apparent that there were also Justices of the *Curia
Regis* as distinguished from the ancient *Curia Regis* regarded as a whole. Many of them were the same persons
as the Justices in Eyre, but were clearly acting in a different
capacity, and not acting solely within the limits assigned
to them respectively in their circuits as Justices in Eyre.
Thus, in Yorkshire pleas, William Fitz-Ralph, Bertram de
Verdun, and William Basset [1] acted as Justices of the *Curia
Regis* in 1176, whereas Ranulf de Glanvill, Robert de Vaux,
and Robert Pikenot were the Justices in Eyre for the same
county [2]. So also, in the pleas of Buckinghamshire and
Bedfordshire. Fitz-Ralph, Verdun, and Basset are found to
be Justices of the *Curia Regis* even in the preceding year [3],

In 1176 there were Justices of the Curia Regis, dis-tinguished from the Curia Regis as a whole, and from the Justices in Eyre.

---

[1] *Great Roll of the Exchequer*, 22 Hen. II, Yorkshire; and again
the Roll of 23 Hen. II (both cited by Madox, *Hist. Exch.*, cap. iii. § 5,
notes).

[2] *Ib.* ; Bened. Abb. (Rolls Series), vol. i. p. 108.

[3] *Great Roll of the Exchequer*, Bucks and Beds, 21 Hen. II (cited
by Madox, as above).

CHAP. IV. and the same persons (Verdun and his companions) again in
1176 [1], whereas the Justices in Eyre for those counties were
in 1176 Walter Fitz-Robert, Hugh de Cressi, and Robert
Mantell [2].

The Eyre
of 1179:
the Lord
High
Treasurer
and a
Bishop
among the
Justices.

The creation of a limited *Curia Regis* as distinguished
from the whole Court known by that name was, therefore,
not as has sometimes been supposed, merely the outcome
of the suppression of the Eyres of 1176. Those Eyres in
fact had barely been ended before new Eyres were put in
commission. In the year 1179 the kingdom was divided
not into six, but into four circuits, and Justices to the
number of no less than twenty-one were divided among
the four districts—six Justices to one, and five to each
of the others. The names are of singular interest as showing how some, though not all, of the Justices in Eyre must
have been members also of the great *Curia Regis*, while
others apparently were not qualified to be members, unless
indeed there was already arising a Council within a Council.
In three out of the four circuits a Bishop presided, in one
of the three the Treasurer was one of the Justices, in the
second the King's Chaplain, and one of the King's Clerks,
and in the third also one of the King's Clerks. There is
nothing to show that the other Justices in these three
divisions were Bishops, Abbots, Earls, or Barons.

The
Justices of
one Circuit
were the
Justices of
Common
Pleas.

The fourth division, however, was the most remarkable
of all. There were in it six Justices, not one of whom
appears to have been Bishop, Abbot, Earl. or Baron, and
of these six it is said that they were also appointed Justices
in the King's Court (*Curia Regis*) to hear the claims or
plaints (*clamores*) of the people [3]. The Justices to hear
the claims of the people can only be, under another name,
the Justices to hear Common Pleas, as distinguished from
those who had jurisdiction in Pleas of the Crown. As

---

[1] *Great Roll*, 22 Hen. II, Bucks and Beds (cited by Madox, as above).

[2] The same *Great Roll*; also Bened. Abb. (Rolls Series), vol. i.
p. 107.

[3] Bened. Abb. (Rolls Series), vol. i. pp. 238–9; Hoveden (Rolls
Series), vol. ii. pp. 190–1.

Justices in Eyre in the Northern Counties the six would
have both jurisdictions. As Justices of the King's Court
to hear the plaints of the people they had only one.

Shortly afterwards Ranulf de Glanvill, who was one of *Indications*
these six Justices, became Chief Justiciary (in A.D. 1180)[1], *of the*
existence,
and partly from what has been told of him, partly from *by delega-*
what he has told us himself, it is possible to discern the *tion, of the*
Court
Court *Coram Rege*, afterwards known as the King's Bench, *Coram*
Rege (after-
having by delegation a distinct existence apart from the *wards*
Court of Common Pleas. In the year 1184 it would seem *known as*
the King's
that the expression *Coram Rege* (before the King) no *Bench` in*
1184.
longer signified necessarily before the King in person. In
that year one Gilbert de Plumpton was accused of felony
Coram Rege. In this case the action of the Court is clearly
seen to be distinguished from that of the King. Plumpton
was condemned either by or at the instigation of Glanvill,
who was his enemy. The King, however, afterwards remitted the capital punishment by advice[2]. The King's
Court *Coram Rege* still followed the King, and was held in
the place in which he might happen to be. He was often,
no doubt, present in Court, but not always, and his presence
was perhaps beginning to become one of the fictions of
the law, though the Court of King's Bench was always
known as 'the Court of our Lord the King before 'the
King himself.'

In the year 1187 (the thirty-third year of the reign of *The*
delegated
Henry II) the Court of Common Pleas was also in existence *jurisdic-*
still more plainly than in previous years, as will be apparent *tion of the*
Court of
to any one who is familiar with the style of the Court, and *Common*
with its jurisdiction. It was always known as 'the Court *Pleas, as*
described
of our Lord the King of the Bench,' and its Justices as 'the *by Glanvill*
Justices of our Lord the King of the Bench.' The expression *in 1187.*

---

[1] Hoveden (Rolls Series), vol. ii. p. 215.
[2] Hoveden (Rolls Series), vol. ii. p. 286. His diction is a little
obscure. The story is somewhat differently told by Benedictus Abbas
(Rolls Series), vol. i. pp. 314–317. The latter makes Glanvill exhort
those who were to give judgement in the case to pass sentence of
death. In either case the King was not present at the trial.

CHAP. IV. 'King's Bench' does not seem to have been known before the reign of Edward I. The Common Bench in later times had jurisdiction in real actions, and it was the Court in which fines of land were levied. So also it was, though not with an exclusive jurisdiction, in 1187, according to the testimony of Glanvill himself. The 'concord' or the 'fine,' which was to be the end of the proceedings in any action, was to be put into writing by mutual consent of the parties; it was to be brought before the Justices of the Lord the King sitting[1] on the Bench; and a counterpart was to be delivered, in the presence of the Justices, to each of the suitors. The form of the concord is set out and is obviously the foundation of the fines of lands of later date. The concord might be made in the King's Court, or made elsewhere, and afterwards recorded and enrolled in the King's Court; but the King's Court was, in both cases, not the full *Curia Regis* of previous reigns and of the early part of the reign of Henry II, but the King's Court of the Bench, before the King's Justices of the Bench. When the final concord was made in the King's Court, it was, according to the form given by Glanvill. made before the chief Justiciary and four persons named, together with some others. When it was made elsewhere, it was to be recorded in the King's Court at Westminster before persons named (two Bishops and the Chief Justiciary, in the form given) being then and there present. There is no longer any suggestion that the King in person and all the Bishops, Earls, and Barons constituted the Court. The Court was the Court of Common Pleas, of which the Justices might or might not have been trained lawyers, but of which, except in exceptional cases to be hereafter noticed, the number of Justices might be limited[2]. It differed from the later Court of the same name chiefly in the fact that one of its constituent members was the Chief

---

[1] *Residentibus.* This was the term commonly used at the time to express 'sitting,' not necessarily, as has been sometimes supposed, residing.

[2] Glanvill, lib. viii. caps. 1, 2, 3.

Justiciary who presided also over the Court *Coram Rege*, CHAP. IV.
and that the Court *Coram Rege* and even the Exchequer
seem also to have had a concurrent jurisdiction.

In these times the Fine of Lands was regarded not as The
the conclusion of a fictitious action on a writ of covenant, *Capitalis*
Curia
but as an agreement between the parties in an action *Regis* of
which had really been commenced and come into Court. and its two
A similar agreement might at this time be made in actions divisions,
other than those relating to land[1], and might be made in *Domino*
the Court *Coram Rege*; and the distinction between the *Rege*,
two Courts is again clearly drawn by Glanvill. 'Whatso- *Justiciis*.
ever anyone has acknowledged that he has to do, whether
Coram Domino Rege (that is to say, in the Court subsequently known as the King's Bench) or in the Common
Bench (*Coram ejus Justiciis*). thereof let him keep his
engagement[2].' The two Courts taken together were distinguished by Glanvill from the Court before the Justices
in Eyre as the Head or Chief Court of the King[3]. The
two branches, however, not only were. but continued to be
distinct ever afterwards. In the Eyre Rolls of the reign of
Richard I (to which the name of *Rotuli Curiae Regis* was
assigned by some person who made a calendar of them
long ago, and whose error has been perpetuated to the
present time) there is frequent mention of 'the Bench,' the
invariable title for the Common Bench or Court of Common
Pleas[4].

A cause of confusion has arisen from the fact that in Glanvill's
Glanvill's time, and subsequently, the King's Court (*Curia* distinction
between the
Regis) was commonly mentioned in contradistinction to the jurisdiction
of the
County Court or Court of the Sheriff. Glanvill, in fact, King's
uses as the heading of his first book the words 'Of the Court and
that of the
pleas which belong to the King's Court or to the Sheriff.' Sheriff.
The expression 'the King's Court' has generally. been
supposed to mean a single and indivisible Court. It is

[1] Glanvill, lib. viii. cap. 1.
[2] *Ib.*, lib. viii. cap. 5.
[3] *Ib.*
[4] *Rot. Cur. Reg.* (ed. Palgrave), vol. i. 217, &c.

CHAP. IV. clear from the evidence given above, that this is not the
meaning. Such an interpretation would be as little
warranted as would be the interpretation that 'the Sheriff'
means only one Sheriff with one Court. The respective
jurisdictions of the two Courts (*Coram Rege* and *Coram
Justiciis*) may not have been so sharply defined in
Glanvill's time as in the time of Edward I—could not have
been, indeed, when the same Justiciary sat in both. Yet
this very fact illustrates the growth of the two Courts and
explains how in later times a writ of Error lay from the
Court of Common Pleas to the Court of King's Bench over
which the Chief Justice of England presided.

The
jurisdiction
of the
Common
Bench
inferior to
that of the
King's
Bench, and
to that of
the Eyre.

The inconvenience of the Common Pleas following the
King's Court, or, in other words, of the Court of Common
Bench sitting only when and where the King held his
Court (the word Court being used in more senses than one)
was felt and remedied before the time of John's Great
Charter. It was remedied, to some extent, by the appointment of Justices in Eyre, who heard common pleas as well
as pleas of the Crown. They, as delegates from the King's
Court to carry justice into the Shires, took with them the
full jurisdiction. The Court of Common Pleas was inferior
to the Court of the Eyre, just as it was inferior to the Court
of King's Bench. When the Eyre was in any county, the
jurisdiction of the Common Bench immediately ceased in
that county, and the common pleas of the county were at
once removed into the Court of the Eyre.

The full
*Curia
Regis* still
hears
causes of
great im-
portance;
Case of the
Kings of
Castile and
Navarre in
1177.

The King's Court itself, however—the full Court—appears
to have still retained its original constitution for occasions
and causes of great weight and moment. In the year 1177
the Kings of Castile and Navarre submitted their disputes
to the judgement of the 'Court of the King of England.'
This Court, to which the term 'General Council' was also
applied, consisted, when it first assembled, of the Archbishop of Canterbury, several Bishops, and Abbots, Priors,
Earls, and Barons of England. The disputants were
required to put their respective cases in writing, because,
until that was done, 'neither the King nor the Barons of

the Court' could understand the matter of complaint. Chap. IV.
Afterwards, 'the Earls and Barons of the Court of the King
of England'[1] gave judgement, which was embodied in the
form of a charter, just as decisions in the Court, Council, or
Parliament of the Conqueror had been embodied before.
The Charter was described as a 'Charter of Henry, King
of England, touching the judgement given in his Court
between the King of Castile and the King of Navarre[2].' It
was attested by the Archbishop of Canterbury, fourteen
Bishops, seven Earls, nine Barons named, and others of the
clergy and laity.

Even when there began to be other Justices besides the *Barons still occasionally sat in the Courts with delegated jurisdiction.* Chief Justiciary and the Justices in Eyre, the Barons might
still constitute a part of the King's Court. Thus when
Robert de Aubeney quit-claimed, released, or surrendered
Didcot to Henry II, it was 'in the King's Court at Westminster, before the King and his Barons and Justices then
and there present[3].'

The Court of Common Pleas (the Court before Jus- *An Earl and Barons in the Court of Common Pleas in the reign of Richard I.* tices and not before the King himself), also retained for
a time some of the characteristics of the old undivided
Curia Regis, when cases of exceptional importance were
to be heard, or concords or fines of exceptional importance
to be recorded. Thus in the ninth year of the reign of
Richard I, in a case in which a demand was made against
the Prior and Convent of Christ Church, Canterbury, and
considerable interests were involved, there were not only
Justices constituting the Court, as well as the Chief
Justiciary, but also an Earl and various Barons and others
of the King's lieges. A concord or fine was made *Coram
Justiciis*, but not *Coram Rege*. Here the Court was the
King's Court, but the Court of his Bench. though Barons

---

[1] *Comites et Barones Regalis Curiae Angliae.*
[2] Benedictus Abbas (Rolls Series), vol. i. pp. 138–154; Hoveden
(Rolls Series), vol. ii. pp. 120–131.
[3] This appears from a recital of a charter produced in Court in the
eighth year of the reign of King John. Printed *Placitorum Abbreviatio*, 54 b.

CHAP. IV. again sat as they had sat in the original King's Court of old [1].

The full Curia Regis or Common Council of the Realm, acting as a Court superior to the more limited Curia Regis in the reign of John. The distinction between the old and full *Curia Regis*, however, and the Courts *Coram Rege* and of the Bench was, in the reign of King John, becoming marked by the use of the Council of the Realm, which was in fact the ancient full *Curia Regis*, as a superior Court—if not a Court of Appeal, certainly one into which causes could be removed from the Courts or branches below. It was laid down by Glanvill that all actions touching Baronies must be tried in the King's Court [2]. In the reign of Henry II a convention, agreement, or fine had been made touching a Barony, but not in the King's Court. The person who had agreed to the transfer, afterwards, in the reign of King John, redemanded the Barony on this ground, in the King's Court. The matter was not then settled in ordinary form but by the Council of the Realm and the will of the King [3].

Various senses in which the terms *Curia Regis* and *Council* are used in Chronicles and Records. In the division of functions now becoming manifest there appears also, not perhaps unnaturally, a great confusion of terms, a confusion from which even the records are not free, but which is most conspicuous in the writings of the Chroniclers. The King's Court is a term used sometimes to express the Common Council of the Realm, sometimes the King's Council, sometimes the Court *Coram Rege*, afterwards called the King's Bench, and sometimes the Court of Common Pleas. The Council means sometimes the Common Council of the Realm, sometimes a Court sitting to hear causes which it might have been supposed would be brought before the Court of King's Bench or the Court of Common Pleas and sometimes a committee of the Common Council of the Realm appointed to consider petitions.

[1] Printed in Madox's *History of the Exchequer* (cap. iii. § 7, note), from one of the original Feet of Fines among the archives of Christ Church, Canterbury.
[2] Glanvill, lib. i. cap. 3.
[3] Hoveden (Rolls Series), vol. iv. pp. 117–8.

It was established, as already mentioned, in 1178, that
the permanent Justices of the Common Bench, or those who
had to hear the ordinary causes between party and party,
were not to proceed in important or difficult cases without
referring the matter to the King and his *Sapientes* or *Witan.*
On these occasions the Court would naturally be reinforced
by members of the fuller *Curia Regis*, which had merely
delegated its functions in relation to minor causes. In like
manner the functions of the Court *Coram Rege*, afterwards
called the King's Bench, were not at first absolutely severed
from the full *Curia Regis.* Thus, even in the reign of
Henry III, when an advowson was given and granted to
the Bishop of Bath in frank-almoign, this was done *Coram
Rege et Magnatibus*, and seisin was given *Coram Rege* by
a pair of gloves[1].

In the time of Henry III, the Council, not qualified by
any epithet, is seen to be exercising various functions,
some perhaps, peculiar to itself, others of the same nature
as those exercised by the Court of King's Bench, and the
Court of Common Pleas. In the twenty-first year of the
reign there are records of cases before the Lord the King at
Worcester. In one of these[2] it was pleaded, under Magna
Charta, that Common Pleas ought not to follow the King,
from which fact it is clear that the distinction between the
Court *Coram Rege*, and the Court of Common Pleas was
fully recognized. In another case the decision appears to
have been given by the King and his Council under the head
of the Court *Coram Rege*[3]. In the twenty-seventh year
of the reign the Council, without any mention of the King,
takes cases of *Quo Warranto*[4]. The Archbishop of York
and the Council, in the same year, deal with an action of

The severance of the Courts of King's Bench and Common Pleas from the full Curia Regis long incomplete; though commencing earlier than commonly supposed.

'The Council,' the 'Whole Council.' and the Court Coram Rege; records of cases before these tribunals on the same rolls in the reign of Henry III.

---

[1] *Rot. Lit. Pat.*, 10 Hen. III, m. 5. Printed in Madox's *Hist. Exch.*, cap. iii. sec. 7, note.

[2] *Placita coram Rege*, 21 Hen. III, R°. 3, printed in the *Plac. Abbr.*, p. 105 a.

[3] *Ib.*, in relation to a claim of the King of Scotland, touching the Earldom of Huntingdon.

[4] *Placita coram Concilio Domini Regis*, 27 Hen. III, R°. 2, printed in the *Plac. Abbr.*, p. 118 b.

CHAP. IV. assise [1], and with some real actions between party and party, as well as with cases of *Quo Warranto* and various matters in which the King was interested [2]. In the thirty-eighth year the Council hears (among others more immediately affecting the Crown) a number of cases of trespass and of offences against the peace which might in later times have been determined in the Court of King's Bench [3]. In the fifty-sixth year of the reign there were pleas *Coram Rege* (the style of the Court of King's Bench of later reigns), and among them occurs a case in which a writ was directed to the Justices of the Bench (Common Pleas) requiring them to send the records of two cross actions which were before them to the King. They sent the records before the King and his Council. The parties afterwards came before the King and Council, by whom judgement was given [4].

In the forty-third year of the reign is a remarkable intermixture of the Court *Coram Rege* or King's Bench, 'the King's Council,' and 'the King's whole Council.' In an assize of Novel Disseisin it appeared that the King's interests might be affected. The cause was adjourned in order that the King might be consulted, and a day was given, *Coram Rege ubicumque*, &c. On the appointed day the King 'before his Council' [5] at Westminster acknowledged and recorded certain matters. There was again an adjournment, and a day was again given *Coram Rege ubicumque*, when the plaintiff appeared in the King's presence. There were further adjournments, and at length the plaintiff came before the whole Council of the King [6], and prayed seisin. It was then ordered that the rolls of the Exchequer should be searched as to certain facts, and that the *Magnates*

---

[1] *Placita coram Concilio Domini Regis*, 27 Hen. III, R⁰. 3 d, printed in the *Plac. Abbr.*, p. 118 b.

[2] *Ib.*, Rⁱˢ. 7–24, printed in the *Plac. Abbr.*, pp. 119–20.

[3] *Ib.*, Mich., 37–38 Hen. III, Rⁱˢ. 5–11, printed in the *Plac. Abbr.*, pp. 129–131.

[4] *Placita coram Rege*, Hil., 56 Hen. III, printed in the *Plac. Abbr.*, p. 182 a, b.

[5] *Coram concilio ejus.*   [6] *Coram toto concilio Domini Regis.*

of the Council should be certified thereon, and there was
again an adjournment *Coram Rege ubicumque*[1], or into the
King's Bench, as the Court was subsequently called.

The proceedings of the Council, indeed, seem to be
indistinguishable from those of the Court *Coram Rege* or
King's Bench. In the forty-fifth year of the reign of
Henry III, among a number of cases headed 'Pleas before
the Lord the King,' it appears that Isabella de Fortz,
Countess of Albemarle, comes before Hugh le Despenser,
the King's Chief Justiciary, and other Magnates of the
Council of the Lord the King, and there prefers her claim
to a wardship. Judgement was given in her favour[2].

In the time of Edward I, 'the whole Council' was
stated to include, though not to consist exclusively of,
the Chancellor, the Treasurer, the Justices of the two
Benches. and the Barons of the Exchequer[3]. In a roll
of pleas, *Coram Rege*, of the thirty-third year of that
reign, James, formerly Seneschal or Steward of Scotland,
acknowledged a certain instrument to be his deed, before
the Chancellor of England, the Chief Justice of England,
the Justices of the two Benches, the *locum tenens* of the
Treasurer, John de Berewyk, and several others of the
King's Council, and the Barons of the Exchequer[4].

So also in the reign of Edward I.

We know from a different source[5] that 'the Court of
the King in his Council in his Parliament,' was now in
existence, and that in it sat Prelates, Earls, Barons, *Proceres*, and other learned persons. There doubts respecting
judgements were determined, there new remedies were
established for new wrongs, and there justice would be
awarded to every one according to his deserts. A truly
perfect Court! From the same source we know that the
Court of King's Bench. though recognized as a separate
Court, still had only an inferior jurisdiction, which was, to

The Courts of the King in his Council in his Parliament, and of the King's Bench, in the reign of Edward I.

[1] *Plac. Abbr.*, pp. 145–6 (43 Hen. III).
[2] *Placita coram Rege*, Mich., 44–45 Hen. III, printed *Plac. Abbr.*, p. 151.
[3] *Plac. Abbr.*, p. 260 b, Easter, 35 Ed. I.
[4] *Placita coram Rege*, Mich., 33 Ed. I, *Plac. Abbr.*, p. 298 b.
[5] Fleta, lib. ii. cap. 2.

CHAP. IV. some extent, concurrent with that of the King's Court in his Council in his Parliament. The Justices of that Court, ' as well Knights as Clerks,' were the King's *locum tenentes*. The King was always supposed to be in the place in which they were sitting, and they were supposed to sit only in the place in which the King was. They had criminal jurisdiction, and jurisdiction in false judgement and error, and their jurisdiction was exclusive, except in so far as it was shared by and subordinate to that of the King and Council, and that of any special commissioners appointed for special purposes.

The *Curia Regis*, Council, and King's Bench in the reign of Edward II. At a still later date the *Curia Regis* makes it appearance in close connexion with the Council on the one hand, and with the King's Bench on the other. The Court of King's Bench had in the reign of Edward II a well-established jurisdiction in cases of error from the Court of Common Pleas. In cases of exceptional difficulty and importance, however, the Council was still called in, and not only the ordinary official Council [1] but the Barons and Magnates as well. Thus, when a fine of lands had been levied in the Court of Common Pleas and the family of the Despensers was interested, error was alleged, and the case was in the usual course brought into the King's Bench. It was not, however, settled by the ordinary Judges of the Court. Frequent deliberation was had with the Justices of both Benches. the Chancellor. the Treasurer, and the Barons of the Exchequer, as well before them all as before the Barons

---

[1] The expression, ' ordinary official council,' has been used here, and elsewhere, not in any technical sense, but to distinguish this more or less official or legal body from ' the whole Council.' The term *Concilium Ordinarium* is used by Sir Matthew Hale in a different and apparently more technical sense, but there appears no sufficient warrant for his two divisions, *Concilium Privatum* and *Concilium Ordinarium*, taken as legal definitions. His third division, the *Magnum Concilium*, had an existence in the reign of Edward II, as distinguished from the *Secretum Concilium*, which he does not mention. His fourth division, *Commune Concilium*, which, as he alleged, consisted of the two Houses of Parliament, was in existence before the House of Commons came into being. See Hale, *Jurisdiction of the Lords' House*, p. 5, et seq.

and other Magnates of the King's Council[1].' Thereupon CHAP. IV. it appeared to the King's Court (*Curiae Regis*) that the fine ought to be annulled.

A remarkable illustration of the variety of Councils and The King's Great Council, of their connexion both with the Court of King's Bench and with the Chancery occurs in the sixteenth year of and Secret Council : Edward II. The King, being at Bishopthorpe near York, remarkable caused to be summoned before him to his Council there case of Henry de the Archbishop of York, the Bishop of Norwich who Beaumont. was also Chancellor, the Bishop of Exeter who was also Treasurer, Edmund Earl of Kent the King's brother, the Earl of Pembroke, Hugh le Despenser Earl of Winchester, the Earl of Athol, Hugh le Despenser the younger, William de Ros of Hamelak, and several other Barons and Nobles (*Nobiles*) of his realm, together with the Justices of both Benches, the Barons of the Exchequer 'and others of his Council.' Among the Nobles (*Nobiles*) was Henry de Beaumont, a Baron, and one sworn of the Great and of the Secret Council of the King. When asked for his advice, Beaumont disrespectfully refused to give it. He was angrily commanded by the King to quit the Council; and, as he went, he said, in the same tone as before, that it would please him much better to be out of the Council than in it. The King then bade the Magnates and others of the Council to consider what judgement should be passed on him, inasmuch as being the King's liege, and a Baron, and sworn of the King's Secret Council, he had refused to give his advice and used opprobrious words. The Magnates and the rest of the Council, after careful deliberation, and after he had been called back into their presence and that of the King, passed judgement that he should be committed to prison for contempt and disobedience[2].

The Court of King's Bench was at this time at York, The King's

---

[1] *Placita coram Rege*, Hil., 8 Ed. II, *Plac. Abbr.*, 320 a.

[2] *Rot. Lit. Claus.*, 16 Ed. II, m. 5 d (printed in *Parliamentary Writs*, vol. ii. div. 2. part 1. p. 285). *Placita coram Rege*, Trin., 16 Ed. II (printed in *Plac. Abbr.*, p. 342).

CHAP. IV. following the King ; and the rolls of the Court were used,

Bench and as in so many earlier cases, for the purpose of recording
Chancery the judicial proceedings of the Council. The Chancery
rolls used
to record also followed the King, as had recently been declared
proceed- anew [1] ; and the rolls of the Chancery were used in like
ings before
the manner both in this and in other instances. The result
Council :
the Council in this instance is a double enrolment The matter is of
not fully some little importance because no separate records of the
separated
from other proceedings of the Council of earlier date than the tenth
Courts be- year of the reign of Richard II are known to be in ex-
fore the
reign of istence. The natural inference seems to be that the absolute
Richard II. separation of the Council from the original *Curia Regis,* or
from the Court about the King, or from the Courts of
Justice which followed the King, or from the Parliament,
was not complete much before this time. There are many
other facts which point to the same conclusion.

The several It is clear from the records to which attention has been
kinds of
Councils drawn that there were many kinds of Council known to
enumer- the law. There was the Common Council of the Realm
ated.
summoned, perhaps, only on great occasions ; there was
the Great Council, which must have been a different and
a more permanent body because a Baron could be sworn of
that Council ; there was the Secret Council which must
have been different, not only from the last-mentioned. but
also from the official, legal, or ordinary Council, because
we find a Baron, without office or technical qualification,
belonging to it ; there was the ' Whole Council ' which
may or may not have been identical with the Great
Council and which seems to have included necessarily the
Chancellor, the Treasurer, the Justices of the two Benches,
and the Barons of the Exchequer, if not others ; and there
was the Council without any qualifying epithet, which may
have been sometimes the last-mentioned body, sitting with
a part only of its members, or sometimes any Council
except the Common Council of the Realm.

Thus far the King's Court and Council have been traced

---

[1] 28 Ed. I, stat. 3. cap. 5.

in detail only in relation to the Court of King's Bench and CHAP. IV.
the Court of Common Pleas. A very important attendant The
at the King's Court and member of his Council, however, Common ›
was, during the earliest times after the Conquest, the Chan- of the
cellor. He seems always to have had charge of the Great Realm, the
Seal. From the Chancery issued the Original Writs, duly and
sealed, for the trial of actions in the King's Courts of Original
Justice. The Chancery, moreover, appears to have been, Writs.
from the first, an office of the Common Council of the
Realm, as afterwards it was an office of Parliament. Even
the Original Writs did not issue on the authority of the
Chancellor alone. Some writs were 'writs of course,' and
could be had in the prescribed form upon application
in the Chancery, but even these were originally allowed
and approved by the Common Council of the Realm [1].

In the reign of Edward I, power was given to the clerks The
of the Chancery to issue writs '*in consimili casu*' where 'Parlia-
matters fell under the same law and required like remedy. ment' and
If, however, the clerks could not agree upon the form, they the framing
were to refer the cases to the next Parliament so that of writs.
a writ might be framed by men learned in the law [2]. This
provision, with its reference to the sages of the law, obviously has reference not to a Parliament in the modern
sense of the term, but to one of those other bodies or
councils to which the term 'Parliament' was commonly
applied in the reign of Edward I, and for some time
afterwards. It clearly was not the intention that writs
should be considered and framed by the Lords Spiritual
and Temporal, and the Commons in Parliament assembled,
but by a body possessing special aptitude for the task.
That body, there can be little doubt, was 'the King in his
Council in his Parliament,' the resolutions of which, when
promulgated, had the authority of the whole assembly.
It would seem to follow that this later expression furnishes
the interpretation of the phrase 'the Common Council of

[1] Bract. 413 b.
[2] Stat. 13 Ed. I (Westm. 2), cap. 24.

CHAP. IV. the Realm.'   The body which was to devise new writs in
. the reign of Edward I, must have been, allowing for differences of phrase and circumstances, the body which had
framed the recognized 'writs of course' current in the reign
of Henry III.   Great attention had been given to the study
of the law in the interval, and a class of men had arisen
who were experts in the subject.   To them naturally fell
the actual task of settling the forms to be used, but their
authority alone was not considered sufficient.   They were
summoned to the so-called Parliament, as members of
the Council, but Archbishops, Bishops, Earls, and Barons
were summoned also, and gave additional solemnity to the
additions which were to be made in the Chancery Register
of Original Writs.

Various
signifi-
cations in
which the
word 'Par-
liament'
was used.
About the reign of Edward I a new cause of confusion is
introduced by the use of the word 'Parliament' in more
senses than one, but a confusion through which it is,
perhaps, possible to arrive at clearness.   It is sometimes
a Parliament, in the modern sense of the term, to which
Lords Spiritual and Temporal and Commons are summoned.
Sometimes it is a different kind of assembly.   Thus in the
twenty-third year of the reign the Archbishops and Bishops,
and other Prelates, including forty-two Abbots and eleven
Priors, were summoned, together with sixty-four Earls and
Barons, to a 'Parliament' which was to meet on August 1.
The Justices of both Benches, the Justices in Eyre, the
Justices of Assize, the Deans sworn of the Council, and
other Clerks of the Council were also summoned [1], but
not the Commons.

According to the marginal description on the roll,
a 'Parliament' was to meet at Salisbury, on February 27,
in the twenty-fifth year, to which neither Prelates nor
Burgesses were summoned, but only ninety-four Earls,
Barons, and Knights [2].   In the same year there were sum-

---

[1] *Rot. Lit. Claus.,* 23 Ed. I, m. 9 d (printed in *Parliamentary Writs,*
ed. Palgrave, vol. i. pp. 28–9).
[2] *Rot. Lit. Claus.,* 25 Ed. I, m. 25 d (*Parl. Writs,* vol. i. p. 51 et seq.).

moned to attend the King's son, on September 30, five CHAP. IV.
Bishops, two Earls, two Barons, two Archdeacons, eight
Clerks of the Council, six Justices, and two Friars, and by
other writs the Archbishop of Canterbury, six other Bishops,
seventeen Abbots, four Priors (as well as in particular the
Prior of St. John of Jerusalem), the Master of the Knights
of the Temple, eight persons who were apparently Barons,
and two more Earls. In the margin of the writ to the
Archbishop of Canterbury this assembly also is called
a Parliament [1].

The word Parliament, however, does not appear to have *The word*
been used in relation to every kind of Council, and, in par- *applied to*
ticular, not to the official or legal Council. Thus in the *but not*
twenty-sixth year of the reign, when twenty-two persons *kind of*
only were summoned, the assembly was described as a *Council*
Council in the margin of the roll. It consisted of the
Bishops of London and Ely, nine other ecclesiastics, the
Justices of the two Benches, and the Barons of the Exchequer [2].

In the following year nearly all the same persons were *Meaning of*
called, as members of the Council, to attend a 'Par- *in his*
liament.' The Bishop of London was summoned, but *Council*
simply in the capacity of Bishop. The Bishopric of Ely *liament'*
had fallen vacant. Of the rest seventeen were summoned *precisely*
as of the Council, with four others, among whom was *tained.*
John de L'Isle, a newly-appointed Baron of the Exchequer.
Two out of these four had been mentioned in earlier
writs as being of the Council. The distinction between
this assembly and that of the twenty-sixth year lies in
the fact that the Council was now summoned to meet
at the same time as the Prelates and *Proceres*, among
whom were two Archbishops, eighteen Bishops, thirty-five
Abbots, four Priors, eleven Earls, and seventy-nine Barons.
In the margin of the roll the meeting is described as

[1] *Rot. Lit. Claus.*, 25 Ed. I, m. 6 d. (printed *Parl. Writs*, vol. i. pp.
55–56).
[2] *Ib.*, 26 Ed. I, m. 12 d (printed *Parl. Writs*, vol. i. p. 65).

E

CHAP. IV. a Parliament, though the Commons were not in attendance[1]. The appointed day was Sunday, March 8. On the
twenty-fifth day of the same month the Mayor and Aldermen of London elected certain persons to further the
business of the city 'before the King and Council in Parliament,' which had commenced its sittings on the previous
ninth of March[2]. The body before which the representatives of the city of London were to appear could only have
been that which was to attend the King at London on
March 8. It follows, therefore, that we know precisely
what was meant by the expression ' the King in his Council
in his Parliament,' which is of frequent occurrence in the
records of important cases reported in the Year Books.
This kind of Parliament was not necessarily a Parliament including the Commons, but a Parliament of Lords
Spiritual and Temporal with the King and his Council
sitting therein.

In this assembly (the King in his Council in his Parliament) it seems. too, that we must recognize the ancient
Common Council of the Realm, modified, it may be, by time
and circumstances. but still the nearest equivalent of that
Common Council of the Realm which Bracton mentioned as
the necessary authority for the form of an original writ.
It was, as will presently appear, known by the name of
' full Parliament.' It was the fountain of justice, the source
to which men commonly went if they felt aggrieved by the
manner in which their causes were being heard in the Court
of Common Pleas, or in the Court of King's Bench. It had
not, even as late as the reign of Edward III, lost its hold
over the Courts which had sprung from it, but controlled
their proceedings, before judgement was pronounced or
error alleged, and it gave its directions to those Courts
on petitions made by the parties.

Control of   It is sometimes possible, with the aid of the Year Books
the King

---

[1] *Rot. Lit. Claus.*, 27 Ed. I, m. 18 d (printed *Parl. Writs,* vol. i.
pp. 78–80).

[2] Lib. C. in *Archivis Civitatis Lond.* fol. 28 (extracted and printed
in *Parl. Writs,* vol. i. p. 80).

(or early law reports), the records of the Courts of Common CHAP. IV.
Pleas and King's Bench, and the rolls of Parliament, to in his
follow out the whole mode of practice. There was in the Council in his Parlia-
reign of Edward III a family dispute which must have ment over
caused no little anxiety to the disputants. One Geoffrey the pro-ceedings of
de Staunton brought an action in the Court of Common the Court
Pleas against one John de Staunton and Amy his wife. In of Common Pleas;
the course of the pleadings the question whether a certain case in
averment was admissible or not was warmly disputed. illustration.
Geoffrey presented a petition to the King in his Council in
his Parliament praying. among other matters, a decision on
the point. It was agreed in Parliament that the averment
was admissible, and a writ was sent to the Justices of
the Common Pleas instructing them to proceed. Nothing,
however, was done; and a second writ was sent directing
the Justices either to proceed, or to signify the reason why
they did not. Upon this there was a new argument in the
Court of Common Pleas. It was urged that the decision in
Parliament, having been given in the absence of one of the
parties, was unjust, and the Chief Justice of the Common
Pleas declared it to be altogether bad law. An acting
and a late Chief Justice of the King's Bench were consulted,
and differed in opinion from each other. The result was
that no judgement was given, and the Justices did not, as
they had been directed, signify the cause.

Geoffrey then presented another petition to the Council
praying that they would command the Justices of the
Common Pleas either to give judgement or else to bring
their rolls, record, and process, into Parliament, so that
judgement might be given, one way or the other, before
the end of term. It was thereupon 'agreed by all in full
Parliament, and command was given by the Prelates, Earls,
Barons, and others of the Parliament to Sir Thomas de
Drayton, Clerk of the Parliament, that he should go to
Sir John de Stonore, and his companions, Justices of the
Common Bench,' and tell them to proceed to judgement
before the rising of the Bench, without further adjourning
or delaying the parties. In case they should be unable to

CHAP. IV. agree they were to come into Parliament, and the Chief Justice was to bring with him the rolls and the record of the plea into Parliament, there to take final agreement what judgement should be given.

Stonore and his companions did bring the record into Parliament, where were assembled the Chancellor, the Treasurer, the Justices of both Benches, the Barons of the Exchequer, and others of the King's Council. The process and record were viewed and read in Parliament, and it was there agreed at length that Geoffrey should recover against John and Amy. The decision was entered upon the Common Pleas roll thus:—'and thereupon advice having been had as well of the Prelates and Magnates, as of the Justices and others of the Council of the Lord the King being in the full Parliament last held,' judgement is given according to the direction of Parliament.

Control of the King in his Council in his Parliament over the proceedings of the Court of King's Bench. It might have been supposed that the matter was now at an end, but it was not. The Court of King's Bench had jurisdiction in error over the Court of Common Pleas. After all these delays, after the exertion of all the powers of the Council in Parliament, and after judgement had been given in accordance with the opinion of the highest legal and other authorities, there comes, in legal phrase, the lame and impotent conclusion that 'a writ of error was sued.'

The stages of the hearing in the King's Bench dragged on as slowly as those in the Court below, and were interrupted by similar petitions. John and Amy presented a petition to the King in his Council in his Parliament. representing that the Justices of the King's Bench had delayed proceeding to the correction of the errors assigned; . This called forth a writ directing the Justices of the King's Bench to proceed after consultation with those of the Common Bench and others learned in the law. The cause, however, was again and again adjourned, and petitions were again presented to the King in his Council in his Parliament, both by Geoffrey on the one hand, and by John and

Amy on the other. In the end John and Amy abandoned the case, and did not appear when called in Court. Geoffrey then prayed execution of the original judgement, and had it [1].

In the case of the Stauntons, though the matters in dispute were brought before the King in his Council in his Parliament, the petitions when presented remained 'in the Chancery [2].' The plea is described as having come into the Chancery [3], and one of the King's writs directed to the Justices contains a clause in which it is expressed that the record and process had been brought 'before us in our Chancery [4].' It is to be observed too, that the petitions presented, during the progress of the case, to the King in his Council in his Parliament have a resemblance in form to the Petitions or Bills presented to the Council, and in later times addressed to the Chancellor, for the purpose of commencing a suit. They have the characteristic words 'pur Dieu' (for God's sake). The Chancery is the office of the King in his Council in his Parliament   The writs issuing from it issue in virtue of that higher authority. If the usual forms prove insufficient, justice has to be aided by the source from which it originally flows—the King in his Council in his Parliament—though the Chancery is used as the channel.

The Chancery was the office of the King in his Council in his Parliament.

It is not necessary for the purposes of this history to trace the whole of the steps by which the functions of the Common Council of the Realm in relation to the Chancery were gradually delegated to the Council of another kind— to the official or legal Council of men learned in the law—or to show the growth of common law practice in the Chancery,

The Council in Chancery, and the King's High Court of Chancery.

---

[1] The facts in relation to the very illustrative case of the Stauntons have been put together from the following sources :—The *Year Book*, Mich., 13 Ed. III, No. 15 ; the *Placita de Banco*, Mich., 13 Ed. III, R⁰. 107 d ; the *Rolls of Parliament* (printed 2 Rot. Parl. 122–125) ; and the *Placita coram Rege*, Hil., 15 Ed. III, R⁰. 41. See also the introduction to the volume of *Year Books*, 13–14 Ed. III (edited by the present writer in the Rolls Series), pp. xxxvi–xliii.

[2] *Rolls of Parliament*, vol. ii. p. 123 a.

[3] *Ib.*   [4] *Ib.*, p. 125 b.

CHAP. IV. and the development out of it of the equity practice[1]. It is necessary, however, to bear in mind that the Chancery, like the Courts of King's Bench and Common Pleas, was the King's Court, and owed its existence to that greater King's Court or *Curia Regis* of which the Chancellor was a member. By degrees it became the custom for the King's Council—his legal or official council—to hear certain causes in the Chancery. Parties were required to appear 'before our Council in our Chancery,' and 'to do and accept as Our Court shall adjudge[2].' Here we see the Council in Chancery recognized as the King's Court or *Curia Regis*, and when petitions at a later date were addressed directly to the Chancellor and he decided causes on the principles of equity, it was in the King's High Court of Chancery.

The Treasurer: the Barons of the Exchequer Peers of Earls and other Barons.

Like the Chancellor, the Treasurer was a high officer commonly attendant on the King from the Conquest downwards, and so, in a certain sense, one of the King's Court. It has been disputed whether the Exchequer can be traced back, with a separate existence, as far as the Conquest. or was only a later outgrowth of the *Curia Regis*. The question is not of much importance in the present history, except in relation to the fact. that Barons of the Exchequer were Peers for the purpose of assessing the amercements of Earls and Barons, and that the Treasurer and Barons usually formed a part of the King's Council, and of his Council in his Parliament. It may, however, be worth noting that as soon as there was a Treasurer he must have had a department, with subordinates, just as the Chancellor had. There is consequently nothing unreasonable in the supposition that there was an Exchequer as well as a Treasurer in the time of the Conqueror, and it is quite possible that some matters relating to the revenue may even then have been brought before the Treasurer and some

---

[1] As to this, see an article by the present writer in the *Law Quarterly Review*, vol. i. p. 443. See also below, p. 296.

[2] This form appears on *Rot. Lit. Claus.*, 20 Ed. III, p. 2, m. 4 d, whence it has been cited in Palgrave's *Original Authority of the King's Council*, p. 132.

selected Barons, though the Chief Justiciary may have had CHAP. IV.
the supreme jurisdiction in the absence of the King.

There was, no doubt, a tradition in the Exchequer, as The Court
early as the reign of Edward III, that its special laws, of Ex-
customs, and privileges grew up (*inoleverunt*) in the time of from
William the Conqueror, and were used and reduced to to Edward
writing in the times of his successors. These privileges III :
included the right of the officers of the Exchequer to plead and others,
in the Exchequer itself touching all wrongs and trespasses Barons,'
against themselves. In case error should be alleged, the sitting in it.
Barons of the Exchequer themselves, having some of the
King's lieges associated with them, were to consider and
amend the error if necessary[1]. This is a very elaborate
organization for the time of the Conqueror, and it is to
be observed that, when the Barons of the Exchequer
living in the reign of Edward III specify particular
kings in whose reigns these privileges existed, they mention none earlier than Henry III. It is most probable
that, although the Exchequer, and even the Court of
Exchequer, may have existed under William I, various
changes were effected analogous to those which clearly
distinguished the Court of Common Pleas from the Court
of King's Bench, and that the various branches of the
Exchequer, including the Exchequer of Pleas, did not all
spring simultaneously ready-armed from the head of the
Conqueror. It does, however, seem clear that, in the
comparatively early stages of development, the Exchequer
possessed some judicial functions, and was a King's Court.
In the reign of Henry II[2] we find an account of a con-

---

[1] This appears in a certificate of the Barons of the Exchequer sent
to the King and enrolled on the Lord Treasurer's Remembrancer's
Remembrance Roll, Hil., 11 Ed. III, '*Adhuc recorda.*' The certificate is also enrolled on the King's Remembrancer's Roll of the same
term. There is another copy of it in the *Rubeus Liber* of the Exchequer, but this, as it now stands, was not inserted before the reign
of Henry VI, and is not, in all respects, perfectly accurate.

[2] *Reg. Roffen.* ff. 47-8, cited in Madox's *Hist. Exch.*, cap. iii. sec. 2,
note. It has been doubted whether the Exchequer may not here be
interpreted to mean the place of sitting rather than the Court. A simi-

CHAP. IV. cord or fine at Westminster at the Exchequer, as well as instances of Pleas at the Exchequer. We also find sitting at the Exchequer certain Bishops and others the ' King's Barons.' Some of the nobles about the King, those of his Court in the general sense of the term, were thus delegated to perform certain functions in the Exchequer; and so the Barons of the Exchequer were then and for some time afterwards the peers of Earls and Barons in general.

lar case, however, occurs ' *coram Baronibus de Scaccario* ' in the *Great Roll of the Exchequer*, 1 John, London and Middlesex.

CHAPTER V.

THUS far we have traced only the outlines of events *Chap. V.* down to the reign of Henry I, and the consti- *Necessity* tutional details affecting the Royal Court, the Councils, *of details* and the ' Parliaments,' down to the reign of Edward III. *relating to the* The status of the classes and individuals composing those *classes of* *which the* assemblies has hardly been touched in the foregoing *King's* pages. It is a subject necessarily involving the considera- *Court,* *Councils,* tion of some details which may, at first sight, appear to be *and Par-* of no great importance, but the statement of which is *liaments* *were* essential for the full comprehension of principles relating *composed.* to the growth of the House of Lords.

The hereditary principle, which, in one sense, appears to *An earl-* have been firmly established in Normandy before the *dom an* *administra-* Conquest, could not, in the nature of things, be said to *tive office,* have become as firmly established in England immediately *not strictly* *hereditary,* after it. When Englishmen were dispossessed by French- *imme-* *diately* men the latter held their newly acquired lands and titles of *after the* honour by purchase (to use a later legal phrase) and not by *Conquest.* inheritance, and the terms in which the grants were made have in most instances not been handed down. An earldom seems to have been still regarded as an office, which might indeed descend by hereditary succession, but which did not so descend of necessity.

If we turn to Northumbria we find Copsi, or Copsig, apparently with the assent of the Conqueror, expelling

CHAP. V. Osulf, the previous Earl, by force of arms, only to be himself defeated and put to death by Osulf. It is said that
The   Robert Comyn or de Comines was the next nominee of the
Earldom
of the   Conqueror[1]; but, at any rate both he and Osulf were
Northum-
brians.   killed very soon after the death of Copsi. The earldom, it
is said, was then bought of the Conqueror by Cospatric,
a descendant of that Northumbrian house of which members had frequently held the earldom before the Conquest.
He took, however, not by right of inheritance, but, in every
sense of the term, by purchase, and, as the chronicler ex-
presses it, 'administered the earldom' He fell away from
his allegiance, and the earldom was then conferred by the
Conqueror upon Waltheof, a son of Earl Siward by a daughter
of Earl Aldred (both Northumbrian Earls before the Conquest). Waltheof, like many of his predecessors, met a violent
death, and then the earldom was given to Bishop Walcher.
He, in his turn, was killed, and Alberic, or Aubrey, whose
name appears as a witness to a charter already cited. was
set in his place. Aubrey, it is alleged, resigned; and was
succeeded by Robert de Mowbray, from whom the earldom
was taken by William Rufus, and retained in the hands
of the Crown[2]. During the Conqueror's reign the Earls
appear to have been officially known as Earls not of
Northumbria but of the Northumbrians. It would probably
be difficult to prove that either Earl Aubrey or Robert de
Mowbray did or did not leave heirs. but after Robert de
Mowbray's time the earldom seems to have remained in the
hands of the Crown, or to have been non-existent, during
many years. Before Aubrey became Earl, however, the
principles, if they deserve the name. on which the earldom
devolved, in Northumbria, from one person to another,
were practically indistinguishable from those which prevailed before the Conquest. They may be summed up as
a regard for the claims of certain houses or families,

---

[1] Simeon of Durham (Rolls Series), vol. i. pp. 98–99, 245 ; A. S.
Chron., *anno* 1068.

[2] Simeon of Durham, vol. ii. pp. 197–199, 382–384 ; Flor. Worc.
vol. ii. pp. 251–252.

tempered by the military exigencies of the position, and CHAP. V.
a due consideration of the necessities of finance.

The official character of the earldom which seems to be The
marked in the title Earl of the Northumbrians, rather than of the East
of Northumbria, is marked in a similar manner in the title Angles.
of Alan Earl of the East Angles—not, be it observed, of
Norfolk and Suffolk. This earldom also appears under the
same name in the hands of Hugh Bigod during the reign of
Stephen though Hugh Bigod was subsequently created Earl
of Norfolk by Henry II.

There is no known instance of the creation of an Earl Earldoms
by patent, or by any written instrument, before the year ecclesi-
1140, and consequently no distinct proof of limitation to astics.
the heirs of the grantee. The Earldom of Chester offers,
perhaps, the nearest approach to a grant of this kind in the
time of the Conqueror, because the terms of its grant to
Hugh d'Avranches were, as alleged, to hold as freely by the
sword as the King himself held England by the Crown.
A County Palatine, however, was in a position different
from that of other Earldoms, and the principles applicable
to the one were not necessarily applicable to the others. It
must, indeed, be accepted as certain that an earldom was
not regarded as being absolutely hereditary in the early
days succeeding the Conquest, because earldoms were
commonly granted to ecclesiastics. as in the case of Odo
Bishop of Bayeux and Earl of Kent, and in the case of
Bishop Walcher, Earl of the Northumbrians[1].

At this time also it would seem that, so far as the King, No differ-
the Earls, and the Barons were concerned, there was no the Con-
difference of privilege or of status suggested between those queror's
who at a later period were designated Lords Spiritual and between
those who were designated Lords Temporal. The Church the status
was one of the roads of promotion to secular offices—to the leges of

---

[1] The charter of William de Warenne to the Priory of Lewes, in
which it is recited that William Rufus made him Earl of Surrey,
does not prove an express limitation to his heirs, though his heirs did
in fact have the third penny of the county of Surrey. The charter is
printed in Dugd. *Monast.*, v. 12.

CHAP. V.   highest secular offices in the land—to that of Chief Jus-

Lords   ticiary, to that of Chancellor, and to that of Earl. The

Spiritual   Bishops certainly had it in their power to secure absolute
and those
of Lords   equality with the Earls in all points, and might have secured
Temporal.   the right of trial by Peers at a later period had they not
thought fit to struggle for immunity from all secular jurisdiction. But the clergy had already entered on a conflict
with the lay authority, in an attempt to secure exceptional
privileges. It will, however, be most convenient to trace
the course and issue of this policy in a later chapter, when
the efforts of Becket and Stratford on behalf of their order
are considered.

The first   As the growth of hereditary earldoms cannot be distinctly
known
grant of an   traced before the reign of Stephen, it may be suspected
earldom,   that the exigencies of the war between him and the Empress
with limi-
tation to   Maud, daughter of Henry I, gave a stimulus to royal
the grantee   generosity. The first known documents which prove quite
and his
heirs,   clearly that an earldom was conferred upon the grantee
made in   and his heirs are charters of King Stephen and the
the reign of
Stephen.   Empress Maud. Geoffrey de Mandeville had creations or
grants from both to the effect that he and his heirs should
be Earls of Essex [1]. Maud also created Milo (or Miles)
de Gloucester Earl of Hereford, giving him the castle of
Hereford, and the 'third penny' of the pleas of the County
Court in fee and inheritance [2].

The   From this time onwards the creation of Earls to hold to
hereditary
succession   the grantees and their heirs is common. There is, how-
to an   ever, apparent a very remarkable feature which still to
earldom
at first   some extent qualifies the hereditary succession. In the
qualified   reign of Henry II Hugh Bigod was created Earl of Norfolk,
by the
necessity   receiving the third penny from Norwich and Norfolk. He
that the   and his heirs were to hold of the King and his heirs [3]. His
heir should

---

[1] The two charters have been printed by Mr. Round (the one from
Cott. Chart., vii. 4, the other from *Cott. Chart.*, xvi. 27, collated with the
Dugdale and Ashmole MSS.) in *Geoffrey de Mandeville*, pp. 51 and 88.

[2] Rymer's *Foedera* (1816), i. 14, from the Cotton Collections.

[3] *Cartae Antiquae*, S. n. 13, printed in *Reports on the Dignity of
a Peer*, vol. v. p. 2.

son Roger Bigod was nevertheless created Earl of Norfolk by Richard I, just as if he had no right of inheritance[1]. It is, indeed, possible that Hugh may in this case have been considered to have forfeited his earldom for traitorous practices, and that Roger may have been restored by a new grant. But there are other examples which show that the son did not at any rate become a full Earl upon the death of his father.

Geoffrey Fitz-Piers or Fitz-Peter, Earl of Essex, died, it is said, in the year 1213. He had been girt with the sword of the earldom, at the Coronation of King John[2], and he appears as a witness to several charters by the designation of Earl of Essex. He had married a grand-daughter of the heiress of William de Mandeville, Earl of Essex, but it is not clear that he was supposed to have a title to an hereditary earldom. His eldest son, Geoffrey, was eventually recognized as Earl of Essex, but not immediately after his death. The fact is curiously shown by the record of a cause of Michaelmas term in the fifteenth year of John's reign (A. D. 1214). Geoffrey de Say demanded the manor of Pleshey, together with the honour which had belonged to William de Mandeville, Earl of Essex. Geoffrey de Mandeville (the son of Geoffrey Fitz-Piers) pleaded that much was wanting to him of the honour which had belonged to Earl William. that William was Earl of Essex and girt with the sword of an Earl, and in receipt of the third penny, whereas Geoffrey de Mandeville was neither an Earl, nor girt with the sword, nor in receipt of the third penny[3].

At the beginning of the reign of Henry III also it seems that the son and heir of a deceased Earl did not immediately become Earl, and that he was not even in full possession of his earldom after having had livery of his lands. Thomas, son and heir of Henry Earl of Warwick, appears to have had livery of his lands in the thirteenth year of the

---

[1] The second grant is printed in the *Reports on the Dignity of a Peer*, vol. v. p. 4, from *Cart. Antiq.*, 1 Ric. I, S. n. 14.
[2] Hoveden (Rolls Series), vol. iv. p. 90.
[3] Printed in the *Plac. Abbr.*, p. 93.

CHAP. V. reign, but it was not until the seventeenth year (four years afterwards) that the following precept was sent to the sheriff of the county of Warwick: 'The King hath girded Thomas de Warwick with the girdle of the Earldom of Warwick, and the sheriff of Warwick is commanded that he cause the same Earl to have of the County aforesaid that which he ought to have in the name of Earl of Warwick and whereof his predecessors, Earls of Warwick, were seised as belonging to them in the name of the Earldom of Warwick [1].'

It might have been supposed *a priori* that when it was necessary for an Earl to be girt with the sword by the sovereign, the girding of the ancestor could not enure (or operate) to the benefit of the heir. When the heir of any tenant *in capite* had to sue out livery of the land held by his ancestor, it could hardly be possible that the heir of an Earl could gain possession of his Earldom without the ceremony of girding with the sword. The instances above cited are probably sufficient to prove the point, and the point when proved goes far to qualify the principle of absolutely hereditary succession. The succession was hereditary, but subject to the approval of the sovereign as expressed by the ceremony of investiture with the sword and belt.

Another principle distinguishable in the reign of Henry III: earldoms associated with an estate of inheritance in lands: the earldom of Lincoln.   There was, however, another principle coming into operation in the reign of Henry III, and one closely associated with the doctrine of barony by tenure. Every Earl, as forming part of the baronage, was a baron also. A man who succeeded to an estate of inheritance in a barony appears to have been subject to the burdens and to have had a right to the privileges of his predecessor. The theory that an Earl had a purely official or administrative rank was now on the wane, though not yet extinct. The theory that the rank followed an estate of inheritance in the lands seems now to have been entertained, though not yet fully estab-

[1] Cited in Dugdale's *Antiquities of Warwickshire*, p. 270, from *Anon. Evesh.* MS. (in the Bodleian Library), fo. 50 a.

lished. Thus Ranulf Earl of Chester and Lincoln, executed CHAP. V. a deed conveying to his sister, Hawise de Quency, the county (*comitatum*) of Lincoln (so far as it belonged to him), to hold to her and her heirs, of the King and his heirs, with all its appurtenances and with all the franchises thereto belonging, in order that she might be Countess thereof (*inde Comitissa*)[1]. The 'county, so far as it belonged to' Ranulf, can in this instrument hardly mean anything but those possessions in the county which had been held by the Earls of Lincoln. The word *comitatus* has sometimes been otherwise translated—sometimes as the earldom in the sense of the dignity[2], and sometimes as the third penny attaching to the earldom[3]. It is, however, impossible that the word could have been used in either of those two senses. Ranulf wished his sister to be Countess of Lincoln, not Countess of the earldom, which would be a phrase without meaning. He wished her to have not barely the third of the proceeds of the County Court, but an estate of inheritance also in the lands with which the earldom of Lincoln was associated; and although *comitatus* is a word used to express the County Court as well as the county, it would not be used to express a third part of the proceeds alone.

Hawise de Quency, it appears, wished her son-in-law, John de Lacy, to be recognized as Earl of Lincoln in her lifetime, and King Henry III, at her instance, granted to him the third penny of the County Court of Lincoln, as previously received by Ranulf Earl of Chester and Lincoln. It is mentioned in the grant that Ranulf had in his lifetime given this third penny to his sister. The royal grant, however, differs from the terms of the deed made by Ranulf. According to the latter the *comitatus* or county was conveyed to Hawise in fee simple. Henry's grant settled the

---

[1] The deed is printed in Selden's *Titles of Honour*, p. 653.
[2] E.g. in *Cruise on Dignities* (2nd edition), pp. 109-111.
[3] E.g. in the *Third Report on the Dignity of a Peer*, vol. ii. p. 238.

CHAP. V. third penny in special tail to John de Lacy and his heirs by Margaret his wife, daughter of Hawise [1].

It is sufficiently clear from these transactions that the word county or *comitatus* in a conveyance was held not to be, but to include the third penny received by the Earl from the proceeds of the County Court. It seems clear also that the third penny could not be treated as a charge on the issues of the County Court which might be conveyed away at his pleasure by a person having the fee simple. A licence to alienate was of course necessary, and the Crown could therefore interfere to prevent any alienation which had not the royal approval, and would certainly regard with a very jealous eye any alienation which affected a part of the royal revenue.

Partition between coheirs: effect of one county or earldom alone falling to coheirs: the Earldom of Chester. If an Earl held a county, together with lands in other counties, and died without male heir, partition could be made between his female coheirs, and one of them could receive the 'county' as her share, though many cases show that, for some centuries after the Conquest, the death of an Earl who was Earl of one county only, and left only female coheirs, was a cause of perplexity. In the twenty-third year of the reign of Henry III it was decided that 'if the *Earldom* of Chester descend to coparceners, it shall be divided between them just as other lands, and the eldest shall not have that seignory (or lordship) entirely to herself [2].' The confusion, in this passage, between the earldom and the lands of the earldom is a sufficient indication that there was some connexion between the two. There is no evidence that the first Earls of Chester after the Conquest, though invested with the sword, held a dignity apart from the lands. They must, indeed, having Palatine rights, have been in the same position with regard to the lands of the county, as the King with regard to the lands of England generally, and have been chief lords over them all.

---

[1] *Rot. Lit. Pat.,* 17 Hen. III, m. 9, No. 35 (printed in *Reports on the Dignity of a Peer,* vol. v. p. 8).

[2] Fitzherbert's Abridgement, *Particion,* 18 (23 Hen. III), and see Co. Litt. 165.

When the lands were held to be partible (A.D. 1239), the CHAP. V.
point must have arisen in view of the recent decease of
John the Scot, Earl of Chester, without heir male. He had
himself succeeded [1] to the earldom in right of his mother,
one of the coheirs of Ranulf, Earl of Chester. Partition of
lands had been made between Ranulf's sisters and coheirs,
or their representatives, and the whole County of Chester
had been allotted to the eldest sister Matilda, John's
mother, the other sisters receiving lands of proportionate
value [2]. When John died, however, it was no longer
possible to make partition between his sisters, or their
representatives, in such a way as to give the County of
Chester to one, because the other possessions of Ranulf had
already been allotted. According to strict law, therefore,
the county would have had to be divided, or otherwise to
be held in coparcenary. The difficulty, however, was
evaded by giving other lands as compensation to the
coheirs, and by retaining those of the earldom in the
hands of the King [3].

In the reign of Richard II, it is clear, the legal mind
was familiar with the idea that the earldom was to be
identified with the County or *Comitatus*, and that the
County or *Comitatus* was equivalent to the possessions
attaching (and, as it would appear, inseparably attaching)
to the earldom. The same idea was then also attributed
to lawyers as far back as the time of Henry III.

The title
to the
County of
Chester, in
the sense of
the lands
and pos-
sessions
of the
earldom,
regarded as
identical
with the
title to the
earldom
itself from
Henry III
to Richard
II.

Richard wished to establish his right to nominate a
person to receive a pension or annuity from the Priory of
Coventry. The Prior disputed the claim on the ground
that the Priory (or, as it had once been called, the Abbey)
was not of royal foundation. According to the plea on his

[1] *Successit* is the word used both in Wendover (Rolls Series),
vol. iii. p. 40, and in Knighton (Rolls Series), vol. i. p. 211, though it is
sometimes said that John was created Earl.
[2] *Rot. Lit. Pat.*, 22 Hen. III, m. 4, and m. 11, and 25 Hen. III,
m. 1, and *Rot. Lit. Claus.*, 22 Hen. III, m. 12 (cited in Dugdale's
Baronage, vol. i. p. 46), and Knighton (Rolls Series), vol. i. p. 212.
[3] *Rot. Lit. Pat.*, 31 Hen. III, m. 6 (cited in the *Third Report on the
Dignity of a Peer*, vol. ii. p. 130).

F

CHAP V. behalf, the House had been founded before the Conquest, and the *advocatio*, advowson, or patronage had always been with the Earls of Chester. It is not necessary to accept as accurate the pedigree by which the inheritance is traced from Leofric, who was Earl of Chester before the Conquest, through Hugh d'Avranches, as a son of Leofric's sister, to Ranulf, the last of that name who was Earl of Chester and Lincoln, and from Ranulf to his four sisters. The pedigree differs in many particulars from the facts as stated in contemporary documents. The principle enunciated, however, was very clear, and was not disputed. On Ranulf's death. it is said, the advowson or patronage of the Priory, together with the whole county (*Comitatus*) of Chester and its appurtenances, was allotted to Matilda, one of Ranulf's sisters, in satisfaction of her share, while various other castles, manors. lands, and tenements were allotted to the other sisters. The advowson or patronage, it is said, 'together with the whole County of Chester,' descended from Matilda to her son John the Scot. Earl of Chester. It is also said that John afterwards gave the advowson, together with the whole County of Chester, to King Henry III, and the devolution (always including the whole County of Chester) is then traced through successive Kings to Richard II [1]. It thus appears indisputable that from the time of Henry III to that of Richard II the title to the county (or possessions of the earldom) of Chester was regarded as identical with the title to the earldom itself.

The Earldom of Pembroke held to be the right of one who succeeded to a part of the inheritance, as descen-   A different course was taken in relation to the Earldom of Pembroke (like that of Chester, a Palatine earldom) in the reign of Edward III, but here also it is evident that the descent of the earldom was associated, according to the prevalent ideas, with the inheritance of the lands. The inheritance of Aymer de Valence, Palatine Earl of Pembroke, devolved upon his sisters, to be divided between them and their heirs in due proportion. Nothing appears

---

[1] *Placita coram Rege*, Hilary, 14 Richard II, *Rex*, R°. 20.

to have been done with regard to the earldom immediately, CHAP. V.
but Lawrence de Hastings, who *succeeded to part of the* dant of an
inheritance, as descendant of the eldest sister, was held by eldest
the lawyers to be entitled to the 'prerogative of the name sister.
and honour.' The name of Earl of Pembroke was therefore
confirmed to him by the King 'willing and granting that .
Lawrence do have and hold the prerogative and honour of
Earl Palatine *in the lands which he holds of the inheritance
of the said Aymer*, as fully and in the same manner as
Aymer had and held them at the time of his decease [1].' It
was clearly in virtue of his part of the inheritance that his
claim to the earldom was recognized.

It is probable that as early as the reign of Edward I the Earldoms
ceremony of girding a newly-created Earl with a sword by tenure
in the
enured to his heirs without the absolute necessity of a new reign of
ceremony on succession. It is probable also that the idea Edward I.
of an earldom by tenure, or associated with the holding of
certain lands, was not unfamiliar at this period, and had
grown up since the Conquest. In this reign an Earl was
summoned to Parliament in a manner which can hardly be
reconciled with any other hypothesis than that of holding
the earldom by tenure of the lands.

Gilbert de Clare, Earl of Gloucester and Hertford, The
married, as his second wife, Joan, a daughter of King Earldoms
of

[1] There are some curious mistakes with regard to the authority for
this matter in the *Third Report on the Dignity of a Peer* (vol. ii.
pp. 180–181). It is there said that the Letters Patent are cited in 'the
third Institute' but that they had not been found on the Roll. They
are in fact cited in 4 Inst. 221, and they do appear on the Roll
of Letters Patent, 13 Ed. III, Part 4, m. 12. Coke's reference is
perfectly correct with the exception that he omitted to insert the
words 'Part 4'; but the omission would cause little difficulty to
any one who is familiar with records. It is suggested in the same
passage, in the *Third Report on the Dignity of a Peer*, 'that there
was a difference between the term 'Earl of Pembroke,' and the
term 'Earl Palatine,' and that the dignity of Earl was something
different from the prerogative and honour of Earl Palatine; but the
words 'prerogative and honour' are used in relation to the Earl of
Pembroke, and there does not seem to be any ground for this very
subtle distinction.

CHAP. V. Edward I. Upon that occasion he surrendered his lands to
Gloucester the King, and new settlements were made, the terms of
and Hert-
ford settled which are fully set out in the Charter Roll of the time[1].
by a settle- The lands in Ireland were settled in one form, those in
ment of England and Wales (with which alone we are now con-
the lands.
cerned) in another. All the castles, manors, and lands in
England and Wales, with all their appurtenances, were
granted and confirmed by the King to the Earl and his
wife, and the heirs of their bodies, to be holden by the
same services as before the surrender, as freely, fully, and
honourably (*honorifice*) in all rights, royalties. honours, lordships, free customs, and all other things appertaining to
the castles, manors, and lands as the Earl held them on the
day of the surrender, without any reservation. If the Earl
should die without heir of their two bodies, or if the heirs
of their bodies should die without heirs of their bodies, and
Joan should survive, she was to have and to hold, at her
will for ever all the castles, manors. and lands, with all their
appurtenances, rights, royalties, liberties, and all other things
appertaining thereto as her own inheritance. If, however.
there should be heirs of their two bodies, Joan was to have
no power to make any alienation of the lands. and if she
should die without heirs of their two bodies, and the Earl
should survive, all the castles and lands were to ' remain and
wholly revert ' to him and his heirs as if the surrender and
settlement had not been made.

Case of   The Earl died, leaving (with other issue) a son, Gilbert,
Joan,
widow of by his wife Joan. She was then, according to the terms of
Gilbert, the settlement, tenant in special tail of the castles, lands,
Earl of
Gloucester and everything granted according to the King's charter.
and Hert- During her widowhood she was attracted by the manly and
ford, tenant
in special graceful appearance of one Ralph de Monthermer, who. at
tail of the that time, was not a peer, or even a knight[2]. She married

---

[1] Charter Roll (Chancery), 18 Ed. I, nos. 59 and 60. Thesé
are cited, but not by any means correctly, in Dugdale's Baronage,
which has served as the basis of statements in many subsequent
Peerages.

[2] Trokelowe, *Annales* (Rolls Series), p 27.

him without asking her father's consent. Apart from any
question of want of filial respect, this was a serious offence
from a feudal point of view, as Joan was what was termed
a King's widow—the widow of one holding *in capite*, who
could not, except at her own risk, marry without the
King's licence. The lands were consequently seized into
the King's hands. The King, however, was afterwards
appeased, and the lands were restored.

According to the law of the period. though Joan was now
tenant in special tail, it was only in subordination to her
husband, who held the lands in her right, without whom
she could not sue or be sued, and who was bound to perform
the services by which the lands were held. Ralph de
Monthermer, however, was not only summoned to perform
military service, but was summoned as Earl of Gloucester
and Hertford[1]. He was also summoned as Earl of
Gloucester and Hertford to give his advice in Parliament[2].

It is usually said that Monthermer was summoned as
Earl in right of his wife, but before that proposition can
even be entertained it must be clearly proved that the
wife herself had an earldom. If she had it. she could
certainly have had it only as an appurtenance or part of
the castles, lands, and rights previously the inheritance of
her' first husband, her estate in which was acquired by the
King's charter effecting the new settlement. In that charter
there is no express mention of any earldom, and, if any
passed by the terms of the grant, it could have passed
only in one of two ways—either as included in some of
the other terms used, or as included under the word appurtenances. These two ways, however, resolve themselves
into one only, for it matters little whether an earldom
could pass under words relating to lands by various desig-
nations or under the word appurtenances. As there was

---

[1] *Rot. Lit. Claus.*, 27 Ed. I, m. 9 d (printed in *Reports on the Dignity
of a Peer*, vol. iii. p. 112.
[2] *Rot. Lit. Claus.*, 28 Ed. I, m. 17 d ; and subsequent years (printed,
p. 113, &c.).

CHAP. V. no express mention, if any carldom passed at all, it passed
with the lands and castles.

Gilbert,   Another consideration also suggests itself here. Gilbert,
the heir,
did not, on son of Gilbert de Clare and Joan, was the heir to the
his father's carldoms, and must have succeeded on his father's death,
death,
succeed   if the earldoms were strictly hereditary, and not capable
to the   of being made the subject of a new settlement. What,
earldom.
then, happened after the settlement was made upon the
marriage of his father and mother? What was his position,
with regard to the earldoms, when his father died? When
Ralph de Monthermer was recognized as Earl, were there
two Earls of Gloucester, or only one? Clearly, if there
was only one, the succession to the earldom was interrupted
by the settlement of the lands; and it is absurd to suppose
that Gilbert and Ralph were both Earls of Gloucester at
the same time.

Indications   The difficulties, however, vanish at once on the theory
that the
earldoms   that the earldoms of Gloucester and Hertford were earl-
were   doms by tenure. On that supposition, but on no other,
earldoms
by tenure. Ralph de Monthermer was in the same position with
regard to the earldoms as with regard to the lands. As
long as his wife lived, he had, by law, the same rights and
the same liabilities (including that of summons to Parliament) in respect of the lands as the wife would have had
if a male. If a male holder of the land in fee tail, or
otherwise having an estate of inheritance, would have been
an Earl, then her husband was of necessity an Earl also;
but she could not, apart from the lands, give him any
dignity as an Earl, because her legal status would have
been only Joan, wife of Ralph de Monthermer. Contemporary records, however, show that her status actually was
Joan, wife of Ralph, Earl of Gloucester and Hertford[1]—not,
be it observed, Joan, Countess of Gloucester and Hertford,
wife of Ralph de Monthermer, for such a designation was,
at that time, unknown to the law.

---

[1] In Michaelmas Term, 28-29 Ed. I, Ralph de Monthermer and
Joan his wife were defendants. The case is printed in the *Plac. Abbr.*,
p. 242. They are mentioned, under the same description, on p. 255.

There are several cases, in the reports of the period, which prove the same point, and show incidentally that the Earl suing with Joan, as wife, claimed the rights of the preceding Earl and his ancestors[1]. Of course the husband was liable for the military services due in respect of the lands which he held in right of his wife, and everything in relation to Monthermer's position is perfectly intelligible, and quite usual except the application to him of the title of Earl of Gloucester and Hertford.

It is not known that Ralph de Monthermer was created Earl by patent, or girt with the sword of earldom by the King, nor is it in the least degree probable that he ever was. He had no estate of inheritance in the earldoms, as they went to Gilbert, heir of Gilbert de Clare. He had not even the earldoms for life, as they departed from him as soon as his wife died. As long only as his wife lived, her estate of inheritance in the lands was for all practical purposes his, and for that reason, to all appearance, he enjoyed the earldoms.

When Joan died, the lands, under the settlement, im- Gilbert, heir in special tail mediately became the right of young Gilbert de Clare, son of her and her first husband, and heir in special tail. He of the lands, is recognized was a minor, and the wardship of his lands belonged to the King. Ralph de Monthermer, being no longer in possession as Earl only after of the lands, and having in his own person no claim to an his mother's estate of inheritance, ceased to be Earl[2]; and this fact in death. itself affords a very strong presumption that the earldoms followed an estate of inheritance in the lands. Edward II

[1] E.g. *Year Book*, E, 32 Ed. I, pp. 177–9, and T, 32 Ed. I, pp. 209–213.

[2] Some very curious mistakes in relation to this point appear in the *First Report on the Dignity of a Peer*, p. 432, where it is said that Ralph de Monthermer was summoned as Earl of Gloucester during the minority of his 'son-in-law,' 'the son-in-law, after he attained his age, being summoned as Earl of Gloucester.' Gilbert, the heir, was not son-in-law, but step-son, of Monthermer. The fact of his being step-son has no direct relation to the subject, and, as will be seen, his summons to Parliament preceded his attainment of full age.

CHAP. V. who had just succeeded to the throne showed great favour
to his nephew. Gilbert's lands were restored, while he was
yet a minor, in order that he might be knighted [1]. He was
summoned as Earl of Gloucester and Hertford, in January
1307–8, when he was not yet seventeen years of age, to
be present at his uncle's coronation [2]. He was summoned
to Parliament as Earl of Gloucester and Hertford, one day
later [3], and he was summoned, as Earl of Gloucester, to
perform military service against the Scots, on June
21, 1308, when he had just completed his seventeenth
year [4].

Monther-
mer then
ceased to
be sum-
moned as
Earl, and
was sub-
sequently
summoned
as a newly-
created
Baron.

If further proof were needed that the earldoms followed
the estate of inheritance in the lands it would be shown in
the fact that after Joan's death Monthermer ceased for
a short time to be summoned to Parliament at all. In
March 1309, however, he was again summoned, no longer
as an Earl, but among the Barons [5]. According to modern
ideas this summons followed by a sitting in Parliament,
was Monthermer's creation as a Baron.

Hugh de
Courtenay;
the Earl-
dom of
Devon
declared to
follow an
estate of

Another instance of earldom by tenure, an instance in
which an earldom followed an estate of inheritance in
certain lands, may be discerned in the early Earldom of
Devon. William de Fortz (or Fortibus), Comte d'Aumarle [6] married as his second wife Isabella daughter of

---

[1] *Rot. Lit. Claus.*, 1 Ed. II, m. 15.
[2] *Ib.*, 1 Ed. II, m. 12 d.   [3] *Ib.*, 1 Ed. II, m. 11 d.
[4] *Ib.*, 1 Ed. II, m. 2 d.   [5] *Ib.*, 2 Ed. II, m. 11 d.
[6] He was *Comes Albae Marliae*, of which the French translation is,
no doubt, Comte d'Aumarle or Aumâle. Whether the expression can
rightly be translated Earl of Albemarle, may, perhaps, be open to
doubt, as the title was of French origin, and the place from which it
was taken in Normandy. The succession to that title is, in itself,
a subject of much interest, but, in the absence of proof that it relates
to an English earldom, it would hardly be relevant to enlarge upon
the subject. In more instances than one, the husband of an Albemarle
heiress became *Comes Albae Marliae*. Thus after Hawise, daughter of
William le Gros, *Comes Albae Marliae*, married William de Mandeville, he was '*factus Comes Albae Marliae* ' (*Chronicle of Robert de
Torigny*, Rolls Series, p. 282). Her third husband, Baldwin de
Bethune, was *Comes Albemarliae, dono Ricardi Regis* (Hoveden, Rolls

Baldwin de Ripariis, Redvers, or Rivers, Earl of Devon. On the death of her brother who had succeeded to the earldom, she inherited his lands, and with them apparently the earldom. This happened after her husband's death, and she was then described sometimes as Countess of Albemarle, sometimes as Countess of Devon, and sometimes as Countess of Albemarle and Devon. In the fifty-second year of Henry III she brought, as Countess of Albemarle and Devon, an assise of Mort d'Ancestor against the Prior of Brommore, as Countess of Albemarle an action against one Adam de Newmarch and others, and as Countess of Devon against one Roger de Lancashire and others[1]. It is probable that there was in each case a reason for the particular description, and one connected with the tenure of lands, for in the following reign, when the King asserted his right of presentation to a church, as having in his hands by escheat the lands of the Earl or Count of Albemarle, it was disputed whether the lands to which the advowson appertained belonged in fact to the Earl of Albemarle or to the Earl of Devon[2].

CHAP. V.

inheritance in the lands in the reign of Edward III.

Her children died during her lifetime without issue, and her next heir was Hugh de Courtenay, a descendant of Mary, daughter of William de Redvers (or Vernon), Earl of Devon, who died in the year 1216. The fact that he was heir does not appear to have been at any time disputed. but when he claimed certain lands held by Isabella de Fortz, and in particular the whole of the Isle of Wight, his claim was contested on the ground that she had conveyed these particular lands to the King for the sum of six thousand marks. The proceedings appear in the rolls of Parliament of the eighth year of the reign of Edward II, when the matter was held over for further consideration[3].

Series, iii. 306). In both cases the title seems to have been given by the Crown. Hawise's second husband, William de Fortz, was also *Comes Albae Marliae*, as was their son after her death.

[1] Mich., 52 Hen. III, printed in *Plac. Abbr.*, pp. 172–3.
[2] *Placita coram Rege*, Easter, 24 Ed. I, R°. 2. *Plac. Abbr.*, p. 262.
[3] *Rot. Parl.*, 8 & 9 Ed. II, No. 1 (printed, vol. i. pp. 334–6).

CHAP. V.   It was probably by reason of doubts and disputes relating
to portions of the inheritance that Hugh de Courtenay was
not for ·some time recognized as Earl of Devon, though
he was summoned to Parliament among the Barons as
early as February 6, 1298–9 (27 Ed. I) and for many
years afterwards. Though not called Earl, however, he
received the third penny (or third part of the proceeds of
the County Court) of Devonshire, in the same way as
the Countess and previous Earls had received it. An
objection was at length made that a person who was not
an Earl ought not to receive this third penny. The
payment ceased and the claim was disallowed.

Courtenay, however, in the reign of Edward III had had
his right recognized if not to the whole of the lands which
Isabella had held, at any rate to so much of them as constituted the inheritance of the Earls of Devon. He then
presented a petition to the King in relation to this matter
of the third penny, and the King caused enquiry to be
made at the Exchequer. The Treasurer and Barons of the
Exchequer certified that the money had been withheld
because Courtenay had not used the name and title of
Earl. The King thereupon sent a writ or ' letter close ' to
Courtenay, reciting the facts, and commanding him to take
the name and honour of an Earl, for certain reasons, which
deserve attention. 'Because the *inheritance* of the Countess
and of her and your predecessors, Earls of Devon, has descended to you by right of inheritance, and you at this present
do hold the inheritance . . . . . we will and command you that
you cause yourself henceforward to be called Earl of Devon.'
The King promised that the third penny should in future
be paid to him as it had been paid to the Earls of Devon
his predecessors [1]. The King also directed a writ to the
Sheriff of Devonshire to make proclamation that Courtenay
was to be esteemed and called Earl of Devon, and directed

---

[1] *Rot. Lit. Claus.*, 9 Ed. III, m. 35 d. It is erroneously stated in
the *Reports on the Dignity of a Peer*, vol. ii. p. 176, that the declaration
was by Letters Patent. This is a very serious mistake, as Letters
Patent might imply a new creation.

the Treasurer and Barons of the Exchequer to cause the third penny to be paid to him, by the name of Earl, in the same manner as to his ancestors.

It is difficult to interpret the reasons given by the King in any other sense than that the earldom followed or ought to follow the rest of the inheritance Courtenay was to take the title of Earl of Devon, not because that dignity itself and by itself had descended to him, but because the inheritance of the Earls of Devon had so descended and was already held by him. There was no new creation, no investiture or girding with a sword, but a simple direction to assume the name in virtue of the inheritance already held.

From one point of view this may be regarded as a re- *The con-* cognition of an earldom by tenure, but not as a recognition *veyance of the* of the proposition that the earldom absolutely followed *lands to a* the lands. The descent to the Earl by right of inheritance *might* is an essential feature of the reasons given, and it does not *perhaps deprive* follow that a purchaser of everything included in the in- *the heir* heritance of the Earls of Devon would acquire the earldom *of the* by the purchase. It does, however, seem to follow that *without* a conveyance of the lands to a stranger in fee would *conferring* deprive an heir of his succession to the earldom. *stranger.*

While some earlier earldoms had thus come to be *It was a* associated with the tenure of certain lands, some later *recognized doctrine in* earldoms were associated with the grant of lands to *the reign of* support them. Thus when William de Bohun was created *Edward* Earl of Northampton in the year 1337, he had not only *Earl must* a fixed charge of twenty pounds *per annum* on the issues of *to support* the county[1], but also a grant to him and the heirs male *his earl-* of his body of various castles and manors[2]. In the same *dom.* year several other Earls were created, and at the same time commonly received lands to the value of a thousand marks *per annum*, as well as a certain sum from the revenues of

[1] *Rot. Chart.*, 11 Ed. III, no. 49 (printed in *Report on the Dignity of a Peer*, vol. v. p. 30).

[2] *Originalia* Roll, Exchequer, 11 Ed. III, R°. 50 (cited in Madox's *Baronia*, p. 149).

Chap. V. the county. William de Clinton was made Earl of Huntingdon on those terms [1], Robert de Ufford Earl of Suffolk [2], and William de Montague Earl of Salisbury [3]. In each case certain specified lands were assigned in whole or part satisfaction of the claim thus given to a thousand marks *per annum*. In each case the lands were given to the newly-created Earl and the heirs male of his body, with reversion to the Crown, though, whether from inadvertence or otherwise, the rent charged upon the county was to be held by the Earl and his heirs, of the King and his heirs, for ever.

All these Earls were created and belted in ' Parliament,' but not all in the same kind of Parliament. The Earl of Huntingdon, the Earl of Northampton, and the Earl of Suffolk were so made by the common consent and advice of the Prelates, Earls, Barons, and others of the Council in Parliament. The Earl of Salisbury was so made at the request of the Prelates, Proceres. and Commonalty of the realm in Parliament. In each of these instances, however, it was clearly recognized on all hands that an Earl must have lands to support his earldom.

The first Duke (of Cornwall) girt with a sword; like an Earl; lands inseparably attached to the dukedom. The subject receives further illustration from the terms in which the first Duke was created. He was Edward the Black Prince, son and heir of Edward III. His charter was constructed on lines similar to those of the Earls newly made in the same year. His dukedom was in fact only a superior kind of earldom. It was conferred, like most of the earldoms of the period with the common consent and advice of the Prelates, Earls. Barons, and others of the King's Council in Parliament, and without any reference to the Commons. He was girt with a sword in the same manner as the Earls. He had the shrievalty of Cornwall

---

[1] *Rot. Chart.*, 11 Ed. III, nos. 34, 41, and 42 (printed in *Rep. Dig. Peer*, vol. v. pp. 27–30).

[2] *Ib.*, 11 Ed. III, nos. 51 and 52 (printed in *Rep. Dig. Peer*, vol. v. pp. 31 and 38), and *Rot. Lit. Pat.*, 11 Ed. III, part i. m. 5 (printed, p. 33).

[3] *Ib.*, 11 Ed. III, nos. 54 and 55 (printed, pp. 32 and 34).

granted to him in such a manner that he could constitute a Sheriff of Cornwall at his pleasure. In this respect he had the functions of an Earl of the olden time, his nominee being the Vice-Earl, as the Sheriff always should have been according to the etymology of his Latin and French de- signations[1]. Vast possessions were also assigned to him, but only as Duke of Cornwall[2]; and they were annexed and united to the dukedom for ever, and made inseparable from it[3]. The grant of them was only to the Black Prince and the first-born sons of him and his heirs, being Kings of England, and to Dukes of Cornwall by succession of in- heritance. Thus there could be no Duke of Cornwall without the lands assigned to the dukedom, and the lands assigned to the dukedom must always be in the hands of the Duke when not in the hands of the Sovereign[4].

The grants of lands by the King, though probably not Acts of usually made without due consideration, occasionally gave Parliament to restrict rise to disputes in matters of detail. Sometimes, it was the grant said, the King was 'deceived in his grants.'. For this Lands in reason it was enacted in the year 1399 that he should the reign of Henry IV. always have the advice of the sages of his Council with regard to matters touching his estate and that of the Realm. All persons asking for lands, rents, offices, or other profits from the King were also to make, in their petitions, express mention of the value not only of those lands or profits, but also of any others which they might have had by gift from the King or any of his predecessors.

---

[1] *Vicecomes, Vicounte.*

[2] '*Sub nomine et honore Ducis dicti loci.*'

[3] '*Quae quidem omnia . . . praedicto ducatui praesenti carta nostra pro nobis et heredibus nostris annectimus et unimus eidem in perpetuum remansura, ita quod ab eodem ducatu aliquo tempore nullatenus separentur, nec alicui seu aliquibus aliis quam dicti loci Ducibus per nos vel heredes nostros donentur seu quomodolibet conce- dantur.*'

[4] *Rot. Chart.*, 11 Ed. III, no. 54 (printed, *Rep. Dig. Peer*, vol. v. pp. 35-38). It is said in the *Third Rep. Dig. Peer* (vol. ii. p. 108), that 'the dignity of the Duke of Cornwall . . . was clearly personal,' but the actual words of the grant do not seem to warrant the state- ment

CHAP. V. Failure to comply with this condition was to render void any letters patent of grant [1]. A remedy was at the same time provided for persons wrongfully dispossessed by 'colour' of such letters patent [2]. Grants of lands by the King were further restrained in the year 1402, by the provision (somewhat difficult of interpretation) that none were to be made except to deserving persons [3]; but in the year 1404 the Queen and princes of the blood were exempted from the provisions of the Act of 1399 relating to petitions for grants [4]. In the year 1429 it was enacted that all lands which had been seized into the King's hands should be retained until a month had elapsed after the return of the Inquisitions in which the facts were set forth. Any letters patent of grant made before that time were to be void, in order that any one disputing the King's title might have due opportunity of proving his case [5].

They had little effect at first.   The effect of these Acts there can be little doubt, was to check by degrees the grant of Crown lands, and so to prepare the way for the grant of the higher dignities of the peerage without any corresponding assignment of lands. It was not, however, until the fourth year of the reign of Henry V that the Acts appeared to have had any effect upon official instruments relating to the creation of Dukes, Marquesses, and Earls. The Sheriff of Devonshire having been commanded to pay to the Duke of Exeter forty pounds *per annum* out of the issues of his county, a clause was at the same time introduced (apparently with reference to the Act of 1 Henry IV), · Notwithstanding the preferment of ten thousand pounds made in our Parliament lately held at Westminster [6].'

Grants of lands associated with dignities in Normandy   The English successes in France were followed about this time by the grant of various dignities in Normandy to men of English birth. John de Gray obtained the county of Tancarville in terms which indissolubly associated the

---

[1] Stat. 1 Hen. IV, cap. 6.   [2] Stat. 1 Hen. IV, cap. 8.
[3] Stat. 4 Hen. IV, cap. 4.   [4] Stat. 6 Hen. IV, cap. 2.
[5] Stat. 8 Hen. VI, c. 16.
[6] *Rot. Lit. Claus.*, 4 Hen. V, m. 10 (*Rep. Dig. Peer*, vol. v. p. 183).

dignity with the lands [1]. The Earl of Salisbury acquired the county of Perche [2], and William Bourchier the county of Eu [3], in a similar manner. So also Gaston de Foix was created Comte de Longueville, and had a grant of the county of Longueville in support of it [4]. It is apparent from these instances how familiar the minds of men living in the reign of Henry V must still have been with the idea of a county or earldom associated with the tenure of lands.

CHAP. V.

in the reign of Henry V.

It was not until Henry VI had been more than ten years upon the throne that distinct references began to be made to the Statutes in restraint of the grants of lands in the hands of the King. Humphrey, Duke of Gloucester, a son of Henry IV, presented a petition to the King in Parliament. He had, it seems, been created Earl of Pembroke and Duke of Gloucester, for life, by his brother Henry V [5], who granted to him and the heirs of his body, just before the creation, the county of Pembroke with all its issues and profits under the name of the Castle and Lordship of Pembroke, and the Castle and Lordship of Tenby. Through some inadvertence a grant had been made, out of the issues of the same county, of twenty pounds *per annum* for the better support of the earldom, and of forty pounds *per annum* for the better support of the dukedom, and this of course was nugatory, since the Duke, as Earl of Pembroke, already enjoyed the whole of the county revenue. The possessions of the alien Priories having been seized into the King's hand in the eighth year of the reign of Henry V, the Duke now prayed that he might have a grant of the possessions

The earldom of Pembroke still associated with the county in the reigns of Henry V and Henry VI.

---

[1] *Rot. Lit. Pat. Norm.*, 6 Hen. V, part ii. m. 41, no. 78 (printed, *Rep. Dig. Peer*, vol. v. pp. 186-7).

[2] *Ib.*, 7 Hen. V, part i. m. 63, no. 232 (printed, *Rep. Dig. Peer*, vol. v. p. 187).

[3] *Ib.*, 7 Hen. V, part i. m. 4 (printed, *Rep. Dig. Peer*, vol. v. p. 188).

[4] *Ib.*, 7 Hen. V, part i. m. 35, no. 64 (printed, *Rep. Dig. Peer*, vol. v. pp. 188-9).

[5] *Rot. Lit. Pat.*, 2 Hen. V, part i. m. 36 (printed, *Rep. Dig. Peer*, vol. v. p. 171).

CHAP. V. of the alien Priory of Pembroke, to him and the heirs male
of his body in satisfaction of the sums of twenty and forty
pounds *per annum* which had been granted to him, and
from which he had received no profit. He at the same
time prayed that he might have a grant of the earldom
and dukedom to him and the heirs male of his body
instead of for life only. Here he introduced a clause which
recurs again and again in the same or similar form in later
grants of dignities—'Notwithstanding that express mention
is not made in this petition of the true value of the priory, &c.,
or of that which the petitioner has of your gift or the
gift of your progenitors, and notwithstanding any statute or
ordinance to the contrary.' He obtained the earldom and
dukedom in the terms desired, but the priory during the
King's pleasure only [1]. These very instructive transactions
tell us how the Earldom of Pembroke was still associated
with the county of Pembroke in the reign of Henry V,
and lead us almost insensibly to that new state of affairs
in which earldoms and higher dignities became strictly
personal.

The earl-
dom of
Arundel
held to
depend
upon an
estate of
inheritance
in the
castle and
honour of
Arundel in
the reign of
Henry VI.
One of the great essentials of earldoms by tenure seems
to have been that the holder must have taken the lands
by inheritance, and not by purchase, except of course when
he acquired them directly from the Crown. Thus in the
famous case of the Earldom of Arundel, when John
Fitz-Alan, the heir in tail male of Richard Fitz-Alan, and
tenant in tail male of the castle and honour of Arundel,
was admitted in Parliament to be Earl of Arundel, he was
so admitted, not simply as being in possession of the castle
and honour, but because they had descended to him by
special right of inheritance [2]. The admission, too, was
evidently made with much hesitation, not because there
was a doubt whether any one having by descent the fee
simple of the castle and honour was Earl of Arundel, but
because John Fitz-Alan's estate of inheritance was not a fee
simple like that of Richard Fitz-Alan, from whom he derived

---

[1] *Rot. Parl.,* 11 Hen. VI, no. 36.   [2] *Ib.,* 11 Hen. VI, nos. 32-35.

his title. It was probably for this reason that a clause was CHAP. V. introduced to save the right not only of the King, but also of John Mowbray Duke of Norfolk (then a minor), who, as the representative of one of Richard's daughters and coheirs, opposed Fitz-Alan's claim.

The doctrine that the Earldom of Arundel was an Earldom by tenure seems to have been, at this time, admitted on all sides. The opposition of the Duke of Norfolk was itself made on the ground that Fitz-Alan's title to the castle and honour was not good, and that, if he were recognized as Earl, those who had a better claim would be prejudiced.

In the fourteenth year of the reign of Henry VI, it is It was an clear, the common opinion was that there could be no Earl accepted opinion in without lands. In a case which was then argued it was the same reign that stated by counsel that proceedings to outlawry could not there could be taken against an Earl in a civil action because it was not be an earldom a principle of law that, unless he had lands, a man could without not be understood to be an Earl. Counsel on the other lands. side did not dispute the proposition, and merely said that this was not the only cause which exempted an Earl from proceedings to outlawry, but that another cause existed in the dignity of his name, as such proceedings could not be taken against a Duke, an Earl, or a Baron [2].

Seven years later the reversion of the Earldom of Pem- Grant of broke was granted by the King to William de la Pole, the rever- sion of the Earl of Suffolk, and Alice his wife, and the heirs male of Earldom and County their bodies, should Humphrey, Duke of Gloucester, die of Pem- without heir of his body. They were also to have, with broke, with a 'notwith- the same limitations, the castle and lordship of Pembroke, standing' and the castle and lordship of Tenby, under which de- clause referring to scription the county of Pembroke had passed to Humphrey, the Acts in restraint of Duke of Gloucester. The earldom and the county were the grant

---

[1] Subsequent disputes respecting this earldom were settled by Act of Parliament (3 Charles I, cap. 4). It seems unnecessary to discuss this particular case at greater length, because the general principles affecting earldoms and lands are capable of better illustration from cases which have not given rise to heated controversies.

[2] *Year Book*, 14 Hen. VI, no. 9. fo. 2.

G

CHAP. V. thus still united, but the 'notwithstanding' clause was
of Crown introduced into the patent [1]; and the Acts to restrain the
lands. grants of Crown lands seem afterwards to have had some
effect in dissociating dignities from lands.

The clause   For the ancient custom of granting to an Earl the
afterwards
became third part of the proceeds of the county court, there
merely had long been substituted the practice of granting a fixed
formal,
and was annual sum to be paid out of the issues of the county to the
introduced Earl, Marquess, or Duke. This continued to be the custom
when no
lands had long after the 'notwithstanding' clause was introduced into
been the patents or charters of creation, but it soon came to be
granted.
the only mark of territorial connexion between the Earl,
Marquess, or Duke, and any county from which he might
happen to take his title. At first the clause had reference
to actual grants of lands made in connexion with the
creation of the Earls and others. It was afterwards introduced, as a mere form, in accordance with precedent,
in cases in which there had not in fact been any grant of
lands, or even of other profits, beyond the conventional
allowance out of the revenues of a county, known as creation
money. In this way also it seems to have been used in
some of the creations of baronies by letters patent.

Illustration   When, in the reign of Edward IV, a marriage between
from the
case of George Neville and the King's daughter Elizabeth was in
George contemplation, the King created his proposed son-in-law
Neville
Duke of Duke of Bedford. He and the heirs male of his body
Bedford, were, as usual, to have forty pounds a year out of the
in the
reign of revenues of the counties of Bedford and Buckingham. The
Edward IV. 'notwithstanding' clause was introduced into the charter [2],
according to the usage, but subsequent events show that it
was, in this case, founded on a fiction.

He was   In virtue of this charter George Neville bore for some
degraded
by Act of years the title of Duke of Bedford, but eventually lost it
Parliament because he had not lands to support it. His case is unique

---

[1] *Rot. Lit. Pat.*, 21 Hen. VI, part ii. m. 1 (printed, *Rep. Dig. Peer*,
vol. v. p. 240).

[2] *Rot. Chart.*, 8–11 Ed. IV, no. 3 (printed, *Rep. Dig. Peer*, vol. v.
pp. 377–378).

in the history of the peerage. He did not marry the King's CHAP. V.
daughter, and he did not obtain any grant of lands. At because he
the time of the proposed marriage ' for the great love ' the had no estate to
King bore to George's father, he ' intended to have given support his
to the said George, for sustentation of the same dignity, dukedom.
sufficient livelihood.' George's father, John Neville, Marquess of Montague, however, was concerned with the Earl
of Warwick in restoring Henry VI to the throne, and fell
at the battle of Barnet, fighting on the Lancastrian side.
He was attainted after his death, and, by corruption of
blood, George became incapable of inheriting his lands or
his dignities. An Act was therefore passed in the seventeenth year of the reign of Edward IV, to degrade George
Neville from his dukedom. Its English words are remarkable: ' For so much as it is openly known that the
same George hath not, nor by inheritance may have, any
livelihood to support the said name, estate, and dignity,
or any name of estate, and oft times it is seen that when
any Lord is called to high estate, and have not livelihood
conveniently to support the same dignity, it induces great
poverty, indigence, and causes oft-times great extortion, em-
bracery, and maintenance to be had, to the great trouble of
all such countries where such estate shall hap to be inhabited.
Wherefore the King by the advice and assent of his Lords
Spiritual and Temporal and the Commons in this present
Parliament assembled, and by authority of the same,
ordaineth, establisheth, and enacteth that from henceforth
the same erection and making of Duke, and all the names
of dignity given to the said George or to the said John
Neville his father be from henceforth void and of no effect,
and that the same George and his heirs from henceforth
be no Dukes, nor Marquess, Earl, nor Baron, nor be reputed
nor taken for no Dukes nor Marquess. Earl, nor Baron, for
no erection or creation afore made, but of that name of
Duke, and Marquess, Earl and Baron in him and his heirs
cease and be void and of none effect, the said erection or
creation notwithstanding [1].'

[1] *Rot. Parl.*, 17 Ed. IV, no. 16 (printed, vol. vi. p. 173).

G 2

CHAP. V.   Thus it was admitted that George, Duke of Bedford,
His dignity could bear the title as a personal dignity not associated
was purely with the tenure of lands, and without any means of sup-
personal.
porting the honour. It was at the very same time declared
to be inconvenient and mischievous that he or others of
high estate should be in such a condition. The remedy of
degradation had never before been applied for the same
cause; it could hardly have been then applied had the
earlier course been followed and a grant of lands been
made to support the dukedom at the time of its creation.
All sub-   The degradation of the Duke of Bedford for want
sequent
creations of means was never used as a precedent. The form
purely of creation used in his case was, however, followed in
personal.
subsequent grants of earldoms, and dignities of higher
grade. The clause 'notwithstanding,' as in the charter to
George Neville, was uniformly introduced in the later
creations of the reign of Edward IV. It appears in the
Letters Patent making Edward Plantagenet Earl of Salisbury[1]. It appears in the charter by which William
Herbert was created Earl of Huntingdon on surrendering
the Earldom of Pembroke[2]. It appears in the charter by
which Edward, Prince of Wales, son of Edward IV, was
created Earl of Pembroke[3], and in the charter by which
he was created Earl of March[4]. It appears in the charter
by which William, Lord Berkeley, was created Viscount
Berkeley[5], and in the charter by which Lord Lovel was
created Viscount Lovel[6]. In these cases there had not
been, it is believed, any specific grant of lands preceding
and relating to the grant of the dignity[7].

[1] *Rot. Lit. Pat.*, 17 Ed. IV, part ii. m. 16 (printed, *Rep. Dig. Peer*,
vol. v. p. 413).
[2] *Rot. Chart.*, 15–22 Ed. IV, no. 11 (printed, *Rep. Dig. Peer*, vol. v.
pp. 417–418).
[3] *Ib.*, no. 10 (printed, *Rep. Dig. Peer*, vol. v. p. 419).
[4] *Ib.*, no. 9 (printed, *Rep. Dig. Peer*, vol. v. p. 419).
[5] *Ib.*, no. 6 (printed, *Rep. Dig. Peer*, vol. v. pp. 420–421).
[6] *Ib.*, no. 1 (printed, *Rep. Dig. Peer*, vol. v. p. 421).
[7] Castles and lands in Wales and the Marches were granted to the
Prince of Wales just before he was created Earl of March, but they

As soon as the 'notwithstanding' clause had become
a mere form, and the grant of lands in association with
a dignity a fiction, a newly-created title of honour could
have been only personal. In this light it must have been
regarded, so far as grades in the peerage above that of
Baron were concerned, at the end of the reign of Edward IV.
The transition from the idea that newly conferred dignities
were personal to the idea that all were personal alike was
natural, and, indeed, inevitable.

were not expressly associated with any dignity. *Rot. Lit. Pat.*,
17 Ed. IV, pt. 2. m. 24). And, four years after he was created Earl of
Pembroke, an exchange was effected between him and William
Herbert, Earl of Huntingdon, in virtue of which the castle, town, and
lordship of Pembroke, and various lands became annexed to the
Duchy of Cornwall, but they were no longer described as 'the County
of Pembroke.' (*Rot. Parl.*, 22 Ed. IV, no. 12.)

CHAPTER VI.

CHAP.VI.

Barons distinguished from Earls as having no official dignity.

THE history of earldoms, and of the manner in which they became hereditary, and became associated with the tenure of land, may be of some service as a guide in tracing the hereditary dignity of Baron, and its early association with the tenure of land also. It must, however, be remembered that a Baron, merely as Baron, never had, like an Earl. any official position, and consequently never had, like an Earl, an official dignity.

Thanes sometimes described as Barons.

It has been sometimes supposed that the Thanes who existed in England before the Conquest were in a position similar to that of the Barons who existed afterwards. Unfortunately the writers who lived near the time of the Conquest, whether French or English, made somewhat rough and ready translations of words in the two languages. The French authors who lived a little later than the Conquest, naturally also reduced the events they were describing as far as they could into the language of their own time. We thus find the higher grades of society in England, during and even before the reign of Edward the Confessor, described precisely as if they were Norman or other French nobles. When Earl Godwin was brought to trial, according to Geoffrey Gaimar:

> 'There was present a great Baronage,
> Earls, and Barons, and many a Sage[1].'

The accusation was described by the French word *appel*, or

[1] 'Isci aveit mult grant Barnage,
Contes, Barons, maint home sage.'

appeal, and with regard to that and his answer Godwin was Chap. VI.
made to say, ' Let all these Barons speak what is just [1].'

As there were Earls before the Conquest so there were Difference
Lords to whom their 'men' owed a certain obedience. between the Pre-
There was thus a kind of likeness between some, at any Norman
rate, of the Thanes and the Norman Barons. The Thanes Thanes and the Barons
who were great landholders might, so long as they retained of the French
their possessions, naturally be called Barons by the French, type.
and, when the French gained the same possessions, they
too, were naturally called Barons. There appears, however,
to have been this great distinction, that before the Conquest,
the Thanes or other Lords did not hold their land by
knight-service as the Barons did after the Conquest. The
word Baron did not exist in the English (or rather *Englisc*)
language before the · Conquest, but was introduced from
France. With it came tenure in chivalry, or by knight-
service, together with all the feudal incidents.

In this fact we have the key to the position of the early The
Baronage in England—to the position of the great tenants- Baronage after the
in-chief of the Crown—who were landholders owing military Conquest
service to the King, and suit to his Court. It is true that consisted of the
the change was not complete on the morrow of the battle great
of Hastings, and that, in the absence of records, the process tenants-in-chief of the
by which it was effected cannot be traced in detail with Crown, owing
absolute precision. There is, however, no doubt, as has military
already been shown, that the Baronage had practically service to the King,
become denationalized in the reign of Henry I. It con- and suit to his Court.
sisted chiefly of foreigners owing allegiance to a King who
was the son of the Conqueror by a daughter of Baldwin,
Comte de Flandre. Their ideas of government, of the
tenure of land, and of the administration of justice, were
French.

A few of the Barons were Earls also, who, having
originally an official dignity, differed in that respect from

---

[1] Geoffrey Gaimar (Rolls Series), ll. 4900–4916. The last passage
is in French :

> ' De vostre apel et de mon respons
> Dient en dreit tut ces barons.'

CHAP. VI. their compeers.   The Barons, however, merely as Barons,

The held no office, and the descent of their lands was un-
Baronies trammelled by any of the difficulties incident to the
were
hereditary, descent of offices.   The hereditary principle which pre-
but subject vailed in Normandy was naturally applied to the lands
to the
payment of acquired by the new comers in England.   As soon as we
the feudal find any clear light upon the subject, we find the barony
relief.
descending to the heir without doubt or question, but
subject of course to the usual feudal burden of relief.   'As
soon,' says Glanvill, who lived in the reign of Henry II,
' as one of the King's chief Barons dies, the King immediately retains the barony in his hand until the heir
(though of full age) has given sufficient security for his
relief[1].'   The amount payable for a barony in chief was
at the pleasure and mercy of the King[2].   This restraint
on the succession seems to have constituted one of the
grievances of the Barons in the reign of King John.   It
was provided in his Great Charter that, when one of the
King's Earls or Barons died, and the heir was of full age,
he should have his inheritance on payment of the ancient
relief, which was defined to be one hundred pounds for
the entire barony, whether of an Earl or of any other
Baron[3].

The Baron   This was in the transition period before the earldom
a holder of had lost its official character, and become more closely
an entire
barony or associated with the tenure of lands of the county.   Similar
of part of a
barony. words were introduced into the Great Charter of the ninth
year of the reign of Henry III, though the readings of the
various manuscripts vary.   According to the better text,
which agrees with the words of Bracton, the Earl had
then to pay one hundred pounds as the relief for an entire
county (or earldom), and the Baron one hundred marks
as the relief for an entire barony[4].   As, however, it rarely
happened that the possessions of an Earl (except in the
case of a county Palatine) were exactly co-extensive with

[1] Glanvill, lib. ix. cap. 6.   [2] *Ib.* cap. 4.
[3] *Magna Charta* (King John), cap. 2.
[4] *Magna Charta*, 9 Hen. III, cap. 2 ; Bract. 84.

the boundaries of a county, it can hardly be said that very CHAP. VI. great precision was attained by the words of the later charter with regard to earldoms. With regard to baronies other than earldoms, the words are, if possible, still more obscure, because, although Barons are again and again described as tenants-in-chief of the King as of his Crown, it does not appear that there was any uniform rule to determine the extent of their holdings. It would also seem that whatever may have been at first supposed to constitute an entire barony, it was quite possible for any Baron to hold either less or more. In later times, when the burdens of a Baron were in question, it was necessary for any one wishing to escape them to prove that he did not hold either a barony or part of a barony.

Whatever vagueness, however, there may be with regard His military character: 'the strength of war.' to details, it seems perfectly clear that until the end of the reign of Henry III, at any rate, a Baron was a person holding lands of the Crown, and owing military service to the King. It is hardly necessary to consider the etymology of the word, which is, perhaps, the equivalent of 'man.' According to Bracton it meant 'the strength of war[1],' and the use of this expression shows with sufficient plainness that the Baron was a great landholder, bound by the feudal obligations under which he held his possessions, to bring into the field a force proportionate to their extent.

It has sometimes been maintained that the Greater Tenants by Grand Sergeanty not of necessity Barons, nor of necessity summoned to Parliament: an instance. Barons of the reign of John and of previous reigns were those only who held by Grand Sergeanty[2]. This has, however, not been proved, though the tenure was in later times held in the highest estimation, and though it survived the Act of Charles II which changed other tenures into socage. There is no proof that Grand Sergeanty was in equal honour in the time of Edward I, and still less that it gave the sole claim to the degree of a Greater Baron in earlier times. It is not even clear that a tenure by Grand

[1] Bract. 5 b, 'robur belli.'
[2] Nicolas, *Historic Peerage of England*, ed. Courthope, p. xviii.

CHAP. VI. Sergeanty was at first necessarily a tenure of the King *in capite*, though in Littleton's days it was[1]. Britton, on the contrary, refers by implication to cases in which fees are held by Grand Sergeanty, but not directly of the King[2], and Bracton uses similar language. It is, however, certain that the lineal descendant and heir of a Baron who held by Grand Sergeanty in the time of the Conqueror was not necessarily summoned to Parliament as a Baron in the time of Edward I. Reginald de Argenton, for instance, held by Grand Sergeanty[3] in the reign of Richard I. He was the son of a Reginald de Argenton who lived in the reign of Henry I, and the grandson of another Reginald de Argenton who had a grant from the Conqueror[4]. Yet, the descendants of these Barons were not summoned to Parliament in later reigns, and if any descendant and heir were now living, he would have no right to the hereditary dignity of a Baron on the ground of his descent from a Baron by writ of summons.

The character of Baronies not altered in the reign of Henry III.

It is usual to describe the Barons, who in legal documents are styled 'the King's Barons,' or 'the King's Chief Barons,' or 'the Greater Barons' as 'Barons by tenure' until the reign of Henry III, and then to assume a violent change of status, and to regard all Barons as 'Barons by writ,' until one was created by Patent in the reign of Richard II. There is, however, no evidence of any such revolution. The idea seems to have sprung from a misconception—itself arising out of a tendency to forget the difference between ancient and modern conditions of society.

As yet no individual title of Baron: descent of lands.

It is the fact that persons holding land under certain conditions were collectively known as Barons. It is the fact that they were regarded as men of power subordinate to the King[5]. It is not the fact that each of them had

---

[1] Litt. Sec. 156.

[2] Britton, lib. iii. cap. 4. sec. 4; Bract. 35 b.

[3] *Per sergantiam Pincerniae*, Eyre Roll, Hertford, 10 Ric. I (printed in 'Rotuli Curiae Regis,' i. 162).

[4] 'Rotuli Curiae Regis,' 1 John (printed, vol. i. p. 392).

[5] Bract. 5 b.

individually a title of honour as Baron A, or Baron B. Chap. vi.
Each of them was liable to perform certain duties, and, as
will be shown in a subsequent chapter, enjoyed certain
privileges, but he bore hardly any resemblance to a Baron
of the nineteenth century. His lands, subject to the feudal
relief, descended to his heir, and with them his duties and
his privileges. They might even descend to a female heir, as
when he left only one daughter, or to female coheirs, as when
he left several daughters. They might be divided, with the
restriction that where there was only one castle, or capital
messuage or dwelling of any earldom or barony, it was not
partible but went to the eldest of the coheirs, as a symbol of
indivisible strength descending from a time when it was
said that the realm was composed of earldoms and
baronies[1]. The military services for the lands had to be
rendered whether in the hands of one person or of many.
The King could summon to his Court, his Council, or his
Parliament the husband of any of the coheirs if he saw fit.
In certain cases he had even greater power. There was an
important difference between the case in which a Baron,
tenant in fee. died leaving three unmarried daughters, and
the case in which he left two elder married daughters and
one youngest unmarried daughter as his coheirs. In the
latter case the marriage of the unmarried daughter of one
of the King's Barons who held of the King in chief belonged
to the King. He could give her, together with the whole of
the inheritance of which her father died seised, to any one of
his knights whom he might select, and her sisters could not
recover anything against her during her life. This was the
law at the beginning of the reign of Henry III, and it was
then believed to have prevailed since the time of the
Conquest[2].

In this instance it will be observed that there was no
separation of the dignity from the inheritance. The

---

[1] Bract. 76–76 b ; Britton, lib. iii. cap. 8 ; Fleta 313.

[2] Fitz-Herbert's Abridgement, Tit., *Prescripcion*, 56 (3 Henry III).
This case is cited in Co. Litt. 165 a, but the use there made of it is
hardly warranted by the actual words of the report or abridgement.

CHAP. VI. youngest daughter remained, as it is expressed in the report, 'in her father's inheritance.' The husband of course represented her in all rights and liabilities, and, as her estate was regarded as an estate of inheritance so was that of the husband so long as they both survived.

A barony did not necessarily give 'a voice in Parliament.'

Though, however, the appellation 'Baron' was thus indissolubly associated with the tenure of lands, that tenure could not have had the effect which has sometimes been attributed to it. The theory that 'till the time of King Richard I, or of King John, each man to whom the Crown gave lands to hold by knight's service *in capite* was thereby made a Baron and Peer of the Realm, and had a voice in Parliament,' may at one time have been the 'received orthodox opinion amongst all heralds and antiquarians [1],' but it has no solid basis of fact. It is doubtful whether, in those early days after the Conquest, there was any such right as a right to a voice in Parliament, and it has yet to be proved that the term 'Peer of the Realm' was known in England.

No evidence from Henry I to Henry II that a summons was regarded as a privilege.

There is no trace of any desire on the part of the Barons to be summoned to the King's Great Council as a privilege and an honour before the reign of John. Earlier charters [2] contain many of the points for which the Barons then contended, but not any reference to the summons to the Common Council of the Realm, which was a prominent feature in John's Charter.

Even the summons conceded by John's *Magna Charta*,

Even in John's reign, too, the summons was desired not as an honour but as the means of mitigating demands for money [3]. It was only when an exceptional aid or scutage was to be assessed that the Barons wished to be called

---

[1] John Smyth, of Nibley, *Lives of the Berkeleys* (ed. Sir John Maclean), vol. ii. p. 50.

[2] For instance, the Charter of King Henry I, A.D. 1100. See also the two Charters of King Stephen, and the Charter of King Henry II, in all of which the Charter of Henry I is mentioned. These have been conveniently brought together in the notes to Blackstone's Tracts, 286–288 (*The Great Charter*). They are also printed in the Statutes of the Realm.

[3] King John's *Magna Charta*, cap. 12 and cap. 14.

together. In that case the King agreed that he would cause the Archbishops, Bishops, Abbots, Earls, and Greater Barons to be summoned individually, and that he would also cause to be summoned collectively, by his Sheriffs and Bailiffs, all those who held of him *in capite*, that in every summons he would express the reason for which it was made, and that the particular business in hand should proceed on the appointed day, and be settled by the advice of those present.

CHAP. VI.

was desired as a protection against extortion, rather than as an honour.

The classes of persons to whom the separate writs of summons were to be directed were, no doubt, the classes of persons who were subsequently known as Peers of the Realm, and constituted the House of Lords. They had already acquired some privileges which were afterwards enjoyed by Peers, but it does not, therefore, follow that the laymen among them had as yet attained the position of hereditary legislators, or legislators by tenure. That was gained by a sort of prescription in a later generation.

The Barons had not yet acquired the position of hereditary legislators.

The doctrine that between the accession of King John and the death of King Edward I (or as it is sometimes more precisely stated, in the reign of Henry III [1]), the position of a Baron ceased altogether to depend upon territorial possessions and became merely personal, is contradicted by the strongest evidence. At the very time at which this change has been said to have been complete, there issued, by royal authority, a famous law book, in which there is a passage not to be reconciled with the theory that a Baron's dignity was independent of lands held by barony. 'Kings may not aliene the rights of their crown or of their royalty so as not to be revocable by their successors. It is nevertheless permissible for baronies and other demesnes and liberties to be granted by Kings, sometimes in frankalmoign, and sometimes in order to have the prelates, and the other discerning persons of the realm as part of the

In the reign of Edward I the reason expressly alleged for the grant of baronies (in the sense of lands) was that the grantees might be liable to a summons to Parliament.

---

[1] The statement is made in the preface to Camden's *Britannia*, but the existence of the alleged law is not precisely indicated, and it has never been traced to any document of authority.

CHAP. VI. Council, in such manner that they may be capable of being summoned to the King[1].'

All holders of baronies were, however, not necessarily summoned. From this important and authoritative statement of the law it is clear that as late as the twenty-second year of the reign of Edward I the summons to any Council, whether the Common Council of the Realm or any other, was, if regarded as a privilege, certainly regarded not less as a burden, incident to the possession of land. It is also clear that the King might summon as a Baron whomsoever he pleased, if the person was liable to the summons by reason of holding a barony, but there is not the least indication that a person holding a barony could claim to be summoned, or would even wish to be summoned on all occasions, if the King did not desire his presence. When the object for which the Common Council of the Realm, or Parliament, was called together was the grant of an extraordinary aid to which the Baron would have to contribute. it might seem that he would have the right to be summoned under the provisions of King John's *Magna Charta*, if he ranked as one of the *Barones Majores*, but this provision had already disappeared from *Magna Charta* as confirmed by Henry III

The summons was at the discretion of the King. Particular instances are found to be in harmony with the general principles involved in Britton's statement of the law. It would be very difficult to show that any of the laymen beneath the rank of Earl who were called to advise the King in the reign either of Henry III or of Edward I did not hold a barony or part of a barony. It may be true that some of those who were summoned on any occasion held less land than some others who were not summoned, but the reason is apparent. In times of trouble and danger a wise King, such as was Edward I, would not wish for the advice of men deficient in wisdom. He probably knew personally or by repute the character. and abilities of his Barons, he probably had his own likes

---

[1] Britton, lib. ii. cap. 3. sec. 3.   There are similar passages in Bracton, 14, and in Fleta, 3, 4, 183, though not so clearly expressed.

and dislikes, and he probably desired the presence of those who were agreeable and who might be expected to be useful to himself. When wars arose, moreover, it was useless to send a formal summons for attendance in Parliament to men whose services were required in the field.

For many generations the best proof that a man was *In the reign of Edward III a Baron could not prove his status without showing that he held by barony or by part of a barony.* a Baron was the proof that he held lands by barony. When Barons wished to assert their privilege of exemption from being sworn on juries, even at the end of the reign of Edward III, the mere summons to Parliament was not sufficient to prove their right. Ralph de Everden, knight, brought into the Court of Common Pleas a writ from the Chancery, and also a writ of Privy Seal, reciting that he was a Baron, and commanding the Justices to discharge him from taking any oath on any jury whatsoever. The Chief Justice examined him, enquiring whether he held by barony, whether he and his ancestors had always held by barony, and whether they had always come to Parliament as a Baron should. He answered that he held by a certain part of a barony, and that he and his ancestors had so held always. And thereupon, after good consideration, he was absolutely discharged [1], or, in other words, his privilege as a Baron was admitted.

According to the established legal opinions, therefore, a Baron was still a person whose status could be proved only by his tenure. This rendered him liable to military and Parliamentary service; this gave him any privileges which, as a Baron he was entitled to enjoy.

The transition from the stage in which the summons to *Stages of transition from burden to privilege.* Parliament was regarded solely as a burden to that in which, though still associated with the tenure of lands, it was regarded as a privilege may be traced, in one way, by the transition from the period when the number of Barons summoned appears merely capricious to that in which it becomes nearly uniform.

The number of Barons summoned in the reign of *The number of*

---

[1] *Year Book*, M., 48 Ed. III, fo. 30. no. 18.

CHAP. VI.   Edward I varied with almost every Parliament, even when
Barons   the word Parliament is interpreted according to modern
summoned   ideas, and not according to the far less precise use of the
capri-
ciously   term in the contemporary records.   For the Parliament (invariable   cluding Lords Spiritual and Temporal, and Commons), which
in the
reign of   was to meet on November 13, 1295, there were nine Earls
Edward I. and forty-one Barons summoned[1], but for the Parliament
which was to meet on November 3, 1296, only six Earls
and thirty-seven Barons[2].   For the Parliament which was
to meet on March 6, 1299–1300, there were eleven Earls
and ninety-nine Barons summoned[3]; but for the Parliament
which was to meet on January 20, 1306–1307, only
eighty-six Barons, with twelve Earls, including the Prince
of Wales, as Earl of Chester[4].

And in the   In the first year of the reign of Edward II (1307)
reign of
Edward II. a Parliament was to meet on October 13, but only nine
Earls and seventy-one Barons were summoned[5].   For the
Parliament to meet on April 27, 1309, nine Earls were
summoned and eighty-one Barons[6].   Towards the end of
the reign of Edward II (when a Parliament was to meet
on July 15, 1321), nine Earls and ninety Barons were
summoned[7].   To the Parliament which was to meet on
November 14, 1322, ten Earls were summoned and fifty-two
Barons[8]; and one Earl (of Surrey), whose name has not

---

[1] *Rot. Lit. Claus.*, 23 Ed. I, m. 3 d (printed in *Parl. Writs*, ed. Palgrave, vol. i. p. 31, as well as in *Reports on the Dignity of a Peer*).
[2] *Ib.*, 24 Ed. I, m. 7 d (printed, *Parl. Writs*, vol. i. p. 42, as well
as in *Rep. Dig. Peer*).
[3] *Ib.*, 28 Ed. I, m. 17 d (printed, *Parl. Writs*, vol. i. pp. 82–83, as
well as in *Rep. Dig. Peer*).
[4] *Ib.*, 34 Ed. I, m. 2 d (printed, *Parl. Writs*, vol. i. pp. 181–182, as
well as in *Rep. Dig. Peer*).
[5] *Ib.*, 1 Ed. II, m. 19 d (printed, *Parl. Writs*, vol. ii. div. ii. p. 2, as
well as in *Rep. Dig. Peer*).
[6] *Ib.*, 2 Ed. II, m. 11 d (printed, *Parl. Writs*, vol. ii. div. ii.
pp. 25–26, as well as in *Rep. Dig. Peer*).
[7] *Ib.*, 14 Ed. II, m. 5 d (printed, *Parl. Writs*, vol. ii. div. ii. p. 235,
as well as in *Rep. Dig. Peer*).
[8] *Ib.*, 16 Ed. II, m. 26 d (printed, *Parl. Writs*, vol. ii. div. ii. p. 262,
as well as in *Rep. Dig. Peer*).

been found among the writs of summons, sent a proxy[1].
To the Parliament which was to meet on February 23, 1323–
1324, ten Earls were summoned but only forty-nine Barons[2].
To the Parliament which was to meet on November 18,
1325, only four Earls and forty Barons were summoned[3].
In each of the cases mentioned the Parliament was
a true Parliament from the modern point of view, as it
included the Lords Spiritual and Temporal and the
Commons.

At the beginning of the reign of Edward III a similar Similar irregularity in the early part of the reign of Edward III.
uncertainty still prevailed with regard to the number of
Lords Temporal who were to come to Parliament. Thus in
the first year six Earls, and forty-six persons who were presumably Barons[4] were summoned to meet with the Prelates
and Commons at Lincoln on September 15. To the
Parliament which was to meet in the following February
(in the second year) at York, six Earls were summoned,
and fifty Barons[5]. In the fourth year eleven Earls and
fifty Barons were summoned to a Parliament to meet at
Winchester, in January[6]. In the seventh year twelve
Earls and sixty-three Barons were summoned to a Parliament to meet at Northampton, in the February of the eighth
year[7]. In the eleventh year there was summoned to meet
in September an assembly which it is difficult to distinguish
from a Parliament in the modern sense of the term. Writs
issued to all the counties for the election of knights of the
shire and burgesses. The Bishops were summoned in the

---

[1] Original Proxies preserved among Parliamentary Petitions (printed, *Parl. Writs*, vol. ii. div. ii. p. 267, no. 30).
[2] *Rot. Lit. Claus.*, 17 Ed. II, m. 27 d (printed, *Parl. Writs*, vol. ii. div. ii. p. 289, as well as in *Rep. Dig. Peer*).
[3] *Ib.*, 19 Ed. II, m. 27 d (printed, *Parl. Writs*, vol. ii. div. ii. pp. 334–335, as well as in *Rep. Dig. Peer*).
[4] *Ib.*, 1 Ed. III, part ii. m. 16 d (printed in *Rep. Dig. Peer*, vol. iv. p. 377).
[5] *Ib.*, 1 Ed. III, part ii. m. 3 d (printed in *Rep. Dig. Peer*, vol. iv. pp. 379–380).
[6] *Ib.*, 4 Ed. III, m. 41 d (printed, pp. 392–393).
[7] *Ib.*, 7 Ed. III, part ii. m. 3 d (printed, pp. 422–424).

H

CHAP. VI. usual form. and Abbots also. Thirteen Earls were summoned and only thirty-three Barons[1]. In some subsequent years we find the number of Earls who were summoned varying from eight to thirteen, and the number of Barons rising again to more than forty. In the twentieth year, however, there were but five Earls and eleven Barons summoned to the Parliament which was to meet at Westminster in September[2]. The reason, no doubt, was that many of those who would otherwise have been called, were engaged with the King in military service in 'parts beyond the sea.' It is quite possible, too, that in previous years the wars with Scotland and France, as well as, perhaps, in some cases other political events may have caused, wholly or in part, the striking differences in the numbers of the Temporal Lords who were required to attend successive Parliaments.

In the twenty-first year of Edward III, eleven Earls and thirty Barons were summoned to meet in Parliament at Westminster, in the February of the following year[3]. The same numbers occur in the first writs of summons to Parliament in the twenty-second year ; but somewhat later, fifty-six Barons were summoned to meet at Westminster in the following February, and again when Parliament was prorogued. This prorogation, caused by the Black Death, was followed by another, which was a postponement *sine die*[4], and the notification of which was addressed to fifty-five Barons. In the twenty-fourth year fifty Barons were summoned to the Parliament to meet at Westminster in the February of the following year[5], the reduction in numbers having been caused probably by the ravages of the pestilence and the minority of some of the heirs of the Barons previously summoned.

---

[1] *Rot. Lit. Claus.*, 11 Ed. III, part ii. m. 40 d (printed in *Rep. Dig. Peer*, vol. iv. pp. 479–481).

[2] *Ib.*, 20 Ed. III, part ii. m. 25 d (printed, p. 559).

[3] *Ib.*, 21 Ed. III, part ii. m. 9 d (printed, pp. 573–574).

[4] *Ib.*, 23 Ed. III, part i. m. 19 d (printed, p. 585).

[5] *Ib.*, 24 Ed. III, part ii. m. 3 d (printed, pp. 588–589).

About this time, however, there appears to be a more
definite principle at work in the issue of writs of summons. The
The same names occur again and again, and the omission of normal
a familiar name can usually be explained by the minority number of
Barons to
of the heir or by some grave reason of state. In the twenty- be summoned
fifth year of the reign of Edward III a Parliament was ranged,
summoned to meet at Westminster in the February of the about the
middle of
following year. Those who received a summons were the the reign,
from fifty
Duke of Cornwall (Prince of Wales), the Duke of Lancaster, to fifty-five.
eleven Earls, and fifty-two Barons [1]. It thus seems that
the normal number of Barons to be summoned about the
middle of the reign of Edward III ranged between fifty and
fifty-five, when there were no special circumstances to
diminish it. The special circumstances, however, and notably
the wars with the French, were frequently in operation.
Thus in the thirty-fourth year of the reign only twenty
Barons and only four Earls were summoned to the Parliament which was to meet at Westminster in May[2]. In the
same year, however, after the return of the King to England,
writs of summons issued in November for a Parliament to
meet in the following January, and were directed to the
Prince of Wales, the Duke of Lancaster, eleven Earls, and
forty-four Barons[3]. During the remainder of the reign
the Barons summoned commonly fell short of the normal
number, and sometimes very far short.

In the reign of Richard II it becomes apparent that The
the normal number of Barons summoned had undergone number
reduced in
a permanent diminution as compared with the early part succeeding
of the reign of Edward III. During the first nine years reigns,
and the
of Richard's reign the number of Barons called to Par- summons
to Parlia-
liament varied between forty-four and forty-nine. In the ment
tenth year it fell to forty-two. In the eleventh year hereditary.
it rose to forty-five, and was destined in the end to rise
much higher from a new cause which first came into

[1] *Rot. Lit. Claus.*, 25 Ed. III, m. 5 d (printed in *Rep. Dig. Peer*,
vol. iv. pp. 591–592).
[2] *Ib.*, 34 Ed. III, m. 35 d (printed, p. 623).
[3] *Ib.*, 34 Ed. III, m. 4 d (printed, pp. 625–626).

CHAP. VI. operation in that year—the creation of Barons by Patent. Partly, however, through the protracted civil wars, and partly from the sparing use of the modes of creating new Barons, either by writ or by patent, the number summoned fell rather than rose in the reigns immediately following. Thus the summons to Parliament gradually became hereditary, and no longer dependent on the caprice of the Sovereign.

The word Baron still not used as a term of individual dignity.

During all this time there appears nothing to show that the word Baron was known to the law as a term of individual dignity before the creation of a Baron by Letters Patent in the reign of Richard II, or that it was even then a description necessary for purposes of legal identification. There is, indeed, a very strong presumption to the contrary. Cases occur in the 'Year Books' or old Law Reports in which writs are held to be bad because the 'addition' of 'Earl' has been omitted, but no cases have been found in which a writ failed for want of the 'addition' or description of 'Baron.' This, however, is not all. When an Earl sues, or is sued, his dignity is always stated, or, if not, counsel raises an objection. No cases have been found in which the addition of Baron occurs, and no cases in which any exception is grounded on the omission. Persons who were summoned to Parliament as Barons were of course frequently engaged in law-suits, and it is consequently impossible that the term Baron should have been universally omitted when they were concerned, and that no exception should have been grounded on the omission, if the word had been, in law, a name of dignity in the same manner as the word Earl.

An Earl had always to be described as Earl in legal proceedings, but not a Baron as Baron.

In order to establish a proposition which may, perhaps, be somewhat startling, it may be necessary to cite a case in which the omission of an Earl's dignity proved fatal to a writ, as well as a case in which a Baron sued without any name of dignity, and in which nevertehless neither counsel nor judges raised any technical objection. In the fourteenth year of Edward III an action of replevin was brought against Hugh de Audley, Earl of Gloucester, and another. In the writ the Earl was described simply as Hugh de

Audley. Counsel at once took exception, on the ground that Chap. VI.
he was not described as Earl; and the writ failed as against
him, though held good as against the other person joined with
him as defendant[1]. On the other hand, when Henry Fitz-
Hugh, of Ravensworth (who is described in the Peerages
as Baron Fitz-Hugh, and who was in fact summoned to
Parliament as Henry Fitz-Hugh[2]), brought an action of
ravishment of ward in the same year[3], he is nowhere
described as a Baron in the reports of the case or in the
corresponding record. No exception was taken on the
ground of the omission, which, in the case of an Earl, would
have been a simple and sufficient reason for abating the
writ; but, on the contrary, exception was taken on another
point of a far more difficult and technical character.

Long after the reign of Edward III, too when the wars A Baron
of the Roses were giving new power to the Barons, the old need not
ideas still prevailed in the Courts of Justice, and a Baron described
was still not as another peer. As late as the eighth year of reign of
Henry VI it was expressly decided that there was a differ- Henry VI.
ence between a lord who was only a Baron and a lord who
was an Earl or a Duke, and that when a writ was brought by
or against an Earl or Duke, he must be named by his name
of dignity, but not when the writ was brought by or against
a Baron[4]. In this case the plaintiff, 'Lord' Lovel, was
described as knight or 'chivaler,' as persons not of higher
rank than Barons commonly were in the summonses to
Parliament. This word 'chivaler,' however, was itself a
name of dignity[5], and the omission of it in a case in which
the party was entitled to it was fatal to a writ in which the
omission occurred[6].

Moreover, it was not only in the superior Courts of In early

---

[1] *Year Book*, T., 14 Ed. III, no. 34.
[2] *Rot. Lit. Claus.*, 14 Ed. III, m. 33 d (printed in *Rep. Dig. Peer*,
vol. iv. p. 517).
[3] *Year Book*, M., 14 Ed. III, no. 45.
[4] *Ib.*, 8 Hen. VI, no. 22, fo. 10.
[5] Fitz-Herbert's Abridgement of the Law, *Nomen Dignitatis*, 3.
[6] *Year Book*, H., 14 Hen. IV, no. 26, fo. 21.

CHAP. VI.

times a Baron was not so described even in Parliament itself.

Justice that the designation Baron was usually omitted when particular individuals who were summoned among the Barons were described. The individuals are commonly mentioned without the description of Baron, and almost as commonly without the description of Lord, in the Rolls of Parliament themselves. Thus as late as the ninth year of the reign of Edward II, Hugh le Despenser, the younger, having been accused in Parliament of an assault in Lincoln Cathedral, was committed to the custody of the marshal. He was afterwards released on bail or mainprise, and his sureties or mainpernors were all noblemen of such rank as a summons to Parliament among the Barons could confer on them or their ancestors. Yet not one of them was called in the Roll of Parliament either Baron or Lord, though one, who was an Earl (a Scottish Earl) had due recognition of his title (Robert de Umfravill, Earl of Angus). The rest were called simply Roger de Mortimer of Chirk, Theobald de Verdon, Ralph Basset, William de Ferrers, and Robert de Hastings [1].

The holder of a barony, having originally military but no official duties, was regarded after knighthood as a 'chivaler.'

The most reasonable explanation of these facts appears to be that an Earl was originally described as Earl in Parliament and Courts of Justice by reason of his official dignity, but that a Baron was not usually so called because he was regarded only as the holder of a barony or part of a barony. Ranks in the peerage above that of Earl were, as has been shown, but superior kinds of earldoms, associated at first with lands in the counties, from which they took their titles. Though, however, Barons never had any official duties, their military duties were of great importance, and it was, perhaps, for this reason that their ordinary legal designation, as soon as they had received the necessary knighthood, was ' chivaler [2].'

A Baron's

The dignity of a Baron could not have been considered

---

[1] *Rot. Parl.*, 9 Ed. II, no. 2 (printed, vol. i. p. 352).

[2] Even this, however, was omitted until the end of the reign of Edward III. In the reign of Henry VI it came into common use. It afterwards survived even the abolition of feudal tenures, and was handed down to modern times.

exclusively personal until a comparatively late period, and still less the right to sit in Parliament. The fact that husbands were summoned to Parliament, as it is commonly expressed, in right of their wives, is alone sufficient evidence on the point.

Husband and wife, it is true, were one person in law ; by marriage the husband became the owner of the wife's chattels, and acquired power over her realty during the time of coverture. The reason of this, however, was that her personality was lost in that of her husband, not that his personality was lost in hers. It was an established principle in the reign of Edward III that when a woman married she lost every surname except that of ' wife of ' her husband [1]. It would be altogether inconsistent that the husband should take a name of dignity as husband of the wife. The husband's powers over the wife's lands were, however, in the first instance acquired because he was capable of performing the military and other services by which the lands were held. It was therefore quite reasonable that he should receive a summons to Parliament to which a male holder of her lands would be liable. It must originally have been the land which was subject to the burden of the summons, whether to military service or to attend in Parliament.

Husbands
summoned
to Parlia-
ment in
virtue of
the lands
but not
of the
dignities
of their
wives.

Hugh Stafford, who was summoned to Parliament in the twelfth year of the reign of Henry IV [2], and subsequently, apparently on the ground that he had married Elizabeth, the daughter and heir of Bartholomew Bourchier, was summoned simply as Hugh Stafford, without any mention of a Bourchier peerage. Bartholomew Bourchier had been summoned simply as Bartholomew Bourchier in the first, second, third, fifth, seventh, eighth, and eleventh years of the reign. In modern times both Bartholomew Bourchier and Hugh Stafford are often described as Lord Bourchier. On the death of Hugh Stafford, his widow married Lewis Robsart,

---

[1] *Year Book*, T., 14 Ed. III, no. 51, p. 323.
[2] *Rot. Lit. Claus.*, 12 Hen. IV, m. 2 d (printed in *Rep. Dig. Peer*, vol. iv. p. 810).

CHAP. VI. who in his turn was summoned to Parliament. apparently by reason of his marriage, in the third year of the reign of Henry VI [1], and subsequently, but simply as Lewis Robsart, though he, too, is often described as Lord Bourchier. In each of these cases the summons to Parliament is a striking illustration of the legal doctrine that a wife could not confer a name (either of dignity or otherwise) upon a husband, though during her life he gained the benefits and was subject to the burdens attaching to her lands.

Other cases of a less simple character : Robert Hunger- ford, Lord Molines.

There are, however, some cases, usually regarded as cases in which a husband was summoned as a Baron to Parliament in right of his wife, which are of a different character. They are cases in which the right of the Crown to summon had been in disuse, and was exercised anew in respect of an heiress's husband. Thus it is commonly said that Robert Hungerford was summoned to Parliament as Lord Molines in the twenty-third year of Henry VI, because he had married Eleanor, heiress of William Molines. It is true that he was summoned to Parliament as Robert Hungerford, knight, Lord (or lord of) Moleyns [2]. He is the only person of all those summoned among the Barons to whom the word *dominus*, or lord, is applied on the same occasion; and if the word were to be accepted as a title of honour it might at first sight seem to follow that he was the only lord summoned to meet the Dukes, Earls, and Viscount. His wife's father had not even been summoned to Parliament, nor had any of her ancestors since the twenty-first year of Edward III, when one was summoned as John de Molyns [3]. In this case it would seem either that Hungerford was held liable to a summons by reason of his wife's lands, or that he was newly created a Baron.

Edward de Grey, 'Lord Ferrers of Groby.'

In the twenty-fifth year of the reign of Henry VI, how- ever, Robert Hungerford was again summoned, and again styled *dominus de* Moleyns. On this occasion two other persons were summoned, to whom also, and to whom alone

---

[1] *Rot. Lit. Claus.*, 3 Hen. VI, m. 9 d (printed, p. 861).
[2] *Ib.*, 23 Hen. VI, m. 21 d (printed, p. 908).
[3] *Ib.*, 21 Ed. III, part i. m. 28 d (printed, p. 563).

among all the other barons. the word *dominus* was applied.
Each had married an heiress. One was Edward de Grey.
He had married Elizabeth, grand-daughter and heiress of
William Ferrers of Groby, who, and some of whose ancestors,
had been summoned to Parliament. William de Ferrers
had been summoned as 'William de Ferrers, of Groby,
knight.'· The words 'of Groby' formed part of his description, because other members of the Ferrers family had
for many generations been described as of other places.
When Edward de Grey married the heiress Elizabeth,
he also became 'of Groby,' and he was summoned as
Edward de Grey, Lord of (*dominus de*) Ferrers, of Groby,
knight [1]. In this case it might, perhaps, be maintained,
with some show of reason, that Edward de Grey had
acquired, in some manner, the title of Lord Ferrers of
Groby.

The other person summoned after having married an
heiress was Henry Percy, Lord (*dominus de*) Ponynges or
Poynings. In this case 'Poynings' might have been regarded as a territorial designation. and Henry Percy only as
the holder, in right of his wife, of Poynings in Sussex, and
not as Lord Poynings according to modern ideas. It might
be that the reason for designating him, as well as the two
others who had married heiresses, by the title of *dominus*
was that he was summoned to Parliament simply as lord
of certain lands. It might, however, be that the three
'lords' had the title affixed to their names to show that they
were, by courtesy or otherwise, to be called Lord Molines,
Lord Ferrers of Groby, and Lord Poynings.

Two years later a case occurs which hardly admits of any
doubt as to the meaning of the description. William
Bourchier, a knight, had married Thomasine Hankford,
daughter of Elizabeth Fitz-Warine by Richard Hankford.
There had been nine generations in which the name of
Fulk Fitz-Warine had been borne successively by trans-
mission from father to son. Elizabeth was the sister of
the last of this line. Bourchier was summoned to Parlia-

[1] *Rot. Lit. Claus.*, 25 Hen. VI, m. 16 d (printed, p. 916).

CHAP. VI. ment as 'William Bourchier, knight, Lord Fitz-Waryn[1].'
As Fitz-Warine is a purely family name, and no question
of mere lordship over certain lands can arise, it is clear
that 'Lord Fitz-Warine' must have been a name of dignity,
and not a territorial designation. Even here, however,
many difficulties arise. Richard Hankford was never summoned to Parliament, and no Fulk Fitz-Warine had been
summoned to Parliament since the year 1336—for more than
a century preceding the summons to William Bourchier.

In each case the husband may have been summoned in virtue of the wife's lands, or there may have been a new creation.

A careful consideration of the facts—of the fact that
among the Barons summoned to one Parliament the only
persons who were styled *dominus* were those who had
married heiresses, and of the fact that in two at least of
these cases there is no proof of the existence of a barony,
apart from the lands, in the blood of the heiress—suggests
a conclusion quite opposed to the usual statement that
husbands are to be regarded as acquiring the dignity of
Baron in right of their wives. There are two possible
alternatives; one is that the husbands were summoned
because liable to the summons by reason of the lands of
their wives, though the summons in respect of those lands
had been for some time intermitted ; the other is that in
each case there was a new creation.

The particular titles were given to distinguish the bearers from other Peers of the same families.

The reason for designating each of these lords by a particular title appears to have been a desire to prevent confusion.
Hungerford had to be called by some name other than
Hungerford, because he was summoned to Parliament during
the lifetime of his father, who was also summoned among the
Barons. Ferrers of Groby was a title which had already been
used to distinguish the various branches of the Ferrers family
in which there were peerages. Percy was summoned during
the lifetime of his father, Henry Percy, Earl of Northumberland, and not unnaturally took a distinguishing title.
Bourchier, who, two years later, was summoned as Lord
Fitz-Warine, had to be distinguished from his brother, who
(being also Comte d'Eu) was successively Baron Bourchier,
Viscount Bourchier, and Earl of Essex.

[1] *Rot. Lit. Claus.*, 27 Hen. VI, m. 24 d (printed, p. 919).

In other instances also in which there is a summons to CHAP. VI. Parliament of a Baron 'as in right of his wife,' whether his barony is described by his wife's family name or otherwise. the summons, if not in virtue of the lands held by the wife, indicates a new creation. It is almost impossible to distinguish between the one intention and the other. In either case it cannot be maintained that a Baron really enjoyed his dignity in right of a dignity possessed by his wife, because, according to law, her status as his wife was her only status, and because a new creation by summons would ennoble the blood of the husband and not of the wife.

It is nevertheless probable that there were no very precise doctrines on the subject in the reign of Henry VI, and that, as sitting in the House of Peers came to be regarded more and more in the light of a privilege, its original association with land and land-burdens began to be forgotten. Probable want of precise doctrines in the reign of Henry VI.

In the reign of Henry VIII the summons directed to the husband of a woman inheriting a barony appears to have been associated with the idea of tenancy by 'the curtesy of England.' Mr. Wimbish, the husband of Elizabeth daughter and heiress of Gilbert, Baron Talboys, of Kime, claimed the dignity. He had no issue by her, and the King took upon himself to pronounce that 'neither Mr. Wimbish nor none other from henceforth should use the title of his wife's dignity but such as by curtesy of England had also right to her possessions for term of his life.' This was a recognition of the earlier principle, but with a limitation which had not previously existed. In former times the husband was summoned, though he had no issue. as was clearly shown in the cases of Hugh Stafford and Lewis Robsart Each was summoned as the husband of Elizabeth, heiress of the barony of Bourchier, though both lived and died childless. The acceptance of the new doctrine laid down by Henry VIII was an important step towards the extinction of the older doctrine that the possession of land involved the burden or the privilege of a summons to Parliament. The doctrine as to the 'curtesy of England' laid down by Henry VIII.

CHAPTER VII.

CHAP. VII.

Late growth of the doctrine that a writ of summons to Parliament, followed by a sitting, conferred hereditary dignity.

THE doctrine of the creation of an hereditary peerage by the summons of a man to Parliament, without any mention of his heirs, is of far later growth than the early writs of summons by which peerages are said to have been created. It has already been shown that in the reign of Edward I, and for some time afterwards, the number of persons summoned among the Barons varied very widely. This fact in itself is almost sufficient to prove that the idea of the creation of an hereditary barony could not have been in the mind of the sovereign at the time at which the summons issued. We find that men were summoned to one Parliament and not to another; we find that their heirs were sometimes summoned and sometimes not. All this is quite inconsistent with the theory that a single summons to Parliament, followed by a sitting in Parliament, gave a peerage to the person summoned and the heirs of his body. It is not, however, at all inconsistent with the theory that persons holding in chief of the King, as of the Crown, and therefore holding, according to the Constitutions of Clarendon, as by barony, were liable to a summons which might issue or not at the King's pleasure.

Gradual transition from burden to privilege: attendance

The whole of the ideas relating to the creation of a Baron by writ could not have reached maturity until men had forgotten that the summons to Parliament was a burden as inseparable from their lands, as the burden of military service,

or until they had come to regard it as an essential part of
their dignity. The transition was very gradual. It was
beginning, perhaps, at the time when English Peers first
spoke of themselves as Peers of the Realm, in the reign
of Edward II. It had, perhaps, made some progress when
Richard II created John de Beauchamp (who was Steward
of the King's Household) 'one of the Peers and Barons of
the Realm . . . willing that he and the heirs male of his
body should have the status of Barons, and should be called
Lords de Beauchamp and Barons of Kidderminster[1].'
The reasons assigned for this creation were the services
and personal merits of Beauchamp himself, the nobility and
fidelity of the family from which he had sprung, and the
position which he was to take in future Councils and
Parliaments. Attendance in Parliament in obedience to
the King's summons was thus still one of the duties
obligatory upon a Baron, though in Beauchamp's case
obligatory not in virtue of his lands but in virtue of his
dignity. None of his compeers can be shown to have held
their baronies on the same terms.

It might perhaps be suspected that as the Staffords and
the Greystocks commonly had, unlike the rest of the Barons,
a summons directed, '*Baroni de* Stafford' or '*Baroni de*
Greystock,' there had been in each of those families a creation
of a Baron by Letters Patent never yet brought to light.
This conjecture, however, is not only improbable in itself,
but is refuted by the fact that, when Beauchamp, Baron of
Kidderminster, was himself summoned to Parliament, he
was summoned merely as John de Beauchamp, of Kidderminster, while the summons to Greystock was in the form
'Radulfo Baroni de Greystock[2].' The reason for the
application of the expression 'Baron' to members of the
families de Stafford and de Greystock has never yet been
discovered, but it is possible that the word may be only a

---

[1] *Rot. Lit. Pat.*, 11 Ric. II, part i. m. 12 (printed in *Rep. Dig. Peer*, vol. v. p. 81).
[2] *Rot. Lit. Claus.*, 11 Ric. II, m. 24 d (printed in *Rep. Dig. Peer*, vol. iv. p. 725).

CHAP. VII. part of the surname in each case, and may have no reference to the dignity of a Baron. It is true that early instances of hereditary surnames are extremely rare, and that the Barons of Greystock and Stafford can be traced back to the reign of Edward I. Apart from the question of descent from father to son, however, there is ample evidence that 'Baron' was used merely as a *cognomen* without any reference to status or dignity. As early as the reign of King John, one 'Odardus Baro' was a juror[1], and Roger Baron appears as an essoiner in the reign of Henry III[2]. An exact parallel to the names Baron of Greystock and Baron of Stafford occurs among the sureties for a knight of the shire for the County of Lincoln in the reign of Edward I. One was Robert Baron of Wilesthorpe, and another William Baron of the same place[3]. None of these, it need hardly be said, were ever summoned to Parliament.

The creation of John de Beauchamp as Lord de Beauchamp, Baron of Kidderminster, and his summons to Parliament simply as John de Beauchamp of Kidderminster are very apt illustrations of the legal doctrine that Baron was not a necessary addition to the name of an individual Lord of Parliament summoned among the Barons. John de Beauchamp's title was Lord de Beauchamp; and the words 'of Kidderminster' were added apparently only to distinguish him from other members of the numerous family of Beauchamp.

Importance of Lord Beauchamp's creation by patent in relation to the theory of barony by writ.

The Letters Patent by which he was created are, however, of importance in relation to the doctrine of barony by writ of summons   The dignity was limited in a manner different from that which the later lawyers attributed to the ordinary summons of a Baron. This was held to operate in favour of the heirs general of the body of the person receiving the summons, whereas Beauchamp's creation was in favour only of him and the heirs male of his body. Beauchamp was, .

[1] Roll of Easter, 11 John (printed, *Plac. Abbr.*, 66 b).
[2] Roll of 32 Hen. III (printed, *Plac. Abbr.*, 126).
[3] Return endorsed on writ to the Sheriff of London, 26 Sep., 28 Ed. I (printed in *Parl. Writs*, i. 97).

however, afterwards summoned in precisely the same terms
as the other Barons ; and, if the summons operated in favour
of the heirs general in one case, it is not clear why it should
not have had the same consequences in another case. The
only reason that can be assigned is that the effect of the
writ of summons was governed by the Letters Patent ; but
the admission of one exception to the ordinary effect of the
writ of summons at once suggests the possibility of other
exceptions, and the necessity of a very stringent examination
of the general rule.

Beauchamp's creation as Lord de Beauchamp is the first
undoubted instance of a barony conferred as a dignity apart
from any considerations relating to the tenure of land. We
do know for certain that his title of honour was conferred
as a personal distinction in tail male, but we have no certain
knowledge that the dignity of any other Baron was as yet
supposed to be merely personal, and, if it was, we have no
means of explaining why the inheritance should be to the
heirs general by virtue of a summons directed to a particular
individual.

With the idea that a summons to Parliament gave dignity
to the person summoned, there naturally sprang up the idea
that there were degrees of precedence among those who sat
in the same House. When the only temporal Lords were
Earls and Barons, the writs of summons to the Earls were
always placed on the roll before the writs of summons to
Barons, but there does not seem to have been any definite
rule with regard to the order in which the writs of summons
to the Barons were entered. The creation of Dukes and
Marquesses, however, who took precedence of Earls, and
the creation of a Viscount who took precedence of Barons,
must almost of necessity have suggested questions concerning the precedence of Barons among themselves.

Ideas of precedence grew up with the idea that summons to Parliament was an honour rather than a burden.

There is extant a treatise on the mode of holding
Parliament, which, if of no authority in relation to the times
immediately following the Conquest, must, at any rate,
possess some value in relation to the period at which it was
written. In its earliest form it appears to have been

Places of the Lords of the several degrees in Parliament in the

CHAP. VII.
fourteenth
century.

composed about the beginning of the fourteenth century, but there are later copies of it which show important variations. The Earls and Barons are mentioned as persons having lands and rents to the value of an entire earldom or an entire barony, and they, it is said, ought to be summoned and to come to Parliament. The place of the Lords Spiritual in Parliament is described in the earliest copies, but not the place of the Lords Temporal. 'The King shall sit in the middle of the Greater Bench,' on his right the Archbishop of Canterbury, on his left the Archbishop of York, and behind them the Bishops, Abbots, and Priors. Below the King and to his right were to sit the Chancellor, the Chief Justice of England and his companions (the puisne Judges of the King's Bench) 'and their clerks who were of the Parliament.' Below the King and to his left were to sit the Treasurer, the Chamberlain, the Barons of the Exchequer, the Justices of the Common Bench, and their clerks who were of the Parliament [1].'

In later copies (which, however, must refer to a period before the creation of Dukes, Marquesses, and Viscounts, as they are not mentioned) a somewhat different account is given of the Lords Spiritual and a place is assigned to the Lords Temporal. On the King's right were to sit the Archbishop of Canterbury, and the Bishops of London and Winchester, and behind them the other Bishops, Abbots, and Priors. On his left were to sit the Archbishop of York, and the Bishops of Durham and Carlisle, and behind them, in rows or in succession [2], the Earls, Barons, and Lords, 'such division being always observed [3].'

No precedence among Barons as yet indicated.

The passage is unfortunately vague, but it does not necessarily indicate any order of precedence among the Barons. It rather shows that the Lords Spiritual were to be kept distinct from the Lords Temporal, and the Earls from the Barons. It might, perhaps, even be inferred that there were Lords who were Peers and inferior to the Barons,

[1] *Modus tenendi Parliamentum* (ed. T. D. Hardy), p. 37.
[2] *Seriatim.*
[3] *Modus tenendi Parliamentum* (ed. T. D. Hardy), p. 37.

and that they also were to have a distinct place assigned to CHAP. VII. them. As, however, Baron was not a necessary addition, it is more probable that the ' Barons and Lords' were only the Barons who were Lords, and the Lords who were Barons, just as we find in the two first creations of Barons by patent that each of them was to have the status of Baron, and to be called a Lord[1]. Verbiage and grandiloquence have always flourished in the warm and sunny regions of the peerage; and from a very early time the nobles were called *Proceres et Magnates*, though the term *Proceres* by itself or the term *Magnates* by itself would have been quite sufficient to designate them.

Thus far there is no certain sign that one Baron could claim precedence over another. It was not until the reign of Henry VI, that the first Viscount was created (John de Beaumont, Viscount Beaumont)[2], and it was not until the same reign that questions of precedence came into prominence. In Viscount Beaumont's patent it was expressly stated that he was to have a place in Parliaments, Councils, and other assemblies above all the Barons of the Realm. This appears to be the first instance in which precedence in Parliament was thought of sufficient importance to be mentioned in the patent of creation. The earliest Dukes—the first Dukes of Cornwall and of Lancaster —being of royal blood, had precedence of the Earls, as a matter of course, though the point was not touched in their patents. The first Marquess, Robert de Vere, had a charter[3] in which no mention was made of precedence in

Creation of the first Viscount by Henry VI: questions of precedence come into prominence: Dukes and Marquesses.

---

[1] It might, of course, be argued that Lords, other than Earls and Barons, are the bannerets, of whom there is occasional mention in the Rolls of Parliament. The word 'banneret,' however, occurs on so few occasions that it is difficult to arrive at any satisfactory generalization. It is possible that they may have been summoned when special advice was required on special subjects. See *Rot. Parl.*, 18 Ed. III, no. 6 (printed, vol. ii. p. 147), 46 Ed. III, no. 7 (printed, vol. ii. p. 309), &c.

[2] *Rot. Lit. Pat.*, 18 Hen. VI, part ii. m. 21 (printed in *Rep. Dig. Peer*, vol. v. p. 235).

[3] *Rot. Chart.*, 9 & 10 Ric. II, m. 13 (printed in *Rep. Dig. Peer*, vol. v. p. 78).

I

CHAP. VII. Parliament, though the King directed that he should have place below the Dukes and above the Earls [1]. The charter was cancelled almost immediately afterwards, and Robert de Vere was created Duke of Ireland [2].

The doctrine of hereditary barony by writ was now becoming possible.

The more men struggled, however, for precedence as Peers, the more they forgot the old idea that the summons to Parliament was a burden. The legal doctrine that the summons followed by a sitting was equivalent to the creation of a Peer with inheritance to the heirs of his body was now becoming a possibility. It was not a possibility so long as attendance in Parliament was considered only an irksome duty; it was not a possibility in the reign of Edward I, to which the lawyers of a later time have traced back the origin of many so-called baronies by writ. It grew out of the prescription in accordance with which the representatives of the same families were called to Parliament, generation after generation.

The doctrine not clearly established in the reign of Henry VI: sometimes confused with the doctrine of abeyance: the barony of St. Amand.

Even as late as the reign of Henry VI, it is by no means clear that the writ of summons to an ancestor was held to give a peerage to the descendant. This theory has been unfortunately somewhat intermixed with the theory that in cases in which the descent was to co-heiresses the peerage fell into abeyance, but could be called out of abeyance by the Crown. Aymer de St. Amand had been summoned to Parliament in the reign of Edward I. His lands descended to his brother John, who was also summoned to Parliament. as were successively John's son Aymer, and Aymer's son Aymer. The last Aymer died in 1403. He had no male issue. but two daughters, one by his first wife, one by his second. It does not appear that there was any summons to Parliament of any Lord St. Amand between the time of Aymer's death and the summons of the husband of his elder daughter's granddaughter in 1449. It is commonly said that the barony was in abeyance, and so, according to modern ideas, it

[1] *Rot. Parl.,* 9 Ric. II, no. 17 (printed, vol. iii. p. 210).
[2] *Rot. Chart.,* 10 Ric. II, no. 2 (printed in *Rep. Dig. Peer,* vol. v. p. 79).

may have been until the death of the younger daughter, CHAP. VII.
in or before the year 1426. Upon her death without issue,
however, the abeyance must, according to modern ideas,
have ceased, and no act of the Crown was necessary to
terminate it. There is consequently nothing to show that
when William de Beauchamp, the husband, was summoned
among the Barons to Parliament as 'Lord de St. Amand [1],'
he was not summoned merely to perform a service incident
to the lands which had become the right of his wife, or
that he was not summoned in virtue of a new creation.
The doctrine that a mere summons to Parliament, followed
by a sitting, conferred a descendible dignity cannot be
proved from this and similar cases to have as yet come
to maturity.

When the power of the Crown had been weakened by
the incapacity of the King, and by disputes touching the
succession, the power of the Baronage as a whole was
increased, and each individual member of it was more
disposed than before to assert his own dignity. The King,
however, was still the fountain of honour, and the Baron
who wished to obtain precedence above his fellow Barons
could attain his end only with the King's assistance.
Among the Peers of ranks higher than that of Baron, Henry
VI assumed, if in fact he had not, the power of giving precedence without regard to priority of creation. To Henry
Beauchamp, Earl of Warwick, he gave, by charter, precedence over all other Earls [2]. When the Earl was
created Duke, three days later, his position was assigned
as next to that of the Duke of Norfolk, and before that
of the Duke of Buckingham [3]. The Duke of Exeter, who
had been recently created, was given precedence by patent
next to the Duke of York [4]. The Duke of Buckingham

Power assumed by Henry VI of giving precedence in ranks above that of Baron.

---

[1] *Rot. Lit. Claus.*, 27 Hen. VI, m. 24 d (printed in *Rep. Dig. Peer*,
vol. iv. p. 919).
[2] *Rot. Chart.*, 22 Hen. VI, no. 35 (printed in *Rep. Dig. Peer*, vol. v.
p. 242).
[3] *Ib.*, 21–24 Hen. VI, no. 24 (printed, p. 244).
[4] *Rot. Lit. Pat.*, 22 Hen. VI, part i. m. 13 (printed, p. 248).

CHAP. VII. shortly afterwards obtained a charter to the effect that, except in the case of descendants of Henry VI or his successors, no Dukes subsequently created should have precedence of him or his heirs[1].

When civil war is actually existing or impending the laws are apt to be strained, if not broken, and it has often been remarked that statements made or acts done in the reign of Henry VI should not be regarded as evidence of settled principles. It must, however, be remembered, on the other hand, that times of absolute tranquillity in England had always been rare. Since the granting of Magna Charta the only two Kings who had sat firmly on their thrones for any considerable length of time were Edward I and Edward III. The constitution had grown up amidst wars and rumours of wars. The events which actually occurred in the reign of Henry VI are as much a part of history, and of constitutional history, as the events of any other reign. The statements relating to the past which were then made are of no value if at variance with the contemporary documents of the earlier time.

Creation of a Baron to hold to him and his heirs being lords of the manor of Kingston Lisle.

We know from records of the time of Henry VI, that the Crown assumed in certain cases the power of giving grants of precedence, and that the assumption passed without dispute. We know, on the other hand, that many statements were made which it may seem difficult to reconcile with documents of higher authority. Thus when John Talbot was created Lord and Baron Lisle by Henry VI, we know from the charter itself[2] that the creation was to him and his heirs being lords of the manor and lordship of Kingston Lisle. We know, further, that he held the manor and lordship in fee, by conveyance from his father, the Earl of Shrewsbury, and his mother, Margaret, one of the coheirs of Elizabeth, daughter and heir of Margaret the daughter of Warine the last Lord Lisle. His mother Margaret, the wife of the Earl of Shrewsbury,

The tenure of the manor.

---

[1] *Rot. Chart.*, 25 & 26 Hen. VI, no. 31 (printed, p. 257).
[2] *Ib.*, 21-24 Hen. VI, no. 23 (printed, pp. 244-246).

had held the manor and lordship of Kingston Lisle in CHAP. VII. virtue of a partition of lands made between her and her sisters and coheirs. The conveyance made to John Talbot was 'to hold of the chief lords of the fee by the services due and of right accustomed.' The condition on which he and his heirs were to be Barons and Lords Lisle was therefore that of holding the lordship and manor of Kingston, and not of holding it in chief of the King. This was a creation of a very remarkable character, but there is no doubt whatever that it was actually made, and no reason to doubt that the King had the right to make it.

When a history of the barony of Kingston Lisle, as existing before the new creation, is set forth in the charter, it becomes open to criticism on historical principles. Warine, Lord Lisle, it is asserted, and all his ancestors, from time immemorial, had had the name and dignity of Baron and Lord Lisle, in right of the manor and lordship of Kingston Lisle. The alleged terms of the conveyance of the manor to John Talbot show that the tenure of the manor was not supposed to be of the King in chief, as of the Crown. The barony, therefore, was, according to the charter, not a barony by tenure in the ordinary sense, but a barony by tenure of an exceptional character – a barony inherent in the blood of a particular family holding a particular manor of any person whatsoever. Much labour has been expended with the object of showing that the manor of Kingston Lisle was not in fact held directly of the Crown by the family of Lisle, and that the barony of Lisle was therefore never in fact a barony by tenure [1]. As, however, it is nowhere stated in the charter that the manor was held of the King, but the contrary is implied in the document itself, the evidence that the Lisles held of a 'mesne' (or intermediate) Lord, however interesting from a genealogical and antiquarian point of view, does not in any way invalidate the statements made in the instrument. The real question at issue

Recitals in the charter: the new creation made to remove doubts respecting the ancient barony of Kingston Lisle.

[1] *Third Rep. Dig. Peer*, vol. ii. pp. 199–208.

CHAP. VII. is whether one holding of a mesne Lord could be a Baron by virtue of his tenure of particular lands. That question is answered in the affirmative in the charter, but with full recognition of the fact that there were doubts and scruples on the point. The outcome is, therefore, that no barony by tenure of a mesne Lord has ever been recognized in the person of the possessor except in this one case. In this case, too a new creation was made in order to meet the objections of those who did not assent to the principle, for which the Constitutions of Clarendon, at any rate, afford no warrant.

It is, perhaps, reasonable to infer that the doctrine of barony by tenure was still so familiar, that even long tenure of a mesne Lord was, in one instance at any rate, supposed to be evidence of a right to a barony of a particular designation It is not, however, impossible that the persons now styled Barons and Lords Lisle were in previous times tenants in chief of other lands, though they held the manor of Kingston Lisle of a mesne Lord. It was probably to end this, among other doubts and difficulties, that the new creation was made.

No definite order of precedence mentioned in this charter, or as yet indicated elsewhere. Though, as we have seen, the Crown interfered in many instances with regard to the precedence of Earls and Dukes, yet neither in this case nor in relation to other baronies is any precedence of one Baron over another mentioned in the reign of Henry VI. John Talbot, Baron and Lord Lisle was to have his seat in Parliaments and Councils 'amongst the other Barons of the Realm,' just as Warine and his predecessors had had it, but no attempt is made to define the exact position. It is probable enough that 'ancienty' may have determined, at this time, the relative position of the Barons, but, if so, it is quite clear that the first writ of summons to Parliament could not have been the one determining test of ancienty. Whatever the precedence of any previous Lord Lisle may have been, he must have held it on some ground different from that of the date of a summons; and the only reasonable conclusion is either that there was not as yet any definite rule of precedence between Barons, or that, if there was, it CHAP. VII. depended on some principle not yet ascertained.

In the reign of Henry VIII the precedence of Barons (as well as of Peers of other ranks) according to their 'ancienty' was recognized by Act of Parliament [1] (the consent of the King, however, being given only as an act of grace), but no definition or explanation of 'ancienty' was set forth. In many cases probably a Baron of one family had allowed precedence to a Baron of another family, for many generations, without thought or question of the original right, and for no other reason than that his father had done likewise. It was only when a dispute arose and was settled, and when the decision was recorded, that any principle could be said to be established.

The earliest case in which an express decision was given appears to be that of Thomas son of William West, Lord De la Warr, which occurred in the thirty-ninth year of the reign of Elizabeth [2]. His great grandfather Thomas, who had been summoned to Parliament in the third year of Henry VIII, had by a first wife a son Thomas, a younger son who died without issue, and four daughters. By a second wife he had three sons, Owen, George, and Leonard. After his death, which occurred in February, 1525–6 [3], his eldest son Thomas was summoned to Parliament. This Thomas also died without issue in the year 1554. His eldest brother of the half-blood, Owen, had already died in the year 1551 [3], leaving two daughters but no male issue. His second brother of the half-blood, George, had also died in the year 1538 [3], leaving issue, William and

---

[1] Stat. 31 Hen. VIII, cap. 10.

[2] There is in the *Third Rep. Dig. Peer* (vol. ii. pp. 142–145) a long but inconclusive disquisition on the barony of La Warr and the precedence supposed to attach to it before it was enjoyed by the family of West, but no reference is made to the later and very remarkable details set forth below.

[3] These dates are given in Collins's *Peerage*, vol. v. pp. 12–17, as founded on the probates of the respective wills, and so far as they are material, are confirmed by the documents mentioned below.

CHAP. VII. another son.   Leonard also had issue both male and female.

In the time of the first mentioned Thomas, Lord Lawarre, or De la Warr, the greater part of his lands had been settled on his son Thomas in tail male, with successive remainders in tail male to his three other sons, Owen, George, and Leonard.   Upon the death of the second Thomas, without issue, the lands would, in the absence of any settlement, have descended to his sisters of the whole blood, or their representatives, to the exclusion of his half brothers.   After the death of George, however, in 1538, and of Owen in 1551, George's son William became the heir in tail male according to the terms of the settlement.

William West, heir in tail male to the lands of the barony, disabled for life, by Act of Parliament, in the reign of Edward VI.

William, being then a very young man, and being anxious to expedite his succession to the inheritance, mixed some poison in a cup with drink for his uncle Thomas, but had the misfortune, or the good fortune, to be detected before it was administered.   Upon complaint made in Parliament by his uncle an Act was passed by which William was disabled for life from claiming or enjoying ' any dignity or lordship, in any right or estate by descent, remainder, or otherwise [1].'

Attainted for high treason in the reign of Queen Mary.

In the troubled times which ensued during the reign of Queen Mary, William suffered attainder for high treason, and this further complicated the position.   He was, however, in favour with Queen Elizabeth, and at the beginning of her reign we find him corresponding with Secretary Cecil in relation to his affairs.   His statement can, perhaps, best be given in the words of his letter to Cecil of March 19, 1558-1559 :—

---

[1] 11 Rep. 1.   The title of the Act is given among the ' Private Acts ' of 3 & 4 Edward VI in the Statutes at large, but it was in fact never certified into the Chancery, and does not appear on the Parliament Roll either of 2 & 3 or of 3 & 4 Edward VI.   Its validity, however, was never questioned, and it is mentioned in the Calendar of Acts passed in the Session in the *Lords' Journals* of 3 Edward VI (vol. i. p. 389).

'May it please you to understand that where your CHAP. VII.
pleasure is to know what lands I have in possession and Explains
in reversion and who be my heirs, you shall perceive that his position
my late uncle had licence by Act of Parliament to dispose to Cecil
his lands at his will and pleasure during my natural life, accession of
who in his last will gave unto me yearly during my life Elizabeth.
£350 in annuity, with the manors of Offington and Ewhurst
and the parks to the same appertaining, with a house in
London, being together of the value of £132 by the year.
The residue of his manors, lands, and tenements he willed
to his executors to be and go to the performance of his
last will and testament during my life, and after my
decease the whole to remain to my son according to the
remainder in the said Act expressed, who cannot receive
the same unless it might please the Queen's Majesty of her
mere goodness to restore me and my children in blood by
Act of Parliament. And if he be not restored it comes by
the said Act to my brother and to his heirs males lawfully
coming, and for want of such issue to my uncle [Leonard]
West and his heirs male lawfully begotten, who by reason
of my said attainder are my next heirs. And also my
living before expressed by meane of my attainder came
unto the Queen's hands that dead is. And in the time of
my trouble Her Majesty gave unto my wife for the relief
of her and her children one hundred marks yearly out
of the Exchequer, and did let to farm to my said wife
the said manors of Offington and Ewhurst with the house
in London, paying yearly the said sum of £132 for the
same, which grant was but during the Queen's pleasure,
and now by her death frustrate and void. So that is
all the land I have in possession, paying for it yearly yet
the foresaid sum. The rest of my uncle's lands that went
to the performance of his will do yet remain to that use,
the doing whereof the executors presently after my uncle's
death, by earnest request, resigned over to me, finding
them two sureties which be bound for me to save and
keep them harmless, and yearly to yield unto them a true
and a just account of my doings in that behalf, the which

CHAP. VII. estate I assigned over to my sureties for their safety immediately upon the receiving of it out of the executors' hands, the same yet resting with them for that my uncle's will is not fully performed. And after the performation thereof the profits of the said lands yearly to be by the said executors equally divided to my uncle's kinsfolk at the discretion of the said executors. And thus, good Mr. Secretary, is both the whole state of my living and the order of my uncle's will. Beseeching you for that my special trust is in you so to stand my good Master in my cause to the Queen's Highness, that I may be able the better to serve Her Majesty and have just cause (as I have already) to pray for you, life enduring. From my poor house the 19th of March.

Yours always to command,
WYLLYAM WEST [1].

Restored in blood by Act of Parliament, but his life disability as to inheritance not removed. William's application was successful, and an Act was passed for his restitution in blood in the fifth year of Elizabeth [2]. The attainder for high treason in the reign of Mary is recited, but no reference is made to the Act of Edward VI by which William West was disabled. He is described as the eldest son of Sir George West, Knight, whom we know to have been dead from William's letter. Sir George is described as 'son and next heir male unto the Right Honourable Sir Thomas West, Knight, deceased, late Lord Lawarre, father unto the Right Honourable Sir Thomas West, Knight, late Lord Lawarre, also deceased [2].'

The barony of De la Warr was in abeyance according to modern ideas, but the doctrine of abeyance Upon the death of the second Thomas Lord De la Warr (of those above mentioned) it must now be asked what became of the dignity? According to the legal doctrines of a later period it would appear to have fallen into abeyance between the daughters of Thomas's eldest half-brother Owen. If it did not so fall into abeyance, it· must either have followed the lands or have reverted to

---

[1] *State Papers, Domestic*, Eliz., 1559, vol. iii.
[2] *Rot. Parl.*, 5 Eliz., no. 38.

the Crown, and have been at the absolute disposition of CHAP. VII. the Sovereign. When the De la Warr case was argued, was not yet it was already becoming an accepted doctrine that the recognized. descent of the dignity of Baron differed from the descent of lands held in fee simple. When lands were so held, and the holders died without issue, leaving sisters of the whole-blood, and a brother of the half-blood, the sisters inherited to the exclusion of the half-brother. ' Of dignities,' however, ' whereof no other possession can be had but such as descend to a man and his heirs, there can be no possession of the brother to make the sister to inherit, but the younger brother being heir to the father shall inherit the dignity inherent to the blood, as heir to him that was first created noble[1].' It seems to follow that the daughters of the first mentioned Thomas, sisters of the whole-blood to the second Thomas, had no claim to the dignity, though in the absence of a settlement they would have inherited the lands. It is, however, clear from subsequent events not only that no title to the barony was supposed to exist in them or their representatives, but also that no such title was supposed to exist in the daughters and coheirs of Owen, who would, if living, have succeeded to the dignity as heir.

Nine years after his restitution in blood, William was William summoned to Parliament as Lord De la Warr[2]. This West was regarded as a new creation, and William took his to Parlia-seat in the House of Lords as a puisne Baron[3]. As, ment as however, the designation of De la Warr was accorded la Warr: to him, it must certainly have been supposed that no right creation. to it existed anywhere if not in him and his heirs.

William died leaving a son Thomas who was under no

---

[1] *Co. Litt.*, 15 b. Some doubts on the subject appear to have been entertained as late as the year 1641. It was ordered by the House of Lords that the Judges should deliver their opinions on the point ; and they delivered their unanimous opinion that there could not be a ' *Possessio fratris*, in point of honour.' *Journals of the House of Lords*, 29 Jan. and 1 Feb. 1640–1641 (vol. iv. pp. 147, 149–150).

[2] Dugdale, *Summons to Parliament*, p. 526 (14 Eliz.).

[3] 11 Rep. 1.

CHAP. VII.

A sum-
mons at
this time
held to
create an
hereditary
peerage :
the views
of Sir
Edward
Coke.

disability of any kind.   He was free from all corruption
of blood by virtue of the Act of the fifth year of Elizabeth.
The disability by which his father was affected through
the Act of Edward VI was for life only, and in no way
affected himself.   He was summoned to Parliament as
Lord de la Warr, and it is clear from subsequent events
that the summons to his father was held to be the creation
of a heritable dignity.   It is clear also that this was
generally considered good law in the time of Elizabeth,
as it finds its place in Coke's Institutes, though not in
the great work of Littleton who lived in the reign of
Edward IV.   'When a man is called to the Upper House
of Parliament by writ,' said Coke, 'he is a Baron and hath
inheritance therein [1].'   If a man be 'called by writ to the
Parliament he hath a *fee simple* in the barony without
any words of inheritance.'   'This writ hath no operation
or effect until he sit in Parliament, and thereby his blood
is ennobled to him and *his heirs lineal*, and thereupon
a Baron is called a Peer of Parliament [2].'

It will be observed that there is a very curious contradiction in Coke's own words a contradiction which is
of special importance as he was the counsel of Thomas,
son of William, Lord De la Warr, in a successful claim
of precedence [3].   It is obvious that, if a man's blood was
ennobled only to him and his heirs lineal, he had not
a fee simple in the dignity, and these very loose ex-
pressions, when used by a great lawyer, go far to show
that the law, as it subsequently existed, had not yet been
quite clearly defined.   Coke's own view, indeed, that the
possessio fratris did not apply to the descent of a dignity
is only a statement in another form, that in a dignity there
was no fee simple.

The claim of Thomas, son of William Lord De la Warr,

[1] Co. Litt., 9 b.
[2] Co. Litt., 16 b.   This was, of course, law in Coke's time, but a
reference which he gives in support shows clearly that it was not law
in the latter part of the reign of Edward III.
[3] 11 Rep. 3.

was embodied in a petition to Queen Elizabeth, in which *Chap. VII.* he prayed to have the same place in Parliament as his *Thomas,* great grandfather, Thomas, between the Lord Willoughby *the son of William,* de Eresby and the Lord Berkeley. The petition was re- *held to* ferred by her to the House of Lords. A committee was *have in-* then named. The committee had the assistance of the *older* Chief Justice of England, the Chief Justice of the Court *with pre-* of Common Pleas, and other Judges, and, as has already *cedence, as* been mentioned, Coke was counsel for Lord De la Warr, *the new* and won the case. It was objected, in the first place, that *dignity.* the disability of William by virtue of the Act of Edward VI, prevented the descent to his son Thomas of the dignity enjoyed by William's grandfather. As, however, it was distinctly expressed in the Act that William's disability was personal and for life only, the Judges held that Thomas might claim as heir to him or to any of his ancestors. It was objected, in the second place, that William had accepted a new creation from the Queen, and that the new dignity had descended to his son Thomas, and could not be waived. The Judges held that on William's death both the dignity enjoyed by his grandfather and the new dignity conferred upon himself descended to his son Thomas. The Committee reported accordingly to the House of Lords, and the House of Lords to the Queen. In the end 'the Lord De la Warr in his Parliament robes was by the Lord Zouche (supplying the place of the Lord Willoughby then within age), and the Lord Berkeley, also in their robes, brought into the House and placed in his said place . . . Garter King of Arms attending upon them and doing his office [1].'

No more solemn recognition of Lord De la Warr's right *The old* could have been made ; yet it is not manifest on what *idea of barony by* principle the precedence was allowed. It is perfectly clear *tenure* that the summons of William followed by a sitting in *apparently not yet* Parliament, was held to create an hereditary peerage, *extinct.*

[1] *Journals of the House of Lords*, 14 Nov. 1597 (vol. ii. p. 197), and 11 Rep. 1-3.

CHAP. VII. although he could not, in consequence of his disability, have had any lands in barony. The grounds on which it was held that his son had the barony of his grandfather can only be conjectured.

According to more recent doctrines the barony enjoyed by the first Thomas was in abeyance, and the third Thomas (of those above mentioned) had no right to it. According to the alternative theory (sometimes advanced) that a barony descending to coheirs lapsed to the Crown, the third Thomas had still no right to it. and the new creation in favour of his father gave him his only claim to be a Baron. If, again, an old barony, revived after reversion to the Crown, carried the ancient precedence, William himself would have had it, notwithstanding his disability to inherit ; and his son's petition would have been unnecessary. The only clue that we have to the thoughts which passed through the minds of the Judges and of Coke is to be found in the references which Coke, in his commentaries on Littleton, gives in relation to the subject ; and the only reference of importance is to the report of the forty-eighth year of Edward III already noticed [1]. In that report, tenure by barony is distinctly shown to be essential in the case of any one claiming privilege as a Baron. It would therefore seem to follow that in relation to an ancient barony, or barony by prescription, as distinguished from one newly created, the lawyers had not even yet shaken themselves free from the doctrine of barony by tenure. Thomas, son of William, Lord De la Warr, held the lands of his ancestors, and it is extremely difficult to see any other reason for assigning to him the precedence which his ancestors had enjoyed. It may, perhaps, be objected that he did not hold the lands in barony—that he did not hold them in chief, as of the Crown. This is true, in a sense, because tenant-in-tail held in theory of the donor or his heirs, and not of the Crown directly. When, however, the donor was dead, and

---

[1] *Year Book*, Mich., 48 Ed. III, fo. 30. no. 18.

the coheirs were incapable of sitting in Parliament, it does CHAP. VII.
not seem unreasonable that the tenant-in-tail male, being
of the blood of the original tenant-in-chief, should enjoy
the dignity and privileges and perform the services
attaching to the lands.

There is yet another point in relation to this case of The place
Lord De la Warr which seems worth attention. It is said of Lord De
la Warr
in the Journals of the House of Lords, that the place in Parlia-
of Thomas, Lord De la Warr, the grandfather of William, appeared
appears by record [1]. The question which naturally arises 'by
record ':
is : what record? Coke tells us that when issue was joined question
in any action, whether a person was a Baron or not, it as to the
nature of
could not be tried by a jury, but must be tried ' by the the record.
record of Parliament, which could not appear unless he
were of the Parliament [2].' The 'record of Parliament'
might at first sight appear to be in early times the Rolls
showing the proceedings in Parliament, in later times the
Journals of the House of Lords. It is not, however, quite
clear from Coke's Reports in what sense he, at any rate,
used the expression. If persons 'be Lords of Parliament,'
he says, 'it appears by record and therefore by record,
viz. by the King's writ it ought to be certified [3].' Elsewhere he uses language which also lacks precision : 'If
a Baron, Viscount, Earl, or other Lord of Parliament, and
Peer of the Realm be plaintiff in any action, and the
defendant will plead that the plaintiff is not a Baron,
Viscount, Earl, &c., this . . . shall be tried by the record
in Chancery which imports by itself solid truth [4].'

The Chancery was regarded as an office of the Parlia- The Rolls
ment, and, before the Journals of the House of Lords of Letters
Close, the
began to be kept in a separate form, in the reign of Rolls of
Henry VIII, the record in Chancery might have been ment, and
interpreted to mean either the Roll of Parliament, or the the
Journals of

[1] *Journals of the House of Lords*, 14 Nov. 1597 (vol. ii. p. 196).
[2] Co. Litt., 16 b.
[3] 6 Rep. 53, the Countess of Rutland's case in the Star Chamber,
Mich., 3 James I.
[4] 12 Rep. 96, the Countess of Shrewsbury's case, 10 James I.

CHAP. VII.
the House
of Lords.

Roll of Letters Close, on which the writs of summons to Parliament were enrolled. After that time, the Rolls of Parliament began to be merely enrolments of Acts of Parliament without any account of the proceedings. In relation to individual Peers, therefore, it might seem that in Coke's time the record in Chancery could have been only the Roll of Letters Close. It must, however, be remembered that, when he wrote, the change in the character of the Parliament Rolls was comparatively recent. A writ of summons enrolled on the Close Roll affords no evidence of a sitting in the House of Lords, as do sometimes the earlier Rolls of Parliament ; and Coke himself says, 'this writ hath no operation or effect until " the person summoned " sit in Parliament.' It would, therefore, seem erroneous to suppose that the record by which the issue could be tried is the Roll of Letters Close alone, though this appears to be the view taken of Coke's words in some of the text books [1].

A far more precise and intelligible statement of the law was made in later times. When a party in a cause claims to be a Peer by patent the claim is triable by the patent itself; when by descent or prescription, the claim is triable by a jury; when by writ 'he is not a Peer until he has taken his seat : that is to be tried by the record of Parliament [2].' That which has to be tried, therefore, is clearly not whether he was summoned, but whether he sat.

Proofs of
precedence
of Barons :
practically
none before
the reign
of Henry
VIII.

It seems to follow that the record to which reference is made in the Journals of the House of Lords of the year 1597, in relation to Lord De la Warr, is either the Parliament Roll or the earlier journals of the House. As Thomas, Lord De la Warr, the grandfather of William was living when the journals of the House had begun to show the sittings in order of precedence, there can be little doubt that the place of Thomas in Parliament was that which was assigned to him in the Journals of the Lords.

---

[1] E.g. Hubback, *Evidence of Succession.*
[2] 2 Barn. and Cres. 871–875.

This fact, however, brings us to a very important con- clusion with regard to the precedence of Barons. The Journals of the Lords commence only in the reign of Henry VIII, and the first day on which the names of those present are set down in order is February 6, in the third year of the reign. It would, therefore, seem to be impossible to prove the precedence of a Baron as existing in earlier times, and no question of precedence of Barons appears in fact to have been expressly decided before that date.

It was, of course, well understood that Dukes had precedence of Marquesses, Marquesses of Earls, Earls of Viscounts, and Viscounts of Barons ; but the creations of Dukes, Marquesses, Earls. and Viscounts were by solemn investiture, by charter, or by letters patent. The Barons, however, were in a different position. It is, without doubt, possible to show from the Rolls of Letters Close that the ancestor of one Baron had an enrolled summons to Parliament before the ancestor of another, but this is not necessarily a proof of precedence in all cases, though it is commonly accepted as sufficient. The names of the Barons do not always appear in the same order on those Rolls, and it is sometimes possible to show that a Baron sat in a Parliament when the Roll fails to show his summons.

The case of Thomas, son of William Lord De la Warr, is thus in many ways a landmark in the history of the peerage. It is one of the most striking cases in which a claim of precedence on the part of a Baron was settled ; it is, perhaps, the first case in which a mere summons to Parliament, followed by a sitting, was held to confer an hereditary dignity ; and it is closely associated with Sir Edward Coke, whose statements concerning the law on this subject appear to have been the ground of subsequent decisions.

The tree of the later law on barony by writ was now planted and destined to bear fruit in future reigns. Some time, however, was yet to elapse before the doctrine of barony by tenure was declared to be no longer in force,

K

CHAP. VII. and even before the doctrine of hereditary peerage by writ
existence was finally accepted as a principle. In the year 1669,
in 1669. when Benjamin Mildmay was claiming the barony of
Fitz-Walter in opposition to Robert Cheeke, there was
a discussion on the subject in the Privy Council, before
which the matter was brought by order of the King. Then
barony by tenure 'was found to have been discontinued
for many ages, and not in being, and so not fit to be
revived, or to admit any pretence of right to succession
thereupon [1].' The Council had the assistance of Sir John
Kelyng, Chief Justice of England ; Sir John Vaughan,
Chief Justice of the Common Pleas ; Sir Matthew Hale,
Chief Baron of the Exchequer ; the King's Chief Serjeant-
at-Law, and the Attorney and Solicitor-General. The
opinion has, therefore, the highest legal authority of the
time, and we may feel sure that a few years after the
restoration of Charles II, the only recognized roots of
title to a barony were writ of summons to Parliament, and
creation by letters patent or charter.

This most important Order in Council, however, is for
many reasons of little value in relation to earlier times.
The words 'many ages' are too vague to be of any practical use in history. There had been two great revolutions
in less than a quarter of a century. and the events of the
earlier part of the reign of Charles I may well have
seemed ages apart from the events which occurred after
the Restoration. The whole theory of tenure had also
been changed. Tenure by military service had been swept
away by the men of the Commonwealth ; and the men
of the Restoration had followed their example. When
tenure by military service was gone, barony by tenure
had become an anachronism, and the opinions of Kelyng,
Vaughan, and Hale were only the natural expression of
the sentiments of the time. From the historical point of
view the most remarkable fact is that there is no judicial

---

[1] Order in Council, 19 Jan. 1669, Privy Council Office (printed in
Rep. Dig. Peer, vol. iv. app. iv. p. 1008).

decision adverse to barony by tenure, until a statute had CHAP. VII.
put an end to tenure by barony[1].

In the year 1674 the judges expressed an opinion that Hereditary
Gervase Clifton (who was summoned to Parliament in the barony by
writ more
sixth year of the reign of James I), was by virtue of the fully
writ of summons and sitting in Parliament 'a Peer and recognized
in 1674.
Baron of this kingdom, and his blood thereby ennobled,'
and that 'his honour descended from him to Katharine,
his sole daughter and heir, and successively after several
descents to the petitioner' who was his great grand-
daughter. The House of Lords thereupon resolved 'that
the claimant (Katharine O'Brien) had right to the barony
of Clifton[2].' Even this was rather a decision upon a particular case than the enunciation of a general principle.
It appears, however, to have been a sufficient precedent
for all subsequent cases in which the circumstances were
the same, but to have left open the question of the period
at which a summons to Parliament followed by a sitting
first operated to create an hereditary barony.

The doctrine that a barony may be in abeyance, for an The
indefinite time, between coheirs or their representatives doctrine of
abeyance
does not appear to have arrived at maturity when Sir had not
Edward Coke wrote his *Institutes*. He had an idea that arrived at
maturity
the King might confer the dignity upon any daughter in Coke's
time.
of an Earl or Baron who might be one of the coheirs[3],
but he does not distinctly affirm that the King might not
confer it on a stranger in blood. He does not use the
word abeyance in relation to this subject, and he does
not say that when there are two or more coheirs, and
one alone, or a representative of one alone survives, the

---

[1] The question was raised again as late as 1861, in the Berkeley
Peerage case, when, after reference to them by the Crown, the Lords
held that a writ of summons to Parliament could not be claimed on the
ground of holding certain lands.

[2] *Journals of the House of Lords*, 7 Feb. 1673–1674 (vol. xii.
pp. 629–630).

[3] *Co. Litt.*, 165 a. The case which he cites has been mentioned,
and its effect described above, p. 91.

CHAP. VII. one or the representative of the one becomes entitled
to the dignity. It is therefore necessary to seek in
some more recent period for the full development of the
idea.

Case of   A little later—at the beginning of the reign of Charles I
the Earl of
Oxford :   —the doctrine had not made further progress. A very
a barony   important case was then decided with regard to the earl-
descending
to co-heirs dom of Oxford, and the baronies of Bolbecke, Sandford,
held to be   and Badlesmere. In the sixteenth year of the reign of
absolutely
at the   Richard II, the earldom had by Act of Parliament been
disposal
of the   conferred in tail male upon Aubrey de Vere, after the
Sovereign attainder of his nephew Robert in the eleventh year.
in the
reign of   From this Aubrey the earldom descended, according to
Charles I. the limitation, to another Robert de Vere, who was held
to be the rightful heir in the year 1626. The baronies,
however, not being included in the entail, descended,
in a different manner, to the heirs general. Aubrey had
a son Richard who had two sons, John and Robert.
John had a son John, who had issue a son John, and
three daughters, Dorothy, Elizabeth, and Ursula. The last
mentioned John succeeded, in his turn, to the earldom,
but died without issue. The earldom then fell, according
to the limitation, to the male heir of Richard's son Robert,
as was reported to the House of Lords by the Lord
Chief Justice of England, on behalf of himself and other
Judges[1]. 'And as touching the baronies,' to use their
own words, 'their opinion is that the same descended to
the general heirs of John the fourth Earl of Oxon, who had
issue, John the fifth Earl of Oxon, and three daughters, one
of them married to Lord Latimer, another to Winckfield,
and another to Knightly: which John, the fifth Earl, dying
without issue, those baronies descended unto the said
daughters as his sisters and heirs; but, those dignities
being entire and not dividable, they became uncapable of
the same, otherwise than by *gift* from the Crown ; and

---

[1] *Journals of the House of Lords*, March 1, 1625-1626 (vol. iii.
p. 510), and Collins's *Collections*, pp. 269-275.

they, in strictness of law, reverted unto and were in the CHAP. VII.
disposition of King Henry VIII [1].'

There is no sign of the doctrine of abeyance in these
words. When the dignities *reverted* to the King, it is
obvious that they were at his absolute disposal. He could
renew them or not at his pleasure, and give them to
whomsoever he pleased. The coheirs were '*uncapable*' of
inheriting them, and if any one of the coheirs received
any one of them it would be not in virtue of any right but
as a *gift* (or in other words a new creation) from the
Crown. The evidence, moreover, that there was as yet
no conception of the principle of abeyance does not rest
here. The Judges added that the Earls of Oxford who
had succeeded John the fifth Earl had assumed the titles
of the baronies in various documents, and their eldest
sons, while they lived, had been styled Viscount Bolbecke.
It seems, therefore. to be as clear as anything can be that
neither in the popular ideas of the day, nor in the tra-
ditions of the family of de Vere, nor in the learning of
the Judges, had that which is now called 'abeyance' any
place. The Lords themselves accepted the opinion of the
Judges, reporting to the King that the baronies 'are wholly
in your Majesty's hands to dispose at your own pleasure [2].'

In the reign of Charles II, however, there does at length Something
appear to be an acknowledgement by the King, not only like the
principle of
that when a barony descends to female coheirs he may abeyance
declare which of them shall have the dignity, but also by appears to
be first
implication that his power in relation to the barony does recognized
in the case
not extend beyond the coheirs and their representatives. of Lord
Thomas, Lord Windsor, died in the troubled times of Windsor in
the reign of
Charles I without issue. He had two sisters, the elder of Charles II.
whom (Elizabeth) married Dixie Hickman and had issue,
a son Thomas. Immediately after the Restoration the
services of the Windsor family were rewarded by the
restitution to Thomas Hickman of the barony of Windsor.

[1] *Journals of the House of Lords*, March 20, 1625–1626 (vol. iii. p. 535).
[2] *Ib.*, April 5, 1626 (vol. iii. p. 552).

CHAP. VII. This was effected by letters patent which Dugdale professes to have seen[1], and which Collins cites without any
definite reference. There is no doubt that they did actually
pass the Great Seal, though it is difficult to find an
enrolment of them. On June 18, 1660, the new Lord
Windsor 'brought in [to the House of Lords] his patent
of restitution to the title and degree of a Peer of this
Realm. which was read. And he took his place as Lord
Windsor[2].'

According
to a recital
in his
patent of
restitution,
it was for
the King to
declare
which of
two coheirs
should
enjoy a
dignity.

The effect of the patent is set out with sufficient clearness in the contemporary Docket Book of the Privy Signet
Office, an entry in which appears in the following words :—
'Lord Windsor.—A Grant (reciting that Henry Windsor
had and enjoyed the dignity of Baron Windsor to him and
his heirs and that he had issue Thomas, Lord Windsor, his
son and heir [who died without issue] and two daughters,
the eldest whereof married Dixy Hickman, Esq., who are
both deceased, leaving issue Thomas Windsor alias Hickman their son, who now enjoys a great part of the ancient
patrimony of the Lord Windsor, and reciting that it belongeth to his Majesty to declare *which of the said coheirs*
shall enjoy the dignity of their ancestors) of restoration
and confirmation of the said Barony and of the title and
dignity of Baron Windsor, which the said Henry and
Thomas successively enjoyed, unto the said Thomas Windsor alias Hickman and his heirs, in the place of the said
Lord Windsor, To hold to him and his heirs for ever, and
to have the same precedency and place in Parliament and
elsewhere within the Kingdom of England as the said
Henry and Thomas Barons Windsor (whilst they lived)
successively enjoyed, and all other dignities and pre-
eminences to a Baron of England belonging[3].'

There was
no express
legal

Even in this case the contemporary Index to the Docket
Book describes the patent as a 'creation,' and thus shows

[1] Dugdale, *Baronage*, vol. ii. p. 309.
[2] *Journals of the House of Lords*, June 18, 1660 (vol. xi. p. 67).
[3] Signet Office *Docket Book*, June, 1660.

how new was the idea out of which has sprung the modern CHAP. VII
doctrine of abeyance. If, however, it only belonged to the decision on
King 'to declare which of the coheirs should enjoy the the point
dignity of their ancestors,' it would appear that the dignity case of
was now thought to be in the blood of the coheirs, and Lord
was not held to have *reverted* to the Crown as at an earlier Windsor.
time. Still it must not be forgotten that the words of the
Patent do not embody any judicial decision. The Journals
of the Lords are silent, except in so far as they tell how
the Patent was brought into the House. It was by the
grace and favour of the Sovereign, and not by any operation of law, that Lord Windsor gained his dignity and
place in Parliament, and there is still no trace of the
doctrine that upon the death of all the coheirs but one,
or the extinction of all their lines but one, the surviving
coheir or representative has a right to the barony.

It was not until the year 1695 that this right was The right
definitely though not unanimously acknowledged. In of a
                                                     survivor of
February of that year, a motion was made in the House coheirs to
of Lords to appoint a day for the consideration of some a barony
                                                        not
points which had been raised in relation to the descent acknow-
of baronies by writ. The matter was debated on the ledged by
                                                     the Lords
following March 19. The question was then put until 1695,
'whether, if a person summoned to Parliament by writ, and then
                                                        not unani-
and sitting, die leaving issue two or more daughters, who mously.
all die, one of them only leaving issue, such issue has
a right to demand a summons to Parliament.' It was
resolved in the affirmative [1]. Even then, however, some
of the Lords dissented, being of opinion that the barony
still remained at the King's disposal. As has already been
shown, they had, beyond doubt, the earlier precedents in
their favour. In later times, nevertheless, the resolution of
the majority of the Lords has been held to be law, and the
doctrine then asserted has been attributed to previous
ages.

[1] *Journals of the House of Lords*, March 19, 1694–1695 (printed,
vol. xv. pp. 552–553).

CHAP. VII.   In the year 1839 a barony was called out of abeyance
Later state- which was represented as having been in abeyance for no
ments as   less than four hundred and thirteen years.   In the Minutes
to the
doctrine of   of Evidence given before the Committee of Privileges, to
abeyance :   whom the Petition of Thomas Stonor claiming to be senior
the barony
of Camoys,   coheir to the Barony of Camoys was referred, appears 'the
1839.   unanimous opinion of the Judges,' as delivered by the Lord
Chief Justice of the Court of Common Pleas (Sir. N. Tindal)[1].
He laid down the following general rule as being of great
antiquity :—' In the case of a barony descendible either to
the heirs general or the heirs of the body, if the Baron die,
leaving only daughters, or sisters, or other coheirs, the
barony is in abeyance so long as more than one of such
coheirs is in existence, but so, nevertheless that the Crown,
the Sovereign of honour and dignity, may, at any time
during such abeyance, determine it by conferring the
dignity upon whichever of the coheirs it pleases ; but if
the Crown do not exercise such prerogative, and the
lines of all the coheirs but one become extinct, then the
abeyance is at an end, and such only surviving coheir is
entitled, as a matter of right, to the enjoyment of the
dignity.'

Dubious   The Chief Justice was alone responsible for the reasons
cases used   assigned, and presumably also for the actual words of
in support :
the barony   the report.   He, therefore, may have introduced the very
of Crom-   dubious cases upon which he relied as precedents.   He
well.
said, for instance, that Henry VI, 'in the case of the Lord
Cromwell dying without issue male and leaving several
daughters, preferred the youngest.'   The statement is in no
sense correct.   The last Lord Cromwell of the family in
question died leaving his sister Maud his heir.   She married
Sir Richard Stanhope and had issue two daughters, Maud
and Joan.   The second daughter, Joan, married Sir
Humphrey Bourchier and he was summoned to Parliament, in the second year of the reign of Edward IV, but
apparently not before, as Humphrey Lord Cromwell,

---

[1] *Minutes of Evidence*, as above, pp. 314-321 (504-511).

'chivaler[1].' He was also summoned in the sixth and ninth CHAP. VII.
years of the reign of Edward IV as Humphrey Cromwell,
'chivaler[2],' and in the forty-ninth year of the reign of
Henry VI, as Humphrey Bourchier de Cromwell, 'chivaler[3].'
There is nothing whatever to show that the barony was
supposed to be in abeyance between the two daughters of
Maud, or that the King had not absolute power to dispose
of it as he pleased, or to create a new barony of the same
name.

The Chief Justice also asserted that 'John Grey, the *The*
descendant of one of the coheirs of Edward Charleton, *barony of Charleton*
Lord Powys, was summoned to Parliament in the twenty- *de Powys.*
second year of Edward IV, after the attainder and before the
restoration in blood of John, Lord Tiptoft, the other coheir,
enjoying, upon that writ of summons, the seat and precedence
of his ancestor.' This statement again is not borne out by
the facts. The ancestor had been summoned as Edward de
Charleton de Powys. The descendant was summoned as
John Grey de Powes[4], and there is nothing to show that
he had any particular seat or precedence. No reliance can
be placed on the varying order in which the names occur
on the Roll of Letters Close, and, if it could, the Roll
would rather tend to show that 'John Grey de Powes'
took his seat as a junior Baron. There is no reason to
suppose that, when John Grey de Powes was summoned
to Parliament, the summons effected anything but a new
creation.

In a much more recent peerage case there was a reso- *Declara-*
lution of a Committee of the House of Lords declaring that *tion in 1877 by a*
an abeyance occurred in the reign of Edward IV. It must, *Committee of Lords*
however, be submitted, with all respect, that an opinion *that an*
given in the year 1877 is not conclusive with regard to the *abeyance occurred in*

[1] *Rot. Lit. Claus.,* 2 Ed. IV, m. 5 d (printed in *Rep. Dig. Peer,*
vol. iv. p. 958).

[2] *Ib.,* 6 Ed. IV, m. 1 d (printed, p. 966), 9 Ed. IV, m. 23 d (printed,
p. 970).

[3] *Ib.,* 49 Hen. VI, m. 6 d (printed, p. 977).

[4] *Ib.,* 22 & 23 Ed. IV, m. 10 d (printed, p. 985).

CHAP. VII. opinions entertained in the year 1481. In relation to the
the reign of barony of Mowbray a Committee of the House of Lords
Edward resolved on July 26, 1877, 'that on the death of Anne
IV:
baronies of Lady Mowbray and Segrave, Duchess of York and
Mowbray Norfolk, in 1481, the baronies of Mowbray and Segrave
and
Segrave. fell into abeyance between John Lord Howard and William
Viscount Berkeley, as the grandsons and the then coheirs
of Thomas the first Duke of Norfolk.' and further 'that
the abeyance of the said baronies was subsequently, and
previously to the reign of Queen Elizabeth, determined in
favour of the Howard family [1].' It is obvious, from the
words of the resolution that both the abeyance and the
calling out of abeyance had been merely inferred from the
evidence laid before the Committee [2]. The correctness of
the inference must be judged not by the application of
modern doctrines to ancient facts, but by the application
of the doctrines of the time to the facts of the time. There
is no proof whatever that the doctrine of the abeyance of
a barony was in existence in the reign of Edward IV, and
there is evidence that it was not in existence at a much
later period.

Paucity of   The earliest case in which anything like the doctrine of
cases sub-
sequent to abeyance was recognized was, it is almost certain, that of
that of Lord Windsor, in the reign of Charles II. The coheir then
Lord
Windsor had given to him not only the barony but also the precedence
except in and place in Parliament of previous Lords Windsor. Even
the years
from 1829 since the time of Charles II, the instances in which a barony
to 1841. has been called out of abeyance have been rare. In the
hundred and sixty-nine years, from 1660 to 1829, there
were but eleven; and two of these related to the same
barony (of Zouche). From 1829 to 1841 it was the fashion
to call baronies out of abeyance; and no less than eight
(one of which, the barony of Berners, appears on two

[1] *Journals of the House of Lords*, July 27, 1877 (vol. cix. p. 339).
[2] There is a monograph on the determination of the Mowbray
Abeyance by Mr. J. H. Round in the *Law Quarterly Review*, vol. x.
p. 68.

occasions) enjoyed that distinction in twelve years [1], the CHAP. VII.
fortunate Barons taking the precedence enjoyed or supposed to have been enjoyed by their predecessors. Since
1841 the determination of abeyance has been less frequent,
but the principle has not been disputed. It cannot
claim a very high antiquity, but it has probably been
accepted sufficiently often during the last two centuries
to give it an established legal position. The practice,
however, has varied even since the year 1660. Lord
Windsor then had a declaratory Patent. In more recent
times the usage has been (except when a barony has been
confirmed by patent to a Peer already holding a higher
dignity) to call a barony out of abeyance simply by the
issue of a writ of summons to Parliament.

[1] *Return of Baronies called out of Abeyance*, H. L., Session 1858,
no. 289.

CHAPTER VIII.

CHAP.
VIII.

NO history relating to the hereditary peerage would be complete without some reference to the remarkable doctrine as to blood which appears to have been a development of the ideas brought into England at the time of the Conquest, and which was, at any rate, firmly established early in the reign of Edward III. We have seen how the succession of the Counts and Dukes of Normandy continued in the blood of Rollo, how child succeeded to father, though the union of the parents had not received the sanction of the Church. The late period at which Neustria was conquered by the Northmen, and consequently at which they accepted Christianity, may possibly have been one of the causes which subjected Dukes of Normandy and William the Conqueror, among the number, to the aspersion of being bastards.

Blood
after the
Conquest:
corruption
of blood.

The French conquest of England was effected at a time when the power of the Church was increasing, and for that reason, perhaps, no descendant of William not born in Christian wedlock ever ascended the throne. For many centuries afterwards no form of marriage was recognized in England except that which was recognized by the Church. The lawyers, acting in agreement with the ecclesiastics, evolved the doctrine that a child not born in lawful wedlock was fatherless, *nullius filius*, no man's child. Subject, however, to the restriction that all blood had, as it were, to be church-marked, blood became of almost as much importance in law as in later times it has been held by men of

science to be in physiology; and there is the closest possible Cʜ. VIII.
resemblance between the doctrine of the physiologists and
the doctrine of the lawyers. Blood, according to both, had
properties and capacities transmissible from generation to
generation, and could, according to both, be corrupted with
the gravest consequences to the offspring.

It has been said by an eminent writer on the history of The
the Constitution that the doctrine of the ennobling of the doctrine
blood of a Peer is an absurdity, chiefly, as it seems, because, ennobling
according to his view, a younger son does not become of blood
ennobled when his father has a peerage which is hereditary. and con-
Regarded, however, as part of a general principle, the itself.
doctrine is no absurdity at all, but one which is perfectly
intelligible, perfectly consistent with itself at all points, and
as scientific as anything to be found in mediaeval or even
modern literature.

Whenever any person, not being a corporation, held land The in-
in fee simple, there existed in his blood a capacity of heritance
inheritance—a capacity not limited to his eldest son, but inseparable
pervading the whole of his descendants, and, in the absence before the
of descendants, extending still further. It was a capacity reign of
which he himself had no power to destroy. He could not, VIII.
before the reign of Henry VIII (except in virtue of certain
local customs) affect the disposition of the land after his
death by will. If he died seised of his estate in fee simple,
the land could go only to his heir, who might be his eldest
son, or the issue of his eldest son, or failing them a younger
son, or failing a younger son and his issue a daughter or
daughters, and so on according to the law of descent in
relation to consanguinity. He was absolutely powerless
to affect the inheritance or to destroy the virtue of his own
blood. He could affect his heirs only by affecting himself.
He could convey away his land during his lifetime.; and,
in that case, it would of course no longer go to his heir.
but solely because it was not his when he died. He in no
way affected the capacity of the blood to inherit that which
he held himself. There were some things of which a man
could not divest himself at all in favour of another, and

CH. VIII. which, whether he would or not, must of necessity remain in his blood, unless destroyed or extinguished.

Seignory of lands held in frankalmoign inalienable and ineradicable from the blood. If a man gave lands to a Religious House, to hold of him and his heirs in frankalmoign, the seignory of those lands was so fixed in his blood that it could never afterwards be in any blood but his. No conveyance of the seignory to another person, no forfeiture, no recovery by action at law could affect it. As long as one drop of his blood existed on earth, so long did the seignory, if also in existence, attach to it[1]. This particular seignory could be destroyed or extinguished only by failure of his blood, by release to the tenant, or by the tenant's alienation of the lands[2]. The tenant then ceased to hold in frankalmoign of the donor or his heirs, and the particular tenure was at end.

As soon as hereditary peerage was established as a personal dignity, it bore a very strong resemblance to seignory of lands held in frankalmoign, especially in cases in which the inheritance was to the heirs general. It was from one point of view less absolutely in the blood than the seignory, because it was subject to forfeiture by the holder, the corruption of whose blood by attainder would extend the forfeiture to his descendants. From another point of view it was more absolutely in the blood than even the seignory, as soon as the doctrine was accepted that a Peer could not surrender or extinguish his dignity, though not before[3]. It exactly resembled the seignory in that it could not pass directly from the holder to a stranger in blood by any form of conveyance. In both cases we see a capacity or property inherent in the blood analogous to that which causes the posterity of a human being to be human, and the posterity of an individual of another species to be of that other species. As any one who is in the possible line of descent of the Crown is said to be of the blood royal, so any one who is in the possible line of descent of any peerage is of the inheritable blood in which that peerage runs.

---

[1] *Year Book*, Hil., 14 Ed. III, no. 19, pp. 268, 280–283.
[2] *Litt.*, sec. 139, 141 ; 2 Inst. 502.
[3] See below, chapter xii. pp. 271–273.

Until very recent times (January 1, 1834[1]) the doctrine CH. VIII.
of blood was applied in a very remarkable manner so as to
exclude the half-blood from the inheritance of lands. When The
the right of females to inherit was recognized. the capacity lands :
to inherit might be transmitted to the offspring either from common
the blood of the father or from the blood of the mother. doctrine as
The mother, it is true, during the period of her coverture, to the half-blood.
had no status except as the wife of her husband, and
he might even dispose of her lands. From the moment of
his death, however, her rights of blood reasserted themselves, and the lands could be recovered by her or her
heirs. Upon her death the lands descended to her heirs,
subject only to the life estate of her husband, known as
the ' curtesy of England,' should he happen to survive her.
If she had two sons by her first husband, and the elder
inherited after her death, and died without issue, the
younger son was his heir, as being his brother of the whole
blood. If she had only one son by a first husband, and
another by a second husband, and the elder son became
seised of the inheritance and died without issue, the younger
son being only of the half-blood did not inherit. It might
seem, at first sight. that in this case the younger son, having
the mother's blood equally with the elder, should inherit on
his brother's death. According to the old law, however,
the descent, as it was called, was traced directly from
brother to brother, and not backwards from the elder son
to the mother, and from her to the younger son. The same
principles were applied when the inheritance was on the
father's side. His younger sons by his first wife were heirs
to their elder brothers in succession when their elder
brothers died seised without issue, but his sons by a second
wife could never inherit from their elder brothers of the
half-blood.

If no explanation of this curious rule could be found the The
doctrine might thus seem to be at variance with itself, reasons
because the younger son of the half-blood, possessing in for it.

---

[1] Stat. 3 & 4 Will. IV, cap. 106.

CH. VIII. each case the blood of the parent to whom the inheritance had belonged, in an equal degree with his elder brother, was yet excluded from that very inheritance in favour of a more remote kinsman. The reason usually assigned is, however, one which is consistent with the doctrine of blood in its most rigid application. Although it may be true that, upon the death of any particular person, there could hardly be a doubt whether he inherited from his father or his mother, yet, when the kinship had to be traced further back, the true source of inheritance might well be in doubt as between a husband and wife in some remote past generation. If, for instance, upon failure of all issue in the direct line, a descent had to be traced from a great-uncle, who died seised, it might, in the unlettered age of the earlier fiefs, have been uncertain whether he inherited from his father or from his mother. If he inherited from his mother, no half-brother on his father's side could possess that inheritable blood which would give a title to succeed. If, however, he had a brother of the whole blood, it is obvious that this brother must have possessed the true inheritable blood, whether the inheritance descended from the father or from the mother. The descendants of this brother of the whole blood would consequently inherit. The principle, framed in all probability in the interest of the sovereign or other lord, in order that he might not be defrauded of his escheat upon failure of heirs, had thus some plausibility as applied to distant consanguinity, and, perhaps for the sake of uniformity, perhaps still in the interest of the lord, it was also applied where the same grounds could not be alleged.

Possessio fratris. The exclusion of the half-blood sometimes had the effect of causing a female to succeed to the inheritance instead of a male. Thus if any one died seised of land, leaving a son and a daughter by a first wife, and a son by a second wife, and the elder son inherited and died seised without issue, the daughter then inherited and not the younger son. This fact was expressed in the well-known legal maxim, *Possessio fratris facit sororem esse heredem.*

It would appear to follow from this doctrine that when

any one was summoned to Parliament, as in the older times, Ch. VIII.
to perform the service due for any land, the summons *Possessio*
would follow the law applicable to the descent of lands, the *fratris* in-
sister of the whole-blood would inherit, to the exclusion of applicable
to any
the brother of the half-blood, and, when she married, her dignity
husband would have to perform the service, or in other barony by
words to attend in Parliament. As, however, the idea of tenure.
barony by tenure faded away, and the idea gained ground
that to be a Baron was to enjoy a dignity, the lawyers did
not hold the principle of *Possessio fratris* to be applicable
to an honour.

As early as the time of Sir Edward Coke it was held that
there could be no possession of a brother which could cause
a sister of the whole-blood to inherit a dignity to the
exclusion of a brother of the half-blood. The descent was
considered to be to the heir of the person first created noble
and not directly to the heir of the last possessor of the
dignity. On the death of an elder brother, his younger
brother of the half-blood, though incapable of inheriting
his lands, might nevertheless inherit the dignity from their
common father, in whose blood it was supposed to be inherent. This doctrine was applied to all ranks among the
temporal lords, to Dukes, Marquesses, Earls, Viscounts, and
Barons [1].

'Several reasons were assigned for this later diversity Reasons
between the descent of lands and the descent of dignities. for the
different
Noblemen in the higher grades of the peerage held their descent of
honours in virtue of charters or letters patent, Barons in dignities.
lands and
virtue of letters patent or writs of summons. In all these
cases the title to the peerage could be proved only by
record in the Chancery, which necessarily showed who was
the first holder, and consequently in whose blood the dignity
must descend. There was no possibility of a doubt whether
the inheritance was on the father's side or the mother's.
The person claiming either was or was not the heir of the
first of the family created or summoned. If both brother

---

[1] *Co. Litt.*, 15 b.

L

CH. VIII. and sister were of his blood, the brother was of course
preferred.

The law not fully settled before the reign of Charles I.   The Lords themselves, however, seem to have been perplexed by doctrines of succession as late as the reign of Charles I.   In a peerage case then under consideration the Lords submitted to the Judges the question 'whether a *possessio fratris* can be upon a barony by writ.'   The Judges were unanimously of opinion 'that there cannot be a *possessio fratris* in point of honour[1].'   A special reason said to have been assigned by the Judges for this opinion was that no entry could be made upon the dignity of a Baron, and no profit derived from it, and that in these respects it differed from land upon which entry might be made, and from which the person in seisin derived 'esplees' or profits[2].   However applicable this argument might be to a barony just before the Great Rebellion, it certainly could not have been applicable to earldoms of the twelfth century, a common feature of which was that the Earl received the third penny (or one-third of certain revenues) derived from his county.   The principle of an Earl receiving profit from his office had without doubt fallen into oblivion, just as the idea of barony by tenure was, a few years later, held to be an anachronism.

Original effects of attainder and corruption of blood.   Upon attainder for any kind of felony (in which treason was originally included) the blood of the offender immediately became corrupted, and its capacity of inheritance was lost for ever, except, as we have seen, in relation to seignory of lands granted in frankalmoign.   The lands reverted to the lord of whom they were held, and who, in the case of tenants-in-chief, was of course the King.   On attainder for high treason all lands in possession were forfeited to the King directly.   The effect of corruption of blood was not only that no one could inherit from the person attainted, but also that he could not himself inherit

---

[1] *Journals of the House of Lords*, Feb. 1, 1640–1641 (vol. iv. pp. 149–150).

[2] Collins's *Proceedings on Claims*, p. 256.   Paper said to have been obtained from the son of Chief Justice Brampston, one of the Judges whose opinion was given.

from an ancestor. His incapacity thus affected all his CH. VIII.
descendants, and they were debarred from deriving a title
through him from an ancestor more remote.

The law of forfeiture and attainder was to some extent Effect
mitigated by the creation of estates tail[1], because when of the
creation of
a tenant in tail was attainted, the forfeiture extended only estates tail,
to the term of his life. As he did not possess the fee simple until the
reign of
he could not forfeit it, and thus the lands of many persons Henry
VIII.
attainted of high treason remained in the same family,
even when there was no reversal of attainder. In the reign
of Henry VIII, however, an Act was passed which had the
effect of bringing estates tail within the law of forfeiture for
high treason[2].

According to the older doctrine that a Baron was one Forfeiture
of baronies
who held in chief, or by barony, no one could have continued for high
to be a Baron after his lands were forfeited. It has, indeed, treason.
sometimes been maintained that all the dignities of the
peerage, including baronies, are within the category of
'offices of trust and confidence[3].' In that case they could
not of course be held after conviction of high treason. It
has been shown, however, in this history, that although
Earls commonly held baronies, the origin of the dignity of
a Baron was entirely different from that of an Earl, and
had not any relation to any administrative office. When
the Baron acquired a prescriptive right to be summoned to
Parliament, and with it a personal dignity, he was not
bound to perform any duties which had not been performed
in earlier times. He was. however, subject to the same law
of forfeiture in respect of his lands, and according to the
ancient precedents the dignity was lost at the same time.

When an earldom was an office under the Crown, it was Forfeiture
of earldoms
of course forfeited for treason to the Sovereign ; and the and other
precedent sufficed to ensure its forfeiture in later-.times, dignities
for high
when it was an office no longer[4]. The higher ranks in the treason.

[1] Stat. *De Donis Conditionalibus* (Westm. 2.), 13 Ed. I, cap. 1 ; *Co.
Litt.*, 392 b ; *Bl. Com.*, ii. 116.
[2] Stat. 26 Hen. VIII, cap. 13. sec. 5 ; and see Stat. 5 & 6 Ed. VI,
cap. 11. sec. 9.
[3] *Fourth Rep. Dig. Peer*, vol. ii. p. 312.   [4] 7 Rep. 33.

CH. VIII. peerage naturally followed the same rule ; and thus, as a broad general principle, all dignities were forfeited upon attainder of high treason.

Question as to the effect of entails upon attainder of high treason between 1285 and 1534.

The doctrine of corruption of blood was also applicable, and the temporal lord lost his dignities not only for himself but also for his heirs for ever, or until the attainder was reversed by Act of Parliament. The only possible exception was in the case of a dignity held in tail, with regard to which there has been some difference of opinion. A dignity could be entailed [1], but only by the Crown. The earlier Barons and their descendants were, after a time, mostly recognized as Barons only in virtue of the writ of summons, which, when held to give an hereditary right, was held to give it to the heirs general of the body. This, however, was no entail, as there was no specific gift or grant to the person summoned and the heirs of his body, which was the essential condition of an estate tail. There had been but few patents of baronies before the statute of Henry VIII, which placed estates tail in the same position as estates of fee simple with regard to forfeiture. So also, though other dignities of the peerage had been created with limitations by charter, or letters patent, they were comparatively few in number, and circumstances rarely occurred in which the dignity could be claimed by virtue of an entail, after the attainder of the last possessor, and in the absence of any reversal of attainder. The narrowness of the field of search (extending only from the year 1285, when the law of entails [2] begins, to the year 1534, when an entail ceased to afford any protection in attainders of high treason) renders the task of finding illustrative instances extremely difficult [3].

[1] Co. Litt., 20 a.

[2] Stat. Westm. 2 (13 Ed. I), cap. 1 (De Donis Conditionalibus).

[3] Neville's case (7 Rep. 33) is sometimes cited in relation to this subject. It does not, however, really bear upon the question whether an entail protected a dignity between 1285 and 1534. A claim to the Earldom of Westmoreland was set up in 1604 by Edward Neville. The previous Earl, Charles Neville, had been attainted of high treason in 1570. Edward relied upon the grant in tail male to Ralph Neville in 1397, whose heir according to the entail he represented himself to

The Peer who was attainted of felony also suffered CH. VIII.
corruption of blood. His lands, if not entailed, escheated An entail
to the superior lord, who was commonly the King; he lost saves the
his dignity, and his issue could not inherit. The Act of the heir to
Henry VIII, by which all estates of inheritance (including a dignity
estates tail) were rendered subject to forfeiture for high attainder
treason, did not render them subject to forfeiture or escheat of felony.
for felony; and consequently it seems that a dignity entailed
would descend to the heirs of the body of the person
attainted, if a dignity were subject to the same law of
entail as lands.

The best illustration in support of this doctrine is, per- Illustration
haps, the case of John, Baron Stourton, whose ancestor from the
barony of
John had been created a Baron in tail male by Henry VI[1]. Stourton.
His father, Charles, Baron Stourton, had been attainted of
felony in the reign of Philip and Mary. He, however, was
summoned to Parliament, and took his seat on February 11,
1575-6[2]. On the following March 6 a Bill was introduced
for the restitution in blood of him and of his brethren
and sisters, and was read a third time on the following day[3].
That Bill, however, never became an Act[4], and he, nevertheless, continued to sit in the House of Lords. He must,
therefore, have enjoyed the dignity by inheritance, notwithstanding any corruption of his father's blood, or he
must have enjoyed it as a new creation in virtue of the
writ of summons. In the latter case he could have been
succeeded only by the heirs of his body. He died, however, without issue, and his brother Edward was summoned
in his stead. In this case, therefore, as in some others,

be. He was unsuccessful; but it is not certain that, had the case
occurred eighty years earlier, he might not have succeeded.

[1] *Rot. Lit. Pat.*, 26 Hen. VI, part ii. m. 26.

[2] *Journals of the House of Lords* (vol. i. p. 731).

[3] *Ib.*, March 6 and 7, 1575-6 (vol. i. pp. 742 and 743).

[4] If such an Act had passed, it would be upon the Parliament Roll
of 18 Elizabeth. There is no such Act upon that Roll, nor does it
appear that any such Act was passed during the reign. It is said in
D'Ewes's *Journals of the Commons* (pp. 264-265) that the Lords would
not accept a *proviso* inserted in the Bill by the Commons.

CH. VIII.   it seems that the grant of a dignity to a man and the heirs
male of his body had the effect of saving it for the heir when
the holder was attainted of felony.

Prospective   In the reign of Queen Anne (shortly after the Union with
legislation   Scotland) an Act was passed with the object of abolishing,
in 1708, to
save the   at a future time, the effects of corruption of blood, upon
rights of   attainder for high treason.   It was enacted that, after the
heirs of
persons   death of the Pretender James, and three years after the
attainted   accession of 'the Queen's successor to the throne, no
of high
treason.   attainder for treason should cause any heir to be dis-
inherited, or prejudice the right of any person but the
actual offender[1].   When, however, in the year 1744 a rising
was expected under Charles Edward, son of the elder
Pretender James, it was enacted that the operation of the
Act of Queen Anne should be postponed until the decease
not only of James but of all his sons[2].

Restriction   Thus the old law, as it was after the Act of the reign of
of forfei-   Henry VIII, by which estates tail were brought within the
ture in
1814, and   doctrine of forfeiture for high treason, remained practically
practical   unchanged in England, though it did not extend to Scot-
abolition,
in 1870, of   land[3].   In the year 1814, however, forfeitures for felonies
attainder   in general, though not for high treason, petty treason, or
and corrup-
tion of   murder, were restricted to the life-time of the person
blood.   attainted[4].   Forfeiture, except when consequent upon outlawry, was altogether abolished in the year 1870, when it was
enacted that no judgement of or for any treason or felony
should 'cause any attainder or corruption of blood, or any
forfeiture or escheat[5].'

---

[1] Stat. 7 Anne, cap. 21. sec. 10.
[2] Stat. 17 Geo. II, cap. 39. sec. 3.
[3] The law had been otherwise in Scotland before the Union, and the
rights of heirs in tail were guarded shortly afterwards by the 7 Anne,
cap. 21. sec. 4.
[4] Stat. 54 Geo. III, cap. 145.
[5] Stat. 33 & 34 Vict. cap. 23. sec. 1.

CHAPTER IX.

THE POSITION OF THE SPIRITUAL LORDS.

IT has already been shown that in parts of the Roman empire which the barbarians overran, the Bishops commonly became advisers of the Crown as soon as the conquerors accepted Christianity. Their position was anomalous, because, although in feudal times they had their investiture of their temporalities from the King, they obtained their offices by election, and not, like Earls or Counts, on the nomination of the Crown. In the reign of Henry I, after a struggle with Archbishop Anselm, a com- promise was effected, in accordance with which the previous mode of investiture was abandoned, and the King received the homage of the Bishops. At the same time the election of Bishops, which had previously been in the *Curia Regis* by clergy and laity, was placed in the hands of the clergy alone. This arrangement was confirmed by successive charters, and notably by one of King John, in which he undertook not to withhold his licence for the election (*congé d'élire*), or refuse approval afterwards, without just cause[1].

After election, if followed by the King's assent, the Bishop elect was confirmed by the Metropolitan, and then had restitution of the spiritualities, or ecclesiastical juris- diction, which had rested, during the vacancy of the see, with the Guardian of the Spiritualities. This, however, did not place him in possession of the temporalities of the see.

[1] The charter is printed in the *Statutes of the Realm*, vol. i. p. 5. There was a confirmation by the 25 Ed. III, St. 6 (*Provisors*). sec. 3.

CHAP. IX. He was not yet a Baron, for he had not yet obtained those lands which were held in barony in right of the bishopric. He could have livery of the temporalities only on making an oath of fealty to the King. This was commonly done before his consecration, after which he had all the liabilities and privileges of Bishop and Baron, including that of the writ of summons to Parliament.

Similar position of Abbots. The proceedings by which an Abbot was made were similar in cases in which the Abbey was of royal foundation; and this would probably be assumed when successive Abbots of the same House were summoned to Parliament for a long period of time. The Crown sometimes, indeed, asserted a royal foundation, for purposes of its own, when the Abbots warmly disputed the fact [1]. Licence to elect, election by the Convent or members of the religious House, the royal approval, and restitution of the temporalities, which had been taken into the King's hand when the vacancy occurred, were all necessary before the new Abbot could be in full possession of his abbacy or of the lands held in its right.

The power of the Crown in relation to Prelates. There is no need to trace in detail the attempts which were made by Popes to obtain the power of appointing English Bishops. They belong to the domain rather of the history of the Church than to that of constitutional history. They were never more than partially successful, and, while they continued, they were merely an indication of the power of the Church, which was exerting its influence over England in various other ways. Had they been carried so far as seriously to threaten alien interference in the King's Council and Parliament, the Crown had a remedy. It could always withhold approval of the election, and retain the temporalities of the vacant see or abbey in its hands. Such an extreme measure would, no doubt, have added one to the many quarrels which English kings had with the Church. The mere possibility of it, however, must to some extent have acted as a check upon papal

---

[1] E.g. *Year Books*, Trin., 14 Ed. III, no. 46.

pretensions, and generally have secured the appointment of CHAP. IX.
a prelate who was not at the moment altogether obnoxious
to the King. Henry VIII succeeded very adroitly in
obtaining for the Crown the power of nominating the
Bishops. In his reign it was enacted that when any
see became vacant the King might send to the Prior and
Convent or the Dean and Chapter (as the case might
be), which had the power of election, his *congé d'élire*,
together with a Letter Missive containing the name of the
person to be elected. Should they defer the election
beyond twelve days, the King had power to nominate and
present by Letters Patent under the Great Seal[1].

Thus, until the power of the Church was broken about
the time of the Reformation, all the Lords Spiritual sat in
the House of Lords, only after election. Whatever in-
fluences might have been brought to bear before they were
elected, they might be regarded as representatives of those
who elected them. In their case the King was not the
fountain of honour; and although they could not obtain
possession of the baronies belonging to their sees without
his consent, it was not he whom they had to thank for
their elevation.

Bishops and Abbots, it is well known, were summoned,
before the Conquest, to the Witenagemot, and it has sometimes been inferred that they were called to later English
Parliaments by reason of their spiritual office, and not solely
in virtue of the baronies which they held by military service
after the Conquest. It has even been denied that the
Conqueror applied military tenure to Church lands. There
is, however, no doubt that Bishops and Abbots did, after
the Conquest, hold baronies in chief of the Crown by military service; and although strictly contemporary evidence
may be wanting as to the exact date at which they began
to occupy this position, there does not appear to be any
strong reason against the date assigned by Matthew Paris.
According to him, the Conqueror placed under military

[1] Stat. 25 Hen. VIII, cap. 20. sec. 4.

Chap. IX. service all bishoprics and abbeys holding baronies in the year 1070, setting down *at his pleasure* the number of knights to be supplied by each[1]. The statement accords extremely well with the fact that no uniformity can be discovered with regard to the number of knight's fees in a barony, whether lay or ecclesiastical. It is confirmed by testimony which is clearly independent—by the Chronicle of Abingdon[2] and by the History of Ely[3]. It is in harmony with the position of the Bishops in the King's Court according to the Constitutions of Clarendon. It agrees with the remarks of Bracton made in the reign of Henry III, that the King had power to direct process against Bishops by reason of their baronies[4]. It is also quite consistent, as will hereafter be shown, with the subsequent claims of Bishops to be considered Peers of the Realm on the ground of holding by barony.

The Bishops had no desire to be summoned to the early Parliaments.

To speak of a seat in Parliament as a privilege enjoyed by layman or ecclesiastic, in the early days of Parliaments, is to confuse modern with mediaeval ideas. No baron, lay or clerical, wished to be summoned, except to protect himself against inordinate taxation. No Bishop, as Bishop, wished to be summoned except in the interests of his order.

The *Praemunientes* clause in the writs of summons to them.

When the Archbishops and Bishops were summoned to a Parliament including Lords Spiritual and Temporal and Commons, it was usual, from the time of Edward I, to insert a clause in the summons directed to each of them which is commonly called the *Praemunientes* clause. The Archbishop of Canterbury, for instance, was commanded to warn the Prior and Chapter of his Church and all the Clergy of his diocese to attend with himself—the Prior and Archdeacons in person, the Chapter by one Procurator, and the Clergy by two. In other sees the warning was to be

---

[1] Matt. Par., *Historia Anglorum* (Rolls Series), vol. i. p. 13.
[2] *Chronicle of Abingdon* (Rolls Series), vol. ii. p. 3 et seq.
[3] *Historia Eliensis* (Anglia Christiana Society), p. 276. The coinciding evidence of the three sources of information has been pointed out by Mr. J. H. Round in his essays on the introduction of knight service into England in the *English Historical Review*.
[4] Bract. 427, 442 b.

given to the Deans also to be present in person. It will be CHAP. IX.
observed that this summons, affecting the whole body of
the Clergy, resembles the summons to Convocation of
a later period. The summons, however, was to Parliament, as it is distinctly expressed that the clerical persons
and representatives who were to accompany the Bishops
were to treat, ordain, and act with the King and with the
rest of the Prelates, the *Proceres*, and the other inhabitants
of the Realm, and generally to give their consent.

The object, there can be no doubt, was to have the assent The
of the Clergy to the taxes which were to be imposed upon to the
them. It was also with the same object, there can be as Guardian
of the
little doubt, that, during the vacancy of sees, writs were sent Spiritual-
to the Guardians of the Spiritualities of the dioceses com- ities during
the vacancy
manding them to come, or send a procurator or proxy, and of a
warn the other ecclesiastics to be in attendance as usual. bishopric.
The fact that the Guardians of Spiritualities received
a summons has sometimes been used as an argument to
show that, even when the Bishops held baronies, their
summons was in virtue of their ecclesiastical status, and
that they came to Parliament as *Sapientes* or *Witan*, quite
independently of their lay possessions. The summons to
a Guardian of the Spiritualities during the vacancy of a see,
however, cannot have any relation to the supposed wisdom
of a Bishop when the see is filled. The Guardian of the
Spiritualities had spiritual jurisdiction in his diocese, and
he alone could direct the necessary warning to the rest of
the Clergy. The temporalities being in the King's hand,
the Guardian of the Temporalities had to account at the
Exchequer for the profits derived from them, until they were
sued out of the King's hand, but he had no power whatever
to summon the Clergy or to bind the incoming Bishop.

The most conclusive proof, however, that the summons It issued
to the Guardian of the Spiritualities was solely for the because he
purpose of ensuring the consent of the Clergy to taxes or alone had
power to
other matters [1] to which their sanction was desired, appears call the

---

[1] It appears from *Rot. Lit. Claus.*, 21 Ed. III, part ii. m. 21 d

CHAP. IX. in the fact that no such summons was sent without the
rest of the *Praemunientes* clause. When the King required the Bishops,
Clergy of as persons of wisdom or discretion, to attend a Council,
the diocese. he summoned, as might naturally have been expected, the
Bishops themselves, but not any Guardians of the Spiritualities of vacant Bishoprics in that capacity. When
there is a *Praemunientes* clause the Guardians of the
Spiritualities receive a summons; when there is no such
clause they do not. So also when the see was not vacant,
but the Bishop was abroad (*in remotis agens*), there was an
alternative summons to him or his Vicar-General[1], with the
Praemunientes clause, not on account of the wisdom of the
Vicar-General, but in order that the rest of the Clergy of
the diocese might be duly warned, and might duly vote the
supplies. It is true that the clause was preserved in the
writ of summons, as a form, long after the persons who
were to be warned had ceased to come to Parliament, and
had attended Convocation instead. This fact, however,
does not in any way disprove the origin of its insertion, or
tend in any way to prove the superior discretion of the
Guardian.

Abbots   With regard to Abbots and Priors, it is quite clear that
and Priors they were rightly summoned to Parliament only because
summoned
only as   they held by barony, and that, if they did not hold by
holding by
barony,   barony, they could claim to be excused as late as the reign
and excused of Edward III. This, indeed, is what might have been
when not
so holding. inferred from the passage of Britton already cited. The
point is, however, made perfectly plain by the case of the
Prior of Spalding. He, like his contemporaries, regarding
attendance in Parliament not as a privilege but as a burden,
represented that the lands of the Priory were held in
frankalmoign of the Countess of Lincoln, and not of the
King by barony or part of a barony. Neither he nor his

(printed, *Rep. Dig. Peer*, vol. iv. p. 573) that on one occasion at least
the clergy were to be summoned in virtue of the *Praemunientes* clause,
when no aids, tallages, or other taxes were to be imposed.
  [1] *Rot. Lit. Claus.*, 1 Ed. III, part ii. m. 16 d (printed, *Rep. Dig.
Peer*, vol. iv. p. 376).

predecessors had been summoned to Parliaments or Councils
before the second year of Edward II. They had not been
summoned uniformly, but only at intervals, and not of right,
but only when they were willing (*voluntarie*). The Prior,
complaining of the expense and trouble of coming to Parliaments or Councils, prayed a remedy. The facts, as
alleged by the Prior, were established by inspection of the
rolls of Chancery, and by certificate of the Treasurer and
Barons of the Exchequer. The latter showed in particular
that the 'Prior did not hold of the King by barony or
by part of a barony, or in any other manner in virtue of
which he ought to be summoned to such Parliaments or
·Councils.' The King therefore, after advice with his
Council, and full deliberation, and in consideration of an
immediate aid for the war in France, granted, for himself
and his heirs, that the Prior and his successors should not
be summoned to the King's Parliaments and Councils, 'but
should be discharged and quit for ever from coming
thereto[1].'

When a special meaning became attached to the ex- They begin
pression 'Peer of the Realm,' the Bishops and the most to claim the position
powerful of the Abbots began to take precautions that of Peers of
there should be no derogation from their dignity as Peers. the Realm as holding
Under the Constitutions of Clarendon they had been by barony.
required, as tenants *in capite*, or holding by barony, to do
suit to the King, much against their will, and to attend
with the rest of the Barons in the King's Court. By
degrees they came to regard these irksome duties as badges
of temporal superiority, which might be used with effect on
certain occasions. If a temporal lord holding by barony
was a Peer of the Realm, they may have argued, so also
must be a spiritual lord holding in like manner by barony.

The earliest known use of the expression 'Peer of the The first
Realm,' or *Pier de la Terre*, occurs in a document of the use of the expression
year 1322 (15 Edward II): 'For the honour of God and of 'Peer of
Holy Church, and of our Lord the King, and for his profit the Realm' in 1322.

[1] *Rot. Lit. Claus.*, 15 Ed. III, part ii. m. 14 (printed, *Rep. Dig. Peer*,
vol. iv. pp. 535–536).

CHAP. IX. and that of his realm, and for the maintenance of peace and tranquillity among his people, and for maintenance of the estate of the Crown, show unto the King, the Prelates, Earls, and Barons, and the other Peers of the Land, and the Commons of the Realm,' certain charges against Hugh de Despenser the father, and Hugh de Despenser the son. One of the accusations was that the elder Despenser, by procurement of the younger, had caused the King to revoke a grant which had been confirmed in his Parliament at Lincoln 'at the request and with the assent of the Peers of the Land.' Another was that they had caused lands to be forfeited, and had not instead suffered the King 'to take reasonable fines from the Peers of the Land and others within his fee, as had been accustomed.' The charges were found to be true upon 'examination by the Earls, Barons, and other Peers of the Land,' and judgement was given by 'us, Peers of the Land, Earls, and Barons, in the presence of our Lord the King.' The Despensers were to be banished out of the realm of England, and never to return 'except with the assent of our Lord the King, and with the assent of the Prelates, Earls, and Barons, and that in Parliament duly summoned[1].'

The Prelates, though spiritual lords, were Peers only by virtue of their temporal possessions.   It will be observed that among these five passages in which the word 'Peers' occurs there is not more than one in which it is quite clearly applied to the spiritual lords, and there are two in which the spiritual lords cannot be included in the term. They cannot be among the 'Earls, Barons, and other Peers of the Land,' as spiritual lords are always mentioned before temporal lords. Still less can they be among 'us, Peers of the Land, Earls and Barons.' They do seem to be included as Peers in the first passage, 'Prelates, Earls and Barons, and the other Peers of the Land,' though even here the grammatical construction might leave a doubt. The true explanation seems to be that the Prelates, though recognized as spiritual

---

[1] Printed in the *Statutes of the Realm*, vol. i. pp. 181–184, from *Rot. Lit. Claus.*, 14 Ed. II, m. 14, *Cedula*.

lords, were not spiritual peers, and, so far as they were peers at all, were entitled to the name only in virtue of their temporal possessions, or baronies. The Bishops and Abbots are classed together under the one head of Prelates, and their title to the peerage must have been the same.

For most purposes, nevertheless, both Bishops and Abbots summoned to Parliament were, a few years later, regarded as Peers. In the year 1329 (3 Edward III) the Bishop of Winchester was described in a law report[1] as one of the Peers and Judges of Parliament. In like manner the right both of Bishops and of Abbots to some of the privileges enjoyed by Peers in civil actions was undisputed. The privilege of having knights on the jury when a Peer was a party was claimed by a Bishop in the thirteenth year of the reign of Edward III. It was allowed by the Court, and there was not even so much as a suggestion that, for this particular purpose, the Bishop was not to be regarded as a Peer[2]. In the same year another privilege relating to a 'day of grace' was claimed by the Abbot of Ramsey on the ground that he held by barony and was a Peer of the Realm. He failed, for other reasons, to obtain that which was prayed on his behalf, but it was not denied either that he was a Peer, or that his peerage was consequent on his holding by barony[3]. The case of Stratford, Archbishop of Canterbury, in 1341, has some bearing on the claim of the Prelates to be regarded in all respects as Peers of the Realm, and will be considered in relation to the question of trial by Peers.

It was stated by counsel, and to all appearance admitted, in the reign of Edward III that when any question arose as to a name of dignity, there was an important distinction between that of Abbot or Prior and that of Earl. The question whether a man was an Earl could be determined only by record in the Chancery; the question whether he was Abbot or Prior lay in the cognizance 'of the

They enjoyed certain privileges of Peers, as holding by barony.

---

[1] *Year Book*, Easter, 3 Ed. III, no. 32, ff⁰. 18–19.
[2] *Ib.*, Trinity, 13 Ed. III, no. 2. p. 291.
[3] *Ib.*, Easter, 13 Ed. III, no. 24. p. 223.

CHAP. IX. country,' or (in other words) could be tried by a jury [1]. This shows, as clearly as can possibly be shown, that Abbots were not summoned to Parliament in virtue of any ecclesiastical dignity, with which the Chancery (the office whence the summons was directed) was not concerned, but solely in virtue of the baronies which the Abbots held.

They define their own claim to the peerage, as holding by barony in the reign of Richard II. In the reign of Richard II the Prelates defined their claim to be of the peerage in very clear terms. The occasion was the 'appeal' brought in Parliament against Alexander Neville, Archbishop of York; Robert de Vere, Duke of Ireland; Michael de la Pole, Earl of Suffolk; Robert Tresilian, Chief Justice of England, and others. The Archbishop of Canterbury then made solemn declaration that 'of right, and by custom of the realm of England, it belongeth to the Archbishop of Canterbury for the time being, as well as others his Suffragans, Brethren, and Fellow Bishops, Abbots and Priors and other Prelates whatsoever, *holding of the Lord the King by barony*, to be present in person, in all the King's Parliaments whatsoever, as Peers of the Realm aforesaid, and there, with the other Peers of the Realm, and with other persons having the right to be there present, to advise, treat, ordain, establish, and determine as to the affairs of the realm, and other matters there wont to be treated, and to do all else which there presses to be done.' With regard to all and each of these matters, he protested that he and they intended to be present, and take part in that Parliament, 'save our estate and order and that of each of the Prelates in all things. But because in the present Parliament there is question of certain matters, in which it is not lawful for us or any one of the Prelates, according to the Institutes of the Holy Canons, in any manner, to take part personally,' we intend to retire, '*saving always the right of our peerage* [2].' The Bishop of Durham, on his own behalf, and the Bishop of Carlisle, also on his own behalf, made like declaration. The Archbishop of

---

[1] 22 *Li. Ass.* 24.
[2] *Rot. Parl.*, 11 Ric. II, no. 6 (printed, vol. iii. pp. 236–7).

York was of course unable to say anything in relation to himself or the Prelates of his Province as he was one of the persons accused, and did not appear.

We thus know precisely what position the Prelates took up in the reign of Richard II, and that they did not advance any claim to the peerage, except as holding of the King by barony. They did not assert that they were Peers in virtue of any spiritual office, but, on the contrary, expressly saved the rights of their order, whatever those rights may have been, and so drew a distinction between their position as Prelates and their position as the King's tenants by barony, and Peers. They were, no doubt, covertly asserting their ancient pretensions to be as nearly as possible free from all lay jurisdiction when put upon their trial. The assertion made by themselves that they were Peers of the Realm was neither denied nor admitted on this occasion, as they withdrew immediately after making their declaration or protest.

The doctrine as to blood and its capacities is of great importance in relation to the position of Lords Spiritual as compared with Lords Temporal. It is, as we have seen, not to be disputed that Spiritual Lords were in the reigns of Edward III, and Richard II, described as Peers of the Realm. It is, however, certain that neither during those reigns nor at any other time were they in the same position as the Temporal Lords with regard either to their peerages, or to the lands in virtue of which some or all of them were recognized as Peers. *They were never in the same position as Temporal Lords even with regard to their lands.*

A Spiritual Lord held lands by barony, but yet his estate in his lands was never the same as that of a Temporal Peer. It differed in relation to the most important legal doctrine of blood. No Spiritual Lord could, as such, transmit his lands or his dignity to an heir. After his death his lands and his dignity went to his successor. If he committed treason or felony and was attainted, the corruption of his blood had no effect on the succession of his lands or of his dignity. Whether Bishop or Abbot, a Spiritual Peer was always a corporation, either a corporation sole or the head *No corruption of blood affected the succession to their lands or dignities.*

M

CHAP. IX. of a corporation aggregate; and the blood of a corporation could not be corrupted, or rather a corporation had no blood to corrupt. A corporation aggregate could not commit either treason or felony, and could not therefore be subject to the penalties following upon the commission. If a person who, in his official capacity, was a corporation sole, committed treason or felony, he committed it as an individual and not as a corporation, and it was only as an individual that he could suffer the penalty. A parson might be attainted for treason, and executed, but the glebe and the tithes were not forfeited to the Crown. A Bishop or an Abbot might also be attainted, but the temporalities of the bishopric or abbey, though seized into the King's hand during vacancy, still remained the right of the abbey or bishopric, and the succeeding Abbot or Bishop was summoned to Parliament.

A Bishop did not even necessarily hold his particular dignity of Bishop or his lands for life.

Regarded from one point of view a Bishop did not even hold either his particular dignity of Bishop or the lands attached to his bishopric for life. He was subject to deprivation, in which case his lands and his dignity went to his successor. He might be translated to another see, in which case the lands and the dignity of his first see went to his successor during his own life, and he acquired new lands and a new dignity. His dignity, however, was purely ecclesiastical; his summons to Parliament, after the Conquest, was solely in consideration of the lands which he held in barony. He was a Lord of Parliament, and was styled a Spiritual Lord. He was a Peer, but not a Spiritual Peer, as he derived his only claim to that title of honour from his lay fees. He was not summoned and could not sit in Parliament until he had obtained possession of the temporalities of his bishopric.

The peculiar tenure of the Spiritual Lords not necessarily a disqualification for

There is nevertheless good reason to believe that the nature of their tenure would not have disqualified Bishops and Abbots from being Peers in every sense of the word, had they been prepared to act as other Peers on all occasions. The Prior of the Knights of St. John of Jerusalem in England, held his lands in the same manner as any Abbot, and he was not only a Peer in all other senses, but sat in the Court of the Lord High Steward as Baron and Peer, and gave his verdict of Guilty or Not Guilty when a Peer of the Realm was there brought to trial[1]. The Bishops and Abbots might have been no less fully recognized as Peers of the Realm had the canons of the Church not forbidden them to be present where judgements of life or member were concerned, and had they not attempted to render themselves exempt from all secular jurisdiction. They missed their opportunity by grasping at too much.

CHAP. IX.

complete peerage: the Prior of St. John of Jerusalem.

One of the most remarkable facts in the history of the Bishops and Abbots, considered as Spiritual Lords, is that they ceased to be regarded as Peers of the Realm, while the Priors of the Knights of St. John of Jerusalem, who were not fettered, like them, by the canons of the Church, were not only Barons but Peers to the last. The practice of trying Peers in the Court of the Lord High Steward, in which the Lords Spiritual could not say Guilty or Not Guilty, or pass sentence, and to which, as a necessary consequence, they were not summoned, was probably one of the factors in the exclusion of the Lords Spiritual from the rank of Peers. They still held by barony, but as the idea of tenure by barony among laymen gradually died out, the tenure ceased to be of itself a sufficient title to peerage. In the very year in which John Kendall, Prior of the Knights of St. John of Jerusalem, sat among the Barons who tried the Earl of Warwick, the Abbot of St. Albans was, in a law report, styled not a Peer of the Realm but only a Lord of Parliament[2].

The Lords Spiritual let fall their claim to peerage: while the Prior of St. John was Baron and Peer in the reign of Henry VII, an Abbot was styled only a Lord of Parliament.

Early in the reign of Henry VIII the position of the Spiritual Lords received a very curious illustration in a grant to the Abbot of Tavistock. His predecessors had been frequently summoned to Parliament at various times

Grant to the Abbot of Tavistock to be a Lord of Parliament

[1] *Baga de Secretis*, Pouch II (15 Henry VII), Pouch IV, Bundle 5 (13 Henry VIII).
[2] *Year Book*, Trin., 15 Hen. VII, fo. 9. no. 12.

M 2

CHAP. IX.   down to the twenty-third year of Edward III [1], but so far
in the   as is known, not afterwards. In the recital of the grant
reign of   it appears that Henry wished 'the Abbey or Monastery
Henry
VIII.   to enjoy the honour, privilege, and liberties of the Spiritual
Lords of Parliament.' He therefore granted to Richard
Banham, then Abbot of Tavistock, that he and each
succeeding Abbot of Tavistock should be 'one of the
spiritual and religious Lords of Parliament,' and enjoy all
the honour, privileges, and franchises attaching to the rank.
It was, at the same time provided that should any Abbot
of Tavistock be absent from Parliament, when summoned,
he should pay for every absence during any whole Parliament the sum of five marks [2]. This provision was set forth
in the light of a favour allowed by reason of the distance
which the Abbot might have to travel.

The   The doctrine that a Spiritual Lord was a Peer of the
doctrine   Realm was now evidently extinct. He was a Lord of
that a
Spiritual Parliament, and nothing more. The Abbot of Tavistock
Lord was   was in the same condition as many other Abbots whose
a Peer of
the Realm predecessors had been sometimes, but not always, sum-
was now   moned to Parliament, whose predecessors had had the
extinct.   burden of a summons, and had not recognized the dignity
conferred by it. It can, perhaps, hardly be said that Henry
created the Abbot of Tavistock a Lord of Parliament, as
his remote predecessors had sat among the Prelates. But
Henry did, at the least, declare that he and his successors
should be considered Lords of Parliament, whether they
came to Parliament or not. Had the same policy been
pursued in relation to other Abbots, the power of the
Church would have been greatly increased in the House of
Lords, notwithstanding the denial of the coveted title of
Peer of the Realm. The dissolution of the greater monasteries, however, a few years later had a directly opposite
effect.

[1] *Rot. Lit. Claus.*, 23 Ed. III, part i. m. 19. d (printed, *Rep. Dig.
Peer*, vol. iv. p. 584).
[2] *Originalia Roll* (Lord Treasurer's Remembrancer of the Exchequer), 5 Hen. VIII, Ro. 12.

The Spiritual Lords themselves appear to have now accepted their position as merely Lords of Parliament, and not Peers of the Realm. Archbishop Cranmer made no claim of peerage when brought to trial in the reign of Queen Mary. Staunford, who was a Justice of the Court of Common Pleas in the time of Philip and Mary, and whose recollection must have extended many years backwards, compiled an excellent treatise on Pleas of the Crown. Bishops and Abbots, he there wrote, 'enjoy the name of Lord of Parliament . . . . not in respect of their nobility, but in respect of their possessions—of the ancient baronies annexed to their dignities [1].' Sir Edward Coke also wrote to the same effect [2]. In later times this appears to have been held as settled law. The point is of importance, however, chiefly in relation to the mediaeval doctrine of Blood, and to the right of Trial by Peers. Further reference is made to it in the chapter on the latter subject.

CHAP. IX. The Prelates continued to be Lords of Parliament in respect of their ancient baronies.

Though not in all respects on the same footing with the Temporal Lords, the Spiritual Lords had an equal amount of power until the greater monasteries were dissolved by Henry VIII. Upon inspection of the earlier writs of summons it will be seen that the number of Bishops, Abbots, and Priors summoned to Parliament was sometimes in excess of the number of the lay Peers, and that sometimes the conditions were reversed; but after the reign of Henry III there was never a very large majority on either side except, perhaps, when the laymen were absent on military service. New lay Peers were created, but on the other hand lay peerages became extinct, while there was always a successor to the ecclesiastical baronies which were held in mortmain. Just before the dissolution of the monasteries there appear to have been twenty-six Abbots and two Priors who were summoned to Parliament. After the dissolution six new bishoprics were created, and of those six one (that of Westminster) ceased to exist on the translation of the first Bishop to another see in the reign of

Dissolution of Monasteries: loss of power by the Spiritual Lords.

---

[1] Staunford, *Les Plees del Coron*, lib. iii. p. 153.   [2] 3 Inst. 30.

CHAP. IX. Edward VI. The strength of the Spiritual Lords was thus diminished by twenty-three votes.

They continued to grow relatively weaker in the House of Lords.   The Church never regained any of its lost power in the House of Lords, but on the contrary became continually weaker as new lay peerages were created in greater numbers. In the time of Sir Edward Coke the House consisted of twenty-four Spiritual Lords (the Archbishops and Bishops), sitting by succession in respect of the baronies which were ' parcel of their bishoprics,' and one hundred and six Lords Temporal sitting by reason of the dignities which they held by descent or creation[1]. In the reign of Henry VIII the number of the Temporal Lords had been computed to be about fifty-five, and it had thus nearly doubled in about three-quarters of a century. The subsequent changes of proportion are shown more in detail in the chapter on the Changes in the Component Parts of the House of Lords. It may, however, be mentioned here that another blow was given to the status of the Spiritual Lords when it became law that not even the whole of the Bishops should be entitled to a seat in the House.

Some Bishops are now no longer even Lords of Parliament.   In the year 1847 it was enacted[2] that when any vacancy occurred in any see except those of Canterbury, York, London, Durham, or Winchester, the Bishop elected to the vacant see should not immediately be entitled to a writ of summons to the House of Lords, unless translated from the see of a Bishop actually sitting as a Lord of Parliament. The Bishopric of Manchester had then been newly created, and it was specially provided that the number of Lords Spiritual sitting and voting as Lords of Parliament should not be increased by the creation. There would thus be always one English or Welsh Bishop without a seat in the House of Lords. A Bishopric of St. Albans was created in the year 1875, and it was again provided that the number of Lords Spiritual sitting and voting as Lords of Parliament should not be increased, and that when a vacancy occurred in any see except the five previously excepted,

---

[1] 4 Inst. 1.   [2] Stat. 10 & 11 Vict., cap. 108. sec. 2.

a writ of summons should issue to the 'longest appointed CHAP. IX.
Bishop' who had not previously been entitled to it [1]. The
same words were used when the new Bishopric of Truro
was created in the following year [2]. In the year 1878 no
less than four new Bishoprics were created (Liverpool,
Newcastle, Southwell, and Wakefield), and with similar
provisions regarding the seat in the House of Lords [3].
There are thus always seven Bishops without a seat, and
waiting their turn for a writ of summons according to
seniority.

    In relation to the indisputable fact that Bishops once *The
ancient
baronies*
claimed to be Peers of the Realm in virtue of the baronies
which they held, the comparatively recent transfer of the *in virtue
of which*
lands of the sees to Ecclesiastical Commissioners is of some *Bishops*
interest. The Ecclesiastical Commissioners were first in-*claimed to
be Peers*
corporated in the year 1835 [4]. Powers were given to them *now vested
in the Ec-
clesiastical
Com-
missioners.*
to prepare schemes in accordance with the recommendations
contained in the reports of Commissioners 'to consider the
state of the several dioceses in England and Wales with
reference to the amount of their revenues' and other
matters [5]. It had been recommended that there should be
certain rearrangements of the various dioceses, and that, in
order to provide for the augmentation of the incomes of the
smaller bishoprics, such fixed annual sums should be paid
to the Ecclesiastical Commissioners, out of the larger sees,
as should leave an average annual income to the Archbishop of Canterbury of fifteen thousand pounds, to the
Archbishop of York and the Bishop of London of ten
thousand, to the Bishop of Durham of eight thousand, to
the Bishop of Winchester of seven thousand, to the Bishop
of Ely of five thousand five hundred, to the Bishop of
St. Asaph and Bangor of five thousand two hundred, and
to the Bishop of Worcester and the Bishop of Bath and
Wells of five thousand each. Out of the fund thus accruing

---

[1] The Bishopric of St. Albans Act, 1875, sec. 7.
[2] The Bishopric of Truro Act, 1876, sec. 5.
[3] 41 & 42 Vict., cap. 68. sec. 5.
[4] Stat. 6 & 7 Will. IV, cap. 77. sec. 1.   [5] *Ib.*, sec. 10.

CHAP. IX. fixed annual payments were to be made by the Ecclesiastical Commissioners so that the average annual incomes of the other Bishops should not be less than four nor more than five thousand pounds. The scale of payment was to be subject to revision at the end of every seven years[1].

Various modifications were effected by subsequent Acts, and in the year 1860 it was enacted that upon the first avoidance of the see of any Archbishop or Bishop in England all the lands belonging to it (except lands attached to residences in a scheme sanctioned by Order in Council) should become vested absolutely in the Ecclesiastical Commissioners[2]. It was also provided that after the lands of a see had become vested in the Commissioners an arrangement should be made for assigning to its Archbishop or Bishop such lands as might be convenient, and as would secure, as nearly as possible, a net annual income equal to that named in any Act of Parliament or Order in Council in force. and no more[3]. Archbishops and Bishops were further restrained from granting any of the lands assigned as their endowment except from year to year, or for a term of years in possession not exceeding twenty-one[4]. To this low worldly estate fell the successors of those Archbishops and Bishops who had once proudly boasted that they held by barony and were Peers of the Realm.

[1] Stat. 6 & 7 Will. IV, cap. 77. sec. 1.
[2] Stat. 23 & 24 Vict., cap. 124. sec. 2.
[3] *Ib.*, sec. 3.   [4] *Ib.*, sec. 8.

CHAPTER X.

JUDGEMENT BY PEERS TO THE REIGN OF RICHARD II: END OF
APPEALS IN PARLIAMENT: BEGINNING OF IMPEACHMENTS.

I F a passage in the so-called Laws of Henry I[1] may be CHAP. X.
disregarded, the first mention of the 'Judgement of Judgement
Peers' in England occurs in the Great Charter of King John. of Peers
'No free man is to be taken, or imprisoned, or disseised, or out- John's
lawed, or in any way destroyed, nor will we proceed against Great
him, or direct proceeding against him, except in accordance Charter.
with the judgement of his peers, or in accordance with the
law of the land[2].' It would, perhaps, be impossible to
exaggerate the importance of these provisions for the protection of the subject ; but the words 'judgement of his
peers' must, at the time, have had a more restricted
application than is commonly attributed to them.

It is often asserted. and still more often assumed, that the It had no
judgement of a man's peers, in the case of a person of lower connexion
estate than that of a Peer of the Realm, must have been, in by Jury.
some way, the equivalent of trial by jury. It is absolutely
impossible, for two distinct reasons, that the words can have
had any such sense. In criminal cases, trial by jury had
not even been instituted, and the only modes of trial were by
ordeal, by compurgation, and by battle. From the time when
trial by jury first commenced, either in civil or in criminal
cases, to this present end of the nineteenth century, no jury

---

[1] *Leges Henrici Primi, Regis Angliae,* cap. 31.
[2] King John's *Great Charter,* cap. 39.

CHAP. X. ever did or could give judgement on any matter whatsoever. The one persisting function of every jury (except
the accusing, presenting, indicting, or 'Grand' Jury) is, and
always has been, to find a verdict, and not to give a judgement—to inform the Court of the facts, in order that the
judgement may be pronounced by the Court.

It had
reference
to matters
connected
with
feudal
tenure.
King John bound himself in such a manner as to show
that 'judgement of peers' was one thing, the 'law of the
land' another. The 'judgement of peers' was, as will
presently be shown, a very simple matter and well understood at the time. The 'law of the land' included all legal
proceedings, criminal or civil, other than the judgement of
peers. The judgement of peers had reference chiefly to the
right of land-holders to their lands, or to some matters connected with feudal tenure and its incidents. Thus in another
part of the charter a special remedy is provided for cases
in which any one 'had been disseised' or removed by the
King 'without lawful judgement of his peers, from his lands,
his castles, his franchises, or his rights[1].' So also in the
case of Welshmen disseised or removed without lawful
judgement of their peers, any dispute was to be settled by
lawful judgement of their peers in accordance with the law
(or particular custom) in Wales, England, or the Marches,
as the case might be[2].

Suit of
Court:
the *Pares
Curtis* or
Curiae.
The judgement of peers in the case of persons holding
their lands not directly of the Crown, but of a mesne lord,
was the judgement of the other tenants of that lord, who
owed suit to the same Court, and were in that respect all
peers, or equals. A tenant in chief, holding of the Crown
a wide expanse of land, usually (until restrained by the
Statute of *Quia Emptores*) enfeoffed persons, to hold of
him, as their lord, by certain services. One of these services
was almost invariably Suit of Court, or the obligation to
attend the Lord's Court at stated times, if summoned,—
ordinarily once in three weeks. The Court was described
as the Baron's Court, or in the French of the period as *Court*

---

[1] King John's *Great Charter*, cap. 52.   [2] *Ib.*, cap. 56.

Baron. The Peers of the Court (*Pares Curiae* or *Pares* CHAP. X.
Curtis) were known wherever the feudal system prevailed [1].

At the time when John granted his Great Charter, the The *Court*
remedy for the recovery of land by the possessory action of *Baron* and the Writ
Assise of Novel Disseisin was still comparatively new, of Right
though it already formed a part of 'the law of the land.' for under-tenants.
Judgement in assise was given by the King's Justices. The
higher remedy, however, had been, was, and long continued
to be the Writ of Right, the essential feature of which was,
when tenants not holding in chief were concerned, that it
had to be brought in the Court of their superior Lord. It
issued out of the Chancery and purported to be a command
from the King to the Lord to do full right [2]. In later times,
the cause was commonly removed, after commencement in
the Lord's Court, by due process, into the County Court, and
thence into the Court of Common Pleas. In John's reign,
however, the Court Baron was of more importance than it
was when the King's Courts had obtained their full development ; and the cause of a vassal which had relation to his
feudal rights was commonly decided by his fellow-vassals—
by his peers—in the Court of their common lord.

The rights of the Barons in relation to their Courts were The
most jealously guarded in the Charter. 'The writ called *Praecipe*
in *capite*,
Praecipe shall not henceforth be made out for any one in or Writ
of Right
respect of any tenement in such a manner that a free man for one
can lose his Court [3].' This writ, known in later times as holding in chief.
Praecipe in capite, was the Writ of Right applicable to
a tenant in chief of the Crown as distinguished from an
undertenant owing suit to the Court of his Lord. The
effect of using the *Praecipe in capite* in the first instance as

---

[1] Edict. Conrad II (Pertz, ii. 39) ; Constit. Fred. I (Pertz, ii. 114).
See also Cujacius, *De Feudis*, lib. i. tit. i., &c.; J. A. de Sancto
Georgio, col. 299, &c. Even in Domesday Book, among the *Clamores*
of Yorkshire (printed, vol. i. p. 374 a), William de Perci calls his peers
to witness that he was seised of Bodetone, and held it, while William
Malet was living and had the shrievalty of the county.

[2] *Registrum Brevium Originalium*, 1 ; Fitzherbert's *Natura
Brevium*, 1-10.

[3] Cap. 34.

CHAP. X. a remedy for an undertenant, without licence from the lord, would, of course, have been to deprive the lord's Court of its jurisdiction ; and the Barons were evidently as anxious to preserve the courts held under them as to secure the right of themselves and others to judgement by peers.

In the latter the King's Courts (over which the Curia Regis or House of Lords retained control) had exclusive jurisdiction.

When the Common Bench was fully established as a distinct Court, it had exclusive jurisdiction (except in counties in which the Court of the Justices in Eyre was sitting). in all writs of *Praecipe in capite*, or Writs of Right, in which the demandant claimed to hold in chief, as of the Crown. It might consequently appear, at first sight, that undertenants suing in the Court of their lord, had the judgement of their peers, while the tenants in chief, or Barons, who were also equal among themselves, and Peers of the King's feudal Court, failed to secure the same privilege. All the King's superior Courts, however, were, as has already been shown, only offshoots of the original *Curia Regis*, to which the tenants in chief, or barons, owed suit, just as the undertenants owed suit to the Court of the Baron of whom they held. The original *Curia Regis*, or that part of it, which was in later times known as the Parliament, or House of Lords, always remained the Court of final jurisdiction. when any error was alleged in Courts below, and, for a very long period (as has been proved in another chapter) retained a hold upon them, and directed their course of proceeding when petitions were made to it during the progress of an action. It was also expressly provided in John's Great Charter[1] that amercements in Court should not be enforced against Earls and Barons except by their peers. Thus, although the pressing affairs of state, and the increase of legal business caused law proceedings in detail to be entrusted to special courts, those courts were subordinate to the higher jurisdiction of the suitors to the King's Court. or of the House of Lords. Matters affecting the Earls and Barons could therefore never be finally decided otherwise than by their peers, except

[1] Cap. 21.

through their own acquiescence in the decisions of a CHAP. X.
lower tribunal itself owing its origin to the King's Great
Court.

The idea of trial and judgement by peers, being strictly Feudal
of feudal origin, had no direct relation to criminal offences, rights
except in so far as they affected feudal rights by way of forfeiture
forfeiture. The idea itself, however, was familiar to the for Treason
mind of every land-holder ; and, as treason and felony in- or Felony.
volved forfeiture or escheat, it was very natural that trial by
peers should have been desired by tenants *in capite*. When
the Great Charter was obtained from King John he had
himself quite recently been cited, as Duke of Normandy, to
appear before the King (Philip Augustus) and the Peers of
France for felony committed in the murder of his nephew
Arthur. He did not appear ; and sentence was passed
against him that he should forfeit to his superior lord,
the King of France, all his seignories and fiefs in that
kingdom.

It is not necessary to enquire whether the action of the Earls and
French Court of Peers was strictly in accordance with Barons to
precedent; it is sufficient to know that, just before King by Earls
John granted his Great Charter, he had himself suffered not and
a little from the judgement of his peers. It can hardly be Barons,
doubted that, when judgement by peers was mentioned in when dis-
the Charter, the Earls and Barons interpreted it to mean herison
that, in cases of alleged treason and felony, when forfeiture question,
or escheat was involved, they should be judged only by in the
Earls and Barons. Regarded from another point of view— reign of
from the point of view of the Sovereign in relation to the Henry III.
safety of the Crown—the doctrine of trial by peers in cases of
treason was accepted only in a hesitating manner as late as
the reign of Henry III. The King himself, said Bracton [1],
cannot be judge, because he would then be prosecutor and
judge in his own cause. Nor can the Justices, because in
giving judgement they represent the person of the King.
'Who then shall judge? Without prejudice to any better

[1] Bract. 119–119 b.

CHAP. X. opinion, it seems that the Court and Peers shall judge,' especially where, on the prosecution of the King, there is peril of life and member, or peril of disherison.

This judgement by Peers not identical with the later trial by Peers. As soon as this doctrine was accepted, Earls and Barons could clearly be judged only by Earls and Barons[1]. This judgement, however, was not identical with the trial by Peers of a later time, when the Peers not only pronounced sentence but found the accused Peer guilty or not guilty, and then gave judgement on their own finding. Bracton's only idea of the mode of accusation seems to have been that of an 'appeal.' Subject to certain preliminaries the question of guilty or not guilty was, in that case, decided by battle. The trial therefore, the ascertaining of the fact, was, though under the direction and control of the Court of Peers, by battle, but the judgement on the trial by battle was to be given by the Peers.

Courts differently constituted according to gradations in treason. The definition of High Treason, or *Lese Majesté*, was at this time very vague. It was sometimes regarded as a felony, sometimes as a mere trespass, according to the gravity of each particular case. Even the treason-trespass had its degrees, and the lighter forms, as being punishable only by pecuniary fine, were excepted by Bracton from the necessity of judgement by Peers, and placed within the jurisdiction of the Justices. The graver forms, the punishment for which approached disherison. because apparently the transgressor's lands had to be redeemed from forfeiture, were placed in a middle position, and Peers were to be associated with the Justices in giving judgement[2].

Mode of trial still not settled in the reign of Edward II: Gaveston's case. Though punishment of the most severe kind was inflicted for 'treason,' it was long before the definition of treason itself or the doctrine of trial by Peers made much advance towards precision. The troubled reign of Edward II afforded many instances of conspiracy against the King, and of

---

[1] According to the parallel passage in Britton (lib. i. cap. 23. sec. 8) it appears to have been thought that all appeals of High Treason against any persons should be heard by Earls and Barons in time of Parliament.

[2] Bract. 119 b.

execution for treason, but in the midst of arms laws are silent.
Piers Gaveston, the King's favourite, had already been twice
banished and had twice returned. In the year 1311,
a Committee of Lords, known as the Lords Ordainers,
framed, among other articles, one to the effect that for
having given bad advice to the King, and other alleged
offences, he should as a public enemy be banished a third
time from the realm, and, if found within the King's
dominions after a day named, should be treated as a public
enemy[1]. He had had no trial, and no opportunity of
defending himself. He did, however, return to England,
was compelled to surrender while serving the King to the
best of his power, and was afterwards beheaded[2]. His
death was desired by the great majority of the Earls and
Barons, and advantage was taken of their general Ordinance
to put him out of their way. This may have been a judgement, but certainly was not a trial by Peers. According to
several accounts, the four Earls of Warwick, of Lancaster,
of Hereford, and of Arundel, appear to have been concerned
in the execution[3]. According to another account no peers
at all were concerned in the final judgement. The Justices
of Gaol Delivery appointed to deliver the gaol of Warwick,
it is said, pronounced sentence in virtue of the Ordinance
which they regarded as still in force. The beheading of
Gaveston, it is added, the Peers of the Realm having been
neither present nor even summoned, excited undying
animosity between the King and the Earls[4].

The case of Hugh le Despenser the elder, and Hugh le
Despenser the younger had, in its early stages, some show
of proceeding by due course of law, for the Prelates, Earls,
Barons, and other Peers, together with the Commons, are

*Banish-
ment of the
Despensers.
by Peers
of the
Realm.*

·[1] *Rot. Parl.*, 5 Ed. II, no. 20 (printed, vol. i. p. 283).
[2] Trokelowe, *Annales* (Rolls Series), p. 77.
[3] *Annales Londonienses de tempore Edwardi Secundi* (Rolls Series),
p. 207 ; *Annales Paulini* (Rolls Series), p. 271 ; *Vita Edwardi
Secundi*, Auct. Malmesb. 179–180 (Rolls Series) ; *Vita et Mors
Edwardi Secundi* (Rolls Series), p. 298. See also Murimuth (Rolls
Series), p. 17.
[4] *Gesta Edwardi de Carnarvan* (Rolls Series), pp. 43–44.

CHAP. X. represented as having framed the accusation. The 'Earls and Barons and other Peers of the Realm' found 'by examination,' though in the absence of the persons accused, that the alleged misdeeds of the Despensers (nearly of the same nature as those of Gaveston) were notorious and truly alleged. The 'Peers of the Realm, Earls and Barons,' in the King's presence, passed sentence of disherison and banishment, adding that, if found in the kingdom after the day appointed for their departure, the Despensers were to be treated as enemies of the King and of the kingdom [1].

The Earl of Carlisle degraded, and then sentenced as a traitor, without trial or judgement by Peers.

The case of Andrew Harcla, Earl of Carlisle, was very different from those of Gaveston or the Despensers, because the King himself regarded Harcla as a traitor, while the charges against the others proceeded only from those who were opposed to the King's party, and could hardly be described as treason against the King. The accusation against Harcla was that of treasonable correspondence with the Scots who were the King's enemies. He was not, however. judged by his peers, but by a Court constituted by special commission, and consisting of Edmund, Earl of Kent, the King's uncle, John de Hastings, also the King's kinsman, three knights, and the Chief Justice of the King's Bench. The commission which they received was not to try him, but to degrade him from his rank and pronounce judgement on him after degradation, in the terms of the instructions sent to them, for enmity to the King, and sedition. His guilt was established by the simple formula that his misdeeds were 'notorious and acknowledged in the realm ; and our Lord the King records the fact.' His sword of earldom was accordingly taken from him, and his spurs cut away from his heels, and when he had been thus deprived of his dignity, the sentence for treason in all its horror was passed upon him [2].

As Harcla was degraded first, and underwent judgement for treason afterwards, it may be maintained that he was

[1] *Rot. Lit. Claus.*, 14 Ed. II, m. 14, *Cedula* (*Statutes of the Realm*, i. 184).
[2] *Placita coram Rege*, Hilary, *Rex*, R⁰. 34 d.

not judged as an Earl, and consequently that he was not, CHAP. X.
as an Earl, entitled to trial or judgement by Peers. It
must, however, be obvious that, if the King could at his
pleasure, or by recording any statement as being notorious,
degrade a Peer from his peerage, the right of trial or judgement by Peers would be nugatory.

The banishment of the Despensers was, in fact, but the Case of the
triumph of the political party opposed to them. This was Earl of Lancaster.
very speedily followed by their return, and by a reversal
of the sentence against them[1]. Soon afterwards the
Earl of Lancaster, who was at the head of the opposite
faction, fell in his turn into the hands of the King's
party, and was sentenced to die the death of a traitor
(drawing included); but, being of the blood royal, he was
only beheaded. There is little doubt but that he had been
in treasonable correspondence with the Scots; and he was
taken when in arms against the King. From York he was
carried to Pontefract where the King was, and on the
following day he was brought to judgement.' There was
no time for any strictly formal proceedings even of the
nature of a Court Martial. Some peers were present; his
misdeeds were 'recorded' and judgement was pronounced.
He was not even allowed to say a word in defence[2].

At the end of the reign, when the King's cause was lost, The
the Despensers had the misfortune to be taken by their Despensers sentenced
enemies. Each was adjudged to suffer the full penalties of to death,
treason, the younger a little after the elder. Neither was a 'Knight' presiding
allowed to say anything in his defence. Their previous in the Court.
banishment (though the sentence had been annulled) and
their return to the realm, as well as their subsequent acts,
were alleged as the causes of the judgement now given
against them. The Court by which they were sentenced
appears, in each case, to have consisted of Earls and Barons.

[1] *Rot. Parl.*, 1 Ed. III (*Petitions in Parl.*), no. 1 (printed, vol. ii. p. 7).
[2] *Ib.*, 1 Ed. III, no. 1 (printed, vol. ii. pp. 2–3); *Annales Paulini* (Rolls Series), pp. 302–3; *Gesta Edwardi de Carnarvan* (Rolls Series), p. 77; Auct. Malmesb. (Rolls Series), pp. 270–271.

CHAP. X.   It used as its mouth-piece William Trussel, who is described as a knight, and who was appointed Justice for the occasion. He performed some of the functions which would, at a later time. have been performed by the Lord High Steward, as President of the Court [1], but there is no evidence that any William Trussel had, so early as the reign of Edward II. been summoned among the Barons or other Peers to Parliament. He was, however, probably the William Trussel who, soon afterwards pronounced the deposition of Edward II.

Cases of the Earl of Kent, and of Mortimer: judgement but not trial by Peers.   It is, indeed, clear that as each faction obtained the mastery, it took revenge upon its opponents ; and as the lands of traitors were forfeited for treason and could then be granted to others, there were excellent grounds for passing judgement, but none for a fair and impartial trial. As at the end of the reign of Edward II, so at the beginning of the reign of Edward III, the political party which proved itself the stronger wrought its will, in turn, upon the lives and lands of its principal adversaries. The Earl of Kent was treacherously inveigled by the emissaries of Roger Mortimer, Earl of March. into an undertaking for which he suffered death and forfeiture as a traitor; and Mortimer himself was not long afterwards drawn and hanged for treason, by the judgement of Earls and Barons, as Peers and Judges of Parliament [2]. In each case it may be said that judgement was given by the Peers: but in each case the judgement was a foregone conclusion, and depended solely upon the will of a party. Each party said that the misdeeds of the other were ' notorious,' and notoriety sufficed   . in place of any trial in due form. Each party in its turn reversed, when triumphant, the attainders which its members had suffered in times of adversity.

No clear distinction   At this period (at the end of the reign of Edward II and

---

[1] *Annales Paulini* (Rolls Series), pp. 317-320 ; *Gesta Edwardi de Carnarvan* (Rolls Series), pp. 87-89 ; *Auct. Malmesb.* (Rolls Series), p. 289 ; *Vita et Mors Edwardi Secundi* (Rolls Series), pp. 311, 312.

[2] *Rot. Parl.*, 4 Ed. III, no. 1 (printed, vol. ii. pp. 52-53), nos. 11 and 12 (printed, vol. ii. p. 55).

the beginning of the reign of Edward III) it is plain that
neither the doctrine of judgement by Peers, nor the doctrine
of trial by Peers, had been reduced to any precision. The
different modes of proceeding recognized in later times
were not yet distinguished from each other. There was no
clear discrimination between the course to be adopted when
the accusation took the form of indictment, and that to be
adopted when it took the form of impeachment. Bill of
Attainder was not clearly marked off from impeachment;
and impeachment was not as yet even a technical term, but
was used for any kind of accusation. No case (so far as is
known) had hitherto been tried by the Peers in the Court
of the Lord High Steward.

It is nevertheless in this troubled period, ' when Judge-
ment by Peers' was a phrase in common use, when trial by
Peers had yet no settled form, and when the Statute of
Treasons had not yet become law, that the right of the
Spiritual Lords to trial by Peers is, if anywhere, to be
sought.

Much has been written on the subject in later times,
but it is by no means clear that the Prelates, though, as we
have seen, allowed to be Peers of the Realm, had hitherto
claimed that Peers of the Realm should try them or be
their judges in accusations of treason or felony, still less
in accusations of any other kind. It is quite certain that
since the Conquest they had persistently attempted to
render themselves exempt from all lay jurisdiction. In the
reign of the Conqueror, Odo, Bishop of Bayeux, asserted
the clerical privilege saying, ' I am a clerk and minister of
the Lord ; it is not lawful to condemn a Bishop without
the judgement of the Pope.' The Conqueror took the
matter into his own hands, and condemned him not as
a Bishop but as an Earl, because he was Earl of Kent[1].
This, however, did not settle the question of clerical privilege, or prevent its re-assertion in subsequent reigns. In
the reign of Henry II Becket refused to abide by the

[1] Ordericus Vitalis (French Hist. Soc.), p. 189.

CHAP. X. jurisdiction of the King's Court in a matter of account. The Barons adjudged that he ought to be taken and imprisoned. Two Earls went to announce the fact to him, and he said, 'I forbid you, on the part of Almighty God, and under *anathema*, from rendering judgement on me this day, as I have appealed to the presence of the Lord the Pope[1].' In the reign of Richard I it was adjudged, in the King's Council or Court at Northampton, that Hugh de Nunant, Bishop of Coventry, should be peremptorily cited to answer for acting in a manner contrary to the fealty which he had sworn. It was further adjudged that, should he fail to appear within forty days, he should be subject to the judgement of the Bishops in that he was a Bishop, and to the judgement of laymen in that he had been the King's Sheriff[2]. He had in fact been Sheriff of the counties of Warwick and Leicester in the second, fourth, and fifth years of the reign[3]. As an officer, therefore, he was regarded as being subject to lay jurisdiction, though not apparently of necessity that of Earls or Barons ; and as a Bishop he was regarded as being subject only to ecclesiastical jurisdiction.

Doubts in the reign of Henry III. In the time of Henry III Bracton expressed himself with doubting words to the effect that no clerk, of high or low degree, could be outlawed, and he mentioned a Bishop as having the exemption. The reason was that they could have compurgation in Court Christian. If a Bishop could not be outlawed upon an accusation of High Treason, after having fled, it would seem to follow that he could not have any judgement pronounced upon him in any secular Court. Bracton, however, carefully guarded himself by saying that the doctrine as to outlawry was only the opinion of 'some persons[4].' Men were therefore still in some uncertainty as to the law.

---

[1] Hoveden (Rolls Series), vol. i. pp. 224–228.
[2] *Ib.*, vol. iii. p. 242.
[3] *Great Rolls of the Exchequer* of the respective years under the head of Warwickshire and Leicestershire.
[4] Bract. 134 b.

Soon after the accession of Edward II Walter Langton, CHAP. X.
Bishop of Coventry and Lichfield, was accused of having Langton,
committed various offences while holding the office of Bishop of
Treasurer in the previous reign. According to one instru- and
ment he had presumptuously usurped power, under colour Lichfield,
of his office, and effected sales, alienations, and waste of the Justices of
King's lands, to the disherison of the Crown, and in deroga- Oyer and
tion of the King's royal estate[1]. According to another
document he was further accused of intolerable injuries
and oppression, inflicted by means of certain conspirators
and others who were his adherents[2]. Special Commissions
of Oyer and Terminer issued for hearing and determining
the charges. None of the Commissioners were Peers. They
were Brabazon, Chief Justice of the Court of King's Bench,
Hegham, or Hengham, Chief Justice of the Court of Common
Pleas, Bereford, a Puisne Justice of the latter Court, and
William Inge, afterwards also a Puisne Justice of the same[3].
No question as to trial by Peers arose. Neither the word
Treason nor the word *Felony*, it is true, is mentioned in either
form of accusation. The charges, however, bore a very strong
resemblance to some of those brought in the following reign
against Archbishop Stratford, who, it has been sometimes
asserted, successfully claimed the right of trial by Peers.
That claim will be considered in another place. In the
meantime it may suffice to note that Langton was thrown
into prison[4], and was released only on the interposition
of the Pope[5]. Thus, like his predecessor in the see, Hugh
de Nunant (though the ecclesiastical power may have saved
him as a Bishop), he was, as the King's officer, regarded as
being amenable to the jurisdiction of the King's Justices.

The privileges of the clergy were declared and confirmed Benefit of
in the ninth year of the reign of Edward II. It was then 9 Edward
beyond all doubt the law that an ecclesiastic should not II.

---

[1] *Rot. Lit. Pat.*, 1 Ed. II, part i. m. 8 d.
[2] Also *Rot. Lit. Pat.*, 1 Ed. II, part i. m. 8 d.
[3] The two patents as above.
[4] *Annales Paulini* (Rolls Series), p. 257.
[5] *Ib.*, p. 264.

CHAP. X. receive judgement before any secular judge in relation to
any matter by which he could be brought into peril of life
or member[1]. High treason, above all other crimes, involved peril of life and member ; but it seems to have been
supposed, even before the passing of the Act, and it was
certainly held in later times, that privilege of clergy did not
extend to cases of high treason[2].

Case of Adam de Orleton, Bishop of Hereford.   The case of Adam de Orleton. Bishop of Hereford, also
in the reign of Edward II, is perhaps the first in which
there is any authoritative account in detail of proceedings
against a Prelate accused of felony and high treason. The
whole course of action against him is of a very remarkable
character.

The Commission to enquire, and indictment.   The King[3] directed a writ to the Justices of the King's
Bench[4], which was of the nature of a Commission of Oyer
and Terminer. They were to enquire in various counties as
to felonies, robberies, trespasses, meetings, conspiracies, and
confederacies lately moved against the King by his enemies
who had rebelled against him. The word 'Treason' was
not mentioned in the instrument, but in an Inquisition which
was taken in virtue of it, the Jurors presented that Roger
de Mortimer the nephew, and others, with a numerous
army of horse and foot, levied war against the King.
Mortimer, they said, held a secret conference with the
Bishop of Hereford, who on the following day sent some
of his own men-at-arms to reinforce the rebel army,
with which they marched towards Gloucester, committing
various trespasses against the King and people.

Orleton refuses to answer in the King's Bench.   Upon this indictment the Bishop was 'attached.' He
appeared in the Court of King's Bench on January 23,
1323-4, and being asked by the Justices how he would
acquit himself, he said that he was Bishop of Hereford, at
the will of God and of the Pope, that the matters charged
against him were of so high a nature that he ought not to.

[1] Stat. 9 Ed. II (*Articuli Cleri*), cap. 15.
[2] 2 Inst. 634.
[3] *Placita coram Rege*, Hilary, 17 Ed. II, R⁰. 87.
[4] '*Justiciariis ad placita coram nobis tenenda assignatis.*'

answer in that Court, and that he could not answer without offence to God and Holy Church. He was thereupon required to appear in person from day to day to hear judgement. CHAP. X.

The record contains no mention of any intermediate days, but on the following 24th of February the Bishop 'came before the Lord the King himself in full Parliament.' The whole matter was recited in his presence and that of the 'Earls, Barons, and other the King's lieges.' It was also recited that Roger de Mortimer had already been adjudged a traitor for having seditiously levied war against the King, and that one of the men-at-arms sent by the Bishop to aid him had already been found guilty of treason. The Bishop was then asked whether he had anything more to say than he had previously said, and he replied as before that, being Bishop of Hereford, he could not answer without offence to God and Holy Church. The Archbishop of Canterbury thereupon made a demand that the Bishop, as being one constituted in the episcopal dignity, should be delivered to him. This was conceded, but the Archbishop was required to produce the Bishop in the Court of King's Bench on the Monday next before Mid-Lent, for which day the Sheriff of Hereford was to summon a jury. *Refuses to answer in Parliament, because a Bishop: case remitted to the King's Bench.*

, The Archbishop, the Bishop, and the jury, of whom five were knights, came into Court on the appointed day. The jury found not simply a verdict of 'guilty' or 'not guilty,' but a verdict against the Bishop which followed the words of the indictment. Judgement was given that the Bishop should remain in the custody of the Archbishop as a Clerk Convict, and that his goods and chattels, lands and tenements, should be seized into the King's hand. *Is convicted by a jury, but has benefit of clergy.*

The Bishop of Hereford, when arraigned in the King's Bench, thus claimed no privilege of peerage, but only privilege of clergy. Then followed that which is common enough in the civil causes of the period—a reference to the King in Parliament on a point of difficulty, the cause still remaining to be determined in the Court of first instance, into which it was afterwards remitted for trial by a jury. Nothing

CHAP. X. was decided in Parliament, except that in this particular case Orleton should have his clergy [1].

Inaccurate account of the matter sent to the Pope. 　The King (or rather, perhaps, as may be inferred from the style, some ecclesiastic on his behalf) afterwards wrote to the Pope, giving an account of the matter which is not strictly in accordance with the authoritative records of the Court of King's Bench. He said that Orleton 'had taken part with others in the crime of High Treason, and that the whole of the facts had been made clear not by fleeting or merely assertive rumour, but by lawful process in full Parliament, in the presence of Archbishops, Bishops, Nobles, and other Magnates of the Realm, according to the law and custom thereof.' The King also took credit for having dealt leniently with the Bishop, saying, 'although we might have proceeded against him more rigorously, yet, by reason of reverence for the episcopal order, we left him to be judged, in respect of the crimes aforesaid, *in foro ecclesiae* [2].'

The letter is not without value in relation to the subsequent attitude of Stratford, as stated by ecclesiastics rather than by lawyers. It contains the positive, if not true, assertion that the whole case against Orleton was heard in Parliament. It suppresses the fact that the verdict against him was found by a jury in the Court of King's Bench, and that the judgement was pronounced in that Court by the Justices without the assistance of any Peers whatever. Taken by itself it might seem to show that the Bishop of Hereford obtained that trial by Peers, which he not only never claimed, but which he distinctly refused.

At the beginning of the following reign a petition was

---

[1] Sir Edward Coke (2 Inst. 634) has cited Orleton's case in proof of the doctrine that there was, at common law, no benefit of clergy in cases of High Treason. He was misled, as to the facts, as others have been since, by an account of the matter, written long after the event, by Walsingham, and has thus put the case :—' Because he could not · have any privilege of clergy by the common law, the Archbishops of Canterbury, York, and Dublin, and their Suffragan Bishops came to the bar, in that disordered time, and with force took him from the bar, all which was done by pretext and colour of the canons of the Church.'

[2] French and Roman Roll, 15–18 Ed. II, m. 1.

addressed, on behalf of the Bishop, to the King and Chap. X.
Council, complaining that the judgement which had been The
given against him in the Court of King's Bench was judgement reversed by
erroneous. The proceedings which followed, though in Parliament
themselves remarkable, do not indicate that the question in the reign of
of trial by Peers was raised. They were held before the Edward
King and Council, Prelates, Earls, Barons, Magnates, and III, but without
the whole commonalty of the Realm[1]. The reversal of reference to any
judgement, which followed, thus partook more of the nature question of
of later Acts, in which Attainders were reversed, when one trial by Peers.
political faction succeeded in overpowering its previously
triumphant rival, than of proceedings upon a writ of error
in the House of Lords. Several minor technical points are
found among the assignments of error, but the principal
was that the articles under which the Justices of the
King's Bench were to enquire, though extending to felony
and robbery, did not include the levying of war. In
another document[2] much is made of the fact that the Bishop
was convicted by a jury, though he had not accepted that
mode of trial. As has already been shown, however, the
Bishop refused to put himself upon the country, because he
claimed the privilege not of peerage but of clergy; and
there was no irregularity in taking an 'inquest of office'
in such a case. Nowhere is it stated that the jurisdiction of the Court of King's Bench was called in question
on the ground that Orleton was a Peer of the Realm.
When the judgement was reversed, no reasons were given.
For all that appears, therefore, it may have been held as
law, in the reign of Edward II, that a Bishop might be
arraigned for felony in the Court of King's Bench. and
might there plead, and be tried by a jury, if, at any rate, he
did not himself claim to be tried as a Peer.

It is clear that the doctrine of trial by Peers had not, at The Peers object to giving
this time, been reduced to precision even with respect to

[1] *Rot. Lit. Pat.*, 3 Ed. III, part i. m. 33, and see *Rot. Parl.*, ii.
App. 427.

[2] *Rot. Lit. Claus.*, 1 Ed. III, part i. m. 13, ' *licet idem Episcopus in
inquisitionem aliquam inde faciendam se non posuisset.*'

CHAP. X.   laymen. By the King's special desire, the case of Simon de
judgement Bereford was brought before the Peers in the fourth year
on any but of the reign of Edward III. He was accused of being
Peers.
implicated in the treasons of Mortimer. They protested
because he was not their peer; but in consideration of the
supposed enormity of his crimes they did, in the end,
entertain the charge and give judgement. It was, nevertheless, then 'assented and agreed by our Lord the King,
and all the Magnates, in full Parliament, that although the
Peers, as judges of Parliament, have taken upon them, in
the presence of our lord the King, to make and render the
said judgement, yet the Peers that now are or shall be in
time to come, are not bound or charged to give judgement
upon others than Peers,' and that this particular judgement
was not to be drawn into a precedent[1].

As, however, will be shown in due course, the Lords, at
no very great distance of time afterwards, enunciated a
directly contradictory principle. The unsettled state of the
practice, as well as some other circumstances, must therefore be borne in mind when the important case of John
de Stratford, Archbishop of Canterbury, is considered.

Case of   Stratford had, as Chancellor, enjoyed the confidence of
John de
Stratford,   King Edward III. The King being subsequently engaged
Arch-   in a war with France, had the mortification to find that his
bishop of
Canter-   affairs did not prosper, and that his plans were frustrated
bury: he.   by the want of supplies. He attributed his misfortunes to
refuses to
go to the   the malversation of the officers of various departments.
King when   He returned suddenly and unexpectedly to England, on
summoned.
November 30, 1340[2], threw a number of persons, many of
high position, into prison, and caused various commissions,
of the nature of Commissions of Trailbaston[3], to issue for
full inquiry regarding the misdeeds which he suspected.
One of his first acts was also to summon the Archbishop to
his presence. He seems to have attributed a part of his ill-

[1] *Rot. Parl.*, 4 Ed. III, no. 2 and no. 6 (printed, vol. ii. p. 53 and
p. 54).
[2] *Rot. Lit. Pat.*, 14 Ed. III, part iii. m. 11.
[3] *Ib.*, 14 Ed. III, part iii. m. 2 d, and m. 8 d.

fortune to Stratford's negligence in not having paid certain CHAP. X.
sums, as bound, to foreign merchants. Nothing, however,
could induce the Archbishop to obey the King's commands.
A safe conduct was sent to him[1], but still he refused to
appear except in Parliament[2]. Up to this point, at any
rate, there was no charge of treason distinctly formulated
against him, though it is not improbable that some of the
King's courtiers may have called him a traitor.

He began, however, to make very free use of the eccle- His excom-
siastical weapon of excommunication, including in that munica-
tions.
sentence, somewhat vaguely, all laymen who should lay
violent hands on the persons, lands, goods, or houses of
clergymen, all who should violate the liberties of Holy
Church, all who should lessen the privileges granted to the
Barons in *Magna Charta*, all who should falsely accuse him or
any Bishop or person of his Province of treason, or any other
crime[3]. At the same time he suggested that the Prelates,
Peers, and Nobles of the Realm should be summoned and
make strict enquiry as to what had become of the supplies
voted, and that no one should be deemed guilty of wrong-
doing until his answer had been given and due investigation
had been made.

The Commissions of Trailbaston, or other Oyer and
Terminer, everywhere unpopular, incurred the special animosity of the clergy, and of Stratford at their head. Several
persons in orders had been imprisoned, and proceedings had
been taken against them at the same time as against Chief
Justice Willoughby[4]. Stratford was especially indignant
on this ground, and prayed the King and Council to release
all free men taken and detained in contravention, as he said,
of Magna Charta, but especially the ecclesiastics[5].

A great quarrel now arose between the Archbishop and The King
declares

[1] *Rot. Lit. Pat.*, 15 Ed. III, part i. m. 48 (printed in ·Rymer's
Foedera, ii. 1146).
[2] *Rot. Rom.*, 15 Ed. III, m. 4 (printed in Rymer's *Foedera*, ii.
1152–3).
[3] Hemingb. (English Historical Society) ii. 375–380.
[4] *Rot. Lit. Pat.*, 14 Ed. III, part iii. m. 2 d.
[5] Hemingb. ii. 369–371.

CHAP. X. thc King.   The clergy, at Stratford's instigation, threw every
their object possible obstacle in the way of the Justices of Trailbaston,
to be to by denunciations, monitions, and sentences of excommunica-
stir up
sedition. tion, and by inhibiting the Justices from putting persons
upon their oath during Lent [1]. The King expressed his
views with regard to thc course pursued in a letter sent to
the Bishop of London for publication.   Reciting the original
ground of complaint, he went on to the sentences of excommunication, designed, as he said, 'to impair the good
opinion held of the King . . . and traitorously to stir up
sedition among the people committed to our charge, and
finally to withdraw from our Royal Majesty the hearts of
our Earls, Lords, and Barons of our Realm.'   At the same
time the King made various charges against Stratford of
misapplication of public funds [2].

The Arch-   Thc Archbishop, thereupon, took up new ground. He
bishop
declares   had previously been willing to appear in full Parliament,
that, if   and submit himself to the judgement of his peers, with
accused of
Treason,   a saving for the state of Holy Church, for himself, and for
he denies his Order, and had suggested that, as no Parliament was
the juris-
diction of sitting, a Parliament should be summoned [3].   He now
any secular changed his tone, and showed·very plainly what was meant
judge.
by the saving clause for himself, his order. and the Church.
He wrote a letter to the King beginning thus :—' There
are two things by which the world is chicfly governed, the
Holy Pontifical Authority, and the Royal Power. . . . Who
doubts but that the Priests of Christ ought to be considered
both fathcrs and *masters* of Kings and Princes?'   He made
a lengthy answer to some of the charges against him. In
relation to the particular and later charge of stirring up
sedition, however, he said that inasmuch as it seemed to
cast the crime of treason upon his head, in which no King

[1] *Rot. Lit. Claus.*, 15 Ed. III, part i. m. 40 d (printed in Rymer's
Foedera, ii. 1151-2).
[2] *Ib.*, 15 Ed. III, part i. m. 46 d (printed in Rymer's *Foedera*, ii.
1147-8).
[3] MS. Cotton. Claud. E. 8. fo. 252 a (printed in Rymer's *Foedcra*,
ii. 1143); Hemingb. ii. 363-367.

or temporal Lord could be his competent judge, he did not CHAP. X.
intend to prejudice his position, 'but wholly to refuse the
judgement of any secular judge whatever[1].'

In March, 1340-1, the King summoned a Parliament to
meet at Westminster on the Monday next after the Quinzaine of Easter (April 23), and the Archbishop received
his summons in due course[2]. The events which then occurred
have been represented in an impossible fashion by Birchington, a monk who wrote some forty years after the event, and
whose statements have again and again been copied into
various histories. Birchington states that on the morrow
of St. George's day (April 24) the Archbishop came with
the intention of making his way to his place in Parliament,
but was met at the entrance door of the Great Hall by
Stafford, the Steward of the King's Household, and Darcy,
the King's Chamberlain, who told him that he must answer,
in the Exchequer, all that should there be objected against
him, before he could enter Parliament. Stratford, as alleged,
did then go into the Exchequer, where certain articles were
tendered against him, which he said he would consider. He
then, still on April 24, went into Parliament, and said he
would clear himself in full Parliament of the charges laid
against him. Afterwards, as the monk tells us, Stratford
appeared a second time in the Exchequer[3]. On Thursday,
May 3 (*in Festo Inventionis Sanctae Crucis*), several persons
interceded on behalf of the Archbishop with the King, who

---

[1] The Archbishop's reply is given by Birchington (*Anglia Sacra*,
part i), p. 34, whence it has been copied into Parker's *De Antiquitate
Britannicae Ecclesiae*, and thence into Wilkins's *Concilia*. Birchington
is not an authority to be trusted when stating matters in his own
words, but there is no reason to suppose that the text of Stratford's
letter was not preserved at Canterbury and copied by the monk.

[2] *Rot. Lit. Claus.*, 15 Ed. III, part i. m. 37 d (printed, *Rep. Dig.
Peer*, vol. iv. p. 529). The Quinzaine of Easter is sometimes represented as being the period of fifteen days including Easter Day,
seven days before and seven days after it. The Quinzaine is, however,
usually the fourteenth day after the Feast or Saint's Day named. In
the year 1341 Easter Day fell on the 8th of April.

[3] Birchington (*Anglia Sacra*, part i), pp. 38-39.

CHAP. X. thereupon received him into favour, and held him to be in
every respect free from the charges laid against him [1].

Stratford,   With regard to that which really happened in Parliament,
according
to the Rolls the Parliament Rolls themselves constitute the only trust-
of Parlia- worthy authority; the Rolls of the Exchequer constitute
ment, asked
to be   the only trustworthy authority for that which happened in
arraigned   the Court of Exchequer. From the Rolls of Parliament it
before the
Peers,   appears that on Monday, a fortnight after the first meeting
because   of the Parliament (May 7), the King came into the Painted
he was
' notor-   Chamber. whither came also the Archbishop of Canterbury.
iously
defamed.'   the other Prelates and Magnates, and the Commons. Stratford
there humbled himself before the King, and prayed the
King to grant that, inasmuch as he was notoriously defamed
throughout the realm, he might be arraigned before the
Peers in full Parliament, and there answer. To this the
King, in a manner, consented, adding that he wished
business touching the state of the realm and the common
weal to be first set in order, and other business afterwards [2].
Two years later the King commanded that all matters
touching the arraignment of the Archbishop should be
annulled and set aside, as being neither reasonable nor
true [3]. Thus the statement that on May 3, 1341, the Archbishop was held to be innocent of the charges brought
against him, is absolutely devoid of foundation. He was
not held innocent on that day, or on any day in the year
1341, or before the year 1343.

Statements   The story relating to the Exchequer, absurd enough as
of later
historians told by Birchington, deserves, perhaps, more attention, from
that   the extraordinary proportions which it assumed in later
Stratford
had first   times, and in other hands. Always acquiring strength in
appeared,   its progress. it affected the writings of Bishop Stillingfleet.
on a charge
of Treason, of Jeremy Collier, of Hume, of Hallam, and of more recent
in the
Exchequer. historians.   Hallam. in one of his prominent notes [4] relating
to the question · whether Bishops are entitled. *on charges of* .

[1] Birchington (*Anglia Sacra*, part i), pp. 40–41.
[2] *Rot. Parl.*, 15 Ed. III, no. 8 (printed, vol. ii. p. 127).
[3] *Ib.*, 17 Ed. III, no. 22 (printed, vol. ii. p. 139).
[4] Hallam, *Middle Ages*, cap. 8. part iii. note 1.

treason or felony, to a trial by the Peers,' has, in reliance CHAP. X.
upon Collier (who in his turn relied upon Birchington),
committed himself to the following very remarkable statement. The Archbishop 'came to Parliament with a declared
intention of defending himself before his Peers. The King
insisted upon his answering in the Court of Exchequer.'
Collier (who is Hallam's authority) further states that
Stratford actually did appear there, 'received a copy of the
charge, and promised to return his answer after time for
considering the articles [1].'

This is a truly astounding proposition. Stratford, who, The
be it remembered, is set up by Stillingfleet, Collier, and Exchequer
had, in fact,
Hallam as the great vindicator of the right of Bishops to be no juris-
tried by Peers of the Realm, goes meekly to the Court of Treason.
Exchequer and recognizes its jurisdiction, when, according
to his own showing, it is a charge of High Treason which is
brought against him. He then goes back to Parliament as
champion in a struggle in which he had already surrendered,
and most needlessly surrendered too.

It seems hardly necessary, in these days, to say that Strat- The origin
ford never did anything of the kind. The whole story about story.
the Exchequer arose out of a monkish ignorance of law,
and the idle gossip of a monastery. That which actually
did occur can be ascertained, not from Collier or Birchington,
but from the contemporary Exchequer records, which show
that Stratford did not appear in person in the Exchequer
at all.

The Exchequer was a Court of Revenue and Account. The Rolls
The matter in respect of which the Archbishop had to Exchequer
make an 'appearance' (which does not necessarily mean show that
Stratford
a personal appearance) in the Exchequer was not High merely
Treason, or any bond to foreign merchants, but something appeared
there, in
very much more prosaic. Reduced into the actual words relation
of the Exchequer it is neither more nor less than fifteen matter
sacks, and fifty-seven pounds of wool, which were alleged of account,
by at-
to be due from him to the King 'in respect of the wools torney.

[1] Jeremy Collier, *Ecclesiastical History* (1852), vol. iii. p. 89.

Chap. X. lately granted by the Prelates, Religious, and certain others
of the clergy' in the Parliament of the twelfth year of the
reign[1]. The proceeding was not even, as has sometimes
been said[2], by information of the Attorney-General, or by
bill, or by any of the peremptory measures which the
Exchequer, in later times, at any rate, had at its disposal.
There was not, at this time, in the exact modern sense, any
Attorney-General in existence. The Archbishop was
called to the Exchequer by the mildest of its processes
a *Venire facias*[3]. To this he omitted to appear, as
defendants commonly did in all the Courts upon receipt of
a first writ.

In due course a writ of attachment afterwards issued to
ensure the Archbishop's attendance. He then appointed
an attorney, Elias de Waddeworth[4]. 'And the Archbishop,
by Elias de Waddeworth, his attorney, comes and says that
he can sufficiently show to the Court that he ought not to
be charged with the wools, but says that he has not his
evidences ready, and prays to have a further day prefixed
for him.' The prayer is granted, and successive adjournments follow[5]. During the whole of this time Stratford
was appearing not in person at all, but by attorney, and
fully recognizing the jurisdiction of the Exchequer with
regard to the particular matters in dispute.

Further pro-ceedings in Parlia-ment.
The modern idea that Stratford 'was seized by officers
and carried to the bar of the Court of Exchequer[6]' having
been traced to its source, and its true value having been
ascertained, we may now follow some other proceedings in
Parliament. In this part of the field a furious controversy
raged in the seventeenth century, all because some of the

---

[1] *Remembrance Roll* of the King's Remembrancer of the Exchequer,
Easter, 15 Ed. III, '*Adhuc Recorda*,' Kent.
[2] Lord Campbell, *Lives of the Lord Chancellors*, cap. 14.
[3] *Remembrance Roll* of the King's Remembrancer of the Exchequer,
Brevia Retornabilia, Hilary, 15 Ed. III.
[4] *Remembrance Roll*, as above, '*Praesentationes Attorn.*, &c.'
[5] *Remembrance Roll*, as above, '*Adhuc Recorda*.'
[6] Lord Campbell, *Lives of the Lord Chancellors*, cap. 14.

combatants would not sufficiently attend to the Rolls of CHAP. X.
Parliament itself.

Had Edward Stillingfleet (sometime preacher at the These were
Rolls Chapel, and afterwards Bishop of Worcester) never brought
into pro-
been born, it is probable that the case of Archbishop minence
Stratford would have attracted comparatively little atten- by Bishop
Stillingfleet
tion, and that some eminent writers would have been saved in the
seventeenth
from very remarkable errors. It is quite possible to century.
have a smattering of records, and yet be ignorant of the
law which they illustrate, quite possible to be clever in
controversy and yet not infallible in argument, or even
absolutely correct in statement of matters of fact.

Stillingfleet was an eager disputant, of strength, originality, His state-
and judgement. and met another of not less power, and, ments were
inaccurate.
perhaps, of greater accuracy, in Lord Holles[1]. It is not
necessary to follow the arguments of the two champions,
because both of them, in the heat of the contest, missed
some of the most important points. It may, however,
be of use to show how Stillingfleet deceived himself,
and misled others who followed him. His knowledge of
legal terms was defective, and for that reason, without
doubt, he asserted that Stratford, who was not tried at
all, was 'tried'[2] by the Peers. He made another statement that twelve Peers were appointed to examine the
articles against the Archbishop, and then admitted that,
according to the Parliament Roll itself, the twelve were not
chosen for that purpose, but to draw up in form the wishes
of the Peers in general as to a trial by their peers in
Parliament[3].

The ideas of Stillingfleet were adopted by Jeremy Collier, He misled
a Non-juror, and a controversial writer on many subjects, Jeremy
Collier
including the immorality of the stage. He published in the and others
early part of the eighteenth century 'The Ecclesiastical
History of Great Britain.' It shows considerable research,

[1] See Lord Holles, *His Remains*, 1682.
[2] Selden inadvertently made the same statement in his *Judicature
in Parliament*. (Works, vol. iii. part ii. 1588.)
[3] Stillingfleet's Works, vol. iii. p. 856.

O

CHAP. X. but it is a *rudis indigestaque moles* abounding in statements
made with the object of setting forth the particular
ecclesiastical views of history which the particular ecclesiastical writer entertained. It is a book of absolutely no
authority on matters of law, and exhibits, again and again,
a complete ignorance of the meaning of the commonest
technical terms. Reference to Collier's writings would
indeed be needless, had his views not been accepted without question by later writers of more importance. He
copies Stillingfleet's statement regarding the appointment
of twelve Peers to examine the articles against Stratford,
and then copies Stillingfleet's admission that the Rolls
of Parliament afford no warrant for it [1]. He also tells us,
in Stillingfleet's words, that the Archbishop was 'tried, at
the King's suit, and for a capital crime, and yet not tried by
commoners but by his Peers [2].'

Stratford was never arraigned, much less tried, before the Peers.   As a matter of fact, Stratford was never even arraigned,
much less tried, and it is not quite clear on what points he
wished to be arraigned before the Peers. He asked it only
because he was 'notoriously defamed through the realm.'
Had he been arraigned, it would have been open to him to
make any answer he pleased, and to make one answer with
regard to one part of the charges, another to another. Any
answer he might give he was, according to his own words,
determined to make with a saving for Holy Church, for
himself, and for his Order. To the charge of Treason he
had distinctly said that he would not answer at all in any
temporal court. So far as capital offences were concerned,
he was clearly aiming not at trial by Peers but at exemption
from all secular jurisdiction.

A committee, including Bishops, Earls, Barons, and Judges, appointed to report   The committee appointed to make a report on the
general subject of judgement by Peers was constituted in
relation rather to the far-reaching Commissions of Trailbaston, which had recently issued, than to the particular
case of the Archbishop. As enquiry was to be made of
misconduct in every department, charges might of course

----

[1] Jeremy Collier, *Eccl. Hist.* (1852), vol. iii. p. 90.   [2] *Ib.*

be made against Peers, and for this reason, perhaps, some CHAP. X.
Peers were nominated to act with other persons in these on judge-
Commissions. The committee, however, did not, as is ment by Peers in
commonly represented, consist exclusively of Peers. It 1341.
included four Bishops, four Earls, and four Barons, ' *together*
with some Sages of the Law.' Their instructions were ' to
examine in what cases the said Peers should be bound
to answer in Parliament, and in what cases not[1].'

When the report was made, it had the authority of The report was made without
the twelve Peers, but all mention of the ' Sages of the
Law' was significantly wanting. It was to the effect that the assent of the
' Peers of the Realm ought not to be arraigned or brought Judges: it
to judgement but in Parliament and by their Peers.' applied to all cases
Thereupon a new question arose—whether 'if any of the in which
Peers be or have been Chancellor, Treasurer, or other the King was a
officer whatsoever, this privilege should operate as well party.
with regard to their office as in any other manner.' In
relation to this point the Lords declared ' that all the Peers
of the Realm, officers or others, ought not, by reason of
their office, in respect of matters touching their office, or for
any other reason, to be brought to judgement, to lose their
temporalities, lands, tenements, goods, or chattels, or be
arrested or imprisoned, outlawed, or forejudged, and ought
not to answer or be judged otherwise than in full Parliament,
and before the Peers, in cases in which the King is party,
saving to our Lord the King the laws rightfully used by
due process, and saving the suit of parties.' There was an
exception, however, in cases in which any Peer had been
Sheriff or other officer and had received money by reason
of which he was bound to render an account. Then, the
Peers said, their meaning was that any such Peer should
come and account in the accustomed place (the Exchequer)
either in person or by attorney[2].

All this, be it observed, was only a report, not a judicial Protest of
decision, or an Act of Parliament, and a report made with- the Chan-cellor,
out the expressed sanction of any of the expert members of Treasurer,

[1] *Rot. Parl.*, 15 Ed. III, no. 6 (printed, vol. ii. p. 127).
[2] *Ib.*, 15 Ed. III, no. 7 (printed, vol. ii. p. 127).

CHAP. X. the Committee. There is no recorded protest on the part and Judges, of the Sages of the Law at this stage, but it is clear from against the subsequent events that they dissented. The recommenda-Act which followed. tions of the report were shortly afterwards embodied with other provisions in the instrument known as the Statute of 15 Edward III, Statute 1. It is stated in the Rolls of Parliament that all these provisions 'were made by the Magnates and Commons and shown to our Lord the King,' and that they 'were read before the King.' The Chancellor, however, the Treasurer, and some of the Justices protested that they did not assent to the making or to the form of the Statute, and that they could not observe the Statute if contrary to the laws and usages of the Realm which they were sworn to keep [1]. The Sages of the Law, constituting, at this time, a portion of 'the King in his Council in his Parliament,' considered themselves entitled to a voice in the passing of Acts of Parliament, and did not consider that this particular Act was duly passed.

The Act declared null by the King and Council.
The King permitted the Statute to be sealed, though he subsequently said, in a not very dignified manner, that in so doing he dissembled. Shortly after the Act had passed, he took counsel with Earls, Barons, and learned men (the Sages of the Law who had already expressed their dissent), and with their advice and assent declared the Statute to be null. The grounds which he assigned were that its provisions were expressly contrary to the laws and customs of the Realm, that he had never agreed to its promulgation, and that any consent which he had given to it was not given of his own free will. He added, however, that any of the articles which had already been embodied in previous Statutes should be duly observed [2].

The protest made by the Judges and the action of the

---

[1] *Rot. Parl.*, 15 Ed. III, no. 42 (printed, vol. ii. p. 131).

[2] *Rot. Lit. Claus.*, 15 Ed. III, part ii. m. 1 d (printed in Rymer's *Foedera*, vol. ii. p. 1177). The instrument is also enrolled on the Statute Roll, and printed in the Statutes of the Realm, vol. i. p. 297. This repeal (15 Ed. III, Stat. 2) has not only been admitted into the Statutes of the Realm, but has itself been repealed by the Statute Law Revision Act, 1863.

King may have been prompted, so far as the particular CHAP. X.
enactment touching the Peers was concerned, by the idea The Act
that it went beyond the provisions of Magna Charta in its formally
details. We have not now to consider whether, at this by Parlia-
period, the King had the power with the consent of ment.
a Council to revoke, annul, or repeal an Act of Parliament.
Two years later there was a more formal repeal in Parliament, which, it is to be presumed, had the consent of the
Commons as well as of the Lords, since there is nothing to
show the contrary. The words of repeal may be worth
quoting. The Statute ' shall be wholly repealed and annulled
and lose the name of a Statute, as being prejudicial and
contrary to the laws and customs of the Realm, and to the
rights and prerogatives of our Lord the King. But, for
that some articles are comprised in the same Statute which
are reasonable, and in accordance with law, it is agreed by
the Lord the King and his Council that of such articles
and others agreed in this present Parliament there be made
a Statute anew, by the advice of the Justices and other
learned men, and kept for ever[1] '

No such new Statute, however, was made with regard to *Magna*
the trial or judgement of Peers. The Statute of 15 Ed- *Charta*
ward III was ever afterwards treated by the lawyers as written law
non-existent, and Magna Charta, as confirmed by Henry III, trial of
was always considered the statutory basis of the right of Peers by
Peers to be tried by the Peers. In the reign of Henry VI, Peers.
when the existing privileges in relation to trial by Peers
were expressly extended to Peeresses, there was no
mention of any Act except Magna Charta, the operative
passage in which was quoted at length[2]. Staunford in his
Pleas of the Crown, published in the sixteenth century,
cites no authority for the principle except Magna Charta[3],
and he has been followed by a long line of eminent men.

The whole of the Parliamentary events of the fifteenth As yet no
and seventeenth years of the reign of Edward III serve to settled
principles

[1] *Rot. Parl.*, 17 Ed. III, no. 23 (printed, vol. ii. p. 139).
[2] Stat. 20 Hen. VI, cap. 9.
[3] Staunford, *Les Plees del Coron*, lib. iii. fo. 152 B.

CHAP. X.
as to trial
or matters
to be tried
by Peers.

show very clearly that the doctrine of judgement by Peers, though vaguely accepted in principle, had still not been reduced to any precise system. There is some mention of articles against Stratford, but no indication of any definite mode of procedure or of any particular charge. He was not indicted, he was not 'appealed,' and, in the later sense of the term, there is nothing to show that he was impeached. There was much talk of the judgement of Peers in full Parliament, but no indication that there could be a trial of a Peer in the Court of the Lord High Steward when Parliament was not sitting. If the committee of Lords had had their way, the effect would have been that all Crown cases in which a Peer was concerned (and not merely cases of treason and felony) would have had to be brought before the Lords in full Parliament. There can be no doubt that the lawyers did good service in opposing this pretension.

The
Statute of
Treasons
in 1351.

It was not until the year 1351 (25 Edward III) that the crime of High Treason was defined by Act of Parliament [1]. The Statute was, without doubt, in part declaratory, because there are mentioned in it offences which had previously been mentioned by Britton. The necessity of a definition, however, must have been felt at the time; and, until a definition had been given, the cases in which Peers were to be tried by their Peers could not all be specified with precision.

An Abbot,
whose pre-
decessor
had been
summoned
to Parlia-
ment, tried
for Treason
in the
King's
Bench, and
sentenced
to death
in 1357.

By the Statute of Treasons it was declared to be one of the forms of treason to counterfeit the King's coin, or to import counterfeit money. Six years after the passing of the Act, Ralph, Abbot of Missenden, was indicted for having traitorously and feloniously falsified and clipped the King's coin. His predecessors had been summoned in the forty-ninth year of the reign of Henry III to treat and advise with the other prelates and magnates. Representatives of the Commons were summoned at the same time, and the meeting was of the nature of a Parliament. It has been

[1] Stat. 25 Ed. III, cap. 2.

held that a summons to a lay Baron at this period, if Chap. X.
proved, does not give any hereditary peerage to his
descendants—possibly because, as there are no Rolls of
Parliament of the period, it would be difficult, if not
impossible, to prove that he actually sat.   No Abbot
of Missenden appears to have been summoned after the
reign of Henry III, and, therefore, possibly none had the
status of an Abbot holding in barony and liable to be
summoned.   Be that, however, as it may, the indictment
of the Abbot Ralph was in the King's Bench.   He was
arraigned in that Court and asked how he would acquit
himself of the charges.   He pleaded Not Guilty, and put
himself, for good or ill, ' on the country.'   A jury thereupon
found him guilty, and it was adjudged that he should be
drawn and hanged [1].

In this instance it is clear that no question of trial by
the Peers arose.   It may be that, notwithstanding the Act,
degrees in treason were still recognized, as in the days of
Bracton.   It may be that the Lords, who soon after
claimed to judge of matters of great moment, did not
regard a coinage case, though within the Statute of Treasons,
as a matter of high national importance.   It may be that
for some reason, the later Abbots of Missenden were not
liable to the burden or entitled to the privilege of a summons to Parliament.   It is, nevertheless, perhaps worthy of
note that the successor of an Abbot who had been summoned with other Prelates, Earls, and Barons was not tried
and did not ask to be tried by the Peers.

The right which the Peers had claimed in the year 1331 The Lords
to judge Peers and not commoners was practically renounced, claim to
or rather something higher was claimed, in the year 1387, Peers, *with*
when the Peers again came into conflict with the Sages of *others*,
the Law.   They then declared, with the King's assent, that against the
where there had been any very high crime, touching the 1387.
King's person and the state of all his realm, perpetrated
by Peers of the Realm *with others*, the cause should not be

---

[1] *Placita coram Rege*, Mich., 31 Ed. III, R°. 18 d.

CHAP. X. determined in any place but Parliament, nor by any other
law than the law and course of Parliament. It belonged,
they said, to the Lords of Parliament, and to their privilege
and liberty of 'ancient time accustomed,' to be judges in
such cases, and 'to judge thereof with the King's consent [1].'

Appeal
Treason
against the
Arch-
bishop of
York, and
Peers, and
com-
moners.

This remarkable declaration arose out of the proceedings
against Alexander Neville, Archbishop of York, Robert de
Vere, Duke of Ireland, Michael de la Pole, Duke of Suffolk,
Sir Robert Tresilian. Chief Justice of England, and Sir
Nicholas Brembre, the last two of whom, though Knights,
were not Peers of the Realm. They had been 'appealed' of
'high treasons committed by them against the King and his
realm.' The appellors were Thomas Duke of Gloucester,
Constable of England, Henry Earl of Derby, Richard Earl of
Arundel and Surrey, Thomas Earl of Warwick, and Thomas,
Earl Marshal. The King accepted the appeal, and assigned
a day to the parties to take and receive full justice upon it
at his first Parliament to be held at Westminster. By the
advice of his Council he caused proclamation to be made
through all the counties of England that all the persons
appealed should appear on the day named in Parliament.

On the appointed day the appellors prayed, in the presence of the King and the Lords of Parliament, that the
Archbishop of York, the Duke of Ireland, the Earl of Suffolk,
and the Chief Justice, all of whom were at large, might be
called to answer. They prayed that Brembre, who was in
custody, might be brought before them. The Archbishop,
Duke, Earl, and Chief Justice, when called, did not appear.
The appellors prayed the King and the Lords of Parliament
that they would record the default, and proceed to judgement thereupon. The King and Lords took time to
deliberate until the morrow.

The
Judges and
lawyers
(including
civilians)
declare

At the same time the Justices and Sergeants, and others
learned in the law of the realm, together with some learned .
in the civil law, were charged on the part of the King to
give legal advice to the Lords of the Parliament. They all

---

[1] *Rot. Parl.*, 11 Ric. II, no. 6 (printed, vol. iii. p. 236).

deliberated and gave for answer that they had seen and CHAP. X.
well understood the tenour of the appeal, and that it was the appeal
not made or affirmed in accordance with the order that to be not in
either the law of the realm or the civil law required[1].   with law.

It may, perhaps, be not unprofitable to enquire why Reason for
lawyers learned in the civil law were asked for their consulting
opinion as well as the King's Justices, and why they all civilians:
agreed that the Appeal preferred by the Lords Appellors of Chivalry.
was not made in due course of law. The civilians were
probably called in because some lawyers appear to have
held that an Appeal of Treason, the ultimate trial of which
was by battle, appertained to the jurisdiction of the Constable and Marshal, and because in this Court of Chivalry
the proceedings before ' battle joined ' were according to the
civil law[2]. The authority of this Court, if really existing,
was said to have been gained by gradual encroachment[3],
and might therefore reasonably be a subject of doubt and
dispute.

The Lords, after consultation among themselves, made The Lords,
the declaration as to their right of judgement which has King's
already been quoted. They added that the kingdom of assent,
England never heretofore was, nor, as they and the King the appeal
were minded, ever should be ruled or governed by the civil good ac-
law. A cause of such great moment as this appeal, they the laws
said, should never be tried in any place but Parliament, and course
nor by the course, process, and order in use in any lower ment.
Court in the realm. All the lower Courts had but the
execution of the ancient laws and customs of the kingdom,
and of the Ordinances and Statutes of Parliament. It was
therefore adjudged by the Lords, with the assent of the
King, that the appeal was well and duly made and affirmed,
and that the process was, according to the laws and course
of Parliament, good and effectual.

After an adjournment, the prayer that the default of the The
Archbishop of York, Duke, Earl, and Chief Justice might appeal
proceeds in

[1] *Rot. Parl.*, 11 Ric. II, no. 6 (printed, vol. iii. p. 236).
[2] *Year Book*, Easter, 36 Hen. VI, no. 8. fo. 20.
[3] Stat. 13 Ric. II, cap. 2.

CHAP. X.

Parlia-
ment.

be recorded was renewed. The Archbishop of Canterbury, and the other Spiritual Lords withdrew (after asserting their right to be present as Barons) because matters were to be brought to discussion, at which the canons did not permit them to be present.

Sentences.

The default was then formally recorded, and the appellors prayed judgement. The Temporal Lords pronounced that the Archbishop of York, the Duke of Ireland, the Earl of Suffolk, and the Chief Justice were Guilty of Treason, and passed sentence that they should be drawn and hanged. For want of precedent, however, further consideration was to be had with regard to the person of the Archbishop, whose execution was accordingly stayed. Tresilian was shortly afterwards taken, and brought into Parliament, and, having nothing to say in defence, was executed on the same day.

Trial by battle re-fused to one of the appealed, on the in-terposition of the Commons.

Sir Nicholas Brembre, who was already in custody, was brought up, and the articles of appeal were read to him ' in full Parliament.' He pleaded Not Guilty, and offered to defend by his body—that is to say claimed Trial by Battle. The Commons, however, interfered in this case. They said that what was alleged in the appeal was true, and that they would have made an accusation if the Lords had not made their appeal. It is not certain whether the Lords considered that the action of the Commons had the effect of converting the Appeal into an Impeachment, or whether they held that a commoner had no right to Trial by Battle against a Peer. For some reason, however, they decided that Trial by Battle did not lie in this case. They found Brembre Guilty, and gave judgement that he should be drawn and hanged.

Impeach-ments of Treason by the Commons heard by the Lords.

In the same Parliament the late Justices of the Court of Common Pleas, the Chief Baron of the Exchequer, and one of the King's Sergeants-at-law were impeached[1] of High Treason by the Commons. The Lords Temporal resolved that they would examine the matter and circumstances, and

---

[1] 'Accusez et empeschez,' *Rot. Parl.*, 11 Ric. II, no. 6 (printed, vol. iii. p. 240).

render thereon such judgement as should be to the honour CHAP. X.
of God, and the honour and profit of the King and his
realm. In the end they found the persons accused Guilty,
and passed judgement, but afterwards yielded to the prayer
of the Archbishop of Canterbury and other Bishops, and
remitted the sentence of death. Several other commoners
were also impeached of Treason by the Commons, and
among them some knights who pleaded Not Guilty, and
said they would acquit themselves, as knights, in such
manner as the Lords of Parliament should be pleased to
adjudge. The Temporal Lords, after deliberation, simply
found them guilty and passed sentence upon them. The
Commons further impeached the Bishop of Chichester of
Treason, and he also was found guilty by the Temporal
Lords ; but both he and the Justices whose lives had been
spared were banished to Ireland.

After these cases had been decided the Lords Spiritual
and Temporal again claimed as their liberty and privilege that matters of great moment (not simply treason
or felony) touching Peers of the Realm moved in this or
to be moved in future Parliaments, should be debated and
adjudged only according to the course of Parliament, and
not according to the civil law, or according to the common
law of the land as administered in inferior Courts. The
King allowed and approved the claim in full Parliament[1].

The Lords again assert their claim to judge in all matters of great moment affecting Peers.

The very instructive proceedings in this Parliament
reveal, as in a mirror, the hopeless confusion which prevailed in the minds of all classes, except the lawyers,
with regard to the definition of High Treason, and to the
manner in which persons accused of it, whether Peers or
commoners, ought to be tried. The House of Lords was
now shaking itself free from the Council. In the previous
reign the Chancellor and Judges had a voice and made
it heard when the King sat 'in his Council in his Parliament.' The Judges, though still formally summoned, were
now asked to give their opinions, not as having a right to

Diminished power of the Judges in Parliament.

[1] See the whole proceedings in Parliament, *Rot. Parl.*, 11 Ric. II,
no. 6 (printed, vol. iii. pp. 229-244).

CHAP. X. sit and speak their minds in the House, but merely as persons from whom the Lords could claim instruction and advice; and their deliberate opinion was contemptuously set at nought.

The rights of the Lords, as 'Lords of Parlia-ment,' not as ancient as they supposed.

The Lords insisted again and again upon their privileges as Lords of Parliament 'of ancient time accustomed.' They did not perceive, but possibly the lawyers did, that the Parliament of the reign of Richard II differed materially from any assembly known in the reign of John. Though it might be true that one of the Peers of the King's Court could claim judgement by Peers of the same Court, and though the word Parliament, when it came into fashion, might have been loosely used to express a meeting of the King's Court in earlier times, yet there is nothing to show that immediately after the Conquest, or even in the reign of Edward I, every man who owed suit to the Court could claim to be present when another man also owing suit to the Court was to be judged. According to Magna Charta he was to be judged by his peers, but it is nowhere said that the whole of his peers were to be in attendance. When Edward I summoned in one year some of his Barons, and in other years others, to consider grave matters of State, it could never have been in contemplation that all those who had ever been summoned, or their representatives, had gained a right to be present when a Peer was to be judged. The claim could have been advanced only at a time when cer-tain persons appeared to have acquired or to be acquiring a prescriptive right to be called to Parliament. The pre-scription, if it existed, was not of very ancient date. It seems, however, to have been the only warrant for the doctrine that all the Lords had the right to hear, 'in full Parliament,' every serious charge which might be made against a Peer.

No superior tribunal to call in question the prin-ciples

There is, indeed, nothing to show that the lawyers of the period laid any stress on this particular point, and their objections may have had relation only to the form in which the appeal was drawn, or absolutely to the pro-ceeding by appeal in itself. The mode of accusation had

certainly been recognized in the time of Bracton. They
may, however, have taken the view (as the famous Littleton
did in a subsequent reign) that an 'Appeal' not being at the
suit of the King, but at the suit of subjects, did not fall
within the words of Magna Charta, which refer only to
proceedings taken by or on behalf of the King himself.
They may also have considered that the articles of accusation were not in accordance with the Statute of Treasons
passed in the previous reign. These were points on which
they were more competent to give an opinion than any
other persons in the kingdom. The Lords, however, though
they may have placed themselves in a false position by
asking the advice of the Judges and then rejecting it, and
though they may have misconceived their true position in
Parliament, were yet, perhaps, from one point of view,
technically in the right. It was true, as they said, that
other Courts were inferior. It was true that the other
Courts owed their origin to the *Curia Regis* which the
Lords represented in one of its aspects. If they chose to
lay down certain principles with regard to the trial of
certain offences, and had the assent of the King, there was
no tribunal which had authority to contradict them.

It may here be worthy of remark that although the
Archbishop of York was judged by the Peers, he was not
in that respect placed on a higher level than Tresilian the
Lord Chief Justice, or even than Brembre and others who
were simple knights. Knights were appealed before the
Lords together with Peers ; a Bishop was impeached before
them together with knights. A later doctrine that a commoner could be impeached before the Lords for high misdemeanours only, and not for treason or felony [1], had not as
yet come into being, and was not finally held to be law.
Impeachment itself was of quite recent growth (the earliest
case having been in 1376) [2], and had as yet, perhaps, hardly
attained the technical signification which it acquired in

[1] 4 Bl. Com., 256-257.
[2] In that year Richard Lyons, a merchant, of London, and a
farmer of subsidies, was 'empeschez et accusez,' by the Commons,

CHAP. X. after-times.   The word had long been in use to signify any
kind of accusation in any Court, and had originally no
special reference to an accusation brought by the Commons
before the Lords.

The Com-   Towards the end of the reign of Richard II, however,
mons have
their right   impeachment by the Commons becomes a more important
to impeach factor in the history of the constitution.   In the year 1397
recorded
on the   the Commons made protestation before the King, in full
Roll of   Parliament, that they intended, by his leave, to accuse and
Parliament
in 1397.   impeach any person or persons, as often as seemed to them
good, in the Parliament then sitting.   They prayed the
King to be pleased to accept their protestation, and they
prayed that it might be entered of record on the Roll of
Parliament.

They   Richard gave his consent, and on the same day the
impeach
the Arch-   Commons impeached Thomas de Arundel, Archbishop of
bishop of   Canterbury, of High Treason, before the King, in full
Canterbury
of High   Parliament.   The King took time to consider, as the
Treason.   Archbishop was in so exalted a position and a Peer of the
Realm.   The Commons again prayed that there might be
such judgement against the Archbishop as the case demanded.   Then the King 'recorded in Parliament' that the
Archbishop had appeared before him in the presence of
certain Lords, and confessed, and put himself upon the
King's grace.   The King, and all the Temporal Lords and
Thomas de Percy (who had 'sufficient power from the
Prelates and Clergy of the kingdom of England' as
appeared of record in Parliament), adjudged the matters
admitted by the Archbishop to be Treason and the Archbishop to be a traitor.   Sentence was then delivered in
Parliament that the Archbishop should be banished from
the realm of England[1].

We here find in a very short space three very remarkable
statements:—that the Archbishop of Canterbury was a Peer
of the Realm, that the Commons were allowed to impeach

of several deceits, extortions, and other ill deeds done by him to the
King and people.   *Rot. Parl.*, 50 Ed. III, no. 17 (printed, vol. ii. p. 323).
   [1] *Ib.*, 21 Ric. II, nos. 14–16 (printed, vol. iii. p. 351).

a Peer, and that in trials in which loss of life or member
was concerned the Prelates and Clergy, though not present
in their own persons, were represented collectively by one
Procurator.

The attendance of this Procurator or proxy was altogether The Pro-
curator of
the Clergy
represents
the
Spiritual
Lords at
the trial. an innovation. It came about through a petition of the
Commons, who complained that many judgements and
ordinances previously made had been annulled because the
estate of the Clergy was not present at the time of the
making. Their prayer consequently was that the Prelates
and Clergy should appoint a Procurator with sufficient
power to consent in their name to all matters and
ordinances in Parliament. The Spiritual Lords agreed to
give their full power to a layman[1], and thus we find
'Monsieur Thomas de Percy' voting on their behalf at the
trial of an Archbishop for High Treason. The fact that
the proxy of the Prelates sat and voted on a trial for
treason would go far to show that the right to sit and vote
was now considered to be inherent in them if they chose to
exercise it. It might then very fairly be argued that if
they had the right to try other Peers they had also themselves the right to be tried by Peers if only they were
willing to exercise it.

At the end as in the earlier part of this turbulent Another
Appeal of
Treason
in Parlia-
ment: a
better
system
needed. reign. however, it is manifest that the mode of dealing
with charges of treason against Peers and others had not
been reduced to any satisfactory system. At the very time
at which an 'impeachment' was brought by the Commons
against the Archbishop of Canterbury, an 'appeal of Treason
in Parliament' was again brought by some of the Peers
against their enemies. The position of the rival factions in
1397 was the reverse of that which it had been in 1387;
and the Duke of Gloucester, the Earl of Arundel, and the
Earl of Warwick, who had previously been the appellors,
became, in their turn, the appealed[2].

[1] *Rot. Parl.*, 21 Ric. II, nos. 9–16 (printed, vol. iii. pp. 348–351).
[2] *Ib.*, 21 Ric. II, no. 1 (printed, vol. iii. p. 374), and *Ib.*, 1 Hen. IV,
nos. 1–10 (printed, vol. iii. pp. 449–452).

It seems, nevertheless, to have been generally felt, even in these troubled times, that some measures should be taken to set the law on a more secure foundation. Very important changes were consequently effected in the reign of Henry IV, as will be shown in the next chapter.

CHAPTER XI.

I N the first year of the reign of Henry IV, it was enacted CHAP. XI.
that no Appeal should be pursued in Parliament [1]. The Abolition
reason was, in all probability, the abuse of the engine of of accusation by
Appeal in the previous reign. This Statute effected a com- 'Appeal'
plete change of the law with regard to trial by Peers. The in Parlia-ment.
Appeal was the earliest form of accusation in cases of
treason, and, when it was brought against a Peer, it was
carried to a decision before the Peers of the Realm. After
this Act, however, a Peer could be judged by the Peers in
Parliament only when the proceeding was by indictment or
impeachment. At the same time a great innovation was
made by the institution of the Court of the Lord High
Steward as a Court for the trial of Peers by Peers.

The first known instance of trial in the Court of the The first
Lord High Steward occurred early in the year 1400 (the reported trial in the
year in which the Act relating to Appeals was passed). Court of
An Earl, described in the report of the proceedings as Earl the Lord High
of H., was then indicted of High Treason, in London, by Steward.
virtue of a Commission, before the Mayor and Justices.
The accusation was that he and others had agreed to make
a 'mumming' on the night of the Epiphany, during which

---

[1] Stat. 1 Hen. IV, cap. 14.

P

CHAP. XI. they intended to kill the King, who was then at Windsor. Afterwards the King directed a Commission to another Earl described as the Earl of D., in which the charge was recited. The office of Steward of England, being then vacant, was granted to the Earl of D., in order that he might sit in judgement on the Earl of H. All the Lords were commanded to be attendant upon him, as well as the Constable of the Tower, who was to bring the prisoner before him on the day which he might appoint. On that day the Lord High Steward sat apart in Westminster Hall, under a cloth of State; and the Earl of Westmoreland (who appears to have been at this time Constable of the Tower) and all the other Earls and Lords sat at a great space from him, and not on the same bench, 'but on other forms downward in the said Hall.' And all the Justices and the Barons of the Exchequer sat in the midst, around a table between the Lords. Three 'oyes' were solemnly made by the Crier, and the Commission was read. Then the Justices delivered the indictment to the Steward. . He handed it to the Clerk of the Crown, who read it to the Earl of H. The Earl confessed, and thereupon Hill, one of the King's Sergeants, prayed that the Lord Steward would give judgement. The Lord High Steward recounted the whole matter, and then gave judgement that the Earl should go back to the Tower of London, and be thence drawn to the gallows and there hanged, and 'let down' again while still living, and that his entrails should then be drawn out of his body and burned, and that he should be beheaded and quartered, 'and so may God be propitious to his soul.' The Justices said that, had the Earl chosen to deny the treason, it would have been the Steward's duty, as soon as the verdict had to be given, to ask of each Lord separately and openly what each thought in his conscience, beginning with the junior. Had the greater number said Guilty, judgement should have been given as above. 'And no Lord shall be put upon his oath in this matter[1].'

---

[1] *Year Book*, Mich., 1 Hen. IV, no. 1. fo. 1.

No less than four editions of the Year Books, all obviously
printed, either directly or indirectly, from the same manuscript, agree in the form of the report, giving only initials
instead of the names of the Earl who was indicted and of
the Earl who was Lord High Steward. Sir Edward Coke
appears to have been acquainted with the report in another
form, and tells us, with a reference to the Year Book, that
'upon the arraignment of John Holland, Earl of Huntingdon,
the first that was created Steward of England, *hac vice*. was
Edward Earl of Devon [1]. He also adds some details which
are not given in the printed books [2].

The precise date of the trial is not stated in the report,
but it must have been shortly after the commission of the
alleged offence on the sixth of January, 1399–1400. There
was then no Parliament in existence. The Parliament of
the first year of the reign of Henry IV began on St. Faith's
Day (the 6th of October), 1399 [3], and ended on Wednesday,
the 19th of November, in the same year [4]. It is therefore perfectly clear that the Earl of Huntingdon was not
tried in the House of Lords during a session of Parliament. with the Lord High Steward presiding, but in the
Court of the Lord High Steward when Parliament was not
sitting. It cannot, however, be denied that many difficulties
present themselves with regard to the proceedings. It is
asserted by some of the Chroniclers [5], and, perhaps, implied
by others that the Earl was put to death at Pleshey in
Essex without any trial at all. A contemporary says that
the Earl remained in London until the event of the
conspiracy was known, then made several attempts to
escape by sea, and was afterwards captured in Essex,
and taken to the castle of Pleshey to be held in safe
custody. According to this account he was beheaded
there on the 15th of January, in the presence of a .great

[1] 4 Inst. 59.   [2] 3 Inst. 28–29.
[3] *Rot. Parl.*, 1 Hen. IV, Heading (vol. iii. p. 415).
[4] *Ib.*, 1 Hen. IV, no. 93 (vol. iii. p. 432).
[5] The very circumstantial details in *Waurin* do not bear upon them
the impress of truth.

CHAP. XI. number of persons of the district [1]. This is not absolutely inconsistent with the law report, because the Earl may (though it is hardly probable) have been brought to London for the trial, may have been sent back to Pleshey, from the Tower, and may have been there put to death in due course of execution, or by a mob which overpowered the King's officers, and took the law into its own hands. The report is to some extent confirmed by independent testimony. On the 10th of January Thomas de Arundel, Archbishop of Canterbury, wrote a letter in which he described the Earl as being held captive by the King's power [2]. The date is five days earlier than the alleged beheading at Pleshey, and the interval afforded sufficient time to bring the Earl to the Tower, to try him, and even to send him back to Pleshey. Moreover, on the very same 10th of January, the King, with the advice of the Council, sent a precept to the Constable of the Tower to receive the Earl of Huntingdon from the person who would deliver the prisoner into his custody, on the King's behalf [3].

Subsequent judgement by the Lords Temporal with the assent of the King. These contemporary documents of undoubted authority would suffice to outweigh any statements of Chroniclers to the effect that the Earl was put to death without trial, were there not a document also of the highest authority which is apparently on the other side. In the following year (1401) all the Lords Temporal present in Parliament, with the assent of the King, declared and adjudged that Thomas Holland late Earl of Kent, John Holland late Earl of Huntingdon and others were traitors, as having levied war against the King, and that they should forfeit all the lands and tenements which they had in fee simple, notwithstanding the fact that while levying war they had been beheaded by the King's lieges without due process of law [4]. It is quite clear, from this passage, either that the Earl of Huntingdon

---

[1] Walsingham, *Ypodeigma Neustriae* (Rolls Series), p. 390; *Historia Anglicana* (Rolls Series), vol. ii. p. 245.

[2] *Literae Cantuarienses* (Rolls Series), vol. iii. p. 74.

[3] *Rot. Lit. Claus.*, 1 Hen. IV, m. 22 (printed in Rymer's *Foedera*).

[4] *Rot. Parl.*, 2 Hen. IV, no. 30 (printed, vol. iii. p. 459).

was never tried in the Court of the Lord High Steward, or CHAP. XI.
that, if he was, the trial was not recognized by the Temporal
Lords as being in due legal form.

This declaration of the Lords Temporal was in the form
of an Act of Attainder, but without the assent either of the
Lords Spiritual or of the Commons. It may, however, have
been merely a measure of precaution, so far as the Earl of
Huntingdon was concerned. As there was no precedent
for the trial of a Peer when Parliament was not sitting, it
may well have been thought that the effect of the judgement
in the Court of the Lord High Steward was doubtful
with regard to the forfeiture of lands, and that a deliberate
statement in Parliament by the Temporal Lords, who
would in fact have given judgement in Parliament in earlier
times, would serve to prevent any subsequent dispute. It
is impossible to believe that the report in the Year Book,
confirmed as it is by contemporary evidence, was a pure
invention.

We learn from this case that an indictment for High The
Treason against a Temporal Lord was now removed from Spiritual
Lords were
the inferior Court in which it had been found, and brought not tried
before Peers of the Realm for trial. When a Spiritual by Peers
of the
Lord was indicted there was no such removal, the reason Realm,
being, to all appearance, that the Spiritual Lords would not
recognize any lay jurisdiction, and consequently could not
claim the privilege of peerage.

Thomas Merkes, Bishop of Carlisle, had been suspected Thomas
of complicity in the conspiracy of the Earl of Kent and the Merkes,
Bishop of
Earl of Huntingdon, but he was not treated as a Peer of the Carlisle,
indicted
Realm, and does not seem to have made any claim to be of High
tried by the Peers. A commission of Oyer and Terminer Treason.
issued, before which the Bishop was indicted of High
Treason. The Justices of Oyer and Terminer sent their
precept to the Sheriffs of London to summon a jury of
Aldermen and Citizens. The Bishop was brought up by
the Constable of the Tower.

The King directed his 'writ close' to the Justices with
reference to a Statute of the reign of Edward III, in which

CHAP. XI. it had been provided that no Archbishop or Bishop should be accused before Justices of any crime without the King's express command [1]. By the advice of his Council he now directed that if any Archbishops or Bishops were accused or indicted before them they were to proceed as they should see fit, in accordance with right, and the law and custom of the realm. The Bishop was arraigned and asked how he would acquit himself. He said that he was a Bishop anointed, that under the name of Bishop he was indicted, and that he did not think he ought to be arraigned in respect of the crime before the Justices, or that he ought to make any answer. If, however, it should appear to the Justices that by the law of the land he was bound to answer, he was prepared with the answer which he should give. The Justices told him that the charges contained in the indictment extended to the death of the King, and the destruction of the whole realm of England, and consequently the manifest subversion of that Anglican Church in virtue of which he claimed to be privileged. Each and all of these matters, they said, were High Treason in the extreme degree, and the Bishop must answer at his peril or else be straightway held convicted.

Pleads, with a saving only for his ecclesiastical liberty, and is convicted by a jury.

The Bishop said that, saving his ecclesiastical liberty, inasmuch as he was a Bishop anointed, and under protest that his answer must not derogate from the episcopal privilege or dignity, nor be drawn into a precedent with regard to the dignity of others, he pleaded Not Guilty of the treasons and felonies alleged, and thereof for good and evil he put himself upon the jury. The jury found him Guilty. The Justices, not being sufficiently advised with regard to the judgement which should be pronounced, remanded him to the Tower for safe keeping.

Is pardoned by the King.

The indictment and subsequent proceedings were afterwards removed into the King's Bench. In the meantime Merkes ceased to be Bishop of Carlisle, having been translated by the Pope to the Bishopric of Cephalonia. When

[1] Stat. 18 Ed. III, cap. 1.

he was brought into the King's Bench, it was as 'Thomas CHAP. XI.
Merkes late Bishop of Carlisle,' and no longer as an English
Bishop. He was then asked whether he had anything to
say wherefore the Court should not proceed to judgement
against him on the conviction. For reply he only produced
the King's charter of pardon[1].

It will be observed that. from first to last, the Bishop Never
never claimed privilege of peerage. As Becket and Strat- claimed
privilege of
ford had done before him, he denied that he was amenable peerage.
to the secular jurisdiction. He would have exemption or
nothing. To him all lay Courts were alike. Had he asked
for trial by the Peers he would at once have abandoned the
point for which he and his order were contending. If
compelled to plead he would plead, and if he must accept
a verdict he would accept it; but it was a matter of absolute
indifference to him whether the verdict was given by Aldermen and Citizens or by Barons and Earls.

The mode of trial by Peers seems to have remained Absence
in want of clear definition during some subsequent reigns. of settled
rules for
Charges of heresy and sorcery became confused with trial by
charges of High Treason. If any one compassed the Peers.
death of the sovereign by making a waxen image of him
and slowly melting it before a fire, the acts were, from
one point of view, sorcery, from another point of view
High Treason. In the nineteenth year of the reign of
Henry VI the Duchess of Gloucester was brought before
a tribunal consisting of the King, Cardinal Beaufort,
Cardinal Kempe, five Bishops, and some other ecclesiastics,
and sitting in St. Stephen's Chapel, at Westminster. She
was accused of having, with the aid of a woman known
as the witch of Eye, had a waxen image of the King made
and set before a fire, with the design that, as it slowly lost
its form, the King might, through her incantations, slowly
sink into the grave. The offence actually charged against
her was witchcraft, of which she was pronounced guilty, and

---

[1] The whole of these proceedings appear in the *Placita coram Rege,
Rex* (i. e. the Crown Roll of the King's Bench), Hilary, 2 Hen. IV,
R⁰. 4.

Chap. XI. for which she was sentenced to a very humiliating penance, and sent off to die a prisoner in the Isle of Man[1].

Act of Henry VI for the trial of Duchesses, Countesses, and Baronesses, by Peers. Before this time there had been no settled rule with regard to the trial of Peeresses for high treason, or felony, or misprision of either. Duchesses, Marchionesses, and Viscountesses were of comparatively recent origin, as were the titles of Duke, Marquis, and Viscount. There had now and again been a Countess in her own right, and there had been Countesses who were the wives of Earls. The great majority of the baronage, however, consisted of persons who were only Barons; but 'Baron,' as has been shown elsewhere, was not a term of dignity in the same sense as Earl. Except in the sense of a woman holding by barony, the term Baroness hardly appears to have been known before the fifteenth century. The wife of a Baron had no legal name except that of wife of her husband[2], and before the case of the Duchess of Gloucester there had been no special reason for considering how Peeresses ought to be tried.

As a seat in the House of Lords was now regarded as an honour rather than a burden, and as the idea of strict hereditary right was established, it was natural that the position of women who were either themselves of noble

[1] *Rot. Lit. Pat.*, 19 Hen. VI, part ii. m. 16 (printed in Rymer's *Foedera*, x. 851); Fabyan, 19 Hen. VI; *Political Poems and Songs*, Ed. Wright, vol. ii. pp. 205-208.

[2] So, in the reign of Edward VI, it was held that, when the widow of a Baron married an Esquire, she could not be correctly described in a writ as 'Lady,' bearing her former husband's title. A writ of partition was brought against the Duke of Suffolk, and others, by 'Ranulph Haward Esquire, and the Lady Anna Powes, his wife.' Exception was taken to this description as being a misnomer, 'because she ought to have been named by the name of her husband and not otherwise.' Chief Justice Montague and Justice Hales were of opinion that the exception was good, 'because by the law of God the woman was under the power of her husband (*sub potestate viri*), and so her name of dignity should be changed in accordance with his degree, notwithstanding the courtesy shown to ladies of rank and of the Court.' The plaintiffs accordingly brought another writ in which they were described as Ranulph Haward and 'Anna his wife, late wife of Lord Powes, deceased.' Dyer's Reports, M. 6 & 7 Ed. VI, no. 51. fo. 79 b.

blood or were the wives of Peers should be considered.
The trial of the Duchess of Gloucester for sorcery was
a blow struck through her at the Duke of Gloucester by
his enemy Cardinal Beaufort.   In spite of faction, it was
the interest of all the Temporal Lords that they should
not have their dignity indirectly assailed in the persons
of their wives.   For this reason probably an Act was
passed in the following year touching the mode of trial
of 'ladies of high estate, Duchesses, Countesses, or
Baronesses.' They, whether married or sole, were, when
indicted of high treason or felony, to be brought to answer
and judged before Judges and Peers of the Realm in the
same manner as Peers would be judged if indicted or
impeached of the same offences [1]. The legislators of the
day, however, abstained from defining in precise terms
what that mode of trial was.

Though accusation by appeal in Parliament was abolished,
the accusation by appeal elsewhere was still a recognized
mode of procedure.   If a Peer, or a Lady of the rank
mentioned in the Act of Henry VI, committed a murder,
or other felony, there was nothing to prevent recourse to
an appeal against him, or her.   The widow, for instance,
of a peasant might 'appeal' a Duke for the murder of
her husband.   In the reign of Edward IV the famous
Judge Littleton, author of the well-known work on tenures,
enunciated the doctrine that, when an 'appeal' was
brought against a 'Lord of the Realm,' he not only should
not be tried by the Peers in Parliament, but should not
be tried by Peers at all.   He should be tried just as any
common person [2].   A precedent, too, was cited in the case
of Lord Gray of Codnor.   This continued to be the law until
the year 1819, when all proceedings by appeal, together
with trial by battle, were abolished [3].

When, on the other hand, said Littleton, there is an
indictment of felony or treason, which is at the King's

No trial by Peers in procedure by 'Appeal' of murder, &c.

Court of the High Steward,

[1] Stat. 20 Hen. VI, cap. 9.
[2] *Year Book*, Easter, 10 Ed. IV, no. 17. fo. 6.
[3] Stat. 59 Geo. III, cap. 46.

CHAP. XI. suit, as distinguished from that of a subject, a Peer of
apart from the Realm is to be tried by the Peers. Upon the indict-
Parlia-
ment, ment of a Lord, he added, the matter is to be sent into
hardly Parliament, and there the Steward of England is to put
recognized
in the reign him to answer. It appears from this that the Court of
of Edward the Lord High Steward, sitting independently of Parliament,
IV.
was hardly yet recognized as a proper tribunal for the
trial of Peers, though the Lord High Steward might
preside at the trial in the House of Lords.

Right of   Littleton also made another remarkable statement—that
Spiritual
Lords to be when a Peer is put to answer in Parliament, the Spiritual
present by Lords, who cannot consent to the death of a man, are to
one Pro-
curator, make a Procurator to represent them. It thus appears
throughout that a lawyer of no less eminence than Littleton still
the trial of
a Peer, still recognized the right of the Spiritual Lords to be pre-
recognized. sent, by a collective proxy, at the trial of a Peer, and
so practically attributed to them all the privileges of
peerage.

The Court   Not very long after this time, however, the Court of the
of the Lord
High Lord High Steward, sitting when there was no Parliament,
Steward became an accepted institution. When the jurisdiction
fully
recognized of the Lords had been delegated to this Court, it soon
in the reign became customary for the Steward to summon, not the
of Henry
VII: how whole, but only a small number of the Peers. For the trial
constituted. of the Earl of Warwick in the reign of Henry VII, he was
commanded to summon such and so many Lords, peers of
the Earl, as might make the truth the better be known.
Twenty-two only in addition to the Lord High Steward,
constituted the Court. One was a Duke, four were Earls,
and the rest (including John Kendall, the Prior of the
military order of St. John of Jerusalem in England) were
Barons [1]. At the trial of the Duke of Buckingham, in
the thirteenth year of the reign of Henry VIII, there
were nineteen Peers present, of whom one was Thomas,
Docwra, Prior of St. John of Jerusalem in England ; and

[1] *Baga de Secretis*, Pouch II, mm. 1, 2, 3 (Calendared by Sir F.
Palgrave in the Third Report of the Deputy Keeper of the Records,
App. 2. p. 218).

the Prior gave his vote declaring the Duke guilty[1]. This, CHAP. XI.
however, was the last time that a Prior of St. John of
Jerusalem sat in the Court of the Lord High Steward ;
and the corporation of the Knights of St. John was dissolved
in the thirty-second year of the same reign[2]. Those who
afterwards sat in the Court of the Lord High Steward,
were exclusively Peers possessing some heritable dignity,
which no Prior, as Head of the Hospital of St. John in
England, had ever enjoyed.

The practice of summoning only a small number of
Peers to the Court of the Lord High Steward, which
continued for many generations, naturally gave almost
unlimited power to the Crown of securing a conviction.
It also had an important effect in finally extinguishing
the claims of the Spiritual Lords to the rank of Peer
of the Realm. As they could not pass sentence it was
idle to summon any of them to attend. As the members
of the Court were limited in number there was not the
slightest necessity to summon the Procurator of the
Spiritual Lords as a body, even had he had power to
act ; and as he was only their Procurator in Parliament,
it seems doubtful whether he could have sat in the Court
of the Lord High Steward.

, As has been shown, in another chapter, the Spiritual The
Lords began to be called 'Lords of Parliament' and not Spiritual
Peers of the Realm in the reign of Henry VII. They represented
had for centuries struggled to be free from all lay juris- in it : their
diction, and now the Nemesis had come. The Court of the status
the Lord High Steward was one of the engines for their of peerage.
degradation. It was a Court in which they could not
sit, but one in which a true Peer of the Realm could give
verdict and judgement. They were thus marked off from
the peerage by a disqualification of no small importance.
According to their own showing, or that of their predecessors, they were not to be tried by the Peers when accused

[1] *Baga de Secretis*, Pouch IV, Bundle 5. m. 30 (Calendared, p. 233).
[2] Stat. 32 Hen. VIII, cap. 24.

CHAP. XI. of treason or felony; by the march of events they were now precluded even from being present at the arraignment of a Peer according to the most ordinary form of proceeding. It is obvious that only a little was needed to deprive them of the right to be called Peers at all. The reign of Henry VIII was most disastrous to their order, and when the monasteries were dissolved and the Abbots ceased to sit in the House of Lords, the Bishops had no power to enforce a right which the injudicious action of their predecessors had forfeited.

Case of Fisher in the reign of Henry VIII.
One of the most remarkable facts in relation to the history of Trial by Peers is that the advocates of the rights of the Spiritual Lords, and the advocates of the opposite doctrine, have alike cited the case of John Fisher, sometime Bishop of Rochester, as an instance in which a Bishop was tried otherwise than by the Peers of the Realm. The one party would have done well to place no reliance on the precedent, the other might have spared itself some unnecessary lamentations.

He was not a Bishop when tried for High Treason.
The Bishop of Rochester was never tried at all. John Fisher was attainted for misprision of Treason by Act of Attainder in the year 1534 [1], deprived of his bishopric, and kept a prisoner in the Tower. He was afterwards indicted before a special commission of Oyer and Terminer for High Treason in having denied the King's supremacy. There were two distinct indictments. In one of them he was described as John Fisher, late Bishop of Rochester. In the other he was described as ' John Fisher, late of the City of Rochester, in the County of Kent, Clerk, otherwise called John Fisher, Bishop of Rochester,' and, in another place, as in the first indictment, as ' late Bishop of Rochester.' Upon the administration of interrogatories to witnesses in the Tower of London on the 7th of June, 1535, he was described as ' late Bishop of Rochester.' Upon the administration of interrogatories to himself on the following 12th of June, he was described as ' Mr. John

---

[1] Act of 26 Hen. VIII, cap. 3.

Fisher, D.D.[1] He laid no claim to any kind of privilege, CHAP. XI.
either as a Peer or as a Bishop, because, as he was no longer
a Bishop, he certainly had no other title to be considered
a Peer. A jury was empanelled from the neighbourhood
of the Tower of London. Of the twelve who were sworn
two were Knights and the rest Esquires, and they found
him guilty[1]. The legality of the form of proceeding was
never questioned.

Though, however, Fisher was neither indicted nor tried *Cranmer, in the reign of Mary, was tried, while Archbishop of Canterbury, and sentenced, for High Treason, in a Court of Oyer and Terminer.* while an English Bishop, there is no reason to suppose
that had he still been an English Bishop his trial would
have been different. In the first year of the reign of
Queen Mary, Thomas Cranmer, Archbishop of Canterbury,
was brought to trial before a Special Commission of Oyer
and Terminer on an indictment found in the King's Bench.
When arraigned he pleaded not guilty, and put himself
' upon the country,' which was a jury from the county
of Middlesex. Before they retired to consider their
verdict, but after sufficient and probable evidence had been
given on the part of the Queen, as is stated in the record,
the Archbishop withdrew his plea, and pleaded guilty.
Judgement passed in the usual form[2].

The Archbishop thus clearly admitted the jurisdiction *It has since been settled law that Bishops have no right to be tried by Peers of the Realm.* of the Court, and the power of a jury to pronounce whether
he was guilty or not guilty. He could not, from his
antecedents, deny, as Orleton and Stratford had denied,
the jurisdiction of any secular Court. He made no claim
to be tried by the Peers, and no exception was ever taken
to the validity of the proceedings. From this time onwards,
notwithstanding some protests on the part of ecclesiastical
historians, it seems to have been settled law that Bishops
do not enjoy the right of being tried by Peers of the
Realm, either in Parliament, or in the Court of the Lord
High Steward[3].

[1] *Baga de Secretis*, Pouch VII, Bundle 2.
[2] *Ib.*, Pouch XXIII.
[3] Staunford, *Les Plees del Coron*, p. 153; 3 Inst. 30; and many
subsequent authorities.

CHAP. XI.   Spiritual Lords have been, with commoners, 'appealed'
No instance of Treason, and judged by Peers. They have been tried
in which a by the Lords when impeached, as commoners have also.
Spiritual
Lord, in- They have, however, never successfully asserted the ex-
dicted of
Treason or clusive privilege of being tried, as only Peers are tried,
Felony, by Peers alone, upon an indictment of treason or felony,
has been
tried by or misprision of either, found in a Court below, and removed
Peers of into the House of Lords, or into the Court of the Lord
the Realm.
High Steward. It may be that the right was, in early
times, inherent in them, as Peers of the King's Court
holding in barony. If so, it was a right which they did
not choose to enforce, and which even they rejected with
contumely. They again and again expressed their determination to be free not from the jurisdiction of those
among the King's Courts which were inferior to the House
of Lords, but from all secular jurisdiction whatever.

Effect of   The Bishops were never in a position to recover, after
the aboli-
tion of the complete abolition of the feudal tenures at the time
feudal of the Restoration, the privilege which they had in earlier
tenures
on the times rejected. As it was in origin one belonging to the
Bishops feudal *Pares Curtis* or *Curiae*, there was no title on which
after the
Restora- they could rest their claim to it when the King's feudal
tion. Court had come to an end. The privileges of the
Temporal Lords were continued by the Act which
ended tenure by military service, but no privileges could
be continued which were not recognized as being in
existence.

The   When, however, the feudal system was formally abolished
privileges
of peerage in England, the doctrines relating to blood which had
afterwards grown up with it continued to maintain their ground. The
held to
depend on descent of lands, and the descent of dignities remained
blood. precisely as they were before. The result was that nobility
of blood became of even greater importance than ever.
It was from nobility of blood alone that the only persons
now recognized as Peers derived their claims and their
privileges. Their ancestors had owed and rendered services
to the State, which they were no longer under any
obligation to yield. Their blood was the source of their

dignity, and they regarded the admission of a new man
to their order as a very high honour, especially as the
blood of the new-comer became ennobled like their own.

It was from this point of view that the right of trial And among
by Peers was now regarded. The Bishops, it was said, privilege
by the clearest and most popular exponent of English of trial
Law in the eighteenth century, 'have no right to be tried of the
in the Court of the Lord High Steward, and therefore Realm.
surely ought not to be Judges there. For the privilege
of being thus tried depends upon nobility of blood rather
than a seat in the House, as appears from the trial of
Popish Lords [while incapable of a seat there], of Lords
under age, and since the Union [with Scotland] of the
Scots nobility, though not in the number of sixteen
[representative Peers], and from the trials of females, such
as the Queen Consort or Dowager, and of all Peeresses
by birth, and Peeresses by marriage also, unless they
have, when Dowagers, disparaged themselves by taking
a commoner to their second husband[1].'

A Peeress by marriage, it will be observed, is not
necessarily herself of noble blood, and may enjoy her
privilege in virtue of the blood of her husband. This,
however, is quite in accordance with the old common
law of England, according to which a married woman
has no name and no condition except that of wife of her
husband. The doctrine of blood is thus made quite
consistent with itself, as the foundation of all the privileges
of Peerage. It will nevertheless be apparent to every
one who has read these pages that although there was
continuity of descent, the Peerage after the Restoration,
and its privilege of trial by Peers, rested on a different
foundation from that of the Peerage existing before the
Great Rebellion.

The old forms, however, survived, and the Court of Survival of
the Lord High Steward, and the general principles relating of the Lord
to the trial of Peers remained as they had been in the High
days of Henry VIII. The privilege in relation to trial as it had

[1] 4 Bl. Com. 262.

CHAP. XI. by Peers had been carefully guarded on the passing of
been in the every new Act relating to treason or felony.
reign of   Thus when, in the reign of Henry VIII, an Act was
Henry
VIII.   passed concerning the trial and punishment of murder
Privilege and bloodshed within the limits of the King's palace or
of trial
by Peers house, it was expressly provided that the trial of Peers
guarded in for any of the offences mentioned should remain as before [1].
successive
Acts.   So also when certain treasons and misprisions of treason
committed out of the realm were made triable in England,
the privilege of Peers to have trial by their peers, after
indictment, was expressly saved to them [2]. Again, when
on the accession of Elizabeth an Act was passed in relation
to ecclesiastical jurisdiction, by which certain penalties
were provided for certain offences against the Act, and
certain offences were made treason, a Peer indicted of
treason was to have trial by his peers 'in such manner
and form as in other cases of treason hath been used [3].'
On the restoration of Charles II an Act was passed for
his protection, to remain in force only during his life, and
once more it was provided that no Peer should be tried
for any offence under the Act, except by his peers, though,
upon conviction, he was to be disabled for life for sitting
in Parliament unless he received the King's pardon [4].

Act of   During all this time a Peer could, upon indictment of
William
III: all high treason or felony, claim to be tried by Peers of the
the Peers Realm, but not necessarily by the whole of the Peers.
to be
summoned   In the reign of William III, however, an Act was passed
on trial of which had the effect of placing the jurisdiction in trials
a Peer
for certain for treason in the whole body of Peers whether Parliament
Treasons   was sitting or not [5]. After reciting that 'upon trials of Peers
only.

[1] Stat. 33 Hen. VIII, cap. 12. sec. 20.
[2] Stat. 35 Hen. VIII, cap. 2. sec. 2.
[3] Stat. 1 Eliz., cap. 1. sec. 34.
[4] Stat. 13 Car. II, stat. 1. cap. 1. sec. 7.
[5] Stat. 7 Will. III, cap. 3. sec. 11. It has sometimes been argued
that the Lords Spiritual are included in the word 'peers' in this Act;
but as they could not 'vote at the trial,' and have always withdrawn
before judgement, it seems clear that they are excluded.

or Peeresses a major vote is sufficient either to acquit or Chap. XI. to condemn,' the Statute provided that upon the trial of any Peer or Peeress either for treason or misprison of treason, all the Peers who have a right to sit and vote in Parliament shall be duly summoned, and that every Peer summoned and appearing shall vote at the trial. The Act did not extend to proceedings by impeachment, nor did it extend to indictments for counterfeiting the coin of the realm, the Great Seal, the Privy Seal, the Sign Manual, or the Privy Signet, and no mention was made in it of any kind of felony.

The benefit of this Act was extended to offences declared Extended under Queen Anne. to be High Treason by another Act passed in the reign of Queen Anne[1]. These had relation to the government of the Queen's land-forces when serving out of England or Ireland. They included correspondence or treating with the Queen's enemies, or rebels, without her licence, or that of the Commander-in-Chief[2]. Other offences— those of raising sedition or mutiny in the army, refusing to obey, striking or resisting a superior officer—were made felonies[3]. Any Peer of the Realm who had, beyond sea, committed any treason or felony mentioned in the Act, and who had not already been tried by martial law, but had been indicted after his return, was to have his trial by Peers according to custom[4].

In the reign of Queen Anne also provision was made The trial of Peers of Great Britain committing Treason or Felony in Scotland : Acts of Queen Anne and George IV. for the indictment of Peers of Great Britain who had committed 'high treason, petit treason, misprision of treason, murder, or other felonies' in Scotland[5]. No provision, however, was made as to the mode of trial after indictment, except that the proceedings were to be 'in the same method' as those following any inquisition found before Justices of Oyer and Terminer in England. Some doubts subsequently arose with regard to the interpretation of the Act, and it was declared in the reign of George IV,

[1] Stat. 2 & 3 Anne, cap. 20. sec. 43.
[2] Sec. 34.   [3] Sec. 35.   [4] Sec. 42.
[5] Stat. 6 Anne, cap. 23 (or 78). sec. 12.

†   Q

CHAP. XI. that the crimes in respect of which the Commission in the nature of a Commission of Oyer and Terminer might enquire in Scotland were 'all treasons, misprisions of treason, murders, and other crimes which infer a capital punishment by the law of Scotland, and all felonies and other crimes for which, if committed in England, a Peer of the United Kingdom would be tried by his Peers,' but that it should 'not be lawful for the Court of Justiciary, or any other Court in Scotland, to take cognizance of any of the aforesaid crimes; but such Courts shall and may try all other crimes committed by Peers in Scotland, if otherwise competent to try such crimes by the law of Scotland[1].' It was at the same time declared that the provisions of the explaining Act should extend to all Peeresses in their own right, to all wives of Peers, and to all widows of Peers not married to commoners who should commit crimes in Scotland[2]. It was further declared that the Act should not apply to any Peer of Ireland while a member of the House of Commons[3], and finally that it should not alter or affect any law in force with regard to the trial of Peers for high treason or misprision of treason[4].

Privilege confirmed in 1862 in relation to offences under the Mutiny Acts.

In the year 1862 an Act[5] was passed for the more speedy trial of certain homicides committed by persons subject to the Mutiny Acts, and it was again expressly provided that no one claiming the privilege of peerage should be rendered triable under the provisions of the Act[6].

Thus the privilege of trial by Peers has been the most jealously preserved of all the privileges of Peers, from the time of its establishment to the present. Under the Act of William III, indeed, it was strengthened in relation to charges of treason, or misprision of treason in general, though not in relation to some excepted forms of treason, or to felony or misprision of felony. With regard to the

---

[1] Stat. 6 Geo. IV, cap. 66. sec. 1.   [2] Sec. 12.
[3] Sec. 13.   [4] Sec. 14.
[5] Stat. 25 & 26 Vict., cap. 65.   [6] Sec. 19.

last the law remained, to all appearance, as it was before, CHAP. XI.
and it would seem that, if Parliament were not sitting,
a Peer could be tried in the Court of the Lord High
Steward consisting of a limited number of Peers.

It is, perhaps, open to question whether a Peer could Question
waive his privilege of being tried by Peers of the Realm. whether
The Committee of twelve Lords reported in 1341 that any privilege
submission by a Peer to the jurisdiction of an inferior Court of trial by
ought not to prejudice other Peers, or even himself, on any be waived.
subsequent occasion[1]. The possibility of a Peer waiving
his privilege seems, therefore, to have been then assumed.
Under the Act of 1862 it is only a person claiming privilege who is exempted from the jurisdiction thereby
established; and the omission of the claim would appear
to cause the loss of the privilege, so far as any offences
under that particular Act are concerned. As a general
principle, however, Sir Edward Coke[2] maintained that
a Peer has no power of waiver. He founded his opinion
on a decision to that effect in the case of Lord Dacre of
the North in the reign of Henry VIII, and on the twenty-
ninth chapter of Magna Charta.

As between Sovereign and Peers, and as between Peers In trials of
and Peers, however, there is no doubt that every Peer indict-
(including those of Scotland, and of Ireland) has a right, ments of
when indicted of High Treason, of Felony, or of misprision Felony, the
of either, to be tried by Peers. When Parliament is sitting judgement
he has a right to be tried in the House of Lords (technically of the
known as the Court of our Lady the Queen in Parliament), Temporal
and when Parliament is not sitting, in the Court of the alone.
Lord High Steward. In the former case the Spiritual
Lords may be present, as they are required to be according
to the Constitutions of Clarendon, up to the point at which
judgement is to be given, when they have to withdraw,
and have always withdrawn, in compliance with the canons
of the Church. Though present in full Parliament, as Lords
of Parliament, during the early stages of the trial of Peers,

[1] *Rot. Parl.*, 15 Ed. III, no. 7 (printed, vol. ii. p. 127).
[2] 3 Inst. 30.

CHAP. XI. they have never been summoned, as Peers, to the Court of the Lord High Steward, and the only judgement which can be pronounced upon any Temporal Lord, or upon any Peer who is not a Lord of Parliament, on indictments of Treason, Felony, or misprision of either, is that of the Lords Temporal.

Doctrines as to impeachment after the reign of Richard II. The wavering attitude of the Lords in relation to accusations against commoners in the reigns of Edward III and Richard II, and the trials by them of commoners impeached of High Treason in the reign of Richard II, have already been mentioned. In subsequent reigns the trial, before the Lords, of impeachments formulated by the Commons appears to have been a fully recognized institution, though it is sometimes lost from view during considerable intervals of time, and though disputes arose with regard to the offences to which it was applicable.

Among the earliest instances of impeachment are accusations of High Treason brought against persons who were not Peers of the Realm ; and it is strange that so eminent a lawyer as Blackstone should have committed himself to the statement that a commoner could be impeached only of high misdemeanours[1]. As in other matters, the rare use of a particular mode of proceeding and the long intermissions of Parliaments tended, without doubt, to cause uncertainty on the subject of impeachment. The more recent cases were naturally those to which most attention was paid.

Bill of Attainder the more common mode of proceeding. Although there were 'impeachments' in the reign of Henry IV, and even of Henry VI, there were none between the year 1449 (when the Duke of Suffolk was impeached) and the year 1621 (when accusations were made against Sir Giles Mompesson), unless the doubtful case of the Bishop of London in 1534 be regarded as one. There had always been some confusion between the judicial and legislative powers of the Lords, and thus the proceeding by Bill of Attainder appears, for a very long time, to have

[1] 4 Com. 256-257.

superseded the proceeding by impeachment when, at any CHAP. XI.
rate, the offence alleged was High Treason. This may have
tended to obscure the right of the Commons to impeach
a commoner of treason, and the jurisdiction of the Lords to
try him. The subject was still further complicated by the
usual practice of introducing a Bill of Attainder first in the
House of Lords.

Even the impeachment of Mompesson by the House of Hesitation
Commons, in 1621, was effected in a manner which showed as to the
mode of
some hesitation as to the mode of taking action. He was conducting
the im-
accused, not of High Treason, but of high crimes and peachment
misdemeanours. The Commons had a search made for of Mompesson in
precedents, and came to the conclusion that there was no 1621.
power in their own House to inflict any punishment for an
offence of a general character, and not merely affecting the
privileges of their House. They desired a conference with
the House of Lords, and at the conference described in
general terms the nature of the charge, but they did not
draw up, in accordance with the later practice, specific
articles of accusation. The Lords, having found Mompesson guilty, sent a message to the Commons to the
effect that they were prepared to give judgement. The
Speaker, attended by the Commons, then demanded judgement at the bar of the House of Lords, and it was given
accordingly [1].

Within a few days of the impeachment of Mompesson, Pro-
the Commons proceeded, in a not very confident manner, ceedings on
the im-
to impeach one of the greatest, if not the best of men. peachment
A committee was appointed to enquire into abuses in the of Francis
Bacon,
courts of justice. A series of reports was made. Twenty- Viscount
St. Albans.
eight specific charges of corruption were drawn up against
Francis Bacon, Viscount St. Albans, Lord High Chancellor
of England, and laid before the House of Lords in writing,
but Sir Edward Coke was to move that this should not be
drawn into a precedent. Being in ill health, the Chancellor

---

[1] *Journals of the House of Commons*, Feb. 27, 28, and March 3,
1620–1621 (vol. i. pp. 530–532, 535–537), and *Journals of the House of
Lords*, March 26, 1621 (vol. iii. p. 72).

CHAP. XI. sent to the Lords a written statement, in which he confessed his guilt in general terms, and prayed for mercy. With this the Lords were not satisfied, and required him to answer the articles of accusation, one by one. He then made a further 'humble confession and submission,' admitting that there was at least some foundation for each of the charges, and, with an appeal for mercy, concluded: 'I do plainly and ingenuously confess that I am guilty of corruption, and do renounce all defence[1].'

After steps had been taken to ascertain from the sick Chancellor that his confession was indeed his own, the Lord Treasurer and others went to his bedside, and received from his hands the Great Seal. On May 2, 1621, the Gentleman Usher and the Sergeant-at-Arms received instructions from the House of Lords to summon him to appear in person on the following morning, when judgement was to be delivered. He was unable to attend. The articles of impeachment and his confession were read in his absence, and, on the question being put, it was agreed that he was guilty. The Bishops were present, and there was no dissentient. A message was sent to the Commons that the Lords 'were ready to give judgement against Lord Viscount St. Albans, if the Commons should come to demand it.' The Speaker of the Commons then came to the Bar of the House of Lords and demanded judgement against the Lord Chancellor, as his offences required. The sentence was that he should pay a fine of £40,000, be imprisoned in the Tower of London during the King's pleasure, be for ever incapable of holding any public office, place, or employment, and never sit in Parliament or come within the verge of the Court[2].

Discretion of the Lords as to punishment.   This judgement illustrates the power or discretion of the House in relation to punishment, when capital offences are not in question. It was also exercised in the

---

[1] *Journals of the House of Commons*, beginning March 15, 1620–1621 (vol. i. p. 554), and *Journals of the House of Lords*, March 19, 20, 1620–1621, April 14, 30, 1621, and May 3, 1621 (vol. iii. pp. 51–52, 53–55, 84–86, 98–101, 105–106).

[2] *Journals of the House of Lords*, May 3, 1621 (vol. iii. pp. 105–106).

same year, in a fashion which to modern eyes seems cruel,
when sentence was passed upon Floyd for having used
disrespectful words in relation to the Elector Palatine and
his wife.

There is nevertheless very remarkable evidence that the This
principles upon which punishment should be inflicted by discretion
the Lords for high crimes and misdemeanours, after con- by Lord
viction upon impeachment, were not by any means definitely in the case
settled. Three years after sentence had been pronounced of the
on Bacon, Lionel Cranfield, Earl of Middlesex and Lord Middlesex.
High Treasurer of England, was impeached for corruption
and other misdemeanours, and in particular for having taken
bribes from the farmers of customs[1]. He denied the
charges, but used an argument which indicated, in the
clearest manner, the habits of the time. It was that he had
'been a judge these eight years, and no complaint brought
against him for corruption or bribery, which he hoped
would weigh much with their lordships.' He was, however,
found guilty, and the judgement passed upon him was
almost identical with that passed upon Bacon. Yet Edward
Hyde, afterwards Earl of Clarendon and Lord Chancellor,
deliberately stated in his History of the Rebellion, that when
Middlesex was 'condemned in a great fine, to a long and
strict imprisonment, and never to sit in Parliament during
his life,' this latter clause was 'of such a nature as was
never before found in any judgement of Parliament, and, in
truth, not to be inflicted upon any Peer but by attainder[2].

It is difficult to arrive at any certainty on a question of Case of
constitutional law, when a Chancellor makes a statement Fitz-
directly at variance with an undeniable fact. It is, there- a com-
fore, not wonderful that difficulties arose between the Lords peached
and the Commons at a somewhat later period. It is of High
inevitable that, when there are charges of high treason, in 1681
political feeling should run high. Men use arguments and but not
tried by
the Lords.

[1] *Journals of the House of Commons*, beginning April 5, 1624 (vol. i.
p. 755), and *Journals of the House of Lords*, May 13, 1624 (vol. iii.
pp. 382–383).
[2] *Hist. Rebellion*, i. 45.

CHAP. XI. arrive at decisions which in calmer moments they would reject. Thus, when plots and rumours of plots filled the air, in 1681, it happened, for political reasons with which this history has no concern, that one Fitz-Harris was impeached of High Treason. He was already in prison and about to be indicted, if not already indicted, according to the forms of the common law. The Lords refused to entertain the impeachment, and voted that the proceeding against Fitz-Harris should be at common law. Upon this the Commons resolved 'that it is the undoubted right of the Commons, in Parliament assembled, to impeach, before the Lords in Parliament, any peer or commoner for treason or any other crime or misdemeanour, and that the refusal of the Lords to proceed in Parliament upon such impeachment is a denial of justice and a violation of the constitution of Parliaments[1].' The Lords, nevertheless, did not try the case, and Parliament was almost immediately afterwards dissolved. Fitz-Harris was then tried and found guilty by a jury.

This case was, however, not by any means conclusive with regard to the right of the Commons to impeach a commoner for High Treason. It was complicated with an attempt to withdraw a case from the cognizance of the Courts of King's Bench or Oyer and Terminer, and therefore involved something more than a merely Parliamentary question.

Sir A. Blair and other commoners impeached of High Treason and tried by the Lords in 1689.

An opportunity arose, in the year 1689, for a better and a calmer review of the position, without any similar complications. Sir Adam Blair and four other commoners were then impeached of High Treason. The Lords appointed a committee to search for precedents. Upon receiving the report, in which precedents were cited, and after rejecting a motion to take the opinion of the judges, they resolved that the impeachment should proceed[2]. It was thus settled;

---

[1] *Journals of the House of Commons*, March 26, 1681 (vol. ix. p. 711).
[2] *Journals of the House of Lords*, June 26 and July 2, 1689 (vol. xiv. pp. 260, 362–364).

as indeed it could only be settled, if the Lords were to try
impeachments against commoners at all, that they could
try impeachments of commoners for capital offences. They
could of course try Peers, whether the accusation took the
form of impeachment or of indictment.

One of the chief features of an impeachment, which, A pardon
however, was not universally recognized at first. is that it cannot be
cannot be defeated by the pardon of the sovereign. A great bar of an
dispute arose in relation to this subject on the impeachment ment.
of the Earl of Danby in 1679. When required to give his
answer to the charges brought against him, he pleaded the
King's pardon[1]. The Commons then resolved that the
pardon was illegal and void, and demanded judgement at
the bar of the Lords. as against one who had pleaded a void
plea[2]. The quarrel branched off in various other directions,
the Commons even denying, though in vain, the right of the
Bishops to take part in the earlier stages of an impeachment
in the House of Lords. It was ended for a time by the
prorogation of Parliament. The principal question was
finally set at rest by the Act of Settlement, in which it was
declared 'that no pardon under the Great Seal of England
shall be pleadable to an impeachment by the Commons in
Parliament[3].' The power of the Crown to pardon, after the
Lords have given judgement, is not affected by these words,
but no pardon can be interposed between impeachment by
the Commons and trial by the Lords.

It may, perhaps, also be considered a general principle Question
that neither prorogation nor dissolution of Parliament will proro-
put an end to impeachment by the Commons before the gation or
Lords. As early as 1673 it was resolved by the House of can end an
Lords, after enquiry by a committee, that ordinary judicial impeach-
· 'businesses depending in one Parliament or session of Parlia- tradictory
ment have been continued to the next session of the same tions.
Parliament, and the proceedings thereupon have remained
in the same state in which they were left when last in

[1] *Journals of the House of Lords*, April 25, 1679 (vol. xiii. p. 540).
[2] *Ib.*, May 5, 1679 (vol. xiii. p. 553).
[3] Stat. 12 & 13 Will. III, cap. 2. sec. 3.

Chap. XI. agitation[1].'   A few years later another committee reported
to the House of Lords 'that the dissolution of the last
Parliament doth not alter the state of the impeachments
brought up by the Commons in that Parliament,' and the
House resolved accordingly[2]. In this, however, as in many
other cases, the Lords reversed their own decision[3], political
motives obviously having no little weight.

The question whether even a prorogation would not put
an end to an impeachment seems afterwards to have been
brought into doubt, as in the case of the Earl of Oxford in
1717 it was thought necessary, after a search for precedents,
to make a resolution in the negative[4]. There would *a fortiori*
have been a doubt in case of a dissolution.

The doubt removed by special Acts of Parliament in the cases of Warren Hastings and Viscount Melville.

The difficulty was felt in 1786, when articles of impeachment were drawn up against Warren Hastings. It was
then thought prudent to have an Act of Parliament passed
to the effect that the proceedings should not be discontinued by any prorogation or dissolution of Parliament[5].'
So also when Viscount Melville was impeached in 1805,
another Act was passed in identical terms[6]. It is not
improbable that these precedents would be followed upon
any future impeachment, as each of these Acts had reference
only to the particular case under consideration at the time.
The points have often been argued, but would of course be
subject to further argument on the introduction of any new
Bill.

[1] *Journals of the House of Lords*, March 29, 1673 (vol. iii. p. 583).
[2] *Ib.*, March 19, 1678–1679 (vol. xiii. p. 466). The Order applied also
to Appeals and Writs of Error.
[3] *Ib.*, May 22, 1685 (vol. xiv. p. 11).
[4] *Ib.*, May 25, 1717 (vol. xx. p. 475).
[5] Stat. 26 Geo. III, cap. 96.   [6] Stat. 45 Geo. III, cap. 125.

CHAPTER XII.

THE rights and privileges now enjoyed by Peers and Lords of Parliament are not all identical with those which they enjoyed in former times.

It has already been seen incidentally that the right even to sit in the House of Lords in a particular order of precedence was slowly developed out of the burden of a writ of summons calling an unwilling Baron or Bishop to attend the King in Parliament. It has also been shown that the desire of the Barons to be summoned which appears in John's Great Charter was prompted only by the desire for protection when some exceptional tax was to be imposed.

For some generations afterwards it was thought a privilege, not to sit in Parliament, but to be exempt from attendance. This is equally true with regard both to the lay Barons and to the Prelates. Perhaps, however, the fact ought to be established by more details than have yet been given.

In the reigns of Edward I and Edward II one summons to Parliament was not necessarily followed by a subsequent summons of the same person or his descendants. Though the principal reason may have been that the King did not desire or need the presence of the Baron, another reason was that the Baron did not desire to be present. There are even instances in which men who had been summoned, and whose ancestors had been summoned to Parliament, were ready to deny that they were Barons at all. In the reign of Edward II, Thomas de Furnivall tried to show that he was

CHAP. XII.

Modern and ancient privileges not all identical.

Right to sit in the House of Lords an instance.

Efforts of lay Barons to escape summons and sitting: instances.

CHAP.XII. not a Baron [1], nominally to escape a particular amercement, though his ancestor had been amerced as a Baron in the reign of Richard I [2]. He and his descendants were nevertheless summoned to Parliament for some generations, as his ancestors had been before him ; and his barony is one of the few which can be shown to have developed out of a so-called 'barony by tenure' into a so-called 'barony by writ.'

An indication that the temporal lords regarded the summons to Parliament as a burden rather than an honour or a privilege as late as the twenty-seventh year of Edward III is to be found in an exemption then granted by the King to James de Audley. He was, 'during his whole life, to be quit of coming to our Parliaments and Councils and those of our heirs [3].' There are also other and still later instances which show that even when lay lords were disposed to stand upon their dignity and their rights in Parliament, there were some, at any rate, who were anxious to escape the burden of sitting.

Efforts of Prelates to obtain exemption : instances.

The Prelates were at first, at least, as reluctant as the lay lords to attend in Parliament. Even towards the end of the reign of Edward III the Prior of Lewes, whose name appears in some earlier writs of summons to Parliament, desired immunity from attendance. Upon inspection of the Chancery rolls it was found that no Prior of Lewes had been summoned before the fourth year of Edward II, and that the Prior of Lewes had not been summoned on every occasion since that time. His name had been inserted among those of the other Prelates summoned, because he was willing (voluntarie) and not as of right (de jure). The King therefore commanded that his name, where inserted in the rolls, should be 'withdrawn, cancelled, and deleted,' so that in future the Prior for the time being should not

[1] Exchequer, L. T. R. *Remembrance Roll*, 19 Ed. II, *Communia, Rot.* 3 (printed in Madox's *History of the Exchequer*, chap. xiv. § 2). See also Madox's references to show that Furnivall really held by barony.

[2] Eyre Roll, Hertford, 10 Ric. I, m. 2 d (printed among the *Rotuli Curiae Regis*, i. 169).

[3] *Rot. Lit. Pat.*, 27 Ed. III, part i. m. 13 (printed, *Rep. Dig. Peer*, vol. iv. p. 596).

be summoned to Parliament, but should be altogether Chap. XII.
discharged and quit of his coming [1].'

The case of the Abbot of Gloucester also clearly shows
that in the twenty-sixth year of Edward III attendance in
Parliament and in Councils was regarded as a burden
rather than as an honour by some of the Prelates. The
King in his Letters Patent then says: 'On account of
the special affection which we bear and have towards the
Church and Abbey of St. Peter of Gloucester, in which the
body of the Lord Edward, late King of England, of famous
memory, our father, lies buried, we, willing to show special
grace to our beloved in Christ Thomas, now Abbot of that
place, have granted, for ourselves and our heirs, to the same
Abbot, that he, during his whole life, may appear in all
Parliaments, Assemblies, and Councils by his proctor or
attorney, having full power to consent to the matters which
may chance to be done in the same Parliaments, Assemblies,
and Councils of the Common Council of our Realm, and
that he be in no wise compelled to appear in person [2].'
Other Abbots also had similar exemptions.

Even in the reign of Richard II it was found necessary Act of
to pass an Act of Parliament to secure the attendance of Richard II
the Lords as well as of the Commons. It was, no doubt, to attendance.
a great extent declaratory, but it suffices to show that all
the Lords did not even yet look upon the summons to
Parliament as a privilege. Every one who received that
summons ('Archbishop, Bishop, Abbot, Prior, Duke, Earl,
or Baron') and who absented himself when summoned, was,
unless he could reasonably and honourably excuse himself to
the King, to be amerced and otherwise punished according
to the ancient custom [3].

When, however, the creation of Dukes, Marquesses, The idea
Viscounts, and even Barons by Letters Patent became a that the
common practice, there grew up among the Peers, and was a right

---

[1] *Rot. Lit. Claus.*, 39 Ed. III, m. 32 (printed, *Rep. Dig. Peer*, vol. iv.
p. 638). But a Prior was summoned in 1 Edward II.
[2] *Rot. Lit. Pat.*, 26 Ed. III, part i. m. 20 (printed, *Rep. Dig. Peer*,
vol. iv. p. 593).   [3] 5 Ric. II, stat. 2. cap. 4.

CHAP.XII.   particularly among the Barons, a desire for precedence,
associated   which was probably fostered by their increased power in
with later   relation to the Crown during the Wars of the Roses.
ideas of
precedence   Henry VI, as is shown in another chapter, was frequently
in the   induced to interfere in relation to questions of precedence ;
Realm.
             and precedence came to be associated with a particular
place in the House of Lords. That which had formerly
been regarded only as a burden thus came to be more
closely associated with the ideas of dignity and privilege.
The growing influence of the House of Commons, too, was
probably not without its effect. If the higher ranks of the
peerage could assert their position above the lower ranks,
and the Barons of early origin above those of later origin,
even those of latest origin could assert a position superior
to that of the Commons. The Peer's place in the House
of Lords became the outward and visible sign of his place
in the kingdom. He began to look upon his summons as
a right of which he would not willingly be deprived. Early
in the reign of Henry VIII he took pride in having his
presence mentioned in due order of precedence in the
Journals of the House of Lords. Thus by degrees the old
order of things gave way to the new, and the once hateful
summons to Parliament became a source of joy, though
there still continued to be gradually diminishing punishments for non-attendance.

The 'right'   In the reign of Charles I the Lords had completely
to the
writ of   forgotten the reluctance of their ancestors to sit in Parlia-
summons   ment. The summons to Parliament was, in their view, one
in the
time of   of their rights. Certain accusations had been made against
Charles I : the Earl of Bristol, who was neither tried for his supposed
case of the
Earl of   offences nor summoned to Parliament. He presented a
Bristol.   petition to the Lords, and the committee to which it was
referred reported that there was no instance on record in
which a Peer capable of sitting in Parliament had been
refused his writ [1]. It is impossible to imagine a greater
contrast than that between Thomas de Furnivall trying to

---

[1] *Journals of the House of Lords*, March 22, 1625–1626 (vol. iii.
p. 537). *Parliamentary History*, vol. ii. pp. 74–75.

prove that he was not a Baron in the reign of Edward II,
and the Earl of Bristol, three centuries later, endeavouring
to force the King to send him a summons.

The subject is one which possesses more than a merely The question whether a Peer can abandon his peerage by omitting to demand a summons. antiquarian or historical interest, because it has an important bearing upon the question, sometimes discussed, whether any one succeeding to a peerage of the United Kingdom can remain or be newly elected as a Member of the House of Commons if he abstain from demanding his writ of summons to the House of Lords. If the summons were an instrument devised entirely for the good of the person summoned, he might, perhaps, have it or not at his pleasure. As, however, its origin is totally different, the subject must be regarded from a different point of view.

As shown in another page, it has been held that one Proof of peerage necessary, when privilege was claimed in Courts. claiming privilege of peerage in a Court of Justice cannot have it allowed without producing evidence that he is a Peer. The doctrine might, perhaps, even be carried further by analogy, and extended to everything by which anything could be gained for the particular individual. Still, with reference to a constitutional principle, it is not merely the individual that must be considered, nor merely his relation to the House of Commons, but his relation to the constitution as a whole.

In the old feudal times the death of a tenant-in-chief of The Crown officially informed as to the heir by the feudal inquisition. the Crown was followed by an inquisition, in which the name and the age of the next heir were stated. Upon the return of the inquisition the Crown became informed of the facts, and the summons to Parliament could issue. When the feudal tenures were abolished the inquisitions *post mortem* ceased, and consequently the Crown ceased to be officially informed of the name of the next heir. Before this happened the idea that a summons to Parliament was a privilege or a right had overborne the idea that it was a burden. Peers therefore sought to be summoned instead of avoiding a summons.

Thus when a Peer, who is one of the hereditary Lords of Parliament, dies, the heir (or some person on his behalf)

CHAP. XII.   applies to the Lord Chancellor for his writ of summons,

The
modern
practice of
application
to the
Chancellor
for a
summons.
and produces the necessary evidence that he is in fact the heir [1]. He could, of course, omit to make the application, and if it were held that there could be no summons to a Peer by descent who neglected to ask for it, the conclusion might possibly follow that he would not be disqualified for a seat in the House of Commons. According to Statute [2], the Speaker, if he receive, during a recess of the House, a certificate that a writ has issued to summon a member of the House of Commons to Parliament as a Peer, is to send forth his warrant to the Clerk of the Crown to make out a writ for the return of a new member.

The
summons
to the
House of
Lords and
the seat
in the
House of
Commons.
The summons to the House of Lords is here made an essential factor in vacating the seat in the House of Commons. Precedents have also occurred during a session of Parliament. Thus, when a writ had issued for the return of a new member for the borough of Stamford, on the supposition that General Bertie had become Earl of Stamford, and the House of Commons was informed on February 15, 1809, that no writ of summons to the House of Lords had issued, a *Supersedeas* of the writ for the return of a new member was ordered [3].

The
questions
hence
arising
seem to be
for the
advisers of
the Crown
and the
House of
Lords.
From one point of view, therefore, it may seem that the vacancy of the seat in the House of Commons depends not merely upon the inherited right to a peerage, but also upon the actual issue of the writ of summons to the Upper House. But, on the other hand, from this point of view, the rights of the Crown and the privileges of the Lords are both shut out. If the parish registers instituted by Thomas Cromwell in the reign of Henry VIII, and the registers established by the later Registration Acts, have taken the place of the inquisitions *post mortem* as evidence of heirship, does it necessarily follow that the constitution is altered with

[1] May's *Law and Usage of Parliament* (10th edition), p. 149, note 3, and p. 598, note 2.
[2] 24 Geo. III, Sess. 2. cap. 26, sec. 2. See also 15 Geo. III, cap. 36.
[3] *Journals of the House of Commons*, lxiv. 49 ; May's *Law and Usage of Parliament* (10th edition), p. 597.

regard to the position of the Lords? The inquisition was CHAP.XII.
formerly returned officially into the Chancery; the certified extracts from the registers are now sent by the
person interested to the Lord Chancellor. The baronage
formerly owed suit to the sovereign's feudal court ; but the
sovereign's feudal court no longer exists. Can it then be
maintained that the Crown has lost the right to require the
attendance of a Peer *de jure* in his place in Parliament, or
that a Peer *de jure* may, without surrender [1], abandon the
privileges of peerage? Those questions cannot be answered
here, though the course of events has brought them, as
questions, within the domain of history. The one appears
to be a question for the advisers of the Crown, the other,
according to the precedents, for the House of Lords itself.
In relation to this subject it may, however, be remarked
that a member of the House of Commons who becomes by
descent a Peer of Scotland, immediately vacates his seat,
though he neither applies for nor is entitled to any writ of
summons, and has not to establish his peerage to the satisfaction of the Lord Chancellor [2]. Moreover, if a member of
the House of Commons be newly created a Peer, his seat is
vacated when (though not before) the Letters Patent of
creation have passed the Great Seal.

It was long before the principle was evolved that the Non-at-
House of Lords could determine matters relating to its tendance in
                                                         Parliament
own privileges, including matters relating to attendance. supposed
The history of this doctrine runs indeed almost parallel to be pun-
                                                         ishable in
with the development of the idea that a summons was the King's
                                                         Bench in
a privilege out of the idea that it was a burden. In the the reign of
reign of Edward III it was supposed, by some at any rate Edward
                                                         III: case
of the Judges, that any matter relating to attendance was of the
within the cognizance of the Court of King's Bench. The Bishop of
                                                         Win-
Bishop of Winchester was there called to answer because, chester.
after having come to Parliament in obedience to a summons,

---

[1] As to surrender of dignities of the peerage, see below, pp. 269–272.
[2] May's *Law and Usage of Parliament* (10th edition), p. 598 ;
Journals of the House of Commons, Feb. 21, 1840 (vol. xcv. p. 105), and
Feb. 5, 1861 (vol. cxvi. p. 4) ; Hansard's *Debates*, 3rd series, lii. 435–477.

R

CHAP. XII. he had departed without the King's permission. The Bishop appeared in Court in person. His counsel practically claimed privilege, and denied the jurisdiction of the King's Bench. The Peers, he said, met in Parliament for the profit of the King and the people, and therefore when one of the Peers did not come, or, having come, departed without leave, the fault was committed as much against the people as against the King. In matters touching Parliament the Peers were judges, and if one departed without the King's permission, it was a matter for them to record. He submitted that cognizance could not be had in a lower Court of that which had occurred in a higher. Scrope, the Chief Justice, took a different view. 'Those,' he said, 'who are judges of Parliament are judges of their peers, but the King has no peer in his own land, and therefore the matter ought not to be judged by them, and cannot be judged anywhere but here ; and it is the King's pleasure to make suit against those who trespass against him wheresoever he may choose ; therefore be advised.' No judgement, however, was given on this occasion. There was an adjournment, and the sequel does not appear [1].

Later orders made by the House in relation to attendance. The House itself afterwards made many orders relating to attendance, which was not always very regular even after the summons to Parliament had beyond all doubt been recognized as an honour. Occasional absence soon came to be regarded as a venial offence punishable by the not very severe fine of five shillings for every day, unless a good excuse could be given [2]. A fine was also imposed upon a Peer who, though attending, came after prayers [3]. Absence at the first meeting of a Parliament, however, was long considered far more serious, as might have been expected from previous history. In the reign

[1] *Year Book*, Easter, 3 Ed. III, ffo. 18-19, no. 32. The record is in the *Placita coram Rege*, Easter, 3 Ed. III, R⁰. 9 d. It is printed *in extenso* in 4 Inst. 15–16.

[2] *Journals of the House of Lords*, Feb. 25, 1625–1626 (vol. iii. p. 507).

[3] *Ib.*

of Charles I it was resolved that an order should be drawn CHAP. XII.
'whereby the Lords may know the danger they incur of
being absent except they have leave of the King¹.'

By special leave from the King a Lord of Parliament Privilege
might, as we have seen, be excused from attendance in of making
Parliament for life on appointing a procurator, or proxy, to gradually
represent him. He might also, by licence, appoint a proxy restricted and at last
for particular occasions to give a vote on his behalf. Here discontinued.
again may without doubt be traced the original idea that
attendance in Parliament was a burden, rather than an
honour, as proxies were made at a very early period.
Sometimes, as, for instance, when an aid was wanted for
knighting the King's eldest son, appearance by attorney or
proxy was even suggested in the writ of summons². Sometimes, as, for instance, when a Crusade was in contemplation,
notice was given that no proxies or bearers of excuses would
be admitted except upon 'evident and manifest necessity³.'
At first it was not even necessary that the proxy should
be a Prelate or a Temporal Peer⁴, though it was necessary
in the fifteenth century, and other restrictions were afterwards imposed. In later times orders were made by the
House of Lords itself that no proxy should vote upon
a question of guilty or not guilty when there was a trial by
Peers.

Two or more proxies might, in the reign of Elizabeth, be
made by an absent Peer, but they could not vote unless they
all agreed⁵. It was also already held that,⁶if a Peer, after
making a proxy, attended personally in Parliament, the
proxy was revoked⁶. A sharp division was drawn between
Lords Spiritual and Lords Temporal in relation to proxies

¹ *Journals of the House of Lords*, Feb. 25, 1625–1626 (vol. iii.
p. 507).
² *Rot. Lit. Claus.*, 34 Ed. I, m. 15 d (printed in *Rep. Dig. Peer*,
vol. iii. pp. 165–166). Abbesses were summoned on this occasion.
³ *Rot. Lit. Claus*, 6 Ed. III, m. 37 d (printed in *Rep. Dig. Peer*,
vol. iv. p. 408).
⁴ See the Proxies of the year 1322, printed in *Parliamentary Writs*,
vol. ii. div. 2. p. 248 and p. 267.
⁵ 4 Inst. 12.   ⁶ 4 Inst. 13.

CHAP. XII. in the reign of Charles I. It was then ordered by the House 'that all proxies from a Spiritual Lord shall be made unto a Spiritual Lord, and from a Temporal Lord unto a Temporal Lord [1].' It was at the same time resolved that no Lord of the House should be capable of receiving more than two proxies [2].

In 1810 the idea that the King's licence was necessary, even in theory, for the making of a proxy, seems to have been quite forgotten. The 'King's illness' in that year, when George III, through mental incapacity, was unable to sign a commission for a further prorogation of Parliament (which had been formally prorogued until the 1st of November, but was not expected to meet on that day), caused many difficulties, and led incidentally to a consideration of the subject of proxies. A committee was appointed to enquire whether they could then be used. Its report was read on January 4, 1811, and was to the effect that there was no precedent except one in 1788-9, when proxies had been admitted before a commission had been read for holding a Parliament. A motion 'that proxies be now called over' was negatived by a majority of three. The subject was revived on January 4, and again on January 8. On the 23rd the Chancellor pointed out an error in the Report of Committee, as proxies had been entered on March 30 and June 2, 1660, as well as in 1788-9. He said, however, that 'he did not mean to argue the question as applying to the case of the two Houses assembling without the authority of the King's commission, but having assembled by virtue of a prorogation, under the authority of the King's commission, he contended that the right of voting by proxy attached to that House in common with other privileges;' and he proposed four resolutions in that sense. The Earl of Moira moved that the House do now adjourn, and his amendment was carried by a majority of two.

[1] *Journals of the House of Lords*, Feb. 25, 1625-1626 (vol. iii. p. 507).
[2] *Ib.*

In the course of the debate, the inherent right of a Lord CHAP.XII. of Parliament to vote by proxy was maintained without reservation on the one side, while on the other side it was insisted that the House had power to limit, modify, and control the privilege. No one seems to have supposed that there was any necessity for the royal licence[1].

The subject has now, however, lost much of its interest, because the Lords have themselves practically abandoned their own privilege. In 1867 it was recommended by a Committee of the House that the use of proxies should be discontinued; and on March 31, 1868, the House agreed to a Standing Order to carry out the recommendation: 'that the practice of calling for proxies on a division shall be discontinued, and that two days' notice be given of any motion for the suspension of this Standing Order[2].

The privilege, if privilege it can be called, of having Growth entered upon the Journals of the House the protest of any of the individual Lord of Parliament against any vote which may practice of have passed, is sometimes said to be of comparatively late entering dissent origin. This is true to the letter, because the Journals of upon the the House of Lords did not branch off from the older Rolls Journals. of Parliament until the reign of Henry VIII, and consequently nothing could have been entered upon them before that time. It must, however, be obvious that, in any assembly whatever, which has freedom of speech, it is competent for any member to make a protest on any subject whatever, and that the recording or not recording of the protest when made must be in accordance with the rules of the assembly itself. As early as the reign of Edward III a most important protest was made by the Chancellor, the Treasurer, and some of the Justices who then had seats in the House, and was recorded on the Rolls of Parliament. It might, indeed, almost be regarded as a 'protest with reasons.' The dissentients expressed themselves as being not only opposed to the enactment of

[1] Hansard's *Debates*, vol. xviii. 1, 752, 786, 805, 976.
[2] *Journals of the House of Lords*, March 31, 1868 (vol. c. p. 99).

CHAP. XII. certain Statutes, to which reference is made in another chapter, but also as being dissatisfied with the form of enactment, and declared the whole to be contrary to the usages of the realm [1]. Neither the Chancellor (Sir Robert Bourchier) nor the Treasurer (Sir Robert Parning) was at this time summoned to Parliament, as holding by barony, but this fact seems immaterial, as the Council in Parliament sat among the Lords, and could hardly have had a privilege which the Lords had not. Moreover some protests made by Prelates against the Statute of Provisors and upon other occasions are entered on the Rolls of Parliament.

Partly, perhaps, through the long intervals between Parliament and Parliament in later reigns, this privilege, like the authority of the House of Lords in some judicial matters, fell almost into oblivion. In the time of Charles I it came again into prominence, and in the opinion of some persons was greatly abused [2]. After the Restoration protests with reasons were not uncommon, and duly appear upon the Journals of the House [3].

Privilege of being attended in the House by the Judges and others. Among the privileges not of individual Lords but of the House collectively, there came to be included the right to be attended by the Judges of the Courts of King's Bench and Common Pleas, and such of the Barons of the Exchequer as were of the degree of the coif or had been made serjeants-at-law, and the Masters of the Court of Chancery, 'for their advice in point of law and for the greater dignity of their proceedings. The Secretaries of State, the Attorney and Solicitor General, and the rest of the King's learned Counsel being Serjeants were also used to attend the House of Peers, and have to this day,' says Blackstone, about the year 1765, 'their regular writs of summons issued out at the beginning of every Parliament ;

---

[1] *Rot. Parl.*, 15 Ed. III, no. 42 (vol. ii. p. 131). See above, pp. 195–6.
[2] Clarendon, *History of the Rebellion*, iv. 254.
[3] *A Complete Collection of the Protests of the Lords* was made from the Journals of the House by Mr. J. E. T. Rogers, and printed in three bulky volumes. The editor, however, makes no reference to events earlier than the reign of Henry VIII, when the Journals began.

but, as many of them have of late years been members of CHAP. XII.
the House of Commons, their attendance here is fallen into
disuse [1].'

It has already been shown [2] that in the reign of Edward I, The
and long afterwards, the Judges and others who were privilege
members of the Council were regularly summoned to growth:
'Parliament,' and had their places assigned to them among the Judges
the Lords. The form of summons to them differed slightly sat in the
House of
from that of the summons to the Prelates and from that of Lords.
the summons to the Earls and Barons, but it was in no sense
a summons to be in attendance upon the Lords Spiritual
and Temporal. When the King sat with them in Parliament they transacted business there which had the
authority of 'the King in his Council in his Parliament,'
and there is nothing to show that the Lords were their
superiors. When, however, the Council was separated from
the Parliament in the reign of Richard II, the King in
his Council in his Parliament was an assembly no longer
known to the law, and though writs continued to issue to
the Judges and others of the Council, as before, their status
naturally underwent a change.

It is difficult to mention a precise date when the Judges Order for
first lost their ancient places in Parliament. It may have Judges to
attend as
been in the reign of Richard II, it was certainly before the Assistants
in the
reign of Henry VIII. When his 'Act for placing of the reign of
Lords'[3] was passed, no mention was made of them, though Charles II.
provision was made [4] for the case of a Lord Chancellor,
Lord Treasurer, Lord President of the Council, Lord Privy
Seal, or Chief Secretary, who might be under the degree
of a Baron. When they lost their seats in the House of
Lords, the Judges, having to give their advice only if
required, naturally fell into a subordinate position. On
June 4, 1660, just after the Restoration, it was ordered by
the House of Lords ' that the Lord Chancellor do move his
Majesty that he would be pleased to give order for writs

---

[1] 1 Com. 168. [2] Above, pp. 47–48, 195–196, &c.
[3] Stat. 31 Hen. VIII, cap. 10. [4] Sec. 8.

CHAP. XII. to the Judges, whereby they may attend in the House as *Assistants* [1].'

The House of Lords can now call for their assistance.   The Lords can always call for the assistance of the Judges, and have frequently so called, especially in questions relating to the peerage.

Breach of privilege of Parliament: opinion of the Judges in 1453.   Matters touching breach of privilege of Parliament constitute no inconsiderable portion of parliamentary law. Many of them relate rather to the House of Commons than to the House of Lords, and it is not within the scope or limits of this history to treat them in detail. There are, however, some of them which cannot be passed over altogether in silence.

In the reign of Henry VI the Lords were in some doubt with regard to their power in reference to breaches of the privilege of Parliament, though it seems to have been admitted that the power which was not in the Courts of Justice was entirely in the House of Lords, and not in the House of Commons. Chief Justice Fortescue, replying, on behalf of all the Justices, to a question submitted to them by the Lords, said that they ' ought not to make answer, for it hath not been used aforetime that the Justices should in any wise determine the privileges of this High Court of Parliament. For it is so high and mighty in its nature that it may make law, and that that is law it may make no law, and the determination and knowledge of that privilege belongs to the Lords of the Parliament and not to the Justices [2].'

Remarkable features of the case, as affecting the Speaker.   One of the most remarkable features in this case is that the determination of privilege of Parliament in general, and not of the House of Lords alone, was said to rest with the House of Lords. The Commons made a petition to the Lords on behalf of Thomas Thorpe their Speaker, and Walter Rayle, both described as Members of Parliament, and then in prison. The Duke of York had brought an action against Thorpe for having carried away certain

---

[1] *Journals of the House of Lords*, June 4, 1660 (vol. xi. p. 52).

[2] *Rot. Parl.*, 31 Hen. VI, nos. 25-28 (printed, vol. v. pp. 239-240).

goods and chattels belonging to him from the palace of CHAP. XII.
the Bishop of Durham. He had been compelled to proceed in the Exchequer because Thorpe was 'one of the
Court,' and had the privilege of being impleaded there and
not in any other Court. Judgement was given for the
Duke, with damages of £1000 and costs ; and Thorpe was
'according to the course of the law committed to the Fleet
for the fine belonging to the King in that behalf.'

The Duke opposed the liberation of Thorpe, and the
Lords Spiritual and Temporal 'opened and declared to
the Justices the premises and "axed[1]" of them whether
the said Thomas ought to be delivered from prison by force
and virtue of the privilege of- Parliament, or no.' They
then gave the well-known answer quoted above.

The Judges nevertheless added some qualifying words
which ought not to be left out of consideration : 'There be
many and divers *Supersedeas* of privilege of Parliament
brought into the Courts, but there is no general *Supersedeas*
brought to surcease of all processes ; for, if there should
be, it should seem that the High Court of Parliament that
ministreth all Justice with Equity should "let"[2] the process
of the common law, and so it should put the party com-
plainant without remedy, for so much as actions at common
law are not determined in this High Court of Parliament.
And if any person that is a member of this High Court of
Parliament be arrested, in such cases as be not for treason,
or felony, or surety of the peace, or for a condemnation
had before Parliament, it is used that all such persons
should be released of such arrests and make an attorney,
so that they may have their freedom and liberty freely to
intend upon the Parliament.'

The Lords Spiritual and Temporal took the whole *The Lords*
statement of the Judges to imply that they were the *then*
supreme
supreme arbiters with regard to privilege of Parliament *arbiters of*
privilege
and its consequences. They resolved that Thorpe should *as affecting*
both
Houses.

[1] The entry upon the roll is in the English of the period.
[2] *I.e.* obstruct.

CHAP. XII. remain in prison notwithstanding any privilege of Parliament, and notwithstanding the fact that he was ' Speaker
of the Parliament [1].' Their resolution was strictly in accordance with the established view that all judgements in
Parliament or of the King in Parliament were those of the
Lords or of the King and Lords. The Commons accepted
the position, and, without more ado, elected a new Speaker.

Matters
touching
either
House
afterwards
decided
by that
House
alone.

In the time of Sir Edward Coke it was the received
opinion that ' Judges ought not to give any opinion of
a matter of Parliament, because it is not to be decided by
the common laws, but according to the law and custom
of Parliament [2].' The doctrine had, however, been further
developed, and the determination of all privileges of Parliament was now no longer thought to belong to the Lords
alone. It was already an accepted maxim that every
question specially affecting either House of Parliament
ought to be decided in the House to which it relates,
and not elsewhere [3].

Power of
the House
of Lords to
determine
all cases of
privilege
on appeal
from in-
ferior
Courts.

In later times there have been some contradictory decisions with regard to the relation of the Courts of Justice
to the privileges of Parliament. Most of them have had
reference to matters with which the House of Commons
was solely or chiefly concerned, and which have therefore
but little bearing upon the subject of the present work [4].

---

[1] There were some elaborate arguments in relation to this case in
the year 1811, upon the hearing of the cause *Burdett v. Abbott* in the
King's Bench, though Lord Ellenborough, the Chief Justice, thought it
had very little bearing on the question before the Court, 14 East,
1–163.

[2] 4 Inst. 15.   [3] Ib. 363.

[4] Matters relating to privilege of Parliament as affecting the House
of Commons have been laboriously collected and set forth in Hatsell's
Precedents and Proceedings of the House of Commons. Later cases
in the Courts as affecting both Houses have been brought together in
Sir T. Erskine May's *Law and Usage of Parliament* (10th edition) ;·
and the manner of dealing with breach of privilege by each House is
illustrated pp. 61–92. According to Lord Ellenborough the power
of either House to punish by imprisonment was to be inferred from the
Statute, 1 James I, cap. 13. See 14 East, 143 (*Burdett v. Abbott*),
where all the important cases before 1811 are cited.

It may, however, be remarked that one of two propositions CHAP.XII. must be true : either each House has the power of determining its own privileges without reference to the ordinary Courts of Justice, or it has not. If each House has that power it is certainly possessed by the House of Lords. If either House has not that power, and the Courts have in any cases a jurisdiction, the House of Lords still has the final decision, not only with regard to itself, but also with regard to the House of Commons. It is, in its judicial capacity, the final court of appeal from any Court before which a case would probably be brought. It would therefore have, in the last resort, precisely the power which Chief Justice Fortescue ascribed to it, of deciding upon all cases of alleged breach of the privileges of Parliament which could come before the Judges.

The House of Lords has a minor privilege, for the use of *Privilege with regard* which occasion has not often arisen in recent times. When *to con-* there is to be a conference between the two Houses, it *ferences.* prefixes both the time and the place of meeting, whether the desire for the conference originates with it or with the House of Commons [1].

It is commonly said that Peers are individually hereditary *Privileges external to* counsellors of the sovereign, and that the Lords Spiritual *the House:* and Temporal are collectively, when not assembled in Par- *the Lords regarded as* liament, the permanent Council of the Crown [2]. If so, *counsellors* these are great privileges, but it is not quite clear that the *of the sovereign.* warrant for them is anything more than the original constitution of the *Curia Regis*. That body consisted of the Lords, the great officers of State, and, perhaps, from time to time, some experts whom the King might wish to consult. It was rather, however, his desire for their advice than their desire to advise him which was the governing principle when he called them together. The position, too, was greatly altered when the Council separated from the Parliament in the reign of Richard II, and became

[1] May's *Law and Usage of Parliament* (10th edition), p. 413 ; *Journals of the House of Commons*, March 26, 1604 (vol. i. p. 154).
[2] *First Rep. Dig. Peer*, vol. i. p. 14, &c. &c.

CHAP. XII. that permanent body which in later times was known as the Privy Council. The position was further altered when feudal tenures were abolished, and the Lords ceased to be members of the King's feudal court.

The Lords at York in 1640, and at the Guildhall in 1688.   It was probably the idea that Peers were his hereditary counsellors which caused Charles I to summon them all to York in the year 1640, to give him advice when no Parliament was in existence. This was an unfortunate expedient, and if defensible in theory, was not considered applicable to the practical needs of the time [1]. Another great meeting of Lords in Council was held at a not less critical period, when in 1688 James II had fled. They assembled not in virtue of any summons from any King, but of their own will. They were not the whole body of Lords Spiritual and Temporal, but only six Spiritual and twenty-two Temporal Lords. They placed themselves in communication with William Prince of Orange, and took upon themselves the duties and responsibilities of an interim government. On what supposed authority they acted it is difficult to determine. They were aiding in the deposition of one sovereign, and they could hardly, as yet, be called the Council of another, though they may possibly have believed themselves to be acting in that capacity.

Their acts not to be confounded with addresses from the House of Lords in Parliament.   Both the Council of Peers at York in 1640, and the assemblage of Lords at the Guildhall in London in 1688, met when no Parliament was sitting. Their acts, and especially those of 1688, must not be confounded with the right of the House of Lords in Parliament to present an address to the sovereign on any subject. They were the acts, in one case, of the Peers brought together by virtue of a non-parliamentary summons from the Crown— in the other case, of certain Lords meeting in a great emergency to consult as to the welfare of the realm.

Privilege of audience of the sovereign :   Every Peer, according to the generally accepted doctrine, . has the right to demand an audience of the sovereign in relation to public affairs. The historical foundation of this

---

[1] Clarendon, *History of the Rebellion*, ii. 95.

appears to rest upon the accusations against Hugh le Chap. XII.
Despenser the elder, and Hugh le Despenser the younger, its his-
in the reign of Edward II. One of the articles was that torical
they would not suffer the Magnates of the Realm, or the foundation.
King's good counsellors, to speak with the King or approach him except in their presence [1]. It is not, however,
quite clear from this passage that every Peer and Lord
of Parliament necessarily had the supposed right, because
the word Council is used in many different senses, and the
Despensers may have interfered to prevent the King from
having a Council, or counsellors except those of their own
choosing. There may even be a doubt whether the Lords
Spiritual are included in the term Magnates. Some passages in documents of the reign of Edward II are, perhaps,
not altogether inconsistent with that opinion, but the words
Prelates and Magnates are more commonly used to indicate
two distinct classes.

It is not easy to illustrate the exercise of this privilege, Opinions
by trustworthy authorities from reign to reign. The man- on the sub-
ner in which it was exercised in the reign of George IV reign of
has been very clearly recorded by Lord Colchester, who, George IV.
before his elevation to the peerage, was Speaker of the
House of Commons. It was the opinion of himself and
Lord Sidmouth that the Peer who desired an audience
should ask it individually for himself, and go singly. If
more than one went at the same time, it was thought that
there might be a semblance of besieging the sovereign
by a strong minority of Peers. The mode of approach was
not through the Secretary of State, but by application to
some officer of the royal household [2]. Lord Eldon, whose
authority was of great legal weight, was disposed to limit
the application of the privilege. He said that no Peer
can of right carry an address or petition to the King in his
closet, but can only tender advice [3].

---

[1] *Rot. Lit. Claus.*, 14 Ed. II, m. 14, *Cedula* (*Stat. Realm*, i. 184), and
4 Inst. 53.
[2] *Diary of Lord Colchester*, March 7, 1829 (vol. iii. p. 604).
[3] *Ib.*, March 12, 1829 (vol. iii. p. 606).

CHAP. XII.   The Duke of Newcastle, at this time, when there was
How ex-   great agitation with regard to the Roman Catholic Bill,
ercised by   availed himself of the privilege. His request was made
the Duke
of New-   by a note to the Lord in Waiting, and was for leave to
castle.   present an address and for an audience. He was immediately received by the King, with whom, after a long
interview, he left the address together with other papers.
The King also graciously desired the Duke to make known
that he was ready to receive addresses from the hands
of any Peer, and to give audience upon due notice[1].
His willingness to receive addresses from individual Peers
may, of course, have been merely a matter of grace,
and, as Lord Eldon had said, not any indication of a
right.

Privileges   A privilege of great antiquity, which was confirmed by
in the   John's Great Charter[2], came to be regarded as a burden
King's
Courts: at a later period. This was the privilege of Earls and
amerce-   Barons (the Prelates being included in the latter term) to
ment of
Earls and   be amerced by their peers. Thus if one of them was
Barons by
their Peers.   a loser in an action in a Court of Justice, he was said, like
any other subject, to be ' in mercy,' or in other words liable
to a fine of indefinite amount to be subsequently assessed.
The assessment, in his case, could be made only by his
' peers,' but there may arise a question as to the definition of
the word. The answer is practically given by Bracton. In
describing proceedings before Justices in Eyre, he says,
Earls and Barons are not to be amerced but by their
peers—by the Barons of the Exchequer or before the
King himself[3]. It seems to follow that the Barons of the
Exchequer and the persons who constituted the Court
coram Rege (but not the Justices in Eyre) were, as late
as Bracton's time, considered to be the peers of Earls
and Barons.

This   We are thus by a process of inference enabled to carry.
privilege   back this privilege to the reign of Richard I, or in other
at least as

---

[1] *Diary of Lord Colchester*, March 14, 1829 (vol. iii. pp. 606-607).
[2] *Mag. Chart.*, cap. 21.   [3] Bract. 116 b.

words to the time beyond which memory runneth not.
Certain rolls of that reign have been preserved to which
the title of *Rotuli Curiae Regis* has commonly been given.
The term is, in relation to some of them, and in particular
to one which is now to be cited, a misnomer, except in
so far as any of the King's Courts might be called ' *Curia
Regis.*' The Roll is clearly not that of the *Capitalis Curia
Regis*, or either division of it, but that of the Justices in
Eyre on their circuit. The privilege of Barons to be
amerced by their peers is here made manifest, though it
could not have been detected without Bracton's explanation.

In this Eyre Roll occurs a list of amercements. In all
instances, except two, the amount at which the amercement was assessed is set opposite the name of the person
amerced and without any reference to the Exchequer. The
two exceptions occur in the cases of Gerard de Furnivall
and Reginald de Argenton. ' Gerard de Furnivall is to be
amerced *at the Exchequer* for a disseisin.' ' Reginald de
Argenton is to be amerced *at the Exchequer* for a disseisin[1].'
In the latter case the words ' one hundred marks ' are added,
apparently as a suggestion. It was not, however, adopted
at the Exchequer, as the sum which Argenton had to pay
was only twenty marks[2]. Gerard de Furnivall and Reginald
de Argenton were both Barons, and both were amerced
by their peers, the Barons of the Exchequer, while the commoner sort were amerced directly in the Court of the Eyre.
The Justices in Eyre (or *Missi*) were not all peers of the
Capitalis Curia Regis, though Geoffrey Fitz-Piers, or Fitz-
Peter, who was the chief of them, was about to be, if he was
not already, Chief Justice or Justiciary of England.

In the first year of the reign of King John also, long
before his Great Charter, we find that Herbert Fitz-Herbert
was the loser in an action of assise. He was therefore ' in
mercy.' The roll shows that privilege was claimed. It

[1] Eyre Roll, Hertford, 10 Ric. I, m. 2 d (printed among the *Rotuli
Curiae Regis*, i. 169-170).
[2] *Great Roll of the Exchequer*, 1 John.

CHAP. XII. bears in the margin the Latin words for 'Mercy. He is a Baron¹.'

The Barons of the Exchequer, or the King's Council, acted as Peers for the purposes of the assessment. Though Barons, having this privilege, were commonly amerced by the Barons of the Exchequer, they were sometimes amerced by another tribunal which must also have consisted of their peers. Thus in the third year of the reign of Henry III the Justices in Eyre in the County of Kent were instructed that Earls and Barons who were 'in mercy' before them were to be amerced before the King's Council². This is, no doubt, the amercement which Bracton describes as *coram Rege*, the proceedings of the Council in the reign of Henry III being often with difficulty distinguished from those of the King's Bench, and often enrolled on the same rolls. About the forty-second year of the same reign Barons put in mercy in the Eyre also had the amercement assessed *coram Rege*³.

Amercements according to a fixed scale about the time of Edward I: Earls and Barons amerced in ordinary Courts of Justice. The actual amercement, however, either by the Barons of the Exchequer, or *coram Rege*, very soon became rather a form than a fact. It became a recognized principle that Earls and Barons should be amerced according to a definite scale⁴, which may, in the first instance, have been fixed either by the Barons of the Exchequer or by the Council. As soon as this was adopted, Earls and Barons had their amercements assessed in the courts in which they fell 'in Mercy.' Thus as early as the eleventh year of Edward I there were Barons amerced in the Common Bench⁵. In

¹ An abridgement of the case is printed in the *Placitorum Abbreviatio*, p. 24, Hereford.

² *Rot. Lit. Claus.*, 3 Hen. III, m. 13, cited in Madox's *History of the Exchequer*, cap. xiv. sec. 2. note.

³ A 'cedula' among the records of the Lord Treasurer's Remembrancer of the Exchequer, printed in Madox's *Baronia Anglicana*, p. 102.

⁴ This appears in the *Mirror of Justices*, cap. iv. sec. 25. Little as may be the value of the *Mirror* in relation to 'the Coming of the English' and King Alfred, it is a contemporary authority for the end of the thirteenth and beginning of the fourteenth century, and the statement as to amercements is fully confirmed by records and law reports.

⁵ Great Roll of the Exchequer, 11 Ed. I. *Item Essex et Residuum Surr.* cited in Madox's *History of the Exchequer*, cap. xiv. sec. 2. note.

the tenth year of the reign of Edward II also, Earls and Barons were amerced in the same Court, Abbots being included under the head of Barons[1]. Among these was the Abbot of Croyland, who complained to the King in Council that he had been treated as a Baron without due warrant, and alleged that he did not hold any lands or tenements by barony or part of a barony. The matter was referred to the Court of Exchequer. Search was to be made among the Exchequer records, and the Justices of the Common Bench were to be consulted if necessary. Upon examination of the rolls it was found that the Abbot had been amerced as a Baron, in the preceding reign, by the Justices in Eyre[2]. It is also clear, from a case in which the Earl of Arundel was concerned in the reign of Edward III, that when an Earl wrongly brought an action in the Court of Common Pleas, he was amerced in the recognized sum of one hundred shillings[3].

It cannot, perhaps, be said that there was absolute uniformity of practice even as late as the reign of Henry VI, for on the one hand the Earl of Northumberland, in the first year, having made default on a writ of Right, was not amerced in the Common Pleas, but by the Peers[4], and on the other hand, in the ninth year, Lord Fitz-Walter was amerced in the Common Pleas, as a Baron, in two several sums of one hundred shillings for two distinct reasons[5]. The Earl of Northumberland, however, seems to have been exceptionally treated, and many instances show not only that there was a regular scale of amercement for Peers, according to their rank, but that so long as the scale was duly followed, the amercement could be imposed in the Court in which it was incurred. In the reign of Edward IV a Duke was, upon nonsuit, amerced at ten pounds, and an

[1] Exchequer, *Originalia*, 10 Ed. II, m. 2, *in cedula*, printed in Madox's *History of the Exchequer*, cap. xiv. sec. 2. note.

[2] Exchequer, Treasurer's Remembrancer's *Remembrance Roll*, Hil., *Communia*, 12 Ed. II, R⁰. 23, cited in Madox's *History of the Exchequer*, as above.

[3] *Year Book*, 38 Ed. III, 31 (*Quare impedit*). And *see* 2 Inst. 28.

[4] *Year Book*, 1 Hen. VI, fo. 7.   [5] *Ib.*, 9 Hen. VI, fo. 2. no. 5.

CHAP.XII. Earl at a hundred shillings [1]. A Bishop also was amerced at a hundred shillings [2], but this of course could be only in respect of his lay fee, or barony, as, according to Magna Charta [3], no ecclesiastic could be amerced in respect of any spiritual benefice.

A Baron's word sufficient in the Exchequer in the reign of Henry II.   As early as the reign of Henry II (if the *Dialogus de Scaccario* is to be trusted on this point) the King's Barons (*Barones Regis*) had a privilege which is not unlike that of the later Peers, who upon certain occasions gave their word instead of taking an oath. When the King's debts were in demand, and payment was to be enforced, one who held a barony of the King was, after the summons of the Exchequer had been heard, only asked to say to the Sheriff, either in person or by his Steward:—'In respect of this sum and in respect of this summons I will do according to the award of the Barons of the Exchequer on the day of account [4].' With this the Sheriff had to be content until the day came, though the procedure was very different in the case of inferior persons, who held nothing of the King in chief.

Earls and Barons exceptionally treated when 'essoiners.'   When Earls or Barons were essoiners (persons giving an excuse in a Court of Justice for the non-appearance of a party) they were, in the time of Henry III, treated differently from those of inferior rank. The essoin, however, gradually became a mere form, and then fell into disuse. It is therefore needless to pursue the subject further [5].

When a Lord was a party in a civil action there had to be Knights upon the   A privilege of some importance in civil causes appears to have belonged, from a very early period, both to the lay and to the ecclesiastical lords. When one of them was a party it was the custom that there should be knights upon the jury, and if there were none, the 'array' could be success-

---

[1] *Year Book*, 19 Ed. IV, fo. 9. no. 10.
[2] *Ib.*, 21 Ed. IV, 77.
[3] *Magna Charta*, 9 Hen. III, cap. 14.
[4] *Dialogus de Scaccario*, lib. ii. cap. 19.
[5] Full details relating to Earls and Barons as essoiners are given in Bract. 337 b, 351 b, and 352.

fully challenged[1]. This practice led to some abuses, and Chap. XII.
was often a cause of serious delay, but it continued to be Jury until
the law of the land until the year 1751, when an Act was the year
passed providing that no challenge should be taken to any 1751.
panel of jurors for want of a knight [2].

Freedom from arrest in civil actions was, from one point Freedom
of view, a Parliamentary privilege enjoyed by both Lords in civil
and Commons, and for some time even by their servants. actions;
From another point of view it was a privilege enjoyed by remaining
the Lords when no Parliament was in existence. It was of this
once of considerable importance. It belonged both to the privilege.
Prelates and to the Temporal Lords, though the Prelates
seem to have had it as Prelates and not necessarily as
Peers[3]. It was a privilege, however, which in the case of
Barons, at any rate, the Courts would not notice unless
specially pleaded. 'They were not bound to know and
could not know whether one was a Lord of Parliament,
unless the fact were certified to them by writ out of the
Chancery[4].' The privilege was restricted in England to
Peers and Peeresses of England, those of Ireland not
enjoying it in England before the Union ; and a writ
of *Capias* actually issued in England in the reign of
Richard II against the Countess of Ormonde, Peeress of
Ireland, in an action of debt[5]. Freedom from arrest,
though not taken away from the Peers, lost much of its
significance when arrest on mesne process (before judgement was given) was abolished in all but certain special
cases in the year 1838[6]. Its value has been still further
reduced by subsequent legislation, so that comparatively
few opportunities now occur for the exercise of the ancient
privilege[7]. It never extended to criminal offences.

---

[1] *Year Book*, T., 13 Ed. III (Rolls Series), p. 290.   Dyer's Reports,
1 & 2 Phil. & Mary, fo. 107. no. 27, *et alibi passim*.
[2] Stat. 24 Geo. II, cap. 18. sec. 4.
[3] *Year Book*, T., 29 Ed. III, fo. 42.
[4] Fitz-Herbert's Abridgement, *Exigent*, 2 (Mich., 36 Hen. VI).
[5] *Ib.*, *Proses*, 224.   [6] Stat. 1 & 2 Vict., cap. 110. sec. 1.
[7] It appears to be still applicable when one having privilege of

CHAP. XII.   Freedom from arrest carried with it freedom from out-
Freedom   lawry in civil actions, for a purely technical reason. A writ
from out-   of *Capias* (to take the person of the debtor or other de-
lawry in
civil ac-   fendant) was one of the stages in the process of outlawry,
tions : the and as a Lord of Parliament could not be taken, it neces-
privilege
ceased   cessarily followed that he could not be outlawed on civil
with the
abolition   process. Peers and Lords of Parliament have, however,
of the   no longer any privilege in this respect, as outlawry in civil
outlawry
in 1879.   proceedings was abolished in the year 1879 [1]. The privilege did not, at common law, extend to all criminal proceedings, though with regard to some matters the Lords
had special protection by Statute. Thus when the Statute
of Provisors of 25 Edward III was confirmed and extended
during the same reign, there was expressly enacted a saving
clause in favour of the Prelates and other Lords of the
Realm, so that their persons should not be subject to arrest
by force of the Act [2]. A Peer could, nevertheless, be not
only arrested but outlawed also for treason, felony, or breach
of the peace.

Other   In civil actions at common law a Peer had, at one time, some
former
advantages other advantages, which, however, were in part regarded as
in Courts of privileges of Parliament, and shared with members of the
Common
Law.   House of Commons. They were of a technical nature, and
belonged to a mode of procedure long since obsolete. The
necessity of proceeding by 'Original Writ' against a Peer
had, while it existed, the effect of making actions against
Peers more expensive, and consequently more difficult, and
thus operated as a protection, at any rate, against frivolous
proceedings, to which unprivileged persons were sometimes
exposed.

Exemption   Among the minor privileges relating to Courts of
from ser-
vice on   common law is that of exemption from service on juries.
juries and In former times the name of a Lord of Parliament might
appearance
at Sheriffs' be placed on a jury panel, and he might be challenged by .
Tourns.

peerage neglects to obey a judgement or order, after having been served
with due notice.
    [1] Stat. 42 & 43 Vict., cap. 59. sec. 3.
    [2] 38 Ed. III, stat. 2. cap. 1.

the parties, or might challenge himself. He was not, however, compelled to serve [1], and was discharged on giving
proof that he was a Lord of Parliament [2]. In later times
Peers and clergymen have been expressly exempted by
Statutes [3].

Prelates, Earls, and Barons were also early declared
exempt from attendance at the Courts known as Sheriffs'
Tourns, in all ordinary cases. This, however, was hardly
a privilege of peerage, as it was equally enjoyed by all men
and women who were *religiosi* or 'religious professed' [4], and
it has long ceased to be of any practical value.

When Justices of the Peace acquired the power of taking
recognizances from other persons to keep the peace or to
be of good behaviour, they had no power over Peers in this
respect. Peers and Peeresses could not be bound over in any
place except the Courts of King's Bench and Chancery [5]. *Privileges of Peers in relation to recogniz- ances to keep the peace.*

A very curious privilege was given to Lords of Parliament
and Peers of the Realm in the reign of Edward VI. It
can be understood, however, only by the aid of some little
knowledge of the ancient doctrine of benefit of clergy.
When a man was indicted for certain offences, the Bishop
of the Diocese or Ordinary could claim him, if a clerk, and
withdraw him from the jurisdiction of the King's Courts.
The definition of a clerk appears at first to have been one who
had the clerical garb, and the clerical tonsure. As, however,
the ability to read was at one time almost restricted to the
clergy, it came to be held that any man who could read
should be regarded as a clerk, and might have benefit of
clergy. From the time of Henry VI the accused had to
be arraigned in the King's Court, and might then claim the
benefit, either before trial, or after conviction as a 'clerk
convict.' It is only the benefit as applied to a clerk convict
with which we are now concerned. *Privilege conferred in the reign of Edward VI: Benefit of Clergy.*

[1] *Co. Litt.*, 156 b.   [2] *Year Book*, M., 48 Ed. III, fo. 30. no. 18.
[3] Stat. 6 Geo. IV, cap. 50. sec. 2, and 33 & 34 Vict., cap. 77. sec. 9,
Schedule.
[4] Stat. Marlb. (52 Hen. III), cap. 10.
[5] 4 Bl. Com. 251.

CHAP XII.   In the reign of Henry VII[1] a distinction was drawn between persons actually in Holy Orders and those who were entitled to benefit of clergy solely as being able to read. Those in Orders were to be entitled to the benefit as before, and as often as they offended ; those literate persons not in Orders who committed clergyable offences were to be entitled to it once only. Every such literate person, when convicted of murder, was to be branded with the letter M on the brawn of the left thumb, by the gaoler, in open Court, in the presence of the Judge, before being delivered to the Ordinary. Every such person convicted of felony was to be branded in like manner with the letter F. The distinction between offenders actually in Orders and those only able to read was abolished for a short time in the reign of Henry VIII, when it was enacted that the persons actually in Holy Orders should be burnt in the hand in the same manner as the lay clerks, and be in all respects in the same position as lay persons admitted to their clergy[2]. The previous law, however, was restored in the reign of Edward VI. In all cases within benefit of clergy all persons were then to have it in the same manner as they might have had it before April 24 in the first year of Henry VIII[3].

A Peer might commit highway robbery, &c., once without punishment.   At the same time Lords of Parliament and Peers of the Realm were accorded a very remarkable privilege. In any case in which any of the King's subjects might have benefit of clergy, as well as in addition for the crimes of house-breaking, highway robbery, horse-stealing, and robbing of churches, any Peer or Lord of Parliament was, upon claim made, to be held as a clerk convict who might make purgation. This, to use the words of the Act, was 'though he cannot read, without any burning in the hand, loss of inheritance, or corruption of his blood[4].' While he escaped the burning in the hand, however, he could not, like a person in Orders, · have benefit of clergy a second time for any cause.

---

[1] Stat. 4 Hen. VII, cap. 13.
[2] Stat. 28 Hen. VIII, cap. 1. sec. 7, and 32 Hen. VIII, cap. 3. sec. 8.
[3] Stat. 1 Ed. VI, cap. 12. sec. 10.   [4] *Ib.*, sec. 14.

Benefit of clergy, though it had in theory the effect of
causing the clerk convict to be handed over to the Ordinary
for purgation, practically meant exemption from punishment.   In the reign of Elizabeth it was expressly enacted
that any person admitted to benefit of clergy should be
no longer delivered to the Ordinary but discharged by the
Justices, who might, nevertheless, detain him in prison for any
period not exceeding a year [1].   The imprisonment, however,
did not apply to Peers, whose trial by the Peers in cases of
felony was saved to them by the Act of Edward VI [2]; and
a Peer who could or who could not read might still have
robbed one church or committed one highway robbery with
impunity, though an ignorant peasant would have been
hanged.

In the reign of George I an Act was passed to the effect
that persons found guilty of certain felonies within benefit of
clergy, and liable to be burnt in the hand, might instead be
transported to America [3].   As, however, Peers and Lords
of Parliament were not liable to be burnt in the hand their
privilege remained unaffected.   Benefit of clergy was
abolished in the year 1827 [4], but without any express
reference to the Act of Edward VI, and doubts arose,
a few years afterwards, whether the section in favour of
Lords of Parliament and Peers did not still remain in force.
Another Act was therefore passed in the year 1841 to
repeal the section.   It was further specifically enacted that
every Lord of Parliament or Peer, against whom an indictment for felony might be found, should plead to it, and
should, upon conviction, be liable to the same punishment
as any other of Her Majesty's subjects [5].

For a short time in the history of England a Peer might
lose his dignity for life through contempt of Court.   In
1452 a very stringent Act [6] was passed to compel attendance in Chancery, and before the King and Council.   Any

---

[1] Stat. 18 Eliz., cap. 7. secs. 2, 3.   [2] Stat. 1 Ed. VI, cap. 12. sec. 15.
[3] Stat. 4 Geo. I, cap. 11. sec. 1.
[4] Stat. 7 & 8 Geo. IV, cap. 28. sec. 6.
[5] Stat. 4 & 5 Vict., cap. 22.   [6] Stat. 31 Hen. VI, cap. 2.

CHAP. XII. 'person of the estate of Lord, as Duke, Marquess, Earl, Viscount, or Baron,' failing to appear in accordance with due process, was to forfeit all offices, fees, annuities, and other possessions which he had by grant from the Crown, and if he made a second default he was to 'lose and forfeit his estate and name of Lord, and his place in Parliament' for life. If he had nothing by grant from the Crown the penalty for the first default was loss for life of his place in Parliament, as well as of all his lands and tenements. This curious Act, however, expired at the end of seven years, and in later times a Peer was treated with remarkable courtesy by the Chancellor, whenever he had the misfortune to have a Bill in Chancery filed against him.

Subsequent privileges in the Chancery : their disappearance under new practice.
Other persons received a peremptory writ of *Subpoena* to appear in Court ; the Peer received a 'Letter Missive,' from the Lord Chancellor, desiring him, in courteous terms, to give directions for due appearance to be made, on his behalf, to a bill of complaint which had been exhibited against him [1]. If he failed to appear he was still entitled to some exceptional treatment. A Bill in Chancery, however, is no longer a mode of commencing a suit [2], and for that reason a Peer can no longer be apprised in the old form of the fact that it has been filed. The answer to a Bill in Chancery had to be made on oath by a commoner, but was made by a Peer on his honour. This privilege, however, has fallen into disuse along with the Bill and the Answer, though a Peer would still give his verdict on his honour, if sitting in judgement. When examined as a witness he always had to be sworn like other persons.

Privilege in relation to slander : *Scandalum Magnatum* : legislation from
The growth of the privilege relating to that kind of slander which is commonly known as *Scandalum Magnatum* can be traced from its first origin. Early in the reign of Edward I an Act was passed to restrain inventors of tales likely to be the occasion of discord 'between the King and

[1] The form is given in the earlier editions of Daniell's *Chancery Practice*.

[2] Supreme Court of Judicature Act, 1875 (38 & 39 Vict., cap. 77), Sched. i. Order 2.

his people or some high personages of his realm.' If any
one published any false news or tales which might have the
effect of raising such discord, he was to be taken and
detained in prison until he had produced their first author
in Court [1]. It can hardly be said that this law gave any
exclusive advantage to Peers or Lords of Parliament, as its
object seems to have been to prevent all kinds of dissen-
sions which might arise from untrue reports of any kind.
In the reign of Richard II another Act was passed, which
more clearly defined the classes of persons who were to be
specially protected. These were Prelates, Dukes, Earls,
Barons, and other Nobles and Magnates of the Realm, the
Chancellor, the Treasurer, the Clerk of the Privy Seal, the
Steward of the King's Household, the Justices of the Courts
of King's Bench and Common Pleas, and other great
officers of the kingdom. Untrue statements as to their
acts, words, or thoughts, which might create disputes and
differences between the Lords among themselves, or between
the Lords and Commons, were strictly prohibited on pain
of the punishment provided in the previous Act. The
reason assigned was that unless the evil were repressed,
the whole realm would be in danger of subversion and
destruction [2].

The punishment provided in the Act of Edward I, however, appears to have been found inadequate, and another
Act became necessary in the reign of Richard II. It was
then enacted that if any person imprisoned as a dissemi-
nator of a false report could not discover its first author,
he was to be subject to punishment as the Council might
advise [3].

In the reign of Philip and Mary some further enactments
were made in relation to the slander of Magnates or other
persons mentioned in the Acts of Edward I and the second
year of Richard II. Power was given to Justices of the
Peace to hear and determine these offences, and to put the

[1] Stat. Westm. I (3 Ed. I), cap. 34.
[2] 2 Ric. II, stat. I. cap. 5.
[3] Stat. 12 Ric. II, cap. 11.

CHAP. XII. Statutes in execution. A special punishment was assigned for slander of the King or Queen. In other cases the offender was to pay 100 marks, or lose one of his ears and be imprisoned for a month. For written slander his right hand was to be struck off. For a second offence he was to be imprisoned for life, and forfeit all his goods and chattels[1]. This Act was continued by subsequent Acts, one of which was passed at the beginning of the reign of Elizabeth. So far as slander of the Sovereign is concerned, the law was expounded to extend to Elizabeth and the heirs of her body, and would therefore seem to have expired upon her death without issue. So far as others were concerned, however, it appears to have been in force until repealed by the Statute Law Revision Act of 1863.

Abolition of the privilege by repeal of Statutes in 1887 : it was never exclusively a privilege of Lords of Parliament.

Apart from the actual punishment to be inflicted, the Statutes relating to *Scandalum Magnatum* survived until the year 1887. It is, however, to be borne in mind that although all Peers and all Lords of Parliament have been within the privilege or protection afforded by the law relating to *Scandalum Magnatum*, they have not had the exclusive enjoyment of it. All the great Officers of State were hedged round in the same manner, in order that the King's government might not be brought into disrepute by unfounded charges ; and it was, without doubt, supposed in the fourteenth century that the King's government would suffer equally if Prelates and lay Lords were brought into contempt. Thus the Peers and Lords of Parliament, while sharing with the Commons some privileges which have been included under the head Privilege of Parliament, shared also with the great officers of State certain other privileges which may perhaps be called Privilege of Government or of Administration. These, so far as they relate to *Scandalum Magnatum*, were abolished by the Statute Law Revision Act of 1887, by which the Acts of Richard II are repealed[2] ; and any one may now publish false reports, not only of

[1] Stat. 1 & 2 Philip and Mary, cap. 3, continued by 4 & 5 Philip and Mary, cap. 9, and 1 Eliz., cap. 6.

[2] Stat. 50 & 51 Vict., cap. 59.

Peers but of the great Officers of State, without incurring Chap. XII.
any penalties different from those which he would incur if
he published false reports of any commoner or private
individual.

A privilege highly valued, there can be little doubt, at Privilege in
one time, was that of taking deer in the King's forests. the King's
It was enjoyed as early as the reign of Henry III, if not
before, by every Archbishop, Bishop, Earl, or Baron, when
journeying to the King to obey the King's summons, and
when returning home. Not more than two deer, however,
might be taken, and those only in the presence of the
forester, or after winding a horn in his absence [1]. This,
like many of the other privileges, has fallen into disuse
through the altered conditions of life.

All the privileges, external to the House, which were No ex-
formerly enjoyed in England by the Peers of England or clusive
Lords of the Parliament of England exclusively, ceased to individual
be their exclusive privileges after the Union with Scot- Parlia-
land. The Peers of Scotland and the Peers of Ireland, who ment,
have no seats in the House of Lords (except those Peers of their seats,
Ireland who have seats in the House of Commons), enjoy since the
all the other privileges of Peers of the United Kingdom by Scotland.
virtue of the respective Acts of Union.

It is sometimes asserted that Lords of Parliament had, Lords of
in early times, the right of voting at elections of members Parliament
of the House of Commons, or, at any rate, of Knights of the formerly
Shire. Theoretically it might be argued, on the one hand, elections
that, as a Lord of Parliament has a seat of his own, he of Knights
does not need any representative in Parliament, but, on Shire.
the other hand, that as he suffers under a disability with
regard to voting supplies, he ought to be represented by
some one who is under no such disqualification. Practically the election for Knights of the Shire was in the County
Courts [2], and it is hardly to be supposed that Lords of

---

[1] *Charta de Foresta*, 9 Hen. III, cap. 11. This charter was repealed
by the 7 & 8 Geo. IV, cap. 27. sec. 1, so far only as it relates to
punishments for taking the King's venison.

[2] A common form of Sheriff's return to a writ for the election of

CHAP. XII. Parliament could be excluded, if they chose to attend as freeholders, though they could claim exemption from attendance at the Sheriff's Tourn. Where they cared to exert it, they probably had great influence. The mode of returning the names of the persons elected was very irregular, as appears from the complaints made and the Acts passed in consequence[1]. Some of the returns which have been preserved show that among the electors were the attorneys or persons acting on behalf of Peers[2].

Resolu-
tions of the
Commons
that the
Lords have
no right
to vote or
interfere in
elections.

In this matter, however, as in various others, the Commons have, in later generations, taken the law into their own hands. In 1699, after the Earl of Manchester had voted at an election, they resolved 'that no Peer of this kingdom hath any right to give his vote at the election for any member to serve in Parliament[3].' In 1702 the Commons further resolved 'that it is a high infringement of the liberties and privileges of the Commons of Great Britain for any Lord of Parliament or any Lord Lieutenant of any county to concern themselves in the election of members to serve for the Commons in Parliament[4].' Both these resolutions were renewed, session after session, until the Union of Great Britain with Ireland.

After that Union, by the terms of which a Peer of Ireland might represent, in the House of Commons, a county or borough of Great Britain, these resolutions became no longer suited to existing facts, and a committee was appointed to report upon the subject[5]. The recommendations then made were adopted by the House, and the ·

members was 'The community of my whole county having been assembled, the following Knights were elected.' See e. g. Writs & Returns for the Counties of Middlesex and Rutland, 5 Ed. II (printed, *Parl. Writs*, vol. ii. div. ii. pp. 62, 64, &c.).

[1] E. g. Stat. 7 Hen. IV, cap. 15; 11 Hen. IV, cap. 1; 6 Hen. VI, cap. 4; 23 Hen. VI, cap. 14.

[2] Some of these have been printed by Prynne.

[3] *Journals of the House of Commons*, Dec. 14, 1699 (vol. xiii. p. 64).

[4] *Ib.*, Jan. 3, 1701–1702 (vol. ix. p. 654).

[5] *Ib.*, Oct. 30, 1801 (vol. lvii. p. 5).

new resolutions which followed became Standing Orders[1]. CHAP. XII.
One was 'that no Peer of this Realm, except such Peer of
that part of the United Kingdom called Ireland, as shall for
the time being be actually elected, and shall not have
declined to serve for any county, city, or borough of Great
Britain, hath any right to give his vote in the election of
any member to serve in Parliament.' Another, in like
manner, adapted the resolution of 1702 to the altered
circumstances caused by the Union.

There has been no power to create or develop privileges, No power
except by Act of Parliament, since the year 1705, if, now in
either
indeed, any such power existed before. At a conference House to
then held the Lords communicated to the Commons a reso-
create new
lution that neither House of Parliament had power 'by privileges.
any vote or declaration, to create to themselves any new
privilege that is not warranted by the known laws and
customs of Parliament.' To this the Commons assented[2].

A Lord of Parliament has only one place in Parliament, Peers may
and therefore cannot sit in the House of Commons. There be County
Councillors
does not seem to be any similar reason why he might not by Act
have been a member of a County Council without any of Parliament.
special enactment on this subject. By the Local Government Act of 1888, however, it was provided that Peers
might be members of a County Council if owning property
within the county[3]. They thus escaped any possible
disability.

Before the days of Charles I, a Peer might lose his dignity Early
in various ways. He might, if of higher rank than a Baron, doctrine
that the
and if his title was by Letters Patent or Charter, divest higher
himself of it by surrender to the King. Roger Bigod, dignities
of the
Earl of Norfolk, and Marshal of England, surrendered his peerage
could be
Earldom to King Edward I[4]. William Herbert, Earl of lost by
surrender:
instances.

---

[1] *Journals of the House of Commons*, Nov. 17, 1801 (vol. lvii. p. 34),
and April 27, 1802 (vol. lvii. p. 376).

[2] *Ib.*, Feb. 28, 1704–1705 (vol. xiv. p. 555).

[3] Stat. 51 & 52 Vict., cap. 41. sec. 2 (2 b).

[4] *Rot. Lit. Claus.*, 30 Ed. I, m. 14 d (printed, *Rep. Dig. Peer*, vol. v.
app. v. p. 11).

CHAP.XII. Pembroke, restored into the Chancery the Charter by which his father had been created, in order that it might be cancelled [1]. The real object of this proceeding was that Edward, son of King Edward IV, might be created Earl of Pembroke in his stead [2]. William, however, while surrendering the particular Earldom of Pembroke, expressly reserved to himself the general state and dignity of an Earl, and was immediately created Earl of Huntingdon. In the reign of Henry VII, Edmond de la Pole, son of John, late Duke of Suffolk, agreed to surrender his estate of Duke, and that he should thenceforth be taken to be only Earl of Suffolk 'after such estate of inheritance as his ancestors were, afore the estate of Duke by the King's progenitors or predecessors to any of his said ancestors granted [3].' In the reign of Henry VIII, Thomas, Duke of Norfolk, surrendered (for the life of his son) his Letters Patent by which he had been created Earl of Surrey in tail male; and thereupon his son had grant of the dignity for life [4]. The latter grant was confirmed by Act of Parliament [5]. In the same reign Charles Brandon, Viscount Lisle, surrendered his Patent of creation, in order that Arthur Plantagenet might be created Viscount Lisle [6].

Not only were these surrenders made without any doubt of their validity at the time, but some of them were also held to be good by the Law Officers of the Crown in the reign of Charles II,—by John Glanville, the King's Sergeant-at-Law, by Geoffrey Palmer, the Attorney-General, and by Heneage Finch, the Solicitor-General [7].

This did not necessarily involve In every case, however, it will be observed that the surrender was of some dignity higher than that of Baron— of an early Earldom which was once regarded as an office

---

[1] *Rot. Chart.*, 15-22 Ed. IV, no. 11 (printed, *R.D.P.*, vol. v. pp. 417-418).
[2] *Ib.*, 15-22 Ed. IV, no. 10 (printed, *R. D. P.*, vol. v., p. 419).
[3] *Rot. Parl.*, 11 Hen. VII, no. 13.
[4] *Rot. Lit. Pat.*, 5 Hen. VIII, part ii. m. 11.
[5] *Rot. Parl.*, 5 Hen. VIII, no. 3.
[6] *Rot. Lit. Pat.*, 15 Hen. VIII, part i. m. 26.
[7] *Journals of the House of Lords*, July 16, 1660 (vol. xi. p. 93).

—of other honours conferred by Letters Patent which were CHAP. XII.
returned into the Chancery. There had been no surrender loss of the
of a barony—least of all of that which has been called status of
a barony by writ. In every instance the person sur- Peer.
rendering might still have remained a Peer, as holding
a barony in addition to the dignity surrendered, and so
far there seems to be no clear example of the surrender
of the status of Peer of the Realm.

In the fifteenth year of Charles I, however, Roger Stafford, The fine
Esquire, levied a fine, to the King, of the honour, state, the barony
degree, dignity, and name of the barony of Stafford, in of Stafford
order to bar any claim which he might have to them. The reign of
barony (though not the Earldom) of Stafford was one of Charles I:
those known as baronies by writ. The fine was accepted of the
by the King, and was held good by the Law Officers of House of
the Crown in the year 1660[1]. Nevertheless, there does Lords.
not seem to have been any precedent for it, and it was
not recognized by the Lords at the time at which it was
made. They then resolved 'that no Peer of this Realm can
drown or extinguish his honour (but that it descend to
his descendants)—neither by surrender, grant, fine, nor any
other conveyance to the King[2].'

Both the Law Officers and the Lords appear to have The Lords
been under some misapprehension, and each side appears lawyers at
to have overstated its case. The precedents on which variance.
probably the Law Officers relied did not extend to a barony
by writ; the objections against the surrender or other form
of restoration to the Crown of a barony by writ, on which
probably the Lords relied, did not extend to dignities
granted by Letters Patent or Charter.

Ideas on the subject were thus in some confusion about The Pur-
the time of the Restoration, when the so-called Viscount final
Purbeck was also permitted to levy a fine of his honours. resolution
Eighteen years later, when his son laid claim to the Vis- House of
county, the House of Lords declared their unanimous Lords, in
1678, that

[1] *Journals of the House of Lords*, July 16, 1660 (vol. xi. p. 93).
[2] *Ib.*, Feb. 1, 1640–1641 (vol. iv. p. 150).

CHAP. XII. opinion, and resolved and adjudged, that no fine then

no fine levied or at any time to be levied to the King could bar

could bar a a title of honour, or the right of any one claiming such
title of
honour. title under the person who had levied or should levy
such fine [1].

Question The doctrine that a Peer cannot surrender, or in any
whether
the Lords other way restore any dignity at all to the sovereign, is thus
have the Lord-made law of comparatively recent growth. It seems,
power to
preclude at first sight, to contradict the fundamental doctrine that
the Crown the sovereign is the fountain of honour, as it withdraws
from
receiving a from him the power to receive back an honour once
surrender. conferred. There must of necessity be two parties to
a surrender, and it appears to be hardly within the rights
of any particular body so to define its own privileges as
to affect other interests, and in particular those of the
Crown, without the express consent of the sovereign.

Instance It has been suggested that in very early times a dignity
of the
transfer could not only be surrendered to the King, but could, with
of an Earl- the King's consent, be transferred to another person. In
dom from
subject to the reign of Henry III (as already mentioned [2]), Ranulf,
subject : Earl of Chester and Lincoln, conveyed to his sister, Hawise
it was only
by favour de Quency, the 'county' of Lincoln so far as it belonged to
of the him [3]. The King, at the instance of Hawise, gave and
King.
granted to her son-in-law, John de Lacy, the third penny of
the County Court of Lincoln, in the name of the Earldom
of Lincoln (*which Ranulf had given to her* in the name
of the Earldom of Lincoln), to be held of the King by John
in special tail [4]. Thus Ranulf's gift to his sister was
recognized by the King, and he acceded to her request in
relation to the future settlement of the Earldom. It is,
however, clear that, as no such transfer could be made
without the King's consent, the whole transaction can only

---

[1] *Journals of the House of Lords*, June 18, 1678 (vol. xiii. p. 253) ;.
Shower's *Cases in Parliament*, 1-11.

[2] See above, pp. 62-64.

[3] Charter printed in Selden's *Titles of Honour*, p. 653.

[4] *Rot. Lit. Pat.*, 17 Hen. III, m. 9. no. 35 (printed, *Rep. Dig. Peer*,
vol. v. app. v. p. 8).

be regarded as a new grant of the Earldom by the King CHAP.XII.
at the request of subjects upon whom he looked with
favour.

The alienation of a barony in the sense of an honour or No transfer
dignity could hardly have been possible at any period. It is of a barony.
shown elsewhere that in early times ' Baron ' was not a name
of dignity like ' Duke ' or ' Earl,' and that the omission of
the word in describing one of the parties, in legal proceedings,
was immaterial. There was in fact but little for the
possessor to aliene. The Summons to Parliament, to which
Barons holding by barony were liable, was not considered
a thing of value. The summons of later times, which was
held to give a peerage to the person summoned, and to the
heirs of his body, could not give it to any one else. Letters
Patent of creation themselves limited the succession and
did not confer anything alienable, unless the principles of
fines and recoveries could be rendered applicable.

A resolution of the Lords with regard to the alienation Resolution
of a dignity appears therefore to have had better warrant House of
than their resolution with regard to surrender. They Lords in
resolved in the reign of Charles I, 'that no person that hath that no
any honour in him, and a Peer of this Realm, may aliene or Peer could
transfer the honour to any other person [1].' honour.

, There is nevertheless something analogous to the transfer Effect of
of a dignity, though only by licence from the sovereign, to the
and only within the blood of the alienor, when the eldest son House of
of a Peer is called up to the House of Lords in his father's eldest son
barony. If, for example, an Earl holding the Earldom of a Peer
of Arundel holds at the same time the barony of Maltravers, father's
and his eldest son is summoned in the barony of Maltravers[2], barony.
it is plain that the barony is, from that time forward, in the
son and not in the father. The father, however, loses the
barony only for his own life, and when the son succeeds to

[1] *Journals of the House of Lords*, Feb. 1, 1640–1641 (vol. iv.
p. 150).
[2] This happened in 1482 (*Rot. Lit. Claus.*, 22 & 23 Ed. IV, m. 10 d),
and is believed to be the first instance of the heir being summoned
during the lifetime of the Peer.

T

CHAP.XII. the Earldom he is in precisely the same position in which his father was before him. Should the son die before the father, leaving issue, his eldest son would have the barony, but neither would take it otherwise than in accordance with the limitations by which the father held it. When a Baron was first created by Letters Patent, with limitation to him and the heirs male of his body, and was afterwards summoned to Parliament, the summons did not supersede the patent and enlarge the grant to the benefit of his heirs general. So also the patent governs the summons in later generations, and the only effect of calling up a son to the House of Lords during his father's life, in his father's barony, is to hasten the descent of the dignity and temporarily to add one to the number of Peers.

The case is, of course, different when the son of a Peer is summoned to the House of Lords in a barony which his father does not possess. In that event the summons operates as a new creation, for the benefit of the person summoned and his lineal heirs; and this has been held to be the effect even when it has been supposed, though erroneously, that the barony was in fact held by the father.

Change in the law of Attainder : greater security to heirs. In more modern times it has commonly been said that a Peer can lose his nobility in three ways only, by death, by attainder, or by Act of Parliament[1]. It does not seem that he can now lose it even by attainder in the same manner as he could under the old law, because it was enacted in the year 1870 that no confession, verdict, inquest, conviction, or judgement of or for any treason or felony, shall cause any attainder or corruption of blood[2]. Thus the heirs of each individual Peer have been placed in a position of security which they never previously enjoyed. Except in the event of the outlawry and non-surrender of a Peer charged with treason or felony, or through the passing of some Act of Parliament, the heir must now always inherit the dignity. .

Traitors and felons disquali- fied. A Peer, however, convicted of treason or felony, and sentenced would be disqualified for sitting or voting in the

---

[1] 1 Com. 403.   [2] Stat. 33 & 34 Vict., cap. 23. sec. 1.

House of Lords, until he had suffered his punishment or CHAP. XII.
received a pardon[1].

The fact of being an alien has, since the Act of Settlement Aliens dis-
qualified.
of the reign of William III, constituted a disqualification
for a summons to the House of Lords. No person born
out of the British dominions, unless born of English parents,
can, even though naturalized, be a member of either House
of Parliament[2].

In former times insolvency or bankruptcy did not cause Bankrupts
disquali-
fied.
any disability, but since the year 1871 a Peer has been dis-
qualified for sitting and voting in the House of Lords during
bankruptcy, and no writ of summons to him will issue[3].

In early times there seems to have been no strict rule Disquali-
fication of
minors.
with regard to age, and, as has been shown in another
chapter, the young Earl of Gloucester and Hertford was
summoned to Parliament while yet a minor. He was,
however, the grandson of one King, and the nephew of
another, and it is possible that an exception was made in
his favour for that reason. Edward, son of Edward I (the
first Prince of Wales), his son Edward (afterwards Edward II),
Edward, the Black Prince, son of Edward III, and Richard
his son (afterwards Richard II), were all called to Parliament
before attaining their majority. The House of Lords, however, on May 22, 1685, resolved 'that no Lord under the
age of one and twenty years, shall sit in this House,' and
that the resolution should be added to the Standing
Orders[4].

There have been special instances in which sentences Exclusion
by the
House.
have been passed in the House of Lords itself, to the effect
that one of their body should be incapable of sitting, as in
the cases of Viscount St. Albans (Lord Bacon) and the
Earl of Middlesex, which have been mentioned in another
chapter. Here, however, as upon judgement for felony, the
Crown may remove the disability by pardon.

[1] Stat. 33 & 34 Vict., cap. 23. sec. 2.
[2] Stat. 12 & 13 Will. III, cap. 2. sec. 3.
[3] Stat. 34 & 35 Vict., cap. 50.
[4] *Journals of the House of Lords*, May 22, 1685 (vol. xiv. p. 10).

CHAP. XII.   From December 1, 1678, to April 23, 1829, the numbers
Disability   of the Lords Temporal sitting in the House of Lords were
under Acts   somewhat diminished by the disqualification of Roman
relating to
oaths.   Catholics to sit, vote, or make a proxy.   They were by Act
of Parliament excluded[1] unless they would make, subscribe,
and repeat a declaration which denied some of the principal
tenets of their faith.   In the reign of George IV, however,
this portion of the Act was repealed, and Peers were allowed
to sit and vote, upon taking and subscribing an oath, which
was designed chiefly with the object of securing the loyalty
of the subject to the sovereign as distinguished from the
Pope[2].   In 1866 a form of oath to be taken by members
of both Houses of Parliament was set forth in an Act of
Parliament.   The omission to take it, however, does not
seem to cause any absolute disability.   'If any member of
the House of Peers,' it is provided, 'votes by himself, or by
his proxy in that House, or sits as a Peer during any
debate, without having made and subscribed the oath, he
shall for every offence be subject to a penalty of £500, to
be recovered by action in one of Her Majesty's Superior
Courts[3].'

Disquali-   Since the year 1792 some of the Peers of Scotland might
fication
specially   possibly have been under a disability which affected none
affecting   but Scots.   It was enacted that no Peer of Scotland should
Peers of
Scotland.   be capable of being elected one of the sixteen representative
Peers, or of voting in the election of the sixteen, who had
twice in any year been present at divine service in any
episcopal place of worship in which prayers were not offered
for the King, for his heirs and successors, and for the Royal
Family[4].   This Act still remains law.

Schemes of   Some efforts to free the House of Lords from disreputable
1888 and
1889 to   persons were made in the years 1888 and 1889.   In the
disable   former year the Marquess of Salisbury introduced a Bill, in
Peers for
disgraceful which it was proposed that all Superior Courts in the United
conduct.

[1] 30 Car. II, stat. 2. secs. 1 & 2.
[2] Stat. 10 Geo. IV, cap. 7. sec. 2.
[3] Parliamentary Oaths Act, 1866, sec. 5.
[4] Stat. 32 Geo. III, cap. 63. sec. 12.

Kingdom should report to the Lord Chancellor every case CHAP. XII. in which a Peer of Parliament had been proved to have been guilty of disgraceful conduct, inconsistent with his character as a member of the House of Lords, and that the Lord Chancellor should lay the report before the House. Upon presentation of an address from the House of Lords, the sovereign was to have power to direct that the writ of summons issued to any Peer should be cancelled, and that he should not be entitled to sit during the existing Parliament [1].

This Bill was withdrawn, not without an expression of regret from the Earl of Carnarvon [2], who in the following year introduced another Bill of a similar character, in which felony and misdemeanour were expressly mentioned [3]. When its second reading was moved it was set aside by means of the previous question [4]. Some of the clauses were considered impracticable ; and as Peers convicted of felony were already disabled by Statute, it may have been thought that there was no need to legislate further on that subject.

The existing disabilities of Peers seem to have aroused some interest in the House of Commons, which has permitted the introduction of a Bill for their relief. It was presented on February 8, 1893. The proposals which it contained were that Peers of the Realm might be enabled to vote at elections for boroughs, counties, or universities, and might themselves be elected members of the House of Commons. In either case, however, they were to become commoners, and their hereditary titles were to lapse, and not to descend to their heirs. A Peer accepting the office of any of the principal Secretaries of State, First Lord of the Treasury or Admiralty, President of the Board of Trade or Local Government Board, or Chancellor of the Exchequer, was

Peers' Disabilities Removal Bill of 1893.

---

[1]. Discontinuance of Writs Bill, H. L., 1888, no. 162; Hansard's *Debates*, 3rd ser., vol. cccxxvii. 414.

[2] Hansard's *Debates*, 3rd ser., vol. cccxxviii. 471.

[3] Discontinuance of Writs Bill, H. L., 1889, no. 18 ; Hansard's *Debates*, 3rd ser., vol. cccxxxiii. 1394.

[4] Hansard's *Debates*, 3rd ser., vol. cccxxxiv. 333.

CHAP. XII. immediately to become a commoner, and lose, both for himself and for his heirs, his hereditary titles [1]. The Bill, however, does not appear to have advanced beyond a first reading [2].

[1] Peers' Disabilities Removal Bill, 1893, H. C., no. 186.
[2] Hansard's *Debates*, 4th ser., vol. viii. 839.

CHAPTER XIII.

A S the various Courts of Justice separated themselves from the old *Curia Regis*, the judicial functions of the Prelates and Temporal Lords summoned to Parliament necessarily underwent a change. The jurisdiction of the Lords in cases of impeachment by the Commons and in the trials of Peers is treated elsewhere. With regard to other matters the Lords gradually lost all original jurisdiction, except in certain questions relating to the peerage, though, in the end, they retained the power of giving a final decision upon writs of error or appeals from Courts below.

There were three distinct stages in this transformation—that in which the other Courts of Justice diverged from the *Curia Regis*, and Council—that in which the Council separated from the Parliament—and that which followed the separation.

It has already been shown how matters were brought from the Courts before the King in his Council in his Parliament for the purpose of having points decided which had arisen when final judgement had not yet been given, and of compelling the Justices to proceed to judgement when it had been too long delayed. When no Parliament was sitting, however, the petitions of the parties could not be presented, and it was apparently to remedy this evil that an Act was passed in the fourteenth year of the reign of Edward III. It was provided that upon the meeting of every Parliament there were to be chosen a Prelate, two Earls, and two Barons, who, with the advice of the

Ch. XIII.

Successive changes in the judicial functions of the Lords.

The Act of 14 Edward III: new Court representing the King in Council in Parliament.

CH. XIII. Chancellor, the Treasurer, the Justices of the two Benches, and others of the King's Council, were to have power, upon petition delivered to them, to direct the Justices. In cases of exceptional difficulty only they were to bring the cases into the next Parliament, for direction to be given according to the older practice[1]. The new tribunal, having power to act independently of any session of Parliament, was in fact the representative of the King in his Council in his Parliament, its functions being precisely the same so far as they extended.

The Act of 25 Edward III, restricting the original judicial power of the Council. This, indeed, was neither original jurisdiction, nor the jurisdiction of a later time by which a judgement could be affirmed or reversed upon Writ of Error or Appeal. So long, however, as the King sat in his Council in his Parliament, he and his Council sat among the Lords, and the Lords participated in the jurisdiction of the Council. The King and Council were in the habit of exercising some original jurisdiction, both in civil and in criminal proceedings, and it was a subject of complaint that the proceedings were not according to the Common Law. In the twenty-fifth year of Edward III it was enacted that in criminal cases no person should be apprehended on petition or suggestion to the Council, without due indictment or presentment, nor in civil cases without due process founded on Original Writ[2].

Separation of the Council from the Parliament. These provisions were not strictly observed, but the subsequent development of the Council has little in common with the present history. The separation of the Council from the Parliament was completed in or about the seventh year of Richard II. In that year the following regulation appears upon the Rolls of Parliament:—' As to petitions and bills the King wills that those which cannot be expedited without Parliament be expedited in Parliament, and those which can be expedited by the King's Council. be laid before the Council[3].' From the tenth year of the

---

[1] 14 Ed. III, stat. 1. cap. 5.   [2] 25 Ed. III, stat. 5. cap. 4.
[3] *Rot. Parl.*, 7 Ric. II, no. 51 (printed, vol. iii. p. 163).

same reign the Proceedings and Ordinances of the Privy CH. XIII.
Council have been duly recorded, and, in the main, are
extant. The Parliament without the Council, however, was
no longer the same body as the Parliament in which the
Council sat, and the judicial as well as other functions
of the House of Lords underwent a corresponding change.

As the equitable jurisdiction of the Chancery was now Little civil
beginning to grow, and the courts of common law had jurisdiction of first
a well-recognized independent existence, there was but instance
left to the
little jurisdiction in civil cases left to the House of Lords as House of
a court of first instance. It could not, perhaps, be said Lords:
disputes in
with truth that all such jurisdiction had departed from the seventeenth
them; and they made a spasmodic attempt to revive it in century.
the reigns of Charles I and Charles II. There could, from
the nature of things, be but few occasions on which
a remedy could not be found either in the courts of law or
in the courts of equity. In 1668, in the case of *Skinner*
v. *The East India Company*, the plaintiff alleged that he
could not obtain redress elsewhere, and presented a petition
to the King. The matter was referred to the House of Lords,
which undertook the jurisdiction, and gave judgement for
Skinner. The East India Company presented a petition
to the House of Commons against the proceedings of the
House of Lords. A violent dispute ensued between the
two Houses [1]. The House of Commons took up the ground
that if there was no remedy for a wrong in the ordinary
Courts of Justice, it could be provided only by the whole
body of Parliament. If by this they meant that an Act to
create a new remedy could come into existence only in the
usual parliamentary course, they were, without doubt, in
the right. If, however, they meant that original jurisdiction
had never resided in the Lords, and that the Lords had
never had the power of sanctioning a new original writ,
they were forgetting the whole history of the *Curia Regis*,
of the King in Council in Parliament, and of the Courts.

---

[1] *Parliamentary History*, vol. iv. pp. 431–433; Hatsell's *Precedents*,
vol. iii. pp. 368–392; Holles, *The Grand Question concerning the Judicature of the House of Peers* (1689); 8 *Rep. Hist. MSS. Com.* 165–168.

CH. XIII.   Peace was made, after a long quarrel, only on the direct interference of King Charles II. His speech to both Houses contained the following passage:—'I remember very well that the case of Skinner was first sent by me to the Lords. I have, therefore, thought myself concerned to offer to you what I judge the best and safest way to put an end to the difference ; and, indeed, I can find no other. I will myself give present order to rase all records and entries of this matter both in the Council Books and in the Exchequer, and do desire that you will do the like in both Houses, that no memory may remain of this dispute between you. And then, I hope, all future apprehensions will be secured[1].' A resolution was thereupon carried in the House of Commons that all matters 'relating to the business between the East India Company and Skinner' should be erased from its Journals. A similar erasure was silently made in the Journals of the House of Lords. After this time the jurisdiction of the latter House, as a Court of first instance in civil causes, may be regarded as having been at an end.

Limitation of criminal jurisdiction: uncertainty prevailing in the seventeenth century.   In criminal matters the Lords, as is shown in another chapter, had vacillated with regard to their own wishes, sometimes desiring to have jurisdiction over none but Peers, sometimes to have jurisdiction in all momentous charges in which commoners were implicated with Peers. In the seventeenth century they practically asserted an original criminal jurisdiction apart from that of the trial of Peers, and from that of accusations brought before them by impeachment of the Commons. This, however, they would seem to have lost through the Act of the twenty-fifth year of Edward III, which forbade the apprehension of any one without due indictment. The Act, it is true, applied nominally to proceedings on petition to the Council, but as petition to the King in his Council in his Parliament was· at this time one of the usual forms, it precluded arrest on

---

[1] *Journals of the House of Commons*, Feb. 22, 1669-1670 (vol. ix. p. 126).

any such petition; and criminal jurisdiction without power CH. XIII.
of arrest would obviously be nugatory. It is possible that
the Act did not debar the Lords or Council from hearing
cases in which an indictment had been found, but the indictment would necessarily have been found in a Court
below, from which, as in the trial of Peers, it would have to
be removed.

It is not quite clear how far the Lords supposed their
criminal jurisdiction to extend at the time of the Long
Parliament of the reign of Charles I. Their proceedings
have, perhaps, been a little exaggerated partly through the
warmth of political feeling, and partly because questions of
privilege or supposed privilege have been involved in many
of the cases which appear upon the Journals. Among them
are several instances of slander of Peers. If, however, these
be left out of consideration, together with the impeachments duly laid before the Lords by the Commons, there
are still to be found some examples of unnecessary interference by the Lords. When one Philip Bembricke counter-
feited letters of protection under the hand and seal of Lord
Fauconbridge, and sold them for forty shillings[1], it is
possible that the Lords may have ordered the appearance
before them of the accused on the ground of privilege.
But, when they took upon themselves to allow the removal
of an indictment not affecting any Lord of Parliament from
a Court of Quarter Sessions to the Court of King's Bench[2],
and when they ordered printers and sellers of unlicensed
books to appear before their Committee, and empowered
the Master and Wardens of the Company of Stationers to
search for clandestine presses[3], they certainly appear to
have assumed very general powers. When they resumed,
after the Restoration, the seats which they had lost during
the period of the Commonwealth, there was still some
uncertainty with regard to their judicial functions; but

[1] *Journals of the House of Lords*, Jan. 23, 1640–1641 (vol. iv.
p. 141).
[2] *Ib.*, Feb. 15, 1640–1641 (vol. iv. p. 162).
[3] *Ib.*, March 4, 1640–1641 (vol. iv. p. 173).

CH. XIII. their pretensions to act as a Court of criminal judicature concurrently with the other Courts of the King seem to have expired with their claims as a Court of first instance for civil causes, when the King's remedy of oblivion had been accepted in relation to Skinner and the East India Company.

Controverted elections of members of the House of Commons decided by the Lords in the reign of Henry V.
In the early days of Parliament, before the Commons had learned to assert themselves, the Lords sometimes exercised a jurisdiction which the Commons afterwards regarded as their most exclusive privilege. Controverted elections were rare but when they occurred redress was obtained by petition to the King, who acted with the advice of his Council. The mode of proceeding was not always the same, but in all cases it indicated that the Commons were not and did not claim to be the arbiters[1]. Soon after the Parliament had separated from the Council, a remarkable case occurred which showed clearly where they supposed the power of rectification to lie. In an election for the county of Rutland in 1417, the Sheriff returned, as one of the Knights of the Shire, one William Ondeby, instead of Thomas Thorpe, who had in fact been duly elected. The Commons then prayed the King and the Lords in Parliament that the matter might be examined. Thereupon the King commanded the Lords in full Parliament to make examination, and to act according to their discretion. The Lords called both Ondeby and Thorpe before them, and, after hearing arguments, agreed that the Sheriff's return was incorrect, that it must be amended, and that Thorpe must be returned as one of the Knights of the Shire[2].

Subsequent changes.
The Lords enjoyed this jurisdiction but a short time, as the power of enquiring into false returns of Knights of the

---

[1] The earlier precedents from 12 Ed. II to 5 Hen. IV, are set forth in the Preface to Glanville's Reports, pp. xi–xxiii, as well as by Prynne.

[2] *Rot. Parl.*, 5 Hen. IV, no. 38 (printed, vol. iii. p. 530). The case has been cited both in Prynne's *Plea for the Lords and House of Peers*, and in the Preface to Glanville's Reports.

Shire was soon afterwards given by Acts of Parliament[1] to CH. XIII.
the Justices of Assise. The right of petition to the King,
however, on the subject of elections was not abolished, and was
exercised in the reign of Henry VI[2]. In later reigns some
uncertainty seems to have prevailed until, in the first year of
that of Queen Mary, we find a Committee of the House
of Commons appointed to enquire whether one Alexander
Newell, elected a burgess of Looe, might be of the House.
It declared that he could not be a member, because, being
a prebendary, he had a voice in the House of Convocation,
and that the Queen's writ should be directed for another
burgess[3]. The House of Commons also 'required,' a few
years later, that, in a case of double election, 'another
person' should be returned for a borough[4]. In subsequent
times there were some disputes as to the power of the
Chancellor to issue writs for the election of new members
upon the occurrence of vacancies during a recess of Parliament, or while Parliament was sitting. They can hardly
be said to belong to the history of the House of Lords in
general. The Lords appear to have exercised no jurisdiction in relation to controverted elections of members of
the House of Commons since the reign of Henry V.

Claims of peerage and of offices of honour have long been Jurisdic-
brought before the House of Lords, but not without express tion in
peerage
reference from the Crown[5]. It does not even appear that cases on
the Crown is bound to adopt this mode of decision, for in reference
from the
the case of the barony of Fitz-Walter, to which reference has Crown.
already been made, the claim, though originally referred to
the House of Lords, was, after a prorogation of Parliament,
withdrawn from their cognizance and laid, by the King's
direction, before the Privy Council[6].

---

[1] Stat. 11 Hen. IV, cap. 1 ; Stat. 6 Hen. VI, cap. 4 ; and see Stat.
23 Hen. VI, cap. 14.
[2] One of the year 2 Hen. VI has been printed in Prynne's *Brevia
Parliamentaria Rediviva*, 156, et seq.
[3] *Journals of the House of Commons*, Oct. 12, 13, 1553 (vol. i. p. 27).
[4] *Ib.*, Jan. 27, 28, 1557-1558 (vol. i. p. 47).
[5] Hale's *Jurisdiction of the Lords' House*, p. 104.
[6] See above, p. 130.

CH. XIII. The usual course, in more recent times, has been for the claimant to present a petition to the Crown through the Secretary of State. It is referred to the Attorney-General, who makes a report upon it. The Crown then has absolute discretion to refer it to the House of Lords or not, but has commonly proceeded in that manner[1]. The jurisdiction is thus not inherent in the House of Lords itself, but is only created, from time to time, as occasion may arise.

Jurisdiction in relation to representative Peers of Scotland.

There is, however, a more clearly defined jurisdiction in respect of the election of the representative Peers of Scotland, and especially in respect of votes and claims to vote. By an Act of Parliament passed in the year 1847 it was provided that when a vote or claim to vote in right of any peerage had been disallowed by the House of Lords upon trial of a contested election, the House might order that the particular title of peerage should not be called over at any future election[2]. It was also enacted that when a protest was made at any meeting for the election of representatives, by any two of the Peers present, against any vote or claim, a copy of the proceedings must be transmitted to the Clerk of the Parliaments. The House of Lords might then, whether there was any contested election or not, enquire into the matter raised by the protest, and order the person against whose vote or claim the protest had been made to appear. Upon his failure to appear or to establish his claim, the House might make the same order as upon disallowance of a vote after trial[3]. In the year 1851 it was further enacted that after every meeting of the Peers of Scotland to elect representative Peers, there should be transmitted to the Clerk of the Parliaments the titles of any peerages, called at the meeting, in right of which no vote had been received and counted for fifty years. The House of Lords might then make an order to abstain from calling the title at future meetings for elections; and.

[1] For a full description of the proceedings in peerage cases, see Hubback's *Evidence of Succession.*

[2] Stat. 10 & 11 Vict., cap. 52. sec. 2.

[3] *Ib.,* sec. 3.

the vote of any one claiming to vote in right of any such CH.XIII.
peerage could not afterwards be received [1].

By the Act of Union with Ireland in the year 1800, And in
it was expressly enacted that all questions touching the relation to
rotation or election of the Lords Spiritual or Temporal tive Lords
of Ireland to sit in the Parliament of the United Kingdom of Ireland.
should be decided by the House of Lords. Whenever there
had been an equality of votes, and consequently no complete
election, the names of the Peers of Ireland for whom an
equal number of votes had been given were to be written
on pieces of paper, and put into a glass by the Clerk of the
Parliaments, at the table of the House of Lords, during
a sitting of the House; and the Peer or Peers whose name
or names should be first drawn out by the Clerk of the
Parliaments would be deemed the Peer or Peers elected [2].
When, however, on the disestablishment of the Church of
Ireland on January 1, 1871, the representative Bishops lost
their right to sit in the House of Lords [3], the jurisdiction of
the House in reference to the rotation of the Irish Lords
Spiritual came to an end.

The jurisdiction of the Lords in error has a sound Jurisdic-
historical foundation, though doubts have been raised, at Parliament
times, as to whether the Commons do not participate in it [4]. in error:
There are, in fact, some early cases in which the Commons which the
appear, at first sight, to have had a voice in the reversal of Commons
judgement, as for example those of Adam de Orleton, have a
Bishop of Hereford, and Thomas Earl of Lancaster, at the voice.
beginning of the reign of Edward III. In both these
instances, however, there was a want of precision in the
course taken, as it was not sufficiently clear whether the
decision of Parliament was to be regarded as a judgement
or as a statute. In both the proceeding was commenced
by Petition. In both the form was that of a judgement and

---

[1] Stat. 14 & 15 Vict., cap. 87. sec. 4.
[2] Stat. 39 & 40 Geo. III, cap. 67. art. 4.
[3] Stat. 32 & 33 Vict., cap. 42. sec. 13.
[4] As by Sir Matthew Hale. in his *Jurisdiction of the Lords' House*,
&c.

Ch. XIII. not of a statute. In both strong party feelings were at work, and it may have been thought expedient to have the assent of the Commons for political purposes in times of great disturbance. The petitions did not recognize any jurisdiction in the Commons. The Bishop of Hereford presented his to the King and Council alone. The record of the Court below was read and examined before the King and his Council, ' and also before the Prelates, Earls, Barons, and the whole Community of the Realm being in Parliament.' The judgement of reversal was given by the King and his Council with the assent of the whole Parliament[1]. The idea of obtaining the consent of the Commons appears to have been an afterthought. The tribunal recognized by the parties was the King in his Council, which, as Parliament was sitting, was the King in his Council in his Parliament ; but this body, as shown elsewhere, did not include the Commons.

No such cases without political significance. It would not be easy to produce any cases which have no political significance, in which error was alleged to have occurred in the courts below, and in the determination of which the Commons have nevertheless had a voice[2]. On the other hand, there is no difficulty in showing that the King in Council in Parliament, without any interference by the Commons, directed and corrected the ordinary proceedings of inferior Courts.

Parliament retains the jurisdiction when the Council separates from it. When the Council finally separated from the House of Lords in the reign of Richard II, what, it may be asked, became of this jurisdiction? Did it remain with the Council, or with the House of Lords. or did it cease ? According to all analogy it should have remained in existence, and have belonged to the nearest representative of the old *Curia Regis*. That, it might, perhaps, fairly be thought, was the House of Lords. It could hardly be said that the

[1] *Rot. Lit. Claus.*, 1 Ed. III, part i. m. 13.
[2] Or. to use the words of Sir Matthew Hale, 'where Commons are mentioned as determining the matter,' the cases are ' upon petition of parties unduly attaint, or their heirs.' *Jurisdiction of the Lords' House*, p. 127.

House of Lords was an offshoot of the Council, though it CH. XIII. · might, perhaps, be said that the Council was an offshoot of the House of Lords. If the Council had sat with the Lords, so also had the Common Law Judges, as part of the Council. The Courts over which the Common Law Judges presided were clearly offshoots of the *Curia Regis*, in which their proceedings could be corrected and directed. Still, the Council was a more important body than any that had in previous times separated itself from the ancient King's Court, and its possible claims to be a final Court of Appeal can hardly be passed over in silence.

The point seems to have been determined with sufficient precision in relation to Courts of Common Law by the unanimous opinion of all the Judges, entered upon the Rolls of Parliament, a little before the separation of the Council from the House of Lords was complete. The law was that when error occurred in the King's Bench it should be amended in Parliament[1]. The essential part of 'the King in Council in Parliament,' for the purpose of this jurisdiction, was, therefore, at the time considered to be the Parliament; and as the Commons formed no necessary part of 'the King in Council in Parliament,' the word Parliament must be interpreted to mean the House of Lords.

The point seems... *(marginal note:)* The general principles laid down by the Judges just before the separation.

There is, moreover, good reason to believe that the whole subject had been fully considered with reference to the coming separation. For a long time before, as has been shown in the case of the Stauntons[2], it had been the practice to present petitions to the King in Council in Parliament, in the intermediate stages of actions in both the King's Bench and the Court of Common Pleas. The same tribunal must have had, at the same time, jurisdiction to amend a final judgement in the Court of King's Bench, for there is a precedent in the old Register of Writs, showing that error in judgement in the King's Bench was brought before 'the King in his Council in his Parliament,' which is, in another part of the same instrument, described as 'the King's Court

[1] *Rot. Parl.*, 50 Ed. III, no. 48 (printed, vol. ii. p. 330).
[2] See above, pp. 51–53.

U

CH.XIII. of Parliament [1]. The Judges, at the end of the reign of Edward III, while recognizing the jurisdiction of Parliament over errors in final judgement in the King's Bench, distinctly laid down the principle that errors alleged to have occurred in the Court of Common Pleas could not be brought directly before Parliament, but must first be considered in the King's Bench [2]. Interlocutory applications in Parliament, while cases were still *sub judice* in Courts below, appear to have ceased after the division of the Council from Parliament, and the law now took the definite shape which it retained for many centuries. Error in the Court of Common Pleas was amended in the King's Bench; error in the King's Bench was amended in Parliament, which was understood to mean the House of Lords. Their decision was final, and in that respect equal to a decision in the full *Curia Regis* of other days.

The Commons not concerned with the judgements of the Lords in the reign of Henry IV.   At the beginning of the reign of Henry IV the Commons were not only willing but anxious that they should not be supposed to have any concern with the judgements of the Lords, and made a protest to that effect. The King agreed that all judgements should be given by himself and the Lords alone, except on occasions on which, for some exceptional reason, he might desire that the Commons should participate [3].

Case of the Earl of Salisbury in the reign of Henry V.   The exception left an opening for ingenious pleading in relation to assignments of error, but no advantage seems to have been taken of it except in cases of attainder. In the year 1414 Thomas, son of John Montague, Earl of Salisbury, presented a petition to the King, praying that the record and process of the declaration against his father as a traitor in the second year of the reign of Henry IV, might be viewed and examined in Parliament, and the errors re-

[1] *Registrum Brevium Originalium* (published 1531), fo. 17-17 b. *De errore corrigendo per Parliamentum.* This is not a writ of error, but a writ of *Scire facias ad audiendum errores*, which was in later times the usual process following a writ of error.

[2] *Rot. Parl.*, 50 Ed. III, no. 48 (printed, vol. iii. p. 330).

[3] *Ib.*, 1 Hen. IV, no. 79 (printed, vol. iii. p. 427).

dressed [1]. The Earl was one of those who had fallen into CH. XIII.
the hands of some of the Lancastrian party at the beginning
of the reign of Henry IV, and been beheaded without trial.
The Lords Temporal, with the assent of the King, had
afterwards declared and adjudged that, as a traitor having
levied war against the King, he should forfeit all the lands
and tenements which he had in fee simple, notwithstanding
the fact that he had been put to death without due process
of law [2].

The petition and the subsequent assignments of error are Error in
hardly comprehensible according to any acknowledged Parlia-
legal principles. It was asked that errors alleged to have confusion
occurred, not in a Court below, but in Parliament itself, of ideas.
should be corrected in Parliament. Among the assignments
of error were two which had relation to the Commons
In one the original 'declaration and judgement' were regarded as judicial acts; in the other they were regarded as
legislative acts. In the one it was complained that they
had been pronounced only by the Lords Temporal with the
King's assent, whereas the judgement ought to have been
given by the King, as sovereign judge, and by the Lords
Spiritual and Temporal, with the assent of the Commons, or
on their petition. In the other it was again maintained
that the declaration and judgement were bad, as having
been passed without petition or assent from the Commons,
because the Commons 'are of right petitioners or assenters
in respect of *that which is ordained for law* in Parliament [3].'

A petition of error alternating between an attempt to The case
redress in Parliament an error supposed to have been com- has no
mitted judicially in the High Court of Parliament itself, on the
and an attempt to reverse an Act or Ordinance of Attainder, authority
is a political curiosity, but seems very like a legal absurdity. Lords over
It shows only the lengths to which men might be ·carried below.
by political partisanship. In any case it has no bearing
upon the authority to redress error arising in Courts below.

---

[1] *Rot. Parl.*, 2 Hen. V, no. 12 (printed, vol. iv. pp. 17–18).
[2] *Ib.*, 2 Hen. IV, no. 30 (printed, vol. iii. p. 459).
[3] *Ib.*, 2 Hen. V, no. 12 (printed, vol. iv. pp. 18–19).

CH. XIII.   From the time of Henry IV the jurisdiction of the High

Jurisdic-   Court of Parliament (in the sense of the House of Lords), in
tion of the   cases of error arising in the King's Bench seems to have
House of
Lords over   been fully accepted—at any rate in theory. The form of
error in   proceeding was at first by petition addressed to the King
the King's
Bench   and 'the noble lords,' of which instances may be found[1].
from the   The frequent and long intermissions of Parliament, however,
time of
Henry IV   led to much inconvenience, and even caused the powers of
down-   the House to fall into disuse[2]. In an Act of the year 1585
wards.
it was recited that erroneous judgements in the King's Bench
could be reformed only in the High Court of Parliament
(which 'is not in these days so often holden as in ancient
time it hath been'), and that 'in respect of greater affairs of
this realm' they could not be well determined even during
the session of Parliament. All writs of error both in
criminal and in civil cases had previously had the effect of
bringing the judgement directly from the King's Bench into
Parliament, but for the sake of expedition a new and intermediate Court of Error was now instituted. Into this Court
(long known as the Exchequer Chamber) either of the
parties in certain civil actions, in which the sovereign was
not concerned, and which had not been commenced by
original writ, could sue a writ of error[3]. Parliament still
remained the Court of final decision, whether the causes
passed through the Exchequer Chamber or not; and ' Parliament,' as we know from Sir Edward Coke, who wrote not
long afterwards, was, according to the law and custom of
Parliament, 'the Lords in the Upper House[4].'

---

[1] E. g. in *Rot. Parl.*, 1 Hen. V, no. 19 (printed, vol. iv. p. 7).

[2] The following words in relation to this subject seem apposite :—
' From the third of Henry V to the accession of James I there appears
to have been little exercise of judicature in Parliament civilly, or indeed
criminally, unless the cruel precedents of Acts of Attainder without
hearing the accused, and the indulgent precedents of Acts of Restitu-.
tion, without assignment of errors, of both of which the number is
great, are fit to be considered as judicial records.' Hargrave's Preface
to Hale's *Jurisdiction of the Lords' House*, p. viii.

[3] Stat. 27 Eliz., cap. 8. And *see* Stat. 31 Eliz., cap. 1.

[4] 4 Inst. 21.

Jurisdiction in error over causes arising in the Court of Ch. XIII.
Exchequer was also enjoyed from a comparatively early History
period by the House of Lords; but the Barons of the of the
Exchequer were very jealous of their privileges, and the law jurisdic-
tion in
seems to have been in some doubt as late as the time of error of
the House
Edward III. In the eleventh year of his reign it must have of Lords
been supposed by some lawyers that error in that part of over the
Exchequer
the Exchequer commonly known as the Exchequer of as a Court
Pleas, at any rate, could be redressed in the King's Bench, of Law.
for a writ of error in that sense was then directed to the
Barons. They, however, stoutly refused to send the record
of the case, as required, and they certified their reasons to
the King. They gave a brief history of the Exchequer and
its rights from the time of the Conquest, and stated that
errors alleged to have occurred in the Exchequer had
always been amended in the Exchequer itself, the Barons
being directed by the King to associate with them others of
his lieges, to hear the record and process[1]. They were
successful in their assertion that the King's Bench had no
jurisdiction in error over the Exchequer. This, however,
does not seem to have exempted them from the supreme
jurisdiction, in early times, of the *Curia Regis*[2], and afterwards of the King in his Council in his Parliament. The
Act of the fourteenth year of Edward III, by which power
was given to a Committee of the Lords, acting with the
Council, to direct the various Courts to give judgement,
expressly included the Exchequer[3]. As the Statute only
extended to the Committee (during the time when Parliament was not sitting) the power exercised by the King in
his Council in his Parliament, it follows that the Council in
Parliament had the same jurisdiction in relation to the

---

[1] *Remembrance Roll* of the Lord Treasurer's Remembrancer, *Communia de Termino Sancti Hillarii anno xi° Edwardi tertii.* *Adhuc
Recorda.* Printed in the Introduction to *Year Books* (Rolls Series),
14 Ed. III, pp. xxi–xxv, where further information in relation to this
matter will be found.

[2] This seems to be shown by the *Dialogus de Scaccario*, lib. i. cap. 8,
where it is said 'cognitio ipsi Principi reservabitur.'

[3] 14 Ed. III, stat. 1. cap. 5.

Cн. XIII. Exchequer as to the other Courts. When the Council was
separated from the Parliament the Lords alone could thus
constitute the final Court of Appeal.

It does not, however, appear that there was ever a direct
appeal from the Exchequer, as a Court of law, to Parliament.
Before the matter was regulated by Statute, the Barons, as
has been shown, claimed that error should be considered in
the Exchequer itself. In the year 1357 an Act was passed
to the effect that, when complaint was made of error in the
Exchequer, the Chancellor and Treasurer, associating with
them the Justices and other learned persons, should call
before them the Barons of the Exchequer, with the record,
and córrect any error, if found[1]. The hearing was to be
in some Council Chamber near the Exchequer, and this
appears to have been the true origin of the ' Court of
Exchequer Chamber,' the component parts of which differed
according to circumstances. After 1585 it was constituted
in one way for the purpose of considering writs of error from
the Court of Exchequer, but in another way for the purpose
of considering writs of error from the King's Bench.

The Court of Exchequer, as a court of law, was thus in
a position very similar to that of the King's Bench. From
the King's Bench some errors in judgement might be taken
first into the Exchequer Chamber, and thence to the House
of Lords, though others had to be taken directly to the
House of Lords. From the Exchequer, as a court of law
(though not as a court of equity) all errors in judgement had
to be taken first to the Exchequer Chamber, but might be
taken to the House of Lords by a subsequent writ of error.

Impor-
tance of
the form of
Writs of
Error to
Parlia-
ment.

The Writ of Error to bring an erroneous judgement into
the House of Lords always retained the ancient form. It
was a mandate from the sovereign directing the Judges of the
Court below to send the record and proceedings ' to us in
our Parliament . . . that we may further cause to be done .
thereupon, with the assent of the Lords Spiritual and
Temporal[2] in the same Parliament, for correcting that

[1] 31 Ed. III, stat. 1. cap. 12.
[2] Attention has been drawn by Sir Matthew Hale in his *Jurisdiction*

error, what of right and according to the law and custom of CH. XIII.
England ought to be done.' The King in his Parliament
was the Court of last appeal, and represented the ancient
King in his Council in his Parliament; but the House of
Lords was the tribunal that actually heard the cause.

Proceedings in error were not abolished, even in civil The House
actions, until the year 1875[1], and no change had been made practically
in the words of the writ. Even then there was a saving described
with regard to proceedings on the Crown side of the Queen's ment.
Bench, and on the Revenue side of the Exchequer[2]; and
thus, in relation to criminal jurisdiction in error, the House
of Lords has continued to be described as Parliament.

The jurisdiction of the House of Lords in appeals from Jurisdic-
the Equity side of the Court of Chancery, though it might Lords in
fairly be traced to the same origin as its jurisdiction in Appeals
writs of error, had nevertheless a different history. The Chancery:
Chancery, having always been, from the time when Parlia- early
ment first existed, an office of the Parliament, was naturally of the
very closely associated with it and with the Council. All Chancery
'original writs' for the trial of causes in the King's Courts Parlia-
issued out of the Chancery. Certain writs, of which the ment.
forms had been settled, issued 'as of course;' but, when
any difficulty arose in relation to a new kind of writ, the
authority of Parliament, that is to say, of the King in his
Council in his Parliament, had to be obtained[3].

The issue of original writs has usually been regarded
as part of the common law jurisdiction of the Court of
Chancery. It should, however, rather be considered a dis-

<hr>

of the Lords' House, to an early form of writ of error in Rastell's
Entries, in which he supposes that the words 'and Commons' were
added. There is undoubtedly an addition, but, as it stands, it is
meaningless, and is obviously a misprint, the words being *ac comitatum*,
which could only be translated 'and the County,' 'and the County
Court,' 'and the Earldom,' or 'and of the comities.' Rastell's *Entries*,
1574, fo. 284.

[1] Supreme Court of Judicature Act, 1875, Order lviii.
[2] *Ib.*, Order lxii; Supreme Court of Judicature Act (Ireland), 1877,
sec. 65.
[3] Stat. Westm. 2 (13 Ed. 1), cap. 24.

CH. XIII   tinct function, more closely associated with the equitable
jurisdiction than with the common law jurisdiction, so far
as the latter related to the hearing of causes. As the
fountain of justice under the Parliament the functions of
the Chancery were of the widest possible range ; as a mere
Court of Common law its functions were extremely limited,
and even subordinate to the Court of King's Bench. When
it had given judgement, the judgement could be reversed on
writ of error in the King's Bench ; and a reversal actually
occurred as late as the fourteenth year of Queen Elizabeth[1].

Growth of   The line of demarcation between the common law and
the equity
jurisdic- equity, or between the ordinary and extraordinary jurisdiction of the tion of the Chancery, was not at first drawn in the same
Chancery.
manner as in later times. Some of the proceedings which
are usually said to have been at common law, were in fact
the subject of complaint in the reign of Henry IV as being
injurious to the administration of the common law itself[2].
As late as the reign of Edward IV also the same proceedings
(upon *Scire facias* to traverse an office) were referred to the
equitable jurisdiction of the Court[3].

Proceedings of this kind, however, were in early times
not before the Chancellor alone, though in the Chancery,
but before members of the Council, including the Judges,
and it was sometimes expressed that the decision was given
after consultation with the whole of the Council. To the
King in his Council (or, when Parliament was sitting, to
the King in his Council in his Parliament) may in like
manner be traced the whole of the equitable jurisdiction of
the Court. Certain petitions were referred to members of
the Council sitting in the Chancery, until, by degrees, there
grew up a practice of addressing a Petition or Bill directly
to the Chancellor, and cases for which the common law was

---

[1] Dyer's *Reports*, 315 (no. 100), where earlier cases are cited.
[2] *Rot. Parl.*, 2 Hen. IV, no. 95 (vol. iii. p. 474).
[3] Staunford, *Prerog. Reg.*, p. 77. See a fuller discussion of this
matter in the Introduction to the *Year Books*, 12 & 13 Ed. III (Rolls
Series), pp. cvi–cxi, and the article ' Common Law and Conscience in
the ancient Court of Chancery,' *Law Quarterly Review*, vol. i.

supposed to provide no remedy were heard by him. As, Сн. XIII.
when difficulties arose in framing a common law writ in the
Chancery, the matter had to be taken into Parliament, so
when a decree of the Chancellor was thought to be erroneous,
a petition in Parliament might have appeared the only
possible remedy.

Appeals from Chancery decrees, however, at any rate Jurisdic-
under the name of appeals, were necessarily of much later Lords in
growth than writs of error from the courts of common law. Appeals
The equitable jurisdiction of the Chancery was itself of slow Chancery
growth, and, before it had come to maturity, men had at one time
almost forgotten the remedial power of the King in his
Council in his Parliament.   No petition of 'appeal' appears
to have been made before the reign of James I, when the
Lords heard the matters alleged in Sir John Bourchier's
case, though a committee of privileges had reported that
the word 'appeal' was not usual, and that in former times
the petition had been addressed to the King and his Great
Council [1].   In the reign of Charles I, Lady Moulson's
petition to the Lords for reversal of a decree in equity was
referred to the Committee of Petitions [2].   It has often been
questioned by lawyers of eminence whether the jurisdiction
really belonged to the House of Lords [3], without any special
commission from the sovereign, such as there was in the case
of a writ of error to rectify judgement in a court of common
law.   The point is one which has reference to form rather
than to substance.   The Parliament, in the sense of the
King, Lords, Judges, and high officers of State, was the
original fountain of Justice from which flowed remedies not

[1] *Journals of the House of Lords*, Dec. 3, 6, 10, & 11, 1621 (vol. iii.
pp. 179–180, 184, 189, 190–192).
[2] *Ib.*, Jan. 23, 1640–1641 (vol. iv. p. 141).
[3] Spence's *Equitable Jurisdiction of the Court of Chancery*, vol. i.
p. 393. His opinion seems to have been founded on Sir Matthew
Hale's *Treatise on the Jurisdiction of the Lords' House*, p. 193 et
seq., and Hargrave's Preface to it. The proper course, according to
Sir Matthew Hale, was to present a petition to the King (upon which
there should issue a commission to examine the decree and proceedings), or else to obtain an Act of Parliament.

Cii. XIII. to be obtained elsewhere. It might have been technically incorrect to address a petition, in the nature of an appeal, to the Lords alone, but hardly more incorrect than to address a petition in the first instance to the Chancellor alone. The Chancellor, however, was the King's Chancellor, and the Parliament was the King's Parliament. It does not appear that the King's prerogative suffered more by a petition to the Lords in Parliament than by a petition to the Chancellor in Chancery.

But fully admitted since the reign of Charles II.
As late as the year 1675, the appellate jurisdiction of the House of Lords in equity cases was disputed by the House of Commons[1], but they did not succeed in wresting it away[2]. The appeal, when established, was recognized as being directly from the decision of the Chancellor to the House of Lords, though decisions by his subordinates could be reheard by himself. It could, after the year 1726, at any rate, be brought upon any interlocutory matter as well as on a final decree, and, when it had been heard, the House of Lords gave direction to the Court of Chancery to rectify its own decision[3]. The appeal thus very closely resembled the earlier applications to the King in his Council in his Parliament during the progress of causes in the Courts of King's Bench and Common Pleas.

The Equity side of the Exchequer.
The equitable jurisdiction of the Court of Exchequer seems to have arisen in a manner somewhat different from that of the Court of Chancery. It has been maintained that equity had a place in the revenue side of the Exchequer as early as the reign of Edward II. It is the fact that certain proceedings of that period are mentioned as being ' of the Equity of the Court[4],' but the mere word ' Equity ' was used at a much earlier period, and is described by Bracton as mitigating the rigour of the law[5]. This, however, does not in any way show that the idea of distinct Courts for the

---

[1] *Journals of the House of Commons*, Nov. 19, 1675 (vol. ix. p. 381).
[2] Shower's *Cases in Parliament*, 81.   [3] 3 Bl. Com. 55.
[4] *Remembrance Roll* of the Lord Treasurer's Remembrancer, printed in Price's *Law of the Exchequer*, p. 260, note 1.
[5] Bract. 12 b and 23 b.

hearing of causes in equity, as distinguished from common law, had come into existence. On the contrary we find common law Judges, as late as the reign of Edward III, hesitating with regard to their judgement when the law seems to be at variance with that which they describe as ' conscience and the law of God [1].'

The earliest known bills in Equity in the Exchequer are of the reign of Elizabeth, and there can be but little doubt that they were in imitation of the similar bills in Chancery. As the Exchequer had exclusive jurisdiction in revenue matters, the power of the Court of Chancery did not extend to them ; and equitable relief could therefore be obtained only in the Exchequer itself. By a convenient fiction the jurisdiction of the Exchequer in Equity was afterwards extended, as was its jurisdiction in common law, to other subjects, and for a considerable time the Courts of Chancery and Exchequer thus had (except in certain cases which could be heard in one of them alone) a concurrent jurisdiction. During this period the only appeal from the Equity side of the Exchequer was to the House of Lords.

Appeal thence to the House of Lords.

The appeal from the Court of Chancery as a Court of Equity by petition to the House of Lords, being of later origin than the writ of error, was different in form, and was addressed to 'the Lords Spiritual and Temporal in Parliament assembled.' The dispute which arose in the reign of Charles II may, perhaps, have been one of the causes which determined the form of appeal, so that no jurisdiction could be claimed by the Commons. The Equity jurisdiction of the Court of Exchequer was transferred to the Court of Chancery in the year 1841 [2], though the transfer was not held to apply to matters affecting the revenue.

Form of Equity Appeal : ' To the Lords Spiritual and Temporal in Parliament assembled.'

The Acts of Union with Scotland and Ireland were not without effect upon the judicial functions of the House of Lords. It was expressly provided by the Act of Union

Effect of the Union with Scotland.

---

[1] *Year Books*, M., 13 Ed. III, no. 51 (Rolls Series), p. 96.
[2] Stat. 5 Vict., cap. 5. sec. 1.

CH. XIII. with Scotland [1], that no causes in Scotland should be cognizable by the Courts of Chancery, Queen's Bench, Common Pleas, or any other Court in Westminster Hall.   The jurisdiction of the House of Lords as a Court of Appeal was, however. not excluded, and was regulated in relation to Scotland by subsequent Acts.   It was fully recognized in 1809, though it was then (with certain exceptions) limited to appeals from judgements or decrees on the whole merits of a case, as distinguished from appeals from interlocutory judgements of the Court of Session [2].

And with Ireland.

In relation to Scotland, which up to the time of the Union was a separate kingdom with different laws from those of England, even when under the same sovereign, it has not seemed necessary to trace the early stages of judicature before the House of Lords of Great Britain acquired an appellate jurisdiction over Scottish causes.   In relation to Ireland, however, the House of Lords had stood in a different position for many centuries.

Kings of England at first Lords, afterwards Kings of Ireland.

After the conquest of Ireland by Henry II, and before Henry VIII assumed the title of King of Ireland, it was styled only a dominion or lordship.   John, afterwards King of England, succeeded his father as Lord of Ireland, while his elder brother, Richard, was King of England ; but after the accession of John to the English throne, all the Kings of England, until the time of Henry VIII, were Lords of Ireland.

Early relations of the Courts of Justice and House of Lords in Ireland to the Courts of Justice and House of Lords in England.

During this period a Parliament came into existence, and developed in Ireland, which was in many respects analogous to the Parliament of England, but was wanting in some of the powers enjoyed by the English Parliament, and in particular by the English House of Lords   Theoretically the English laws prevailed in Ireland, after they had been established by King John, and still more after the native Brehon laws had been formally abolished in the reign of. Edward III.   The Irish Courts of Justice were, at a very early period, in subordination to the English Courts of

---

[1] Art. 19.   [2] Stat. 48 Geo. III, cap. 151. sec. 15.

Justice, and the Irish House of Lords had not the same CH. XIII.
jurisdiction as the English House of Lords. When error
was alleged in the proceedings of the Court of King's Bench
in England, the matter was decided by the English Parliament or House of Lords. When error was alleged in
proceedings in the Court of King's Bench in Ireland, the
matter was decided by the Court of King's Bench in
England [1]; and if error was again alleged, the final tribunal
was the English and not the Irish Parliament, the English
and not the Irish House of Lords.

On the other hand, Acts of the English Parliament did Restric-
not in ordinary cases extend to Ireland, and the Chief tions upon
the power
Governor or King's Deputy in Ireland held Irish Parlia- of Irish
ments which passed laws of their own. There consequently ments.
occurred some divergence of laws, for a time, until in the
tenth year of the reign of Henry VII it was enacted under
Sir Edward Poynings, then Chief Governor or King's
Deputy, that all Acts of Parliament previously made in
England should be in force in Ireland [2]. This law had no
effect upon future Acts of Parliament which still remained
inapplicable to Ireland, except where Ireland was expressly
mentioned, or included in general words such as 'within
any of the King's dominions.' By other Statutes, however,
passed in Ireland at the same time, the power of the Irish
Parliament was greatly restricted. A Parliament could not
even be summoned in Ireland until the King had been
certified as to the cause, and as to the articles of the
proposed Acts. No Acts could be passed until the King
in Council in England had approved of them. These
provisions were so far relaxed in the reign of Philip and
Mary, that new propositions might be certified to the King,
after the summons and during the session of Parliament [3].
Even thus, however, the Irish Parliament had practically no

[1] This principle may be detected as early as the reign of Edward I,
and was thoroughly recognized in the reign of Edward III. See
Year Books, 13–14 Ed. III (Rolls Series), Introduction, pp. lxxii–lxxiii.
[2] Irish Stat. 10 Hen. VII, cap. 22. *Ib.*, cap. 4.
[3] Irish Stat. 3 & 4 Philip and Mary, cap. 4.

CH. XIII. independent power of initiating any law, and the power of rejecting was of little use, as the Irish Houses of Parliament could reject only after Irish propositions had been so far modified in England as to be no longer agreeable in Ireland. The effect of this legislation, however, was to remove one cause which might have produced differences between the laws of the two countries.

The House of Lords of Ireland declared to have no jurisdiction in Error or Appeals in the reign of George I.   The assumption by Henry VIII of the title of King instead of Lord of Ireland, was of no practical importance, except in so far as, Ireland being recognized as a kingdom, its Parliament may have acquired some new dignity; but as the King of England and Ireland continued to govern in Ireland by a Viceroy, the difference was almost inappreciable. In the reign of George I, it appears that the House of Lords in Ireland had been assuming a power and jurisdiction to examine, correct, and amend the judgements and decrees of the Courts of Justice in the kingdom of Ireland. A declaratory Act was therefore passed in the Parliament of Great Britain, 'for the better securing the dependency of the Kingdom of Ireland, upon the Crown of Great Britain.' It was therein declared that the kingdom of Ireland had been, was, and of right ought to be subordinate to and dependent upon the Imperial Crown of Great Britain, as being inseparably united and annexed thereunto, and that the Parliament of Great Britain had full power and authority to make laws and statutes of sufficient force and validity, to bind the kingdom and people of Ireland. It was further declared and enacted that the House of Lords of Ireland had not, nor of right ought to have, any jurisdiction to judge of, affirm, or reverse any judgement, sentence, or decree given or made in any Court in Ireland, and that all proceedings before the Irish House of Lords upon any such judgement, sentence, or decree were null and void [1].

The appellate jurisdiction over Irish causes taken from   This Statute while expounding, did not in any way alter the relation of the Irish Courts to England, which remained as it had been for ages. At most the Statute brought into greater prominence the fact that an appeal lay from

[1] Stat. 6 Geo. I, cap. 5.

the Chancery of Ireland, not to the Irish House of Lords, but CH. XIII. to the House of Lords of Great Britain. A very important the House change, however, was effected in the reign of George the of Lords of Great Third, only seventeen years before the Union. The Act of Britain in George the First was repealed [1], but as it was in fact only 1783, and transferred declaratory, the repeal had practically little or no effect. to Ireland. A subsequent Act, however, was passed which placed the Irish Courts and the Irish Parliament in an entirely new position. It was enacted that 'the right claimed by the people of Ireland to be bound only by laws enacted by his Majesty and the Parliament of that kingdom in all cases whatever, and to have all actions and suits at law or in equity, which may be instituted in that kingdom, decided in his Majesty's Courts therein finally, and without appeal from thence, shall be, and it is hereby declared to be, established and ascertained for ever, and shall at no time hereafter be questioned or questionable.' No writ of error or appeal in any action instituted in any of the Irish Courts was to be received in any of the English Courts [2].

The effect of this very remarkable Act was, to place the kingdom of Ireland in a position as independent as that enjoyed by the kingdom of Scotland, between the accession of James I and the Act of Union with Scotland in 1707. There was a difference in that the laws of Scotland were different from those of England, while those of Ireland were the same, but in each case the administration was independent, and subject only to the same Crown.

With the Union came another change of policy. It was, But indeed, enacted that all laws in force at the time, and all restored to the House Courts of civil and ecclesiastical jurisdiction within the of Lords respective kingdoms were to remain, though subject to of the United alteration by the United Parliament. It was, however, at the Kingdom same time provided that the jurisdiction over writs of error by the Act and appeals, which had been given to the Irish House of of Union. Lords seventeen years before, should be transferred to the House of Lords of the United Kingdom [3]. Such is the

---

[1] Stat. 22 Geo. III, cap. 53. [2] Stat. 23 Geo. III, cap. 28.
[3] Stat. 39 & 40 Geo. III, cap. 67. sec. 1. art. 8.

CH. XIII. early history of the jurisdiction over Irish causes on appeal, which, as will appear below, the House of Lords
still retains.

Wide range   The House of Lords has had also analogous jurisdiction
of the
Lords'   elsewhere, as, for instance, in appeals from the Chancery of
jurisdiction the Duchy of Lancaster. It has thus had authority to
in Error
and on   affirm or reverse judgement or decree in all the principal
Appeal.   Courts of Common Law and Equity in the realm, and
authority, through the King's Bench, which had a wide
jurisdiction in error, over various other Courts. The many
changes in legal procedure which have been brought to pass
in later years, though they have had far-reaching effects on
the Courts below, have still left the House of Lords,
nominally at least, the Supreme Court of Appeal, the Court
which gives the final decision, except in cases which are
within the jurisdiction of the Judicial Committee of the
Privy Council.

Threatened   In 1873, however, there was a threatened interruption in
loss of
jurisdiction the functions of the House of Lords. By the Supreme
in 1873:   Court of Judicature Act of that year, a Supreme Court
Supreme
Court of   was brought into existence, which included and united
Judicature various jurisdictions previously distinct. It had two divisions.
Act.
One, called the 'High Court of Justice,' comprised the
former jurisdictions of the ancient Courts of Chancery,
Queen's Bench, Common Pleas at Westminster, Ex-
chequer, Admiralty, Probate and Divorce, of the London
Court of Bankruptcy, of the Court of Common Pleas at
Lancaster, of the Court of Pleas at Durham, and of the
Courts of Assise, Oyer and Terminer, and Gaol Delivery.
The other was a Court of Appeal, which could determine
appeals from the High Court of Justice, and which also
absorbed the appellate jurisdiction of the Lord Chancellor,
of the Court of Appeal in Chancery, of the Chancellor of the
Duchy of Lancaster, of the Lord Warden of the Stannaries, .
of the Exchequer Chamber, and, to some extent, of the
Privy Council. No error or appeal was after the commencement of the Act to be brought from the High Court of
Justice or the Court of Appeal, or the Court of the Chancery

of the County Palatine of Lancaster, either to the House of CH. XIII.
Lords, or to the Judicial Committee of the Privy Council [1].
The effect of this Act would have been to abolish the
appellate jurisdiction of the House of Lords in relation to
all Courts in England. It was to have come into effect on
November 2, 1874 [2]. In the meantime, however, there was
an opportunity for further reflection, and by the Supreme
Court of Judicature (Commencement) Act, 1874, the operation of the previous Act was deferred until November 1
in the following year. In 1875 another Supreme Court
of Judicature Act was passed, by which the Act of 1873
was amended in various points, and in which the operation of the section relating to the House of Lords was
again postponed until November 1, 1876 [3]. Jurisdiction
was given to the House of Lords, up to that date, to hear
appeals from the new Court of Appeal, not only in cases in
which appeal or error might previously have been brought
before the House, but also in cases in which the jurisdiction
of the Privy Council had been, in 1873, transferred to the
new Court of Appeal.

The opera-
tion of the
Act twice
deferred.

Before the appointed November 1, 1876, when the House
of Lords was to have lost its ancient character as a Court
of Appeal, another Act was passed, to take effect on the
same day [4], and practically to maintain the House of Lords
in its former position. Under the Appellate Jurisdiction
Act, 1876, an appeal was made to lie to the House of
Lords from the Court of Appeal in England, and from
any Court in Scotland or Ireland, from which error or
appeal to the House of Lords previously lay by common
law or statute [5].

The
jurisdiction
at last
saved by
another
Act.

It was at the same time enacted that every appeal should
be brought by way of petition to the House of Lords,
praying that the matter of the order or judgement. might

A new
form of
Appeal:
a happy
historical
adaptation.

[1] Supreme Court of Judicature Act, 1873, secs. 3, 4, 16, 18–21.
[2] *Ib.*, sec. 2.   [3] Supreme Court of Judicature Act, 1875, sec. 2.
[4] Appellate Jurisdiction Act, 1876, sec. 2.
[5] *Ib.*, sec. 3. And see Supreme Court of Judicature Act (Ireland),
1877, secs. 65, 86.

X

CH. XIII. be reviewed 'before Her Majesty the Queen in her Court
of Parliament,' in order that the Court might 'determine
what of right and according to the law and custom of this
realm ought to be done[1].' This was a happy combination
of the old petition of appeal with the older writ of error.
The petition to the House of Lords was adopted from the
petition of appeal from the High Court of Chancery to the
House of Lords; the other formal words were from the
writ of error in use when the House of Lords received it
from the Courts of King's Bench or Exchequer Chamber.

Provisions
for sittings
during pro-
rogation
or disso-
lution.

Provisions were at the same time made to prevent delays
in the administration of justice, when Parliament was not
sitting. During prorogation the House of Lords could
thenceforward hear appeals in the manner appointed by
the House during the preceding session, and 'Lords of
Appeal in Ordinary,' of whom more is said in another
chapter[2], might also take their seats and oaths[3]. When
a Parliament was dissolved, Her Majesty might, by writing
under her sign manual, authorize the 'Lords of Appeal,' in
the name of the House of Lords, to exercise the jurisdiction
of the House of Lords, in relation to appeals, as if their
sittings were a continuation of sittings of the House of
Lords[4].

Provisions
as to
'Lords
of Appeal.'

In Blackstone's time it was said that the law reposed
'an entire confidence in the honour and conscience of the
noble persons who compose this important assembly, that
they will make themselves masters of those questions upon
which they undertake to decide, since upon their decision
all property must finally depend[5].' This unquestioning
faith is not so fully apparent in the Appellate Jurisdiction
Act of 1876. According to its provisions no appeal can be
heard and determined in the House of Lords, except in the
presence of three at least of the following persons, all of
whom bear the general name of Lords of Appeal:—the
Lord Chancellor of Great Britain, for the time being, Peers

---

[1] Appellate Jurisdiction Act, 1876, sec. 4.
[2] See below, pp. 382–384.   [3] Sec. 8.   [4] Sec. 9.
[5] 3 Com. 56–57.

who have previously held his office, Peers who hold or have
previously held the office of Lord Chancellor of Ireland,
of paid Judge of the Judicial Committee of the Privy
Council, or Judge of one of Her Majesty's Superior Courts
of Great Britain or Ireland, and 'the Lords of Appeal in
Ordinary.'

The 'Lords of Appeal in Ordinary' were called into
existence for the first time in virtue of the Act of 1876.
They were required to possess the qualification of having
held for two years one of the high judicial offices which gave
a qualification to 'Lords of Appeal,' or of having been
a practising barrister in England or Ireland, or a practising
advocate in Scotland, for not less than fifteen years[1].
Though, however, a new safeguard was provided for the
administration of justice by qualified persons, the ancient
jurisdiction of the House was, in theory at any rate, left
unimpaired. The effect may, no doubt, have been to throw
the judicial business more than ever into the hands of the
'Law Lords;' but, except during a dissolution of Parliament, there was nothing in the Act to exclude any members of the House of Lords from the Court of final appeal.
Eleven years later this Act was somewhat modified[2], but
the changes then introduced did not deprive the House of
Lords, as a whole, of its inherent judicial power.

The descent of the ancient jurisdiction of the King in his
Council in Parliament has now been traced, save with
regard to one curious exception, which is a remarkable
instance of the exception proving the rule. When the
Council separated from the Parliament, the Parliament, or
in other words, the House of Lords, retained almost the
whole of the supreme jurisdiction, but not quite. There
was a Council before there was, in name at any rate,
a Parliament. and William of Normandy had a Council of
his own before he became the Conqueror of England, or
had any familiarity with judicial power in England. Jersey
and the other Channel Islands were part of the Duchy of

The House of Lords not the only final Court of Appeal: jurisdiction of the Privy Council.

---

[1] Appellate Jurisdiction Act, 1876, sec. 6.
[2] Appellate Jurisdiction Act, 1887, sec. 2.

CH. XIII. Normandy, and retained their ancient judicial procedure after they became united to the English Crown. As the power of the English Parliament grew, they were not bound by its ordinary Acts, nor did any writ of error lie from the Islands to Parliament. An appeal lay, however, to the King and his Council, not apparently to the King of England as King, but to the successor of the Dukes of Normandy and his Court, or Council.

When Ireland was conquered, the English laws were imposed, and consequently the precedent of the Channel Islands did not apply to judicial proceedings. The Isle of Man, however, which retained laws of its own, had an appeal from a decree of the Lord of the island to the King in Council. Moreover when any one 'claims an island or a province in the nature of a feudal principality, by grant from the King or his ancestors, the determination of that right belongs to His Majesty in Council.' From all the dominions of the crown, excepting Great Britain and Ireland, an appellate jurisdiction (in the last resort) is vested in the same tribunal[1]. Although the circumstances are not the same, the analogy of the Channel Islands would appear to have gained this jurisdiction for the Privy Council and not for the House of Lords. A similar reason may also, perhaps, be assigned for the jurisdiction of the Privy Council in relation to idiots and lunatics. Under feudal institutions, the custody of an idiot belonged to the lord of the fee, and in early times probably there was no very clear distinction drawn between a lunatic and an idiot. In the reign of Edward II, it was made a part of the King's prerogative to have the custody of the lands of born idiots, and to keep the lands of lunatics for their own use when restored to reason[2]. The King's power, however, was still of feudal origin, and an appeal from an order of the Chancellor, in relation to idiots and lunatics, went, perhaps, naturally to the King in Council, and not to the Parliament, when the Parliament was separated from the Council. In

---

[1] 1 Com. 231.

[2] Stat. *Praerogativa Regis*, 17 Ed. II, stat. 1. caps. 9, 10.

appeals from the High Court of Admiralty, which was not CH. XIII.
a common law or equity Court, the Privy Council has
also had jurisdiction, as well as in appeals from ecclesiastical
Courts. Various changes have been effected from time to
time, but it is needless for the purposes of this history to
trace them in detail. It seems only necessary to mention
that some portion of the jurisdiction (as, for example, in
Admiralty and Lunacy appeals), has been indirectly transferred to the House of Lords through the 'Court of Appeal'
in England, and the similar 'Court of Appeal' in Ireland[1].

[1] Supreme Court of Judicature Act, 1873, sec. 18 (5); Supreme
Court of Judicature Act (Ireland), 1877, sec. 86.

CHAPTER XIV.

LEGISLATIVE POWER.

The legislative power before Commons were summoned to Parliament. THE legislative functions of the House of Lords have undergone many changes since the days of the *Curia Regis*. Before representatives of the Commons were summoned to Parliament (and they were not summoned before the time of Simon de Montfort's assembly in the forty-ninth year of Henry III), it is clear that new laws could be brought into being and that existing laws could be modified only by the sovereign and by those persons whom he called to advise him. The burgesses may have sent to the Exchequer representatives with power to make the best bargain they could with regard to the money which they were to contribute to the necessities of the State [1] ; and in this primitive practice may, perhaps, be discerned the germ of that which subsequently developed into the House of Commons. The burgesses, however, had not the slightest power to alter the laws of the land, and their early aspirations appear to have been limited to two principal objects, —one to escape with as light a burden as possible, the other to obtain a new charter, or a confirmation of a real or imaginary old charter for their borough.

The early Charters subsequent to the Conquest. The idea that laws are in continual need of change was not familiar to our ancestors either immediately before or immediately after the Conquest. The King wore his crown and held his Court at stated seasons, and summoned Bishops, Abbots, and Magnates of the land to advise him in times of great emergency. On his accession he com-

---

[1] See below, p. 337.

monly granted a charter, or confirmed charters made by CH. XIV.
his predecessors; and he sometimes agreed to a new charter
(as King John agreed to Magna Charta) under pressure of
circumstances. On all these occasions he was surrounded
by the ecclesiastical and lay dignitaries of the land, some
of whose names appear as witnesses to the charters which
were granted. The documents very rarely purported to be
for the establishment of any absolutely new law. The
Conqueror and his followers brought from France some
laws and ideas of law which were new to the English; and
some of the laws existing in England were new to the
Conqueror and his followers. When a charter of laws or
liberties was granted, it was usually, for some time after
the Conquest, supposed to be in recognition or declaration
of some laws and liberties which actually were or had been
in existence. Henry I, for instance, professed to restore the
laws of Edward the Confessor, with such amendments as
his father the Conqueror had introduced by advice of the
Barons[1]. Stephen confirmed all the liberties and good
laws which Henry I had granted, and all the good laws
and customs in existence in the time of Edward the
Confessor[2]. Henry II in like manner confirmed all the
customs which Henry I had given and granted[3].

,In all these cases the charter of confirmation which The King,
establishes the law is, according to its words, an act of Prelates, and
royal grace, not necessarily made by the advice of any *Proceres*
kind of Council. These charters were, however, made establish the Consti-
chiefly in the interest of the Church and the Barons, and tutions of
were probably the result of some kind of deliberation—the Clarendon in the
embodiment of a treaty between the King upon his reign of Henry II.
accession and his principal subjects. When we come to
the famous Constitutions of Clarendon in 1164 we find that

---

[1] Charter printed from the *Textus Roffensis*, and the Red Book of
the Exchequer, in the *Statutes of the Realm*, vol. i. p. 1, and in Blackstone's Tracts (1771), p. 286, n.

[2] Charter printed from Claud. D 2. fo. 75, in the *Statutes of the
Realm*, vol. i. p. 4, and by Blackstone (Tracts, p. 287 n.).

[3] Charter printed from Claud. D 2. fo. 79, in the *Statutes of the
Realm*, vol. i. p. 4, as well as by Blackstone (Tracts, p. 288 n.).

Cн. XIV.   King Henry II was himself present, and that there were present also Archbishops, Bishops, Abbots, Priors, Earls, Barons, and 'Proceres' of the Realm.   The establishing of the laws then made is described (even by an ecclesiastic who thought them iniquitous and hateful to God) as the acknowledgement and act of placing on record of a certain part of the customs and liberties recognized by Henry I and others [1].

The legislative power in the King and baronage.
Such legislative power as existed then existed in the King and his baronage, under which term were included at that time the Bishops, Abbots, and Earls, as well as others holding lands of the King, in chief, as of his crown.   It was indeed expressly laid down in the eleventh chapter of the Constitutions of Clarendon that Archbishops, Bishops, and all persons holding of the King *in capite* were to hold their possessions as a barony and perform suit and all customs due to the King; and the Archbishops and Bishops were to be present, like the rest of the Barons and together with them, at the judgements of the King's Court, before sentence of death or loss of member.   They were thus all liable to suit of Court—suit to that Court which was afterwards known as the High Court of Parliament.

Magna Charta, and its confirmations.
Even the Great Charter of King John, which was, to all intents and purposes, a treaty between him and his rebellious Barons, purports to be made by the advice of the Archbishops of Canterbury and Dublin, the Bishops of London, Winchester, Bath and Glastonbury, Lincoln, Worcester, Coventry, and Rochester, the Earls of Pembroke, Salisbury, Warren, and Arundel, twelve other nobles who are named, and others his lieges (*fidelium*) [2].   The confirmation of *Magna Charta* by Henry III on his accession (differing materially from the original *Magna Charta* of King John) was also by advice of Bishops, Earls, and other lieges, as

---

[1] Roger de Wendover (Rolls Series), i. pp. 26–30.
[2] John's *Magna Charta,* as printed from the MS. in the Archives of Lincoln Cathedral (collated with the Cotton MSS. and with the Red Book of the Exchequer) in the *Statutes of the Realm,* vol. i. p. 9.   See also Blackstone's Tracts, p. xi.

well as of the Papal Legate [1], according to the earliest form CH. XIV.
of the confirmation itself. It appears by a document of
equal authority that a Council assembled at Bristol, at
which were present 'all the Prelates of England, as well
Bishops and Abbots as Priors, and many Earls and Barons.'
They demanded the liberties and free customs which were
granted to them by the King; they thereupon with one
accord did fealty, and then gladly returned home [2]. The
subsequent confirmation of the Charter by Henry III, in
the ninth year of his reign, purports to be a spontaneous
grant by him, but it is attested by the Archbishop of
Canterbury and ten Bishops, by eighteen Abbots, by the
Chief Justiciary, by ten Earls, by the Constable of Chester,
and by twenty-two others who must be ranked among the
Barons [3].

This confirmation, like the Charter of King John, par-
takes of the nature of a treaty, or bargain, but as Henry III
was still a minor, and as a large number of the chief
personages in the realm were made witnesses, it can hardly
be said that the bargain was made by the King, as an
absolute sovereign, without advice. Another confirmation
was granted after he had attained full age in the twenty-
first year of his reign. It does not purport to be spontaneous like the confirmation of the ninth year, though
both are said to have been prompted by God. It is
attested by the Archbishop of Canterbury, by twelve
Bishops, and two Bishops elect, by eight Earls, by eighteen
Barons, 'and others.'

When yet another confirmation was granted after civil The confir-
war, in the forty-ninth year of the reign, there was a clause 49 Henry
that all former ordinances and articles provided by the III recognizes a

[1] Printed from the Charter in the Archives of Durham Cathedral,
collated with the Red Book of the Exchequer at Dublin, in the *Statutes
of the Realm*, vol. i. p. 14, and in Blackstone's Tracts, pp. xxvi–xxvii.

[2] *Rot. Lit. Claus.*, 1 Hen. III, m. 14 d, and m. 25 d (printed in
Blackstone's Tracts, pp. 308–309, note q).

[3] *Magna Charta*, 9 Hen. III, cap. 37. As to the consideration for
this Charter and the Forest Charter, in the shape of a subsidy, see
below, pp. 337–339.

CH. XIV. King and his Council, which might conduce to the honour
previous of God and the Church, and the welfare of the realm,
power of
legislation should be inviolably observed [1]. From this it is apparent
in the that a legislative power was recognized as having previously
King and
his Council. been in the King and 'his Council,' however that Council
may have been constituted.

This con- This last confirmation of charters to which Henry III
firmation
made assented is remarkable as having been executed at a time
with the when he was in the power of Simon de Montfort, Earl of
assent
of the Leicester, and in the year in which are mentioned the first
Commons. known writs for summoning the Commons—Burgesses as
well as Knights—to a national assembly. It commences
by stating how agreement and provision had been made,
by the unanimous consent and will of the King, of his eldest
son Edward, and of the Prelates, Earls, Barons, and Community of the Realm, that a certain ordinance should be
observed. The ordinance had previously been made with
the unanimous consent of the King, the Prelates, Earls, and
Barons. but not of the Commons. In the passage in which
the actual confirmation occurs the Commons again appear :
—'With the unanimous consent and will of our son Edward,
of the Prelates, Earls, Barons, and Community of our Realm,
it is by agreement provided that the ancient Charters of
Common Liberties and of the Forest heretofore granted
by us to the Community of our Realm . . . shall be inviolably
observed for ever [2].'

But hardly The difference between the provisions made in the
by assent
of the forty-ninth year of Henry III, with the consent of the
Commons *Communitas*, and those previously made without, is very
as a
distinct sharply marked in this document. It cannot, however,
estate of even here be said that the Commons appear as an estate of
the realm. the realm. They are rather included with the Lords
Spiritual and Temporal under the one word *Communitas*.

[1] *Rot. Chart.*, 49 Hen. III, m. 4, collated with Cotton. Claud. D. 2.
fo. 137, and with a MS. in Corpus Christi College, Cambridge, and
printed in the *Statutes of the Realm*, vol. i. p. 31, and in Blackstone's
Tracts, pp. lxix–lxxii.
[2] *Ib.*

The previous Charters and Confirmations are said in the same document to have been granted 'to the Community,' and they were certainly more for the benefit of the Church and the Temporal Lords than of the Commons. Having regard, however, to the writs which issued in the same year for the summons of Knights of the Shires and Burgesses, we can hardly fail to recognize a new factor in the law-making of England. The confirmation was certainly considered to be more solemn because made with the assent of the whole community, whereas previous legislation had been with the advice or assent of a Council consisting of persons who were in later times called Lords Spiritual and Temporal with a few officials.

CH. XIV.

There are, it is true, a few earlier indications that 'the people' (*populus*) were present on some great occasions, as, for instance, when the sovereign upon accession was anointed and crowned. In the absence, however, of anything like a representative system, the populace could have been but little more than the populace of the particular town or city in which the event occurred. If the King was crowned, or wore his crown, at Westminster, a Westminster or a London mob may have shouted. If he wore his crown at Winchester, or York, the shouters would have been from Winchester and its neighbourhood, or York and its neighbourhood, and could not have had the slightest pretensions to speak in the name of the Commons of England. Travelling was extremely difficult, and the difficulty had two effects. It prevented all but persons of wealth from undertaking long journeys, and it preserved local modes of thought and local prejudices in all their narrowness. A national feeling was hardly possible except among the travelled Lords of the Council, or *Curia Regis*, until the principle of representation had been gradually developed.

The 'people,' may have been present at earlier assemblies, had no representative character.

It was long, however, before the word 'Parliament' was used exclusively in the sense in which it is now used in England, and there are some laws earlier and some later than the Confirmation of Charters of the 49th of Henry III, which have found their way into the Statute Book,

The word 'Parliament' not originally used in the modern sense:

CH. XIV. and which yet do not in any manner depend upon the desire,
the 'Pro- authority, or consent of the Commons. The Provisions of
visions of Merton[1] were made in the King's Court, in the presence of
Merton.'
the Archbishop of Canterbury and Bishops, and the greater
part of the Earls and Barons. During the reign of Henry
III, indeed, it is not clear that any law, except the Confirmation of Charters, had the assent of the Commons. The
Statute of Marlborough[2] was enacted by 'the more discerning persons of the realm, as well greater as lesser,' and the
Commons may have been included among the lesser, though
there is nothing to show that they were elected representatives.

The   At the beginning of the reign of Edward I the famous
Statute of
Westmin- Statute of Westminster the First[3] was enacted. Its
ster the provisions are, in the general heading, described as 'estab-
First : the
initiative lissementz' of the King, by his Council, and with the assent
with King of the Archbishops, Bishops, Abbots, Priors, Earls, Barons,
and Coun-
cil, the   and the Commonalty of the Realm, summoned to West-
Magnates minster, though the writs for summoning the Commons are
and Com-
monalty   no longer extant. The initiative and the final assent were
assenting. thus with the King and his Council. The word Council,
however, is here used not in the sense of the whole *Curia
Regis*, or Common Council of the Realm, but with the
limited signification of an inner Council, which must, in this
case, have consisted principally of Judges, because almost
all the enactments are of a very technical and legal
character.

The   The provisions of the so-called Statute *De Bigamis* were
Statute *De*
Bigamis : first recited in the presence of some of the Bishops and
the King's others of the 'Council of the Realm,' which is here again
Council
and the   clearly distinguished from the King's Council. The Com-
Council of mon Council of the Realm is the old *Curia Regis*, the
the Realm.
later House of Lords. The King's Council (without the
word Common) is a Council within a Council possessing ·
technical knowledge. This latter body, 'all of the King's

---

[1] Stat. 20 Hen. III.,   · [2] 52 Hen. III (Stat. Marlb.), heading.
[3] 3 Ed. I.

Council, as well Justices as others,' agreed that the proposed law should be reduced to writing and firmly observed[1]. It was thus first introduced, verbally perhaps, to as many of the Common Council of the Realm as happened to be present, and having received their consent, was drawn up in due form by the King's inner Council with his consent.

The Statutes of Gloucester[2] were enacted, after summons of the more discerning persons of the realm, as well greater as lesser, in the same manner as the Statute of Marlborough. The Statute of Mortmain[3] had no authority but that of the King acting with the advice of his Prelates, Earls, and other lieges of the realm, who were of his Council. The Statute of Acton Burnel, or Statute of Merchants[4] was 'ordained and established' by the King and his Council. The famous Statute of Westminster the Second[5] was given forth by the King in his Parliament, but without any mention of the Estates of the Realm. The Statute of Winchester[6] (for all that appears) was made on the sole authority of the King, though it must be assumed that he did not act without any of his Council. The Statute of Westminster the Third[7] and the Statute regarding Malefactors in Parks[8], though made 'in Parliament,' were made by the King at the instance of the Magnates or Peers, and there is nothing to show that the Commons assented. Other Acts of the reign of Edward I[9] came into being in the King's full Parliament and by means of his Common Council; but as the use of the term Parliament was still vague, and there was a Common Council of the Realm before there were any representatives of the Commons, it is not certain that the Commons had any voice in these enactments.

Among the many Confirmations of the Great Charter and of the Charter of the Forest one was made in the twenty-eighth year of Edward I[10], with provisions to enforce the observance of them. This was done at the request of the

Other so-called Statutes of the reign of Edward I enacted without any express mention of the Commons.

The Commons never, the Lords often initiated legislation

---

[1] 4 Ed. I, stat. 3. [2] 6 Ed. I. [3] 7 Ed. I, stat. 2. [4] 11 Ed. I.
[5] 13 Ed. I, stat. 1. [6] 13 Ed. I, stat. 2. [7] 13 Ed. I, stat. 1.
[8] 21 Ed. I, stat 2. [9] 20 Ed. I, stat. 2, 3. [10] *Articuli super Chartas,*
28 Ed. I, stat. 3.

Prelates, Earls, and Barons in the King's Parliament, without any mention of the Commons. The Statute of Lincoln, relating to Escheators[1], was agreed to by the King's Council in the presence of the King, who himself consented, at a Parliament. The provisions of the Statute of Champarty[2] were made by common accord or agreement, but it is not certain how far that expression should be understood to extend. The Statute called *De Apportis Religiosorum*[3], however, was enacted by the advice of Earls, Barons, '*Magnates*' '*Proceres*,' and other Nobles and the Commonalty of the Realm. Apart from the grant of supplies, there is thus at first hardly a trace of legislative power in the Commons, and absolutely no trace of any initiative power of legislation. Initiation, however, did frequently proceed from the Lords, and from the King's Council.

In the reign of Edward II the Commons acquired a somewhat better recognized position. He renewed and confirmed certain articles of the *Articuli super chartas* not merely at the request of the Prelates, Earls, and Barons, as in the twenty-eighth year of his father's reign, but at the request of his good people[4] of his realm, and he made further provisions also at the request of his good people. The expression 'good people' could hardly have been limited to the Prelates and lay Lords, but must have included the Commons with them. In the seventh year of his reign two enactments were made by him, and by the Archbishops, Bishops, Abbots, Priors, Earls, and Barons, and all the Commonalty of the realm assembled by his command[5]. Legislation, however, in matters chiefly affecting any particular orders in the State seems to have remained still in the hands of the King and Council in Parliament, though the petition might come from the particular order to be affected. Thus the Articles of the Clergy were set forth by the Prelates and Clergy. The King's proposed answers were recited before the King's Council in his

CH. XIV.
in the
reign of
Edward I.

Lords and
Commons
in the
reign of
Edward II.

---

[1] 29 Ed. I.   [2] 33 Ed. I, stat. 3.   [3] 35 Ed. I, stat. 1.
[4] *Ses bones gentz*, stat. 2 Ed. II.   [5] 7 Ed. II, stat. 1, 2.

Parliament (a body not including the Commons), and, CH. XIV.
after correction, the final answers issued by authority of
the same Council[1]. Even in a matter of such national
importance as the regulations concerning the Sheriffs
throughout the realm, the representatives of the Commons
in Parliament had no assenting voice in the ninth year
of the reign, though one of the reasons for the enactment
was the grievous complaint of the people. The Prelates,
Earls, Barons, and other Magnates[2] are alone mentioned
as having, with the King, assented to the provisions made[3].
The Commons were nevertheless steadily gaining ground.
The Statute of York was made with the assent of the
Prelates, Earls, Barons, and the Commonalty of the Realm
there assembled in the twelfth year of the reign[4], and in
the fourteenth year another law relating to Sheriffs was
passed with the assent of the Prelates, Earls, Barons, and
all the Commonalty of the Realm, as well as on the complaint
of the Commonalty of the Realm[5].

The first year of the reign of Edward III shows the
Commons taking the initiative in matters in which during
previous reigns it was taken by the so-called Lords
Spiritual and Temporal or by the Council. It was at
their request, and not, as in the twenty-eighth year of
Edward I, at the request of the Prelates, Earls, and Barons,
that the Great Charter and the Charter of the Forest were
confirmed[6].

The Lords and Council had lost the exclusive power of initiation in the reign of Edward III.

The mode of procedure was, however, very different from
that by Bill in a modern Parliament, for the Commons
went very humbly to work. They presented a petition
to the King in his Council in his Parliament, and it was
granted with the assent of the Prelates, Earls, Barons,
and other Magnates. The actual power of legislating
might thus seem by the turn of a phrase to be again

At first the Commons initiated only by petition.

---

[1] *Articuli Cleri*, Stat. Linc., 9 Ed. II, stat. 1.
[2] The original French word is *Grantz*—a term inapplicable to the Commons.
[3] Stat. Linc., 9 Ed. II, stat. 2.   [4] 12 Ed. II, stat. 1.
[5] Stat. 14 Ed. II.   [6] 1 Ed. III, stat. 2.

CH. XIV. associated with the King and the Lords alone. The assent of the Commons, as appears in a subsequent reign, was not always held to be identical with their petition. In the very next year the Statute of Northampton was made with the assent of the Prelates, Earls, Barons, and other Magnates, and all the Commonalty of the Realm summoned to Parliament. For some time afterwards it was usually recited, in the general heading to the Statutes of a Parliament, that their provisions were made at the request of the Commons with the assent of the Prelates, Earls, and Barons, or when the Commons did not take the initiative, with the assent of the Prelates, Earls, Barons, other Magnates, and the Commons.

King and Council, and King and Lords, still retained the power of making some laws without the assent of the Commons.
The exclusive power of legislation had thus in a general sense passed away from the King and the Council, and from the King and the Lords. As, however, in earlier times all legislation was in their hands, so they retained the power of making some laws without the consent of the Commons. Provisions affecting the administration of Justice were made in the twentieth year of Edward III [1], by the King with the assent of the Magnates and other learned persons of the King's Council. The important so-called Statute of Labourers, passed to meet the paucity of workers and the high demands for wages after the Black Death, had no authority but that of the King, Prelates, Nobles, and others of the Council [2].

Ordinance and Act of Parliament.
Another Statute of Labourers, however, of two years' later date was passed on the petition of the Commons (who represented that the provisions of the previous law had not been observed) and with the assent of the Prelates, Earls, Barons, other Magnates, and the Commons [3]. It is usually said that, after the legislative power of the Commons as one of the estates of the realm had been recognized, any law passed by King and Lords alone, or by King and Commons alone, was an Ordinance but not an Act. The distinction does in fact seem to be drawn in the words of these laws relating to labourers, for the first, being without

---

[1] Stat. 20 Ed. III.   [2] 23 Ed. III.   [3] 25 Ed. III.

the assent of the Commons, is said to have been 'ordained,'   CH. XIV.
whereas the second is said to have been 'ordained and
established.' The difference of form, however, is not
always maintained, for the 'Statute of Money' made in the
ninth year of Edward III, was 'ordained and established'
without any express assent of the Commons[1]. In some
cases, too, the form for a Statute was '*assentu et accorde*,' and
the usage seems to have wanted uniformity. In the thirty-
seventh year of the reign the King agreed to certain
requests or petitions from the Commons, and they were
asked whether they would prefer to have them embodied
in the form of an Ordinance or in the form of a Statute.
They preferred an Ordinance, as being of a more temporary
nature, and more readily repealed[2]. When, however, the
instrument was formally drawn up, it purported to be
'ordained' by the King at the request of the Commons,
and with the assent of the Prelates, Dukes, Earls, Barons,
and other Magnates assembled in Parliament[3]. It would
seem to follow that the use of the word 'ordained' without
the word 'established,' where the Commons had preferred
a petition, but where their assent was not expressly stated,
would, at this particular time, cause a law to be an Ordinance and not a Statute. But in the very next year
a Statute[4] which had the assent both of the Lords and
of the Commons in Parliament was said only to be 'made
and ordained.'

Our forefathers, however, were not very exact in their   Separation
use of language for Parliamentary purposes. As the   of the Council
doctrines concerning legislation were in a state of transition,   from the
we need not wonder that they were not always very clearly   Parliament in the
expressed. It has sometimes been maintained that an   reign of Richard II:
Ordinance of Parliament did not introduce any new law,   end of the
but was made only for the explanation and due execution   exclusive legislative
of laws already in existence. In many instances, at any   power once
rate, this was the case. In the reign of Richard II, the   belonging to the King

---

[1] 9 Ed. III, stat. 2.
[2] *Rot. Parl.*, 37 Ed. III, no. 39 (printed, vol. ii. fo. 280).
[3] Stat. 37 Ed. III.   [4] 38 Ed. III, stat. 1.

Ch. XIV.
and his
Court, or
to the King
and his
Council.

Council was completely separated from the Parliament. the 'King in his Council in his Parliament' became a phrase of the past, and the proceedings of the Council were registered apart from the Rolls of Parliament. The King and Council retained the power of making proclamations to which obedience must be yielded so long as they were in agreement with the laws of the land and used to enforce due execution of those laws. The doctrine that there could be an Ordinance of Parliament, as distinguished from a statute, did not immediately fall into disuse, but the occasions on which a law came into force without the assent of the three estates, or of the Lords and Commons, naturally became more rare when the Council became completely distinct not only from Parliament as a whole, but from the baronage. From this period may be dated the extinction of that legislative power which had once belonged exclusively to the King and his Court, or to the King and his Council, but of which the Commons had acquired a share.

Question
as to the
separation
of the two
Houses of
Parlia-
ment.

Various opinions have been advanced in relation to the time at which the Lords and Commons began to sit in two separate Houses. Regarded from one point of view the question seems almost insoluble; regarded from another it is extremely simple. It is difficult to prove when a permanent physical barrier was set between the two Houses : it is easy to show that the two assemblies were always distinct. The *Curia Regis*, or King's Court, the King in his Council in his Parliament of a somewhat later time, never included the Commons. The great Officers of State and the Judges were summoned to it and sat among the Lords Spiritual and Temporal, but the representatives of the Commons, or, at any rate, the burgesses, never intermixed with them.

It could have mattered but little whether the Commons, who in the early stages of Parliament appear chiefly as petitioners, formulated their petitions at the bottom of a Hall, while the Lords were at the top, or in one chamber or building while the Lords were in another. No wall could make the two bodies more distinct then they already were in nature. On the other hand, however, the King and the three estates were an organic whole, and there were times when they had to act collectively as the Parliament. These occasions arose at dates considerably later than any of those which have usually been assigned to the division of the two Houses. There are several instances in which a Peer newly advanced to a particular dignity takes his seat in the presence of Lords and Commons. This occurs at least as late as the reign of Henry V, when Thomas Beaufort, Earl of Dorset, was created Duke of Exeter in Parliament, and was there commanded by the King to take the seat assigned to him 'in the presence of the Lords Spiritual and Temporal, and of the Commons of the Realm assembled in this same present Parliament[1].' There is no question here of any deputation from either House to the other. The ceremony must have been in full view of all the members of both Houses who were present. The 'Rolls of Parliament,' it may be here repeated, extend to the reign of Henry VII, and there are no separate Journals of the Lords before the reign of Henry VIII.

During the reigns of Richard II and Henry IV some changes were introduced in the mode of describing the assent of the Lords to an Act of Parliament. In earlier reigns and down to the second year of that of Richard II, the assent was commonly said to be that of the Prelates, Dukes (when there were any) Earls, Barons, and other Magnates[2]. In the third year they were described collectively as 'the Lords[3],' in the fourth year as the 'Prelates and Lords[4]'—a phrase not unknown in the reign of Edward III[5]. In the ninth year the old form reappears 'the Prelates, Dukes, Marquess, Earls, and Barons[6].' In the eleventh and twelfth years they are, as in the third, described collectively as 'the Lords[7].' In the thirteenth

The expression 'Lords Spiritual and Temporal' does not occur before the reign of Richard II: the earlier phrases.

[1] *Rot. Parl.*, 4 Hen. V, no. 13 (printed, vol. iv. fo. 96).
[2] 2 Ric. II, stat. 2.   [3] Stat. 3 Ric. II.   [4] Stat. 4 Ric. II.
[5] Stat. 34 Ed. III.   [6] Stat. 9 Ric. II.
[7] Stat. 11 Ric. II, and Stat. 12 Ric. II.

CH. XIV. year a new form appears, 'the Prelates and Lords Temporal[1].' The expression 'Lords Spiritual and Temporal' occurs, for the first time, in an ordinance made by the King in his 'Great Council' in the same year[2]. It was not, however, immediately introduced into Acts of Parliament, as in the twentieth year of the reign we find 'the Prelates and Lords[3].' In the twenty-first year the Prelates, Dukes, Earls, and Barons are again specified[4], as also in the first and second years of the reign of Henry IV[5], but in the latter year the words 'the Lords Spiritual and Temporal' are used also as being synonymous[6].

The expression occurs in the commencing words of an Act for the first time in 4 Henry IV.

In the fourth year of the reign of Henry IV the 'Lords Spiritual and Temporal' are for the first time mentioned in the commencing words of a Statute[7], and although there are some exceptions, this was ever afterwards the usual form.

Question with regard to the 'two estates' of 'Lords Spiritual' and 'Lords Temporal': the idea probably of ecclesiastical origin.

The question here arises whether the Lords Spiritual and the Lords Temporal are to be regarded as distinct estates before the reign of Richard II. So far as the words of most earlier Acts of Parliament are concerned, the Earls are as much distinguished from the Barons, as either from the Prelates. One form of summons was, however, sent to Earls and Barons alike, and a different form to Bishops; but, on the other hand, the form of the summons sent to the Abbots differed from both the others, and in the earliest Acts Bishops, Abbots, and Priors are specifically mentioned[8], just as much as Earls and Barons. The point is of some importance for more reasons than one. If Bishops, Abbots, and Priors were liable to be summoned to Parliament, as holding by barony, and if their claim to be ranked as Peers was, as alleged by themselves, that they held by barony, it is difficult to see why their position merely as Lords of Parliament required a description

---

[1] 13 Ric. II, stat. 1.

[2] Printed in the *Statutes of the Realm*, vol. ii. p. 74, from the Statute Roll.   [3] Stat. 20 Ric. II.   [4] Stat. 21 Ric. II.

[5] Stat. 1 Hen. IV, and Stat. 2 Hen. IV, general heading.

[6] Stat. 2 Hen. IV, cap. 10, 11.   [7] Stat. 4 Hen. IV.

[8] E. g. Stat. Westm. the First (3 Ed. I).

different from that of the lay Lords. As, however, they CH. XIV.
sometimes constituted the majority of the House of Lords,
we may be sure that the distinction was not made without
their assent, both when they were called Prelates and when
they were called Lords Spiritual. They could not, according
to the canons of the Church, be present in the King's Court
or Parliament when a trial reached the stage of passing
a sentence affecting life or member. They would not,
except when absolutely compelled, acknowledge any lay
jurisdiction over themselves, and were always insisting on
the privileges of their order. It is, therefore, most probable
that they drew the distinction between Lords Spiritual and
Lords Temporal as being in accordance with their own
particular ideas The clerical view that the Lords Spiritual
constitute an estate apart from the Lords Temporal has
prevailed in more modern views of the constitution, but it
can hardly be said to have been recognized by the earlier
lawyers.

There occurred but little of moment, so far as the history The assent
of legislative power and legislative methods affects the of the
Commons
Lords, during the warlike reigns of Henry IV and Henry V. recognized
The Commons, indeed, complained that in Acts founded by Henry V
as neces-
on their petitions matters were sometimes introduced which sary to any
law binding
were not in accordance with the petitions themselves, and them.
claimed to be 'as well Assenters as Petitioners.' King
Henry V thereupon granted that nothing should be enacted
on their petitions contrary to that which was asked, so as
to bind them without their assent[1]. This, however, was
a matter between the King and the Commons, and not
between the Commons and the Lords. The Commons
had been asserting and had established the principle that
they should not be bound by any legislative enactment
without their own consent. Both the Commons and the
Lords could now initiate legislation, and the assent of both
was required to an Act of Parliament.

Down to this period it had been customary for statutes Substitu-
to be drawn in permanent form after agreement had been tion of Bills
(in the form

---

[1] *Rot. Parl.*, 2 Hen. V, no. 22 (printed, vol. iv. p. 22).

CH. XIV. given to their proposed substance. It appears by the
of Acts) for heading to the statute *De Bigamis* that, in the earliest
Petitions, days of Parliament, the inner or King's Council, and not
in the
reign of the whole Parliament, had given instructions for the due
Henry VI. execution of this task. When the Council became altogether distinct from the Parliament[1], it was necessary
to devise some new machinery, and commissioners were
appointed[2] to do the work which had previously been done
by the Council or its legal members. It is, however, clear
that the Commons were not then satisfied with the manner
in which the Acts received their final shape, and desired
a change. For this reason, probably, among others, the
mode of legislation began to be altered towards the end of
the reign of Henry VI, when Bills in the form of Acts (as in
the modern system) were introduced into Parliament as well
as petitions. There was, however, practically no further
change in the legislative power before the time of Charles I,
except in so far as the constitution of the House of Lords
was affected by the dissolution of monasteries and consequent absence of the Abbots and Priors.

The assent   In the mean time there grew up an idea that the consent
of the
Lords   of the Lords Spiritual, as distinguished from other Lords,
Spiritual,   was not in itself necessary to give validity to an Act of
as such, not
necessary: Parliament. It has been shown in another chapter that,
growth   at the instance of the Commons, in the reign of Richard II,
of the
doctrine.   a Procurator or Proxy was appointed to represent the
whole of the Spiritual Lords, so that no question might
arise with regard to the due enactment of statutes which
had passed when they were not present. It must then
have been supposed, therefore, by some persons at any
rate, that an Act could not be considered duly made law
unless the spiritual lords, had, in person or by proxy,
consented to it. This idea, however, did not survive beyond the reign of Henry VIII, for in the seventh year of
that reign it was held by all the Judges that a Parliament

---

[1] See above, p. 251, p. 280, and p. 322.
[2] *Rot. Parl.*, 11 Ric. II, no. 19 (printed, vol. iii. p. 256), and *Rot.
Parl.*, 21 Ric. II, no. 74 (printed, vol. iii. p. 368).

in the modern sense might be held without any Spiritual CH. XIV.
Lords at all. The reason assigned was that doctrine which
the Prelates of the reign of Richard II had enunciated, and
which the greatest lawyers have always held—that the
Spiritual Lords have a place in the Parliament House not
in virtue of any spiritual office, but solely in virtue of their
temporal possessions[1].

Twenty years later the distinction between Lords
Spiritual and Lords Temporal as constituting two estates
appears to have been disregarded. Parliament, it was
then said, 'consists of three parts, the King as the head,
the Lords as the chief and principal members of the body,
and the Commons as the inferior members[2].'

Cases have since occurred in which Acts of Parliament The 'Lords Spiritual' excluded from Parliament in 1640.
have been passed in the absence of the Lords Spiritual.
Acts of the sixteenth year[3] of the reign of Charles I,
were passed by authority of the King, 'the Lords' and
Commons. By one of them it was enacted that persons
in holy orders should be disabled from exercising any
temporal jurisdiction or authority, and that no Archbishop
or Bishop should have 'any seat or place, suffrage or voice,
in the Parliaments of this Realm.' The Bishops were
accordingly excluded from the House of Lords.

, After this year[5] there are no Acts of Parliament recog- The Commons assume the whole legislative power.
nized by the law until the twelfth year of Charles II. In
the interval the Commons voted that the House of Lords
was useless and dangerous, and that whatever was enacted
by the Commons had the force of law without the consent
of the King or House of Lords[6].

When King Charles I had been put to death, and after Oliver Cromwell's 'Other
the Commonwealth of England had been in existence some

---

[1] Keilwey's *Reports*, 184 b.
[2] Dyer's *Reports*, 36 & 37 Hen. VIII, p. 60.
[3] E. g. Stat. 16 Car. I, cap. 11, 14, 16, 19, &c.
[4] Ib., cap. 27.
[5] In the Roll of Parliament there is no distinction between the Acts
of the sixteenth, seventeenth, and eighteenth years of the reign.
[6] *Journals of the House of Commons*, Jan. 4, 1648–1649 (vol. vi.
p. 111).

CH. XIV.

House,'
or House
of Lords,
without
Bishops.
years, Oliver Cromwell conceived the idea of reverting to a House of Lords without Bishops. The Commons, not directly objecting to the institution of an upper House, desired that the nominations should be confirmed by themselves. Cromwell would not consent to this. The Commons then resolved that a form of summons should be adopted for members of 'the Other House,' and that the persons summoned should be 'the Other House of Parliament,' and should, 'without further approbation do and perform all such matters as the other House ought to do and perform, and might exercise all such privileges, powers, and authorities as the other House ought to have and exercise.'

The writs of summons to the members of the 'Other House,' about sixty in number, issued in December, 1657 [1]. Among those called were some who had been Peers before the Rebellion, and some men of ancient family, more than one of whom attained a peerage after the Restoration. The others were men who had rendered distinguished service to the Commonwealth or the Protector. The form of summons was not very different from that which had been in use in earlier times. Cromwell's style was 'Oliver, Lord Protector of the Commonwealth of England, Scotland, and Ireland, and the Dominions and Territories thereunto belonging.' He sent greeting to the person summoned, whose presence was commanded 'to treat, confer, and give advice with us and with the Great Men and Nobles.' He was not King, and he said nothing of fealty and allegiance; but, in other respects, he followed the ancient model as closely as possible [2].

Parliament met on January 20, 1657-8. On February 4, following, the Protector, in a message to the Commons, described the 'Other House' as the House of Lords. The

---

[1] Whitelocke, Dec. 11, 1657 (vol. iv. p. 313, in the edition of 1853).

[2] Whitelocke says 'the form of the writs was the same with those which were sent to summon the Peers in Parliament.' There were, however, some necessary differences, as shown above. The form of the writs has been printed in Noble's *House of Cromwell*, i. 370.

Commons who had accepted the fact, proved refractory CH. XIV. with regard to the name; and the Protector almost immediately dissolved the Parliament. His son, and successor in the Protectorate, Richard Cromwell, summoned a Parliament, including the members of the 'Other House' to meet on January 27, 1658–9; but that also was shortly afterwards dissolved[1], and the 'Other House' was heard of no more.

Upon the restoration of Charles II the first Parliament was necessarily without Bishops, as the Act by which they had been excluded, having received the assent of King, Lords, and Commons, was recognized as valid. It was, however, brought together in an irregular manner, the Lords meeting by their own authority, and the Commons in pursuance of writs issued in the name of the Keepers of the Liberty of England. Its first proceeding, when assembled, was to declare the Parliament begun in the sixteenth year of Charles I, dissolved, and the Lords and Commons then sitting to be the two Houses of Parliament[2]. This declaration clearly purported that the House of Lords could be effectively constituted, and that Acts of Parliament were valid, though no Lords Spiritual had a seat or a voice. The Acts of the Convention Parliament, 12 Charles II, by consent of King, Lords, and Commons, without Bishops.

The Convention Parliament, as it has been called, sat from April 25 to December 29, 1660, when it was dissolved, in due form, by the King. It did not restore the Bishops to their ancient places, and it separated without any suggestion of a doubt as to the validity of Acts which had not the assent of the Lords Spiritual. It did not repeal the Act of 1640, which excluded the Bishops.

A new Parliament was summoned by the King and met on May 8, 1661, without any Bishops. It passed an Act to confirm the Acts of the Parliament immediately preceding, so that no question might arise in consequence of the irregularity of the manner in which the Convention Parliament assembled[3]. This confirmation and, with it, the validity of all the Acts confirmed rest entirely on The Parliament of 13 Charles II, without Bishops, confirmed the Acts of the Convention Parliament.

---

[1] On April 22, 1659. Whitelocke, vol. iv. p. 343.
[2] Stat. 12 Car. II, cap. 1.   [3] 13 Car. II, stat. 1, cap. 7.

CH. XIV. the assent of the King, the Lords Temporal, and the Commons.

It after-wards repealed the Act of 1640, and the Bishops were then summoned.

In this same Parliament of 1661, however, the Act in virtue of which the Bishops had been excluded was repealed as having made 'several alterations prejudicial to the constitution and ancient Rights of Parliament, and contrary to the laws of this land,' and as having been 'by experience found otherwise inconvenient[1].' Still there is, in this repealing Act, no mention of the Lords Spiritual and the Lords Temporal, as constituting two estates of the realm, much less any declaration that they are thenceforth to be so held and esteemed, or that every Act of Parliament must have the assent of both. The effect of the repeal was at most to restore the Bishops to the position which they had held before the Act of 16 Charles I, whatever that position may have been.

Many subsequent changes in detail, but no subsequent changes in principle.

Since the time of Charles II there has been no change of principle affecting the legislative power of the House of Lords, as including Lords Spiritual and Temporal, though there have been many changes affecting the constitution of the House with regard to the number both of Lords Spiritual and of Lords Temporal entitled to sit, and with regard to the right by which they had their seats. These changes, however, can be more conveniently described in another part of this work.

The legislative power as affected by the duration of Parliaments.

The burdens or privileges of the Lords in relation to attendance in Parliament have undergone considerable changes at various times. The Peers were, as we have seen. always liable to be summoned to the King's Courts and Councils, whether called Parliaments or not, and to be summoned to Parliaments, whether including Commons or not. They have always been an essential part of Parliament in the modern sense of the term, but they have, like the Commons, had far more power in the management· of the national affairs at some periods than at others.

Disregard of Acts for annual Par-

In the year 1330 it was enacted that Parliament should be held once in every year, or oftener, should there be

[1] 13 Car. II, stat. I. cap. 2.

need[1]. This rule, however, was not by any means strictly followed, and in the year 1362 there was passed another Act to the same effect[2]. Like its predecessor this also fell into disuse. In the reigns of Henry VIII, Elizabeth, and James I, there were intervals of many years during which no Parliament assembled. In the troubled reign of Charles I there was an interval of twelve years—from 1628 to 1640.

CH. XIV.
liaments before the Great Rebellion.

The first Parliament of 1640 sat but a few days. The second passed an Act ' for the preventing of inconveniences happening by the long intermissions of Parliament[3].' A reference was made, in the preamble, to the Act of the thirty-sixth year of Edward III by the words ' Parliament ought to be holden at least once every year for the redress of grievances.' The royal prerogative was in theory recognized by the words ' but the appointment of the time and place for the holding thereof hath always belonged, as it ought, to His Majesty and his royal progenitors;' for practical purposes, however, it was reduced to nullity by the substantive words of enactment. Whenever the existing or any future Parliament was continued by adjournment or prorogation to the tenth day of September in the third year following the last day of its sitting, it was to be' *ipso facto* absolutely dissolved. The Lord Chancellor, Keeper, or Commissioners for the keeping of the Great Seal were then required to issue, within six days, writs for the summoning of a new Parliament, 'without any further warrant or direction from His Majesty.'

Act of 1640 to prevent intermissions of Parliament for more than three years.

Various provisions were made to ensure the assembling of Parliament should the Keepers of the Great Seal refuse or neglect to issue the writs of summons. Among them was one that the Peers were to assemble, and, on their own authority, send out writs to summon the Commons.

Power given to the Peers to summon a Parliament, failing other means.

It is sometimes said that triennial Parliaments were established by this Act, but the effect of it was only to ensure that there should not be an interval of more than

The Act of 1640 did not

---

[1] Stat. 4 Ed. III, cap. 14.   [2] Stat. 36 Ed. III, cap. 10.
[3] Stat. 16 Car. I, cap. 1.

CH. XIV.   three years between the sittings of Parliament, and that

establish   a Parliament prorogued or adjourned for three years should
triennial   come to an end and be succeeded by another. No pro-
Parlia-
ments.   vision was made for the dissolution of a Parliament which
continued its sittings without any interval of the length
mentioned in the Act. The Parliament, indeed, in which
the Act was made, remained in existence, so far as the
House of Commons was concerned, more than twelve
years, and until its sittings were interrupted, not by the
automatic action of a Statute, but through the master will
of Cromwell with his soldiers at his back.

Act of 1664   Four years after the Restoration this Act was formally
for holding
Parlia-   repealed, and declared to have been 'in derogation of His
ments once   Majesty's just rights and prerogative inherent to the Imperial
in three
years at   Crown of this Realm.' It was also stated in the repealing
least.   Act that 'by the ancient laws and statutes of this realm,
made in the reign of King Edward the Third, Parliaments
are to be held very often.' As those statutes provided for
the holding of a Parliament once every year at least, they
can hardly be said to have afforded a very secure ground
for the substantive enactment which followed, that Parliaments were to be held once in three years at least. The
King was thenceforth to issue out his writs for calling
a Parliament within three years of the termination of any
previous Parliament [1].

The dura-   This Act, like that of Charles I, did not in any way affect
tion of a
Parliament   the length of time during which any one Parliament might
not thereby sit, or require the election of new members of the House of
restricted.
Commons at the end of any definite period. The very
Parliament in which it was passed continued in existence
nearly seventeen years. All that was needed was that
some kind of Parliament should be called together at
intervals of not less than three years, just as some kind
of Parliament was to be called together at intervals of not
less than one year at the beginning of the reign of
Edward III.

Effect of   Charles II, at the end of his reign, allowed four years to
long

[1] Stat. 16 Car. II, cap. 1.

elapse without summoning any Parliament.   There was no Ch. XIV.
power, under the Act, to compel him to issue any summons,
and no machinery for summoning a Parliament without his intervals between
consent.   In the reign of William and Mary, also, the first Parliaments.
Parliament (after the Convention) was continued six years
and a half.   So far as the Lords were concerned, the effect
of the long intervals between one Parliament and another
in these and preceding reigns was to lighten their burdens to
no inconsiderable extent, but also to diminish their influence
in the management of the realm.   The time, however, was
at hand when Parliaments were to be held every year
though not under any legal compulsion.

In the year 1694 another Act was passed requiring, like The Act of 1694 for triennial Parliaments: how it affected the Lords in theory.
that of the reign of Charles II, that a Parliament should be
held once in three years at the least.   It contained a further
provision that no Parliament should continue in existence
more than three years [1].   This was of greater consequence in
relation to the House of Commons than in relation to the
House of Lords, because it set a limit, for the first time, to
the period during which representatives could sit in the
House of Commons without re-election.   It was, however, of
very great constitutional importance, and indirectly affected
even the House of Lords.   As the principle was now
established that there could be no 'Parliament' without
representatives of the Commons, a dissolution precluded
the Lords from sitting in any Parliament until the writs
for the summons of a new House of Commons had been
returned, and there was nothing to compel the issue of
the writs until three years had elapsed after a dissolution.
The Parliamentary functions of the Lords, being now
dependent on the existence of a House of Commons, might
thus legally be dormant for no less than three years.
Practically no inconvenience followed, because there has
never since been a year in which a Parliament has not met,
but theoretically, at least, the power of the House of Lords
was curtailed.

In the year 1715 the continuance of Parliaments was

[1] Stat. 6 Will. and Mary, cap. 2.

Cʜ. XIV. extended to seven years[1], but the provisions relating to the
holding of a Parliament once in three years, and to the
summoning of a Parliament within three years of a dissolution remained in force. The sole effect of the new Act
was to give to the representatives of the Commons a longer
period of representation, though subject, of course, to the
Sovereign's power of dissolving. Portions of the Act of
the reign of William and Mary were formally repealed in
the year 1867, but only portions already rendered inopera-
tive by the Act of George I, and portions relating to the
Parliament in which the Act itself was passed[2].

The Act of 1715 for Septennial Parliaments.

It would seem, therefore, that the Parliamentary functions
of the House of Lords, as well as of the House of Commons,
might still be legally suspended for a period of three years,
because the Acts of Edward III relating to annual Parliaments, already superseded by those of Charles II and William
and Mary, were formally repealed in 1863[3]. The security
for annual sessions of Parliament lies in the power of the
Commons to grant or withhold supplies, and in the necessity
for a vote to appropriate them when granted.

The annual sitting of Parliament depends not on Statutes but on Supplies and their Appro-priation.

In none of the Acts relating to Parliaments was the
power of the Crown to dissolve an existing Parliament
abolished or abridged. In none of them was the power of
the Crown to summon a Parliament taken away. Thus as
the doctrine grew up that the advisers of the Crown were
responsible for the Acts of the Crown, the dissolution of
Parliament, before its term had expired, became a political
engine to be used, as occasion might seem to require, by
the political party in power. Questions have arisen in
recent times concerning the advice which ought to be given
to the Sovereign by a Minister when a Government measure
is rejected in the House of Lords after having passed the
House of Commons. Any theory on this subject can be
founded only on comparatively recent precedents—on precedents subsequent to the first formation of a Cabinet
Council. The subject itself is one perilously near to current

Preroga-tive of the Crown: Disso-lution of Parlia-ment.

---

[1] 1 George I, stat. 2. cap. 38.   [2] Statute Law Revision Act, 1867.
[3] Statute Law Revision Act, 1863.

politics, and does not appear to be strictly relevant to a CH. XIV.
History of the House of Lords. It belongs rather to the
sphere of ministerial duties and responsibilities, in common
with any action to be recommended by a Minister upon the
occurrence of any event domestic or foreign.

It may, however, be remarked that the House of Lords Power of
does not, as is sometimes represented, possess a *veto* with either
House to
regard to any measure in any sense in which a *veto* is not initiate,
amend, or
possessed by the House of Commons. With certain excep- reject a
tions relating to money and privilege, either House can measure.
initiate a measure, and either House can amend or reject
it, but neither has any constitutional power to force the
acceptance of any measure upon the other.

There have, indeed, been occasions when the rejection by Action of
the House of Lords of Bills passed in the House of Com- King,
Lords, and
mons has been the cause of popular outcry and commotion. Commons
in relation
The most memorable of these was when the Lords threw to the
out the Reform Bill in October, 1831. The feeling of the Reform
Bills of
country was shown in a manner which could not be mistaken. 1831.
Another Bill was sent up shortly afterwards, and the second
reading was then carried by a majority of nine. In Committee,
however, the opposition was renewed ; and the danger was
thought to be so great that King William IV used his
personal influence with individual Lords in order to per-
suade them to abandon their resistance. In the end he was
successful, and the Bill became law. This was, no doubt, an
instance in which the Lords permitted legislation contrary
to their wishes, convictions, and previous votes. It was not
a case in which the House of Commons, by its own strength,
forced the Lords to adopt a measure, but one in which the
wishes of the Sovereign and external agitation combined
to overcome their antipathy [1].

There are, however, some matters in relation to which Custom of
exclusive powers are claimed, on the one hand, by the Parliament
in relation
House of Lords, and, on the other hand, by the House of to Bills
Commons. Thus, by the custom of Parliament, it has been affecting
the Peer-
said, all Bills which may affect the rights of the peerage, age, &c.

[1] Greville's Memoirs, ii. 303 ; Raikes's Journal, i. 34.

CH. XIV. are to be first introduced into the House of Lords, and to
suffer no changes or amendments in the House of Commons
which has, however, the power of rejecting them altogether[1].
This practice, it seems, cannot be of earlier origin than that
of commencing legislation in the modern form by Bill in
the reign of Henry VI, and the occasions on which any
questions have arisen in relation to it have been rare. It
was entirely ignored by the House of Commons in the last
Parliament of King Charles I, in which bills were introduced not only 'for taking away the Bishops' votes in
Parliament[2],' but also 'for the abolition of the House of
Peers[3].' This was, no doubt, an exceptional period, but
later events have not all been quite in accordance with the
alleged custom or privilege. Notice was given in the year
1832 of an intention to move for leave to bring a bill into
the House of Commons to prevent the members of the
other House of Parliament from voting by proxy. It
was withdrawn, upon a suggestion that it was an interference with the privileges of the House of Lords[4]. A
bill, however, to alter the mode of electing representative
Peers in Scotland and Ireland, and to enable the Crown to
summon Scotch and Irish Peers, who were not representatives, to sit in Parliament for life was read a first time in the
House of Commons in 1869[5].

Bills for restitution in blood, after corruption, and for
restitution of honours, bills of attainder, and bills of pains
and penalties have usually been first introduced into the
House of Lords, but it is not clear that there is any absolute
right or well-defined privilege in these matters. Courtesy
and convenience may count for much in one class of bills ;
the long-established authority of the Lords in legal affairs
may count for something in the other class. Bills of resti-

---

[1] 1 Comm. 168.
[2] Clarendon's *History of the Great Rebellion*, iii. 148 ; iv. 33;
Journals of the House of Commons, March 10, 1640-1 (vol. ii. p. 101).
[3] Clarendon, xi. 247 ; *Journals of the House of Commons*, Feb. 20,
1648-9.
[4] Hansard's *Debates*, vol. xi. 3rd series, 1156.
[5] *Ib.*, vol. cxciv. 3rd series, 988. See also below chapter xv. part 3.

tution, however, differ from the rest in being introduced CH. XIV.
into the House of Lords by command of the sovereign,
and in being sent to the Commons as having already the
Sovereign's assent [1].'

The limitation of the power of the Lords when legis- Disabili-
lating on money bills is a subject with regard to which our Lords in
early history is obscure. Payments of money which were relation to
independent of the ordinary feudal exactions were, per- Bills: their
haps, more familiar to the townsmen than to the great probable
origin:
feudal lords. Some of the towns which had obtained supplies
charters had to send representative burgesses to West- by the
burgesses
minster, to treat with the Chief Justiciary, and render an before the
institution
account, before there was any House of Commons, and of the
consequently before there was any House of Lords (under House of
Commons.
that name) as distinguished from it [2]. As this important
section of the Commons had money dealings with the
Crown before they had even obtained representation in
Parliament, they would naturally take care that they should
not be placed in a worse position afterwards. It was
obviously not for the Lords to say what the Commons
should contribute. The Lords, on the other hand, being
in origin the great feudal land-owners, contributed to the
necessities of the Crown or the State by the very terms on
which they held their lands, and found, at their own
expense, the greater part of the army. This was a matter
between them and the Crown with which the Commons
could not interfere.

In addition to the military services which they rendered, Bargains
the feudal Barons, as well as the Commons, from time to with the
Crown:
time, specially granted money, or the worth of money, to grants of
money in
the sovereign. As, however, the burgesses made the best return for
terms they could at the Exchequer, so also the Barons are concessions
in 1225.
seen, in conjunction with the Commons, to assist the King
for a consideration. In 1225, forty years before that Par-

[1] Instances have been collected (ranging from 1848 to 1855) in May's
Law and Usage of Parliament (10th edition), p. 435.
[2] See, e. g. King John's Charters to Gloucester and Ipswich, (printed
in *Rotuli Chartarum*, pp. 57, 65). See also *Dial. de Scacc.* ii. 13.

CH. XIV. liament or assembly which Simon de Montfort caused to be summoned, the Archbishops, Bishops, Abbots, Priors, Earls, Barons, Knights, freeholders, and all the King's subjects [1], gave a fifteenth part of all their moveables in return for a confirmation of the Great Charter and for the Charter of the Forest [2].

It is not by any means apparent how this grant was obtained from 'all.' The King, according to a contemporary, held his Court, at Christmas, at Westminster. The 'clergy and people' were present with the Magnates. Hubert de Burgh, the Justiciary, spoke, and represented the evil plight of public affairs and the necessity of help from all. He suggested the gift of a fifteenth both from the clergy and from the laity. Upon this 'the Archbishop, and the whole assembly of Bishops, Earls, Barons, Abbots, and Priors, after deliberating,' answered that they would gladly agree to the King's request if he would grant them the liberties which they sought. The King agreed to 'that which the Magnates asked,' and the charters were forthwith written out and sealed [3]. It is clear, both from the attestation of the charters and from the words of the chronicler, that the final bargain was effected between the King, on the one hand, and the nobles and church dignitaries on the other. It is possible that some members of the clerical body (whom the chronicler describes as the clergy) and some knights responding to a general summons, according to the terms of John's Great Charter, may have been at hand, if not in the same chamber with the Magnates. They may have signified to the Earls, Barons, and clerical dignitaries their willingness to accept the proposed bargain, and the latter may then, 'after deliberation,' have assented to it. But there is no evidence of any such transaction, or of the authority of any part of 'the people,' to consent to a tax upon the rest, except, perhaps, in the case of burgesses representing their town in accordance with its charter.

---

[1] 'Omnes de regno nostro.'   [2] *Magna Charta*, 9 Hen. III, cap. 37.
[3] Roger de Wendover, *Flores Historiarum* (Rolls Series), vol. ii. p. 282.

All that can be said is that in some way a bargain was struck between the King and the Bishops, Earls, Barons, Abbots, and Priors, which had the effect of binding all classes. It would almost seem that those who gained the benefits for all were regarded as having power to agree to the price which all would have to pay.

This precedent for striking a bargain was followed in later times, after the establishment of the House of Commons, upon occasions of great emergency, but the Commons were then parties to the grant in Parliament. Thus, when in the fourteenth year of his reign Edward III was brought to great straits by his wars with the Scots and the French, he obtained an extraordinary grant of ninths in one act [1], but he had already made some extraordinary concessions in others [2]. The concessions, in fact, preceded the grant; and it was recited in the act in which the ninths were given to the King that they were given in consideration of these preceding acts. The King released and pardoned arrears of various kinds due to him, and consented to abolish the 'Presentment of Englishry' which had been the badge of the subjection of the conquered English to their French conquerors. The grant was made by the Prelates, Earls, Barons, and Commons.

The principle of the bargain still accepted after the House of Commons was established.

Other similar instances are found upon the rolls. On ordinary occasions, however, the grants appear to have been made, during a long period, without Act of Parliament. The clergy, notwithstanding the *Praemunientes* clause in the writs of summons to the Bishops, ceased to attend in Parliament after the fourteenth century, and taxed themselves independently in Convocation. The Commons taxed themselves in Parliament, but independently of the Temporal Lords. A little later the Commons and Temporal Lords seem to have joined in grants to be levied in the same proportion. In the reign of Richard II they are described as grants made by the Commons with the assent of the Lords. In these cases, perhaps, the Commons made,

Ordinary grants of supplies in early times: Convocation.

---

[1] 14 Ed. III, stat. I. cap. 20. [2] Ib., cap. 2, &c.

Z 2

as it were, a proffer, and the Lords agreed to give of their moveables, at the same rate, and in addition to the military services which they owed. The Commons (now including both knights of the shires and burgesses) made the bargain, so to speak, as some representative burgesses had made it in the days before Parliaments, and the Lords became parties to the transaction.

It cannot, however, be said that the doctrine of supply had, as yet, been laid down with mathematical precision. But, during the reign of Henry IV, a general principle was established and reduced to writing after a short constitutional struggle. The Commons, in the second year, prayed that, before granting supplies, they might receive answers to their petitions. The King, after consultation with the Lords, replied that it had not been usual for the Commons to have their petitions answered before granting subsidies, and that he would not change the good customs of ancient times[1].

In the ninth year, when Parliament was assembled at Gloucester, the King sat with the Lords Spiritual and Temporal in the Council Chamber of the Abbey. A question was put to the Lords as to what aid would suffice and be necessary in view of the dangers which threatened the realm. They answered that, when the King's necessities, on the one hand, and the poverty of his people, on the other, were considered, no less aid would suffice than 'a tenth and a half' from the cities and boroughs, and 'a fifteenth and a half' from other lay people. Thereupon a message was sent by the King's command to the Commons desiring them to send before the King and Lords some of their number to hear and report to the rest as the King should command. They accordingly sent twelve members into the presence of the King and Lords. It was the King's pleasure, they were then informed, that the question which had been put before the Lords and the answer given (both · of which were communicated to them) should be reported to their fellows, in order that their whole body might take

[1] *Rot. Parl.*, 2 Hen. IV, no. 23 (vol. iii. p. 458).

steps to conform, as nearly as possible, to the proposal of CH. XIV.
the Lords.

When the report was made to the Lower House its The prin-
members were greatly agitated. They declared that the ciples then
accepted
proceeding was highly prejudicial and derogatory to their with regard
liberties. At last the dispute was brought to an 'indem-
nity,' of which a memorial was, by the King's command,
entered of record upon the Roll of Parliament. The purport of this instrument was that the King had no desire
that anything should be done which could in any way turn
against the estate represented by the members of the
Lower House in Parliament, or against the liberties of the
Lords. He therefore willed, granted, and declared, with
the advice and consent of the Lords, that it should be
lawful for the Lords to consult among themselves in Parliament, in the King's absence, with regard to the state of
the realm and to the remedies which might be required,
and that it should, in like manner, be lawful for the Commons to consult among themselves on the same subjects.
It was nevertheless provided that neither the Lords nor
the Commons should make any report to the King with
respect to any supplies which had been granted by the Commons and to which the Lords had agreed, nor with respect
to any communications having reference to supplies, until
the Lords and Commons had come to an accord in the
matter, and then only in the manner and form accustomed,
which were defined to be by the mouth of the Speaker of
the House of Commons. It was also the King's pleasure,
with the assent of the Lords, that the communication made
in the Parliament of Gloucester should never be drawn into
a precedent or turn to the prejudice or derogation of the
liberties of the estate which the members of the Lower
House represented [1].   .

We thus find three points accepted in relation to the constitutional method of voting supplies. They were to be granted
by the Commons, to have the assent of the Lords, and to be

[1] *Rot. Parl.*, 9 Hen. IV, no. 21 (printed, vol. iii. p. 611).

CH. XIV. reported to the King by the Speaker of the House of Commons. There was nothing to prevent any suggestions from the Lords to the Commons; but they were not to have any appearance of dictation caused by the use of the King's name, and they were not to be preceded by any report to him.

Grants of supply by Acts of Parliament. The mode of granting supplies, however, had, even yet, but little analogy with that of later days. There were long intervals between Parliament and Parliament, and grants were made sometimes for long periods of time, sometimes for the life of the sovereign. It was only by degrees that the grants took the form of Acts of Parliament. In the reign of Henry VIII some occur in this form, and the subsidies voted in Convocation were then confirmed by Statute [1]. The practice of taxing the clergy in Convocation was not discontinued until the year 1664, after which time they were taxed in the same manner as the laity.

Financial effect of the abolition of feudal tenures. The Great Rebellion, and the abolition of feudal tenures immediately after the Restoration, effected, in theory, at any rate, a complete revolution in the relation of the great land-holders to the State. Their obligation to provide a national army had ceased, and they constituted but a comparatively small portion of the whole population. Everything that was necessary for the public service had now to be raised by taxation in some form; and the members of the House of Commons represented almost the whole of the persons who were to be taxed. When, therefore, they claimed exclusive privileges in regard to Money Bills, they had not only some historical grounds for their pretensions, but also a powerful argument in the interests with which they were charged.

Dispute between the two Houses in 1661. In 1661 the Commons objected to a Bill sent down to them from the Lords, and having for its object the paving of the streets of Westminster. They said that 'it went to lay a charge upon the people,' and that 'it was a privilege

---

[1] See Stat. 32 Hen. VIII, cap. 23; 37 Hen. VIII, cap. 24 and cap. 25. The last confirmation was in 1663 (Stat. 15 Car. II, cap. 10).

inherent in their House that Bills of that nature should first CH. XIV.
be considered there.' They then sent up a Bill of their own,
but the Lords amended it by the insertion of a clause,
which the Commons would not accept because, as they said,
the amendment infringed their privileges. The Lords did
not admit that they had no power in such a matter as this,
and produced some precedents which they considered to be
in their favour [1]. As neither side would give way, no legislation could be effected.

In 1671 the Commons resolved, with reference to an *Resolu-*
amendment introduced into a Money Bill by the Lords, *tions of the*
Commons,
'that in all aids given to the King by the Commons, the *in 1671 and*
rate or tax ought not to be altered by the Lords [2].' In *1678, in*
relation to
1678 they resolved, ' that all aids and supplies, and aids to *the Lords*
His Majesty in Parliament, are the sole gift of the Commons ; *and Money*
Bills.
and all Bills for the granting of any such aids and supplies
ought to begin with the Commons; and that it is the
undoubted and sole right of the Commons to direct, limit,
and appoint, in such Bills, the ends, purposes, considerations,
conditions, limitations, and qualifications of such grants,
which ought not to be changed or altered by the House of
Lords [3].' This resolution did not, in its terms, affect the
power of the Lords to reject a Money Bill, though it denied
them the power of initiating or altering it. The Lords
could not be taxed without their own consent, but they
could not direct the course of taxation.

The proceedings of later times were long regulated, in *The re-*
the main, by this most important resolution of the year *striction on*
the Lords
1678. There have been instances in which the privileges *has since*
been
claimed by the Commons, in this respect have not been *practically*
pressed to their full extent, and in which expedients have *acknow-*
ledged.
been devised for adopting reasonable suggestions made by

---

[1] *Journals of the House of Commons*, July 29, 1661 (vol. viii. p. 315),
and *Journals of the House of Lords*, July 30, 1661 (vol. xi. p. 328).
There was a precedent in the fifth and another in the thirty-first year
of Elizabeth.

[2] *Journals of the House of Commons*, April 14, 1671 (vol. ix. p. 236).

[3] *Ib.*, July 3, 1678 (vol. ix. p. 509).

CH. XIV.   the Lords [1], but the general principle in relation to measures
of importance has never been abandoned.   It may, indeed,
be said that the power of the Lords even to reject a Money
Bill has been threatened, partly by direct resolutions of the
House of Commons, and partly by the indirect method of
including particular money clauses in Bills of more general
application.

New Reso-
lutions of
the House
of Com-
mons in
1860.

In the year 1860 the Commons sent up to the Lords
a bill for the repeal of acts imposing duties upon paper.
The Lords rejected it, and their action of course had the
effect of continuing the duties in accordance with the existing
law.   The Commons re-asserted their rights in a series of
resolutions.   One was, 'that the right of granting aids and
supplies to the Crown is in the Commons alone.'   In
another, though it was admitted that the Lords had on
previous occasions rejected Money Bills, it was declared that
the exercise of the power of rejection was 'justly regarded'
by the House of Commons 'with peculiar jealousy, as
affecting the right of the Commons to grant the supplies,
and to provide the ways and means for the service of the
year.'   A third was to the effect 'that to guard, for the
future, against an undue exercise of that power by the Lords,
and to secure to the Commons their rightful control over
taxation and supply,' the House of Commons 'has in its
own hands the power so to impose and remit taxes, and to
frame Bills of Supply, that the right of the Commons as to
the matter, manner, measure, and time, may be maintained
inviolate [2].'

Present
position of
the power
of the
Lords to
reject a
Money
Bill.

The meaning of the last resolution was soon made plain.
The repeal of the paper duties was included in the general
Customs and Inland Revenue Bill of the year 1861.   The
Lords were (according to the doctrines of the Commons)
powerless to amend it by striking out a particular clause,
and they could not reject it without deranging the whole.

[1] The details relating to these matters are hardly within the range
of the present Work.   They may be found in Sir T. Erskine May's
Law and Usage of Parliament (10th edition), pp. 540-550.
[2] Hansard's *Debates*, 3rd series, vol. clix. 1383-1606, July 5, 6, 1860.

financial scheme for the year. This was of course prac- CH. XIV.
tically impossible, and they had no alternative but to pass
the entire measure, and so reverse their decision of the
previous year [1]. It would seem that, should the Commons
always follow the same policy, the Lords would lose even
the power of throwing out a Money Bill, or would be able
to assert it only at the risk of interrupting all legislation
affecting the public revenue and expenditure [2].

[1] When passed, the Act became the 24 Vict. cap. 20, by the fourth
section of which the paper duties were repealed. See also Hansard's
Debates, 3rd series, vol. clxii. 594, and vol. clxiii. 68.

[2] An Address of the Lords to the King, in 1677, in relation to
amendments, might seem to describe very appositely the more recent
position of the House in relation to the rejection of Money Bills. The
Lords had then made some amendments in a Supply Bill for building
ships of war. The Commons 'disallowed' them. The Lords gave
their reasons, but the Commons remained 'unmoveable.' The Lords
then said :—The Commons 'have put upon us the extreme difficulty
either of shaking our privileges by withdrawing our amendments, or of
hazarding the safety of the nation by letting a bill fall that is necessary
to this time.' They yielded against their judgement, 'and out of
tenderness that the Whole may not suffer by our insisting on *that
which is our undoubted right.' Journals of the House of Lords*,
April 16, 1677 (vol. xiii. p. 119).

CHAPTER XV.

PART I.

THE FEUDAL PERIOD: DISAPPEARANCE OF THE ABBOTS: POSITION
OF THE CHANCELLOR: ABOLITION OF FEUDAL TENURES:
COMMENCEMENT OF A NEW SYSTEM: PEERAGES AS REWARDS
FOR POLITICAL SERVICE.

CHAP. XV. SOME changes in the component parts of the House of
Lords have been incidentally noticed in preceding
chapters, but it has been thought that the subject, as a whole,
could most conveniently be deferred to the last.

Compo-
sition of
the assem-
bly of
1265.
In the earliest Parliaments there were Bishops, Abbots,
and Priors of various religious Houses, the Master of the
Knights of the Temple, the Prior of the Hospital of St. John
of Jerusalem in England (or of the Knights Hospitallers),
as well as Earls and Barons. The numbers of the Abbots,
Priors, and Barons, were, however, subject to great fluctu-
ations, and the numbers of the Earls were not uniform
throughout. Thus in 1265 there were but five Earls and
eighteen Barons summoned, the Archbishop of York, thirteen
Bishops, sixty-five Abbots, and thirty-five Priors, including
the Prior of the Hospital of St. John of Jerusalem in
England, and the Prior of the Order of Sempringham, whose
position was somewhat different from that of the others[1].
There were also separately summoned five Deans, who
would, in later times, have had to attend either by virtue
of the *Praemunientes* clause in the writs to the Bishops of
their respective dioceses, or as members of the Council.

[1] *Rot. Lit. Claus.*, 49 Hen. III, m. 12 d.

When Edward I summoned a Parliament to meet on CHAP. XV.
November 13, 1295, he called nine Earls, and forty-one And of
Barons, two Archbishops, eighteen Bishops, sixty-seven the Parlia-
Abbots, the Prior of the Hospital of St. John of Jerusalem, ment of
1295.
the Master of the Order of Sempringham, and the Master of
the Knights of the Temple [1].

The varying numbers of the Temporal Lords (and Uniformity
especially of Barons) summoned in subsequent years have in the
writs of
already been noticed [2]. All the Bishops usually received summons
to Bishops.
writs. When their sees were vacant, the Guardians of the
Spiritualities were summoned in their stead. There is thus
much more uniformity in their writs of summons than in
those to the Earls who were sometimes engaged in foreign
service, and who were sometimes under age. An earldom,
too, sometimes became extinct by the death of its holder,
a bishopric never; and the creation of a new earldom was
a more common event than the creation of a new see.

The number of Priors and Abbots summoned, however, But not to
varied quite as much as that of the Barons, and, to some Priors and
Abbots
extent, for the same reasons. They were liable to summons before the
reign of
by reason of holding by barony, but they were not sum- Edward
moned unless the King desired their presence. When, in III.
the reign of Edward III, precedent and custom had largely
taken the place of the King's pleasure, with regard to the
persons who should be summoned, there was drawn up
a list of Abbots and Priors whom it had not been usual to
call. They were no less than twenty-eight in number [3].
The catalogue was not by any means accurate, as it included
the Master and Prior of the Order of Sempringham, as well
as the Abbots of Fountains and Furness, whose names
might easily have been found among the earlier writs of

---

[1] *Rot. Lit. Claus.*, 23 Ed. I, m. 3 d and m. 4 d. It may here be mentioned that, on the dissolution of the Order of the Knights of the Temple,
their possessions in England were given to the Prior and Brethren of
the Order of the Knights of St. John of Jerusalem in 1324 (17 Ed. II,
stat. 3). The latter Order survived in England until the reign of
Henry VIII, as shown in another chapter.

[2] See above, p. 96.

[3] *Rot. Lit. Claus.*, 6 Ed. III, m. 36 d.

CHAP. XV. summons, and even among the writs of the same reign. The mere fact that it was made, however, is an indication that the composition of the House of Lords was falling into a groove, the Temporal Lords and the Spiritual Lords alike having to be called in accordance with a recognized usage. Soon after this time, and before the middle of the reign, there was a permanent diminution in the number of Abbots and Priors summoned.

The dignities held by the Temporal Lords at various times.   In addition to Earls and Barons, the Lords Temporal have, at various times, included, if not Kings, at least one whom the English recognized as King, and Princes, Dukes, Marquesses[1], and Viscounts[1]. John of Gaunt, Duke of Lancaster, who assumed the style and title of King of Castile and Leon, was summoned, in the first and in subsequent years of the reign of Richard II, as King of Castile and Leon, and as Duke of Lancaster[2]. Edward, son of Edward I, was summoned to Parliament as Prince of Wales, and Earl of Chester, in 1302[3]. The first Duke summoned was Edward, the Black Prince, son of Edward III, who was also Prince of Wales, and was summoned as Prince, as Duke of Cornwall, and as Earl of Chester[4]. The first Marquess summoned was Robert de Vere, Marquess of Dublin, in 1386[5]. The first Viscount summoned was John, Viscount Beaumont, in 1441[6].

Majorities of Spiritual Lords through extinction of peerages.   As new dignities were but sparingly created between the time of Edward III and that of Henry VII, as old families died out, in the course of nature, or came to an

---

[1] Both Marquess and Viscount were titles introduced from abroad, and inconsistent with all practice and tradition in England. A Marquess should, according to etymology and precedent, have been no more than an Earl having jurisdiction on a March or Frontier. A Viscount, according to all precedent, was only an Earl's Deputy, or Sheriff. There had been Earls of March, or of the Marches towards Wales, before there was any Marquess in England ; and the Sheriffs of England had been known, in the French which was spoken in England, as Viscounts or *Vicountes*, in Latin as *Vicecomites*, since the Conquest.

[2] *Rot. Lit. Claus.*, 1 Ric. II, m. 37 d, *et alibi*.

[3] *Ib.*, 30 Ed. I, m. 13 d.   [4] *Ib.*, 24 Ed. III, pt. 2, m. 3 d, *et alibi*.

[5] *Ib.*, 10 Ric. II, m. 42 d.   [6] *Ib.*, 20 Hen. VI, m. 27 d.

untimely end in the civil and foreign wars of the period, CHAP. XV.
or through attainders of High Treason, the number of
Temporal Lords had a diminishing tendency. Although,
as we have seen, fifty was about their normal number in
the middle of the reign of Edward III, there were but
twenty-nine summoned to the first Parliament of Henry VII.
The number of Abbots and Priors who had seats was about
the same ; and the Spiritual Lords were thus in a majority
equivalent to the whole Bench of Bishops. This majority
was destined to be soon diminished, and not very long afterwards annihilated. In the reign of Henry VII there were
about five [1] creations of new Peers, apart from promotions
in the peerage, and from restorations of honours and confirmations of previous grants. In the first thirty years of the
reign of Henry VIII there were, perhaps, twenty new creations apart from promotions, restorations, and confirmations.
These had some effect upon the relative proportions of
Lords Temporal and Lords Spiritual, but they were followed
by an event of far greater moment.

The most important of all permanent changes ever The disso-
effected at any one time in the constituent parts of the lution of
House of Lords was that which befel when the greater the greater
monasteries were dissolved. It would be beyond the monas-
province of this history to trace in detail all the events teries.
which rendered such a revolution possible, when the
Spiritual Lords having seats in Parliament were commonly
equal, if not superior in number, to the Temporal Lords. It
may suffice to remark that the doctrines of the Lollards,
which afterwards developed into those of the Puritans, had
sensibly affected the whole nation, that the power of the
Crown had greatly increased since the Wars of the Roses,

[1] It is not, as might be supposed, a very simple task to count the
number. There were altogether no less than thirty-nine creations,
promotions, confirmations, and restitutions in the peerage of England.
List compiled by Mr. R. D. Trimmer, and published in the 47th
Report of the Deputy-Keeper of the Records, pp. 79-83. These,
however, cannot of course be all considered to make an absolute
increase in the number of Peers.

CHAP. XV. from the security given to the throne when Henry VII
ascended it, that the enquiries touching the minor
monasteries and their results had created a strong prejudice
against monasteries in general, and finally that King
Henry VIII and his courtiers looked with longing eyes to
the spoil within their reach.

The Act relating to those which were surrendered.   Most of the Abbots and Priors made a voluntary surrender of their possessions, and this, we may be sure, they
would not have done, had they seen the least hope of
gaining anything by resistance. High treason and heresy
were so near akin in those days of burning theological
hatred, and heresy was so nearly identical with difference
from the King's religious opinions, that an Abbot who
attempted to retain his abbey and his spiritual dignity
would almost certainly have paid the penalty with his life.
The Acts relating to the dissolution were very skilfully
worded. The possessions of those Houses which had been
voluntarily dissolved were given to the King, and were to
be within the survey of the Court of Augmentations of the
Revenues of the Crown[1]. Those which came to the
King's hands by attainder of Treason were excepted[2]. It
was, however, provided in the same Act that all monasteries
and their possessions which should in any other way than
by surrender come to the King should also vest in the
King[3]. As soon as an Abbot or Prior was attainted of
Treason the Abbey or Priory became vacant, and the
possessions of his House would (if of royal foundation, as
would probably be assumed) be taken in the ordinary
course into the King's hand, there to remain until
a successor should be appointed, and livery should be
granted. When therefore, the act of taking possession
upon vacancy vested the possessions in the King by Act of
Parliament, all difficulties with regard to the corporate
character of an Abbot or Prior, or his House, were at an
end.

The Act relating to those   By a subsequent Act which placed the franchises and
jurisdictions attached to the possessions of the surrendered

---

[1] Stat. 31 Hen. VIII, cap. 13, secs. 1-4.   [2] Sec. 4.   [3] Sec. 3.

Abbeys under the survey of the Court of Augmentations[1], CHAP. XV.
the similar franchises and jurisdictions attached to the which
possessions of Abbeys which had come into the King's came to
hands through attainder, were placed under the survey of the King's
the Surveyors-General[2]. Thus a separate machinery was attainder.
provided for the possessions of abbeys coming to the
King's hands through attainder, and not through voluntary
surrender. The result, however, after the legal difficulty
had been evaded, was the same in both cases. The
monasteries were dissolved, the Abbots and Priors ceased
to sit in Parliament, and the King had the lands at his
disposal.

The effect was practically to destroy for ever the power Practical
of one of the so-called Estates of the Realm. The Lords destruction
Spiritual, reduced now only to Archbishops and Bishops, power of
could never again command alone a majority in the House one of the
so-called
of Lords. They might still turn the scale, as in fact they Estates of
did, on important divisions in later times. They might the Realm.
sometimes be of use, as a contingent to a political party of
the day, but could not dictate terms as an independent
body. The few new bishoprics created by Henry out of
the spoil of the monasteries still left the Lords Spiritual in
such a minority that the Lords Temporal outnumbered
them in the proportion of about two to one, and their
relative number grew less in later generations.

At the time of this revolution (for it was little less) an The Act
Act was passed 'for placing of the Lords' in their House, 'for
placing of
which, while omitting of course all mention of Abbots, the Lords':
described the seats of the Bishops and of the Lords the Chancellor.
Temporal. The most important personage at the moment
was the King's Vice-gerent for Ecclesiastical Jurisdiction
(Thomas Lord Cromwell), who was to sit above the Archbishop of Canterbury. Certain other great Officers of
State had different places assigned to them according to
their rank, each sitting in one place if below the rank of
a Baron, and in another if a Baron or in a higher grade of
the peerage. If Peers they were to sit above all Dukes

[1] Stat. 32 Hen. VIII, cap. 20. sec. 1.   [2] Sec. 2.

CHAP. XV. except those of the blood royal, if not Peers they were to sit 'at the uppermost part of the [wool] sacks in the midst of the Parliament Chamber.' These officers were the Lord Chancellor, the Lord Treasurer, the Lord President of the King's Council, the Lord Privy Seal, and the Chief Secretary. Except the Lord Chancellor, there is no mention made of the Judges, who had formerly sat as part of the King's Council in his Parliament, though they were still summoned. The Great Chamberlain, the Constable, the Marshal, the Lord Admiral, the Great Master or Lord Steward, and the King's Chamberlain, were to be placed after the Lord Privy Seal, but above all other personages of the same degree as themselves[1].

The Act has, in modern times, lost much of its force, as it is long since there has been a Lord High Treasurer, or even a Lord High Admiral; and Secretaries of State not unfrequently sit in the House of Commons. One of the officers mentioned, however, is so inseparably associated with the House of Lords that it may be convenient, in this place, to give in outline the story of his connexion with the Parliament.

The early Chancellors were ecclesiastics; they received a summons only when Bishops. In early times the Chancellor would seem to have been commonly in close personal attendance on the King. When a law was made, as it often was before the existence of a true Parliament, by charter, the Chancellor was usually present to seal it with the Great Seal, of which he had charge. His presence in the King's Court or Council appears to have been a matter of course. For many generations after the Conquest the Chancellor was always an ecclesiastic, and most frequently a Bishop. When the writs of summons to Parliament commence, we find that the Bishop-Chancellor is summoned not as Chancellor but as Bishop. The distinction may at first sight appear immaterial, but is in fact of some importance. It was only as · Bishop that his summons could contain the *Praemunientes* clause to warn the clergy of his diocese, and it was therefore necessary that he should be summoned in his episcopal

[1] Stat. 31 Hen. VIII, cap. 10.

capacity. When not a Bishop the Chancellor does not seem to have been summoned at all.

The inference to be drawn, however, is not that the As Chancellor was not expected to attend among the Lords, but that his attendance was necessary in virtue of his office, and that it was needless to summon an officer who was himself directing the issue of the writs of summons. The Chancery was an office of the Parliament from which every summons proceeded. The Chancellor consequently knew in his official capacity the appointed day and place of the meeting of Parliament.

A remarkable illustration of the fact that the Chancellors attended in Parliament, though not summoned, occurs in the case of Sir Robert Bourchier, the first layman who held the office. There is no record of the issue of any summons to him. He was not a Peer of the Realm, and had no place in Parliament except as Chancellor. As Chancellor, however, he took his seat, and made that memorable protest which has been mentioned in another chapter. His successor, Sir Robert Parning, also a layman, and not a Peer of the Realm, never received any recorded summons as Chancellor, though, when previously Treasurer, he had been summoned among the Council. The next Chancellor was Robert de Sadington, who, though previously summoned among the Council, as Chief Baron of the Exchequer, was not summoned as Chancellor. His successor was John de Ufford, Dean of Lincoln, but again no summons to him appears. He was neither a Bishop nor one of the Temporal Peers, at the time, and must have been expected to be present *ex officio*.

Several Bishops afterwards succeeded to the Chancellorship, and were summoned as Bishops, but the next lay Chancellors, Thorpe and Knyvet, received no summons in the capacity of Chancellor. So also Sir Richard le Scrope, Chancellor in the second year of the reign of Richard II, had no recorded summons. Michael de la Pole, also a lay Chancellor, was summoned to Parliament, but summoned among the Barons, as he had been before he held the office, and without any reference to it.   John de Scarle, Chancellor at the beginning of the reign of Henry IV, had no recorded summons, nor had Sir Thomas Beaufort, another lay Chancellor.

The place of the Chancellor in the House, if a Commoner.   It appears needless to pursue the investigation further, as it is clear that, in accordance with the practice of centuries, the Chancellor's presence in Parliament was *ex officio*, and not in virtue of any writ of summons.   He has for centuries been regarded, whether Peer or commoner, as the Speaker or Prolocutor of the House.   His place on the woolsack is now usually said to be not technically within the House, though it is difficult to reconcile this opinion with the plain words of the Act of Henry VIII, that the seat is ' in the midst of the Parliament Chamber.'   In that very Act, however, it was said that if below the degree of a Baron of Parliament, he had ' no interest to give any assent or dissent ' in the House.   He has now no voice or vote, if a commoner, though, in the reign of Edward III, he protested aloud.   It seems not impossible that in the days when there were intervals of many years between Parliament and Parliament, his true position was forgotten.   It is, however, manifest that the original idea as to his attendance in Parliament *ex officio* survived the separation of the Council from the Parliament, and that he continued to attend as Chancellor quite independently of the other Judges whose advice could be required by the House of Lords.

Chancellor, Keeper, and Commissioners of the Great Seal.   Though the Lord Chancellor has usually had charge of the Great Seal, there 'have been times when it has been entrusted to a keeper who was not Chancellor.   This was, for the most part, a temporary arrangement, but towards the reign of Queen Elizabeth the arrangement was sometimes of a more permanent nature.   An Act was then passed declaring that the Lord Keeper of the Great Seal for the time being shall have the same place, pre-eminence, and jurisdiction as the Lord Chancellor of England [1].

From a very early period it happened occasionally that the Great Seal was placed in the custody of several persons.

[1] Stat. 5 Eliz., cap. 18.

In later times these were known as Lords Commissioners of CHAP. XV. the Great Seal. Their position was not very precisely defined until the reign of William and Mary, when it was enacted that they should have all the authority of Lord Chancellor or Lord Keeper and should, if not Peers, rank 'next after Peers and the Speaker of the House of Commons [1].'

In relation to the office of Chancellor there is a disability which came into existence under the Test Act in the reign of Charles II, but which does not now affect Lords of Parliament in general. In 1829 an Act [2] was passed which, by removing the necessity for a declaration against transubstantiation, enabled Roman Catholics to sit in either House of Parliament. It was, however, at the same time specially provided that no person professing the Roman Catholic religion should thus be enabled to hold the Office of Chancellor, Lord Keeper, or Commissioner of the Great Seal [3]. They cannot be Roman Catholics.

After the changes effected by Henry VIII, and the settling of the Lords in their places, the character of the House of Lords underwent but little further alteration until the accession of James I. The creations of new Peers were not much in excess of the extinction of peerages, and mere promotions in the peerage did not affect the total number of the Lords Temporal. After the long reign of Elizabeth there seem to have been only some sixty who were capable of sitting and voting in Parliament. The character of the House underwent little change between the reign of Henry VIII and that of James I.

After James I came to the throne, however, the composition of the House of Lords was considerably modified. At one time he increased his revenue by the sale of Baronies for £10,000 each, Viscounties for £15,000, and Earldoms for £20,000. In one day (May 4, 1605) he made or promoted as many as eight Peers [4]. It is computed that he added no less than fifty-four [5] laymen to the House of Lords. Increase of the peerage in the latter reign.

---

[1] Stat. 1 Will. and Mary, cap. 21.   [2] Stat. 10 Geo. IV, cap. 7.
[3] Sec. 12.   [4] *Rot. Lit. Pat.*, 3 Jac. I, pt. 12, mm. 14–21.
[5] This seems to be the number, after deducting from the total of creations, the promotions in the peerage, restitutions, confirmations, and creations of Scottish and Irish Peers.

CHAP. XV. Most of his successors have followed his example, not indeed, in accepting money for the dignities conferred, but by creating new dignities with profusion.

The events of the reign of Charles I and the Commonwealth. It has been mentioned, in the chapter on the legislative power of the House of Lords, that during the reign of Charles I, the Bishops were excluded from the House by Act of Parliament, that the Commons afterwards voted themselves to be the law-making power without the assent of King or Lords, that Oliver Cromwell found himself under the necessity, as he thought, of establishing an 'Other House,' or House of Lords, that there was legislation under Charles II by a House of Lords sitting without Bishops, and finally that the Act by which the Spiritual Lords had been excluded was repealed, and they were once again summoned to Parliament. These were but episodes in the main current of history. but a change which was effected during this period of disturbance had an important and lasting effect.

The abolition of feudal tenures. Feudal tenure by military service, which was an anachronism under the Stuarts, and was abolished during the Commonwealth[1], rose again into a nominal existence with the restoration of Charles II, only to be finally extinguished immediately afterwards. All tenures by knight-service of the King, or of any other person, were swept away, together with escuage, fines for alienation, wardships, liveries, primer seisins, ouster-le-mains, and values and forfeitures of marriages by reason of any such tenures[2].

Its effect in relieving the Peers of their burdens. Though this radical change affected some persons who were not Peers, it affected the Peers in such a manner as to completely change their relation to the King and to the State in general. Under the strict feudal system, and even under the feudal system when somewhat relaxed, there was no Earl and there was no Baron without lands, and the lands of Earls and Barons were held subject to very heavy· burdens. Every Baron and every Earl, as being a Baron also, was in theory a soldier, and in theory bound to give his counsel to the sovereign. He had to provide men and

[1] 1656, cap. 4.   [2] Stat. 12 Charles II, cap. 24.

arms for war. or, if not men and arms, an equivalent in CHAP. XV.
money. He had to come to the King's Councils and to
Parliament when summoned, or, at any rate, to send a proxy
with power to consent to any further burdens which were
to be imposed. By the abolition of military tenure he was
freed from the greatest part of his obligations.

The summons to Parliament, too, had long been regarded Their titles
as an indication of his dignity rather than as a disagreeable of honour
preserved
incident of his position; and a Peer of the latter part of the by special
seventeenth century was as little like a Peer of the reign of enactment.
Edward II as a modern petty jury is like a petty jury of
the thirteenth or fourteenth century. 'Suit of Court' was,
indeed, preserved in general terms, but the feudal as well
as other titles of honour, and the 'right to sit' in the House
of Lords were saved to the Peers by special enactment,
without any mention of attendance in Parliament as
a necessary duty [1].

Not only was the position of those who enjoyed the older The newer
peerages altered, but later peerages were soon to be created creations
thenceforth
under new conditions and for reasons which the Plantagenets of a dif-
and even the Tudors could hardly have understood. The ferent
character.
sovereign began to govern by ministers who formed
a Cabinet, and the Cabinet began to be representative of
one of two opposing parties. The party which had not
power was always striving to obtain it, always, no doubt, in
the interest or alleged interest of the State. Political
power, however, fell more and more into the hands of the
Commons, and the tenure of office by a Cabinet came to
depend on the possession of a majority in the Lower House.
Service to the State consequently became, in a great measure,
identified with service to a party; and service to a party
was very closely associated with a command of votes.
A peerage giving a new dignity, and not encumbered with
any new burdens, was naturally a much coveted reward; and
the creations of Peers since the Revolution, if not since the
Restoration, have been largely in recognition of faithful
adherence to political chiefs.

[1] Stat. 12 Charles II, cap. 24, sec. 5, and sec. 11.

CHAPTER XV.

PART II.

INTRODUCTION OF THE PRINCIPLE OF REPRESENTATION AMONG PEERS: THE UNION WITH SCOTLAND: ATTEMPTS TO LIMIT THE PEERAGE: THE UNION WITH IRELAND.

CHAP. XV.

The Union with Scotland.

WHEN James VI of Scotland succeeded to the English throne as James I of England, there continued to be a separate kingdom of Scotland, and a separate kingdom of England, though the same sovereign was at the head of both. Each had its distinct Parliament and its distinct Peerage. The English House of Lords was consequently not affected by the accession of James I, or by the union of the two crowns, for more than a century. In the reign of Anne, however, a scheme was devised for the complete union of the two kingdoms, and of the two Parliaments.

No addition of Spiritual Lords to the House of Lords.

Articles of Union were drawn up and subsequently confirmed and ratified by Statute[1]. The effect upon the House of Lords was to add sixteen Lords Temporal but no Lords Spiritual, the established Church of Scotland being Presbyterian and consequently without Bishops. The proportion of Spiritual to Temporal Lords was thus again diminished.

Election of sixteen representative Peers for each Parliament.

The sixteen Scottish Peers who, under the Articles of Union, acquired seats as Peers in the Parliament of Great. Britain, were to be elected not as perpetual representatives, or as representatives for life, of the Peers of Scotland, but

[1] 5 Anne, cap. 8. (Statutes at Large.) The articles had been previously ratified and approved by an Act of Parliament in Scotland.

only as representatives for the particular Parliament for CHAP. XV.
which a writ issued directing them to be summoned[1]. So
long as they were representatives they were to enjoy all
the privileges which the Peers of England had previously
had or might subsequently acquire, and in particular the
right of sitting upon the trial of Peers. At trials of
Peers in the interval between the dissolution of one
Parliament and the calling of another into being the sixteen
representatives who had sat in the last Parliament were to
have the same powers and privileges as any other Peers of
Great Britain[2].

It was provided that, after the Union, there should be
one Great Seal for the United Kingdom of Great Britain,
which was to be different from the Great Seal then used in
either kingdom. This was to be used in sealing writs to
elect and summon the Parliament of Great Britain, all
treaties with foreign Princes and States, and all public
acts, instruments, and orders of State which concern the
whole United Kingdom. The Great Seal of England was
to be used as before in all matters relating to England
alone. Another seal was to be kept in Scotland and used
in matters relating to private grants or rights which had
usually passed the Great Seal of Scotland[3]. The Lord
High Chancellor of England, having custody of the Great
Seal of the United Kingdom of Great Britain, became
thenceforward Chancellor of Great Britain, and so continued
to be after the Union with Ireland, which retained an
independent Lord Chancellor.

The Chancellor of England becomes Chancellor of Great Britain.

All the Peers of Scotland (including those who were not
among the sixteen representatives) were, after the Union,
to be Peers of Great Britain, and have rank and precedence
immediately after the Peers of the like orders and degrees
in England at the time of the Union, and before all Peers
of Great Britain of the like orders and degrees to be created
after the Union. They were to be tried as Peers of Great
Britain and enjoy all the privileges of Peers as fully as the
Peers of England, except the right of sitting in the House

Privileges of the Peers of Scotland.

---

[1] Stat. 5 Anne, cap. 8, sec. 1, art. 22.   [2] Art. 23.   [3] Art. 24.

CHAP. XV. of Lords, and the right of sitting upon the trials of Peers, which were to be enjoyed only by the sixteen representatives.

A new principle of representation now introduced.   There was thus introduced into the ranks of the peerage a numerous class of Peers not entitled to sit in the House of Lords. There was introduced also an entirely new principle—that of representation in the House of Lords by means of election. The Sovereign did not send a writ of summons directly to each of sixteen Peers selected by himself as representatives, but a writ to the Privy Council of Scotland [1] commanding that body to cause the sixteen to be summoned. The sixteen were to be named by the Peers of Scotland, and that by open election and plurality of the voices of the Peers present and of the proxies of those absent [2]. There were 165 upon the Roll, the greater part of whom (not being also Peers of England) remained Peers without seats in the House of Lords when their sixteen representatives had been elected.

The Privy Council of Scotland, in virtue of an Act passed very soon after the Act of Union, ceased to have any separate existence [3], and new provisions had to be made for the return of the representative Peers. It was then enacted that when any Parliament of Great Britain was to be summoned and held, 'in order to the electing and summoning the sixteen Peers of Scotland,' a proclamation should be issued under the Great Seal of Great Britain commanding all the Peers of Scotland to meet, at an appointed time and place, in Scotland, to elect the sixteen in the manner before provided [4].

Absence of provisions relating to extinction of old or creation of new peerages of Scotland: conse-quences.   In the Act of Union no provision was made with regard to the extinction of old or the creation of new Peerages of Scotland, and no power was given to Peers of Scotland to serve in the House of Commons of the Kingdom of Great Britain. In these respects the Union of England with Scotland differed materially from the Union of Great Britain with Ireland. It may have been considered that

[1] Stat. 5 Anne, cap. 8, sec. 1, art. 22.   [2] *Ib.*, secs. 12 and 13.
[3] Stat. 6 Anne, cap. 6.   [4] *Ib.*, cap. 23.

the creation of new Peers of Scotland with power of electing representatives would infringe the rights of the electors under the Act of Union. But their number was soon reduced by attainders following the rebellions of 1715 and 1745. Several descendants of those who were attainted were, indeed, restored by Acts of Parliament, in the reign of George IV, to the dignities enjoyed by their ancestors. Among the titles which then re-appeared upon the Roll were those of the Earls of Mar[1] and Carnwath[2], of Viscounts Strathallan[3] and Kenmure[4], and of Barons Nairn[5] and Duffus[6]. The natural process of decay, however, threatens the ultimate extinction of the peerage of Scotland, which is already greatly diminished.

Very soon after the Union the question arose whether a Peer of Scotland could be created and sit as a Peer of Great Britain. James, second Duke of Queensberry, was created Duke of Dover in 1708, and sat in the House of Lords without opposition. In 1711, however, the Duke of Hamilton in the peerage of Scotland had a patent creating him Duke of Brandon in the Peerage of Great Britain. The House of Lords then declared (though only by a majority of five) that 'no patent of honour granted to any Peer of Great Britain, who was a Peer of Scotland at the time of the Union, entitled such Peer to sit and vote in Parliament, or to sit upon the trial of Peers[7].' The reason of this declaration seems to have been that the majority of Lords considered the number of Scottish Peers who could sit in Parliament to be limited to sixteen in accordance with the principle of representation. Their resolution was not very judicious, because, as soon became apparent, the heir of a Scottish Peer could certainly be created and sit as a Peer of Great Britain, and would not lose his dignity when he succeeded to the Scottish peerage.

It was not, however, until the year 1782 that the Lords reconsidered their decision. They then consulted the

Ineffectual attempts to exclude from the House of Lords Peers of Scotland who were created Peers of Great Britain by Patent.

They now sit without question.

[1] 5 Geo. IV, 47. [2] 7 Geo. IV, 52. [3] 5 Geo. IV, 48.
[4] 5 Geo. IV, 49. [5] 5 Geo. IV, 50. [6] 7 Geo. IV, 51.
[7] *Journals of the House of Lords*, Dec. 20, 1711 (vol. xix. p. 346).

CHAP. XV. Judges, who were unanimously of opinion that Peers of Scotland were not disabled by the Act of Union from being newly created and sitting as Peers of Great Britain. They accepted this doctrine, and made no further opposition [1].

Peers of the United Kingdom cannot sit as representative Peers of Scotland.

This reversal of the previous declaration soon brought into prominence the question whether a representative Peer of Scotland acquiring, by inheritance or creation, a peerage of England or Great Britain, vacated his seat as a representative. There had been a case in 1736, when the Duke of Athole, being a representative Peer, established a claim to the English barony of Strange by inheritance, and yet continued to sit as representative. For some reason no opposition was made at the time, and there was consequently no definite decision. In 1786, however, two of the sixteen representative Peers were created Peers of Great Britain. One was William, fourth Duke of Queensberry, who though succeeding to the Scottish dukedom had not succeeded to the English dignities of the second Duke, and now had his patent as Baron Douglas of Amesbury. The other was James, eighth Earl of Abercorn, who had his patent as Viscount Hamilton. In the following year the matter was brought before the House of Lords, which resolved, in accordance with the report of a Committee of Privileges, 'that the Earl of Abercorn and the Duke of Queensberry had ceased to sit as representatives of the Peerage of Scotland [2].'

But, as Peers of Scotland, they may vote for representatives.

It was long held by the House of Lords, that Peers of Scotland, disqualified for sitting as representative Peers, by reason of holding peerages of Great Britain, were disqualified to vote at the election of the representatives [3]. In 1793 , however, though there were some dissentients, the contrary opinion prevailed; and since that time all the Peers of Scotland, otherwise duly qualified, whether holding

[1] *Journals of the House of Lords*, June 6, 1782 (vol. xxxvi. p. 517).

[2] *Ib.*, Feb. 14, 1787 (vol. xxxvii. pp. 594-5) ; *Parliamentary History*, vol. xxvi. 598-607.

[3] *Journals*, Jan. 21, 1708-9 (vol. xviii. p. 609) ; *ib.*, May 18, 1787 (vol. xxxvii. p. 709) ; *Parliamentary History*, vol. xxvi. 1158.

[4] *Journals*, June 6, 1793 (vol. xxxix. p. 726).

separate peerages of Great Britain or of the United Kingdom, or not, have had their votes admitted.

The jealousy shown by the House of Lords just after the Union with Scotland, in their efforts to limit the number of Scottish Peers to the sixteen representatives, was exhibited somewhat later in another fashion. Queen Anne, with the object of securing a majority for the Court party, created no less than twelve Peers at once—a very considerable number in relation to the total of those already having seats. This use of the prerogative was disliked by the Peers of longer standing, and a few years afterwards they made an attempt to prevent any similar action in the future. In 1719 a bill was introduced in which it was proposed that 'the number of Peers of Great Britain on the part of England' should never be enlarged by more than six. There was, however, an exception in favour of Princes of the Blood Royal; and upon the extinction of a peerage the Sovereign might fill up the vacancy. It was also proposed that the principle of electing representative Peers of Scotland should be abandoned, and that twenty-five hereditary Peers should take the place of the sixteen representatives[1].

The third reading of the bill in the House of Lords was adjourned from the 14th to the 24th of April, and Parliament was prorogued on the 18th. In the following November, however, another bill of similar purport, after passing the House of Lords, was sent down to the House of Commons. Had it become law, it would have forced the development of the Constitution in later times into a totally different channel. The Commons saved the prerogative of the Crown; and it was remarked, in a somewhat cynical manner, by Blackstone that their leaders 'were then desirous to keep the avenues to the other House as open and easy as possible[2].' Robert Walpole at any rate strongly opposed the Bill, which was lost by a majority of 269 to 177[3].

The Union with Ireland had the effect of introducing two new representative elements into the House of Lords.

Marginal notes: CHAP. XV.

Attempts of the Lords to restrict the creation of peerages, and alter the terms of the Union.

The attempts defeated by the Commons.

The Union with Ireland: two

[1] *Parliamentary History*, vol. vii. 589-594.
[2] 1 Com. 157.   [3] *Parliamentary History*, vol. vii. 606-627.

CHAP. XV.　The established Church of Ireland being at the time Epi-
new repre- scopal, and not like that of Scotland Presbyterian, the Lords
sentative
elements　Spiritual of Ireland, as well as the Lords Temporal, obtained
added.　representation in the Parliament of the United Kingdom.

Union　　In the year 1800, the two Houses of the two Parliaments
of the
Churches of Great Britain and of Ireland respectively, agreed upon
of England articles for the union of Great Britain and Ireland, in order,
and Ire-
land.　as was said at the time, 'to promote and secure the essential
interests of Great Britain and Ireland, and to consolidate
the strength, power, and resources of the British Empire[1].'
By the fifth article it was provided that the Churches of
England and Ireland, as then established, should be united
into one Protestant Episcopal Church, to be called the
United Church of England and Ireland. A clause was
added which has a strange sound, since, by the irony of
fate, the Church of Ireland has been disestablished : 'the
continuance and preservation of the said united Church as
the established Church of England and Ireland shall be
deemed and taken to be an essential and fundamental part
of the Union[2].'

According to the fourth article four Lords Spiritual of
Ireland, 'by rotation of Sessions,' and twenty-eight Lords
Temporal of Ireland, elected for life by the Peers of
Ireland, were to be the number to sit and vote, on the part
of Ireland, in the House of Lords of the Parliament of the
United Kingdom[3].

The mode of summoning and returning both the Lords
Spiritual and the Lords Temporal was regulated by an
Act passed in the Parliament of Ireland before the commencement of the Union, and incorporated in the English
and Irish Acts of Union.

Four repre- With regard to the Lords Spiritual it was provided that
sentative
Bishops to one of the four Archbishops of Ireland, and three of the
sit by rota- eighteen Bishops of Ireland, should sit in the House of
tion of
sessions. Lords of the United Parliament in each session. The
Primate of all Ireland (the Archbishop of Armagh) was to

---

[1] Stat. 39 & 40 Geo. III, cap. 67, Preamble.
[2] *Ib.*, cap. 67. sec. 1. art. 5.　　　　　　　　　　[3] *Ib.*, art. 4.

sit in the first session, the Archbishop of Dublin in the
second, the Archbishop of Cashel in the third, the Archbishop of Tuam in the fourth, and so by rotation of sessions
'for ever,' the rotation to proceed regularly and without
interruption from session to session, notwithstanding any
dissolution or expiration of Parliament. The three suffragan
Bishops were also to sit according to rotation of sessions
in the order set forth in the Act.

With regard to the Lords Temporal it was provided that Twenty-
the twenty-eight representatives should be elected by the eight repre-
Temporal Peers of Ireland in the manner prescribed. Those Lords to be
chosen by the majority of votes were, during their respec- life.
tive lives, to sit as representatives of the Peers of Ireland
in the House of Lords of the United Kingdom, and be
entitled to receive writs of summons to every Parliament [1].

The four Lords Spiritual sitting by rotation of sessions, Privileges
and the twenty-eight Lords Temporal sitting as repre- of the
sentatives for life, were to have the same privileges of Spiritual
Parliament as those belonging to the Lords of Parliament poral of
on the part of Great Britain, and the same rights in respect Ireland.
of sitting and voting on the trial of Peers. All the Lords
Spiritual of Ireland were to have rank and precedence
immediately after the Lords Spiritual of the same rank
and degree of Great Britain, and enjoy the same privileges,
except those of sitting in the House of Lords and on the
trial of Peers, which were restricted to the four sitting by
rotation. All the holders of temporal peerages in existence at the time of the Union were to have rank and
precedence immediately after all persons holding peerages
of the like orders and degrees in Great Britain. All
peerages of Ireland created after the Union were to have
'rank and precedence with the peerages of the United
Kingdom so created according to the dates of their
creations.' All peerages both of Great Britain and Ireland
were, in all other respects, to be considered peerages of
the United Kingdom. The Peers of Ireland were, as Peers
of the United Kingdom, to be sued and tried as Peers, and

[1] Stat. 39 & 40 Geo. III, cap. 67. sec. 1. art. 4, and sec. 2.

CHAP. XV. were to enjoy all privileges of peerage as fully as the Peers of Great Britain, except those of sitting in the House of Lords and on the trial of Peers, which were restricted to the twenty-eight representatives [1].

Restriction of the number of peerages of Ireland: provisions for new creations. — Special provisions were made with regard to the number of peerages of Ireland which were to continue in existence. No new creation of a Peer of Ireland was to be made until three of the existing peerages had become extinct, but as often as three became extinct one new peerage might be created. As soon, however, as the number had been reduced to one hundred, the Crown might create one Peer whenever any one of the hundred peerages became extinct, so that the Peerage of Ireland might be kept up to the number of one hundred, over and above the number of Irish Peers who might be entitled, by descent or creation, to an hereditary seat in the House of Lords of the United Kingdom [2].

Position of Peers of Ireland as members of the House of Commons. — A Peer of Ireland might, unless he was one of the Irish representative Peers, be elected and serve in the House of Commons of the United Kingdom, as member for any county, city, or borough of Great Britain, but not of Ireland. As long, however, as he continued to be a member of the House of Commons, he was not to be entitled to the privilege of peerage, or capable of being elected one of the Irish representative Peers, or of voting at any election of such Peers, and he was liable to be sued, indicted, and tried as a commoner [3].

The Spiritual Lords of Ireland excluded from the House on the Disestablishment of the Church of Ireland. — The proportion of four Spiritual Lords to twenty-eight Temporal Peers, as representatives for Ireland, was, perhaps, not unfairly arranged in relation to the existing numbers of each class. The effect, however, was to add only four to the total number of Spiritual Lords in the House, and not in any way to give increased power to the Church. Even this small accession of strength to the Lords Spiritual was destined to be lost in seventy years. In 1869 was passed the Act ' to put an end to the establishment of the Church of Ireland [4].' The union of the Churches of England and

---

[1] Stat. 39 & 40 Geo. III, cap. 67. sec. 1. art. 4.
[2] Ib.   [3] Ib.   [4] The Irish Church Act, 1869.

Ireland was then dissolved, and the Church of Ireland Chap. XV.
ceased to be established by law. It was also expressly provided that, after the end of the year 1870, no Archbishop
or Bishop of the Church of Ireland should, in that capacity,
be summoned or qualified to sit in the House of Lords [1].

The representatives of the Temporal Peers of Ireland Changes proposed in
were of course not affected by a Statute which had relation to
reference solely to the Church, and they retained their the representative
right to sit after election, in accordance with the terms of Peers of
the Act of Union. In the same year, however, a bill was Ireland in the same
introduced by Earl Grey with the object of making year.
a change in their position. It was proposed that their
number should be no longer limited to twenty-eight, but
should be not less than twenty-eight and not more than
thirty. It was also suggested each Peer having a right to
vote at the election of representatives should be empowered
to give three votes instead of one, and to give them all in
favour of a single candidate or to divide them amongst two
or three, as he might think fit.

A greater change was contemplated in relation to the And in re-
representative Peers of Scotland. It was proposed that lation to the repre-
instead of sitting only during one Parliament, they should be sentative
elected, like the representative Peers of Ireland, for life; and Peers of Scotland.
that their number should not be restricted to sixteen, but
should be not less than sixteen and not more than eighteen.
Like the Irish Peers, the Scottish Peers were to be allowed
three votes at an election of representatives, and either to
give them all for a single candidate or to divide them [2].

When, however, the second reading of the bill was moved, The pro-
an amendment was carried to the effect that the subject posals not carried.
in general should be referred to a select committee [3]. The
committee was duly appointed, and a report [4] was received
from it, but no further action was taken, and the law concerning the representative Peers of Scotland and Ireland
remains unchanged.

[1] The Irish Church Act, 1869, sec. 13.
[2] H. L., No. 50. Ordered to be printed, April 9, 1869.
[3] Hansard's Debates, third series, vol. cxcv, 1677–1694.
[4] H. L., No. 112, June 3, 1869.

CHAPTER XV.

PART III.

RAPID INCREASE IN THE NUMBER OF PEERS: MODERN ATTEMPTS
TO EXCLUDE THE BISHOPS: PEERAGES FOR LIFE: CONCLUSION.

CHAP. XV.

The number of Temporal Lords at the accession of George I.

Continual increase in the number of Peers: the Reform Bills of 1831.

WHEN George I came to the throne the number of Temporal Lords had already risen to 194, of whom sixteen were the Representative Peers of Scotland. There were thus 178 Peers having hereditary seats in the House of Lords, of whom twenty were minors [1].

From this time forward the process of creating new hereditary peerages has continued, as well as the natural process of extinction ; but, since the accession of George III, the growth of new Peers has far exceeded the disappearance of ancient titles, and has almost kept pace with the rise in the population of the British Islands. Ministry after ministry, whatever its politics, has rewarded its followers with honours, and the creation of the new dignities more and more rapidly outstrips the decay of the old. At the coronation of George IV, and again at the coronation of William IV, there was a large simultaneous creation of new Peers. The dignities conferred by William IV may have had some relation to the struggle over the Reform Bills of 1831 ; and there seemed at one time a probability that this mode of coercing the Lords would be applied on a far greater scale. As explained, however, elsewhere, the difficulty was overcome in another way, and the development of the peerage went on, in even tenour, as before.

[1] List of the Lords Spiritual and Temporal, &c. Printed 1715.

The feelings evoked by the Reform Bills of 1831-2 were
not immediately reduced to an absolute calm, and shortly Abortive
afterwards (in 1834) found vent in a project to exclude the projects to
Bishops, once again, from the House of Lords. The House theBishops
of Commons, nevertheless, refused even leave to bring in from the
House,
a Bill 'for relieving the Archbishops and Bishops of the 1834-37.
Established Church from their legislative and judicial
duties in the House of Peers[1].' The attempt was made
again in different forms in 1836 and 1837, but on each
occasion the Commons negatived, by very large majorities,
the proposed resolutions which reflected on the position
of the Bishops among the Temporal Lords in the Upper
House[2].

Nearly twenty years elapsed before there was any further The question as to
agitation of a serious kind with regard to the constituent peerages
parts of the House of Lords. A question was then raised for life: an
historical
which led to a remarkable controversy in the House of retrospect
Lords itself. It was the cause of much learned argument, necessary.
and of a careful search for ancient precedents. For its due
comprehension a short historical retrospect is necessary.

The power of the Crown to create a subject a Peer for
life has sometimes been contested, sometimes very warmly
supported. It is, however, needless to carry the investigation
further back than the time at which the expression Peer
of the Realm first came into use.

Robert de Vere, Earl of Oxford, was in the reign of Robert de
Vere, when
Richard II created Marquess of Dublin for life[3]. Though, made
however, he acquired a new dignity for life only, he was Marquess
of Dublin
not thus made a Peer, because he was already a Peer when and Duke
he was made a Marquess. Moreover, this creation was not of Ireland,
for life, in
by the King alone, but with the assent of the Lords and the reign of
Commons in Parliament. He shortly afterwards surren- Richard II,
wasalready
dered his patent of creation as a Marquess, and was then a Peer.

---

[1] *Journals of the House of Commons*, March 13, 1834 (vol. lxxxix.
p. 120).

[2] *Ib.*, April 26, 1836 (vol. xci. p. 293), and Feb. 16, 1837 (vol. xcii.
p. 57).

[3] *Rot. Parl.*, 9 Ric. II, no. 17 (printed, vol. iii. p. 209).

CHAP. XV. created Duke of Ireland by a charter which did not confer any rights of inheritance[1]. This again did not make him a peer for life; it gave only an addition to the Earldom of Oxford which he already enjoyed. It did not in any way affect the claim of his heirs to be Peers as Earls of Oxford. It was only a promotion made by the King, to which the Lords and Commons in Parliament assented.

Edward, son of Edmund Duke of York, created Earl for the term of his father's life

Edward, son of Edmund Duke of York, was in the same reign created Earl of Rutland, not for his own life, but for the life of his father. This also was with the assent of the Lords and Commons in Parliament[2]. The case does not seem to have any relation to life-peerages in the ordinary acceptation of the term.

Promotion of Peers in the reign of Richard II.

Eight years afterwards (in the twenty-first year of the reign of Richard II) there were several promotions in the peerage, which though not for life only, have nevertheless an important bearing on the subject of peerages for life. Thomas Holland, Earl of Kent, was created Duke of Surrey; John Holland, Earl of Huntingdon, was created Duke of Exeter; Edward, Earl of Rutland, was created Duke of Albemarle; John Beaufort, Earl of Somerset, was created Marquess of Dorset; and Thomas, Lord le Despenser, was created Earl of Gloucester. All these creations took effect on Michaelmas Day, when the King sat in Parliament, wearing his crown, and holding his sceptre. The charters of creation had been already drawn out and were read in Parliament; and there the ceremony of investiture was solemnly performed. In each case the newly-made Dukes, Marquess, and Earl were to hold their dignities to themselves and the heirs male of their bodies[3]. In none of these cases was there any new Peer created.

[1] *Rot. Chart.*, 10 Ric. II, no. 2 (printed in *Rep. Dig. Peer*, vol. v. p. 79).

[2] *Rot. Parl.*, 13 Ric. II, no. 23 (printed, vol. iii. p. 364); *Rot. Chart.*, 13 Ric. II, no. 5 (printed in *Rep. Dig. Peer*, vol. v. p. 85).

[3] *Rot. Parl.*, 21 Ric. II, no. 35 (printed, vol. iii. p. 355); *Rot. Chart.*, 21 Ric. II, nos. 21, 23. The charter to Beaufort appears on the roll to have been vacated, but the creation in Parliament seems nevertheless to have been considered operative.

When Henry IV ascended the throne, two years later, Chap. XV. all these recently-promoted Peers were degraded to their previous rank, but not deprived of their peerage. A judge- Degrada-ment to this effect was pronounced in Parliament by the same Peers Chief Justice of the Court of Common Pleas as being that in the reign of of the Lords in Parliament with the assent of the King. Henry IV. It was to affect both the persons named and their heirs[1].

The inference from these events is that a promotion in Promo-the peerage was not held to be subject to the same rules as peerage the creation of a new peerage. It gave precedence among not subject to the same Peers, but nothing more. The Crown seems to have rules as claimed the right to give precedence, as one of its pre- new crea-rogatives, but not, perhaps, without limitation. This, too, Peers. would be strictly in accordance with the old idea of the *Pares Curiae* or *Curtis*, or great feudal tenants of the Crown. They all equally owed service to the King's Court, and none could be judged in such a manner as to lose his fief except with the assent of his peers. They thus formed a class apart from the rest of the population, even though the King might, either with or without their assent, assign the position in which they were to sit. When they became Peers of the Realm, instead of *Pares Curtis*, their rank as Peers distinguished them from other subjects in the realm, 'and was independent of their relations one to another. A promotion in the peerage was, therefore, altogether different in nature from the creation of a Peer.

In the reign of Henry V, Thomas Beaufort, Earl of Case of Dorset, was created Duke of Exeter by the King sitting in Beaufort, Parliament, and straightway took his seat in the presence Duke of Exeter, in of the Lords Spiritual and Temporal, and of the Commons the reign of in Parliament assembled[2]. In the Letters Patent bearing Henry V. date the same day (November 18, 1416), the creation purports to be by the King alone, and for life only[3].

---

[1] *Rot. Parl.*, 1 Hen. IV, *Placita Coronae*, no. 9 (printed, vol. iii. pp. 451-452).

[2] *Ib.*, 4 Hen. V, no. 13 (printed, vol. iv. p. 96).

[3] *Rot. Lit. Pat.*, 4 Hen. V, m. 11 (printed in *Rep. Dig. Peer*, vol. v. p. 182).

CHAP. XV. A grant was nevertheless made, at the same time, at the request of the Commons, and with the assent of the Lords Spiritual and Temporal, of one thousand pounds per annum to the Duke and the heirs male of his body, for the better support of the dignity[1]. It seems, therefore, that it was in contemplation to give him more than an estate for life in his dukedom. In any case it will be observed that this is not an instance of a creation of a Peer for life, as Thomas de Beaufort was already a Peer and an Earl, and the loss of his dukedom would not have deprived him of his peerage.

Peeresses for life: these do not affect the constitution of the House of Lords.

In the reign of James I, Mary, Lady Compton. the mother of the King's favourite, George Villiers (successively Baron Whaddon, Viscount Villiers, Earl[2], Marquess, and Duke of Buckingham), was created Countess of Buckingham for her life[3]. This creation, however, did not and could not have any effect upon the constitution of the House of Lords. It was a mere compliment to the lady. The limitation for her life was a matter of necessity, because otherwise the Buckingham title would have descended to her eldest son John, afterwards Viscount Purbeck, and there would have been two Buckingham peerages possessed by two brothers.

There are several other instances of the creation of Peeresses for life only, in the higher grades of the peerage; but, until quite recently, there had been only one creation of a Baroness for life, that of Baroness Belasyse in 1674. None of these cases, however, are of much importance in the history of the House of Lords, because neither the Peeress for life only, nor her issue, as her heir, could have any seat in the House.

Contradictory state-

Sir Edward Coke is sometimes cited as an authority to

[1] *Rot. Lit. Pat.*, 4 Hen. V, m. 13 (printed, pp. 182–183).
[2] This fact is stated somewhat differently by the Earl of Clarendon in his *History of the Rebellion* : 'though she was married to a private gentleman, Sir Thomas Compton, she had been created Countess of Buckingham, shortly after her son had first assumed *that title*.'
[3] *Rot. Lit. Pat.*, 16 James I, part 11. no. 10.

prove the antiquity of peerages for life. His words, however,
do not altogether appear to warrant the meaning attributed
to them. If a baron 'be created by patent,' says Coke,
'he must of necessity have these words, his heirs or the
heirs males of his body, or the heirs of his body, or otherwise he hath no inheritance[1].' The interpretation, however,
is not that he has a peerage for life. Sir Edward Coke
himself tells us exactly the reverse. If a Baron 'be created
by Letters Patents the state of inheritance must be limited
by apt words, *or else the grant is void*[2].' There may be
nobility 'for term of life, by act in law, without any
actual creation; as, if a Duke take a wife, by the inter-
marriage she is a Duchess, and so of a Marquess, an Earl,
and the rest[3].' This again would, of course, not in any way
affect the constitution of the House of Lords.

In another passage, however, Coke does say that 'as
an estate for life may be gained by marriage, so may
the King create either man or woman noble for life, but
not for years, because then it might go to executors or
administrators[4].' He bases this statement solely on one
of his own reports[5], but the report does not seem to be
a sufficient ground for so wide a generalization. The case
which he cites is one having relation not to peerages
generally but to offices, and in particular to the office of
Marshal of the Marshalsea. The point which was determined
was that the grant of the office for a term of years was void.
It was said, *obiter*, by way of illustration, that in ancient
times an Earl had the custody of 'a county and was called
Shire Reeve, and that afterwards this custody was transferred to the Sheriff, who was the Earl's deputy. 'But,
as the King cannot grant to one that he and his executors
or administrators shall be Counts or Earls for years (for
then his executors or administrators, one being appointed
by himself, the other by the Ordinary, would be Earls),
so, without question the King may create an Earl for life,
in tail, or in fee.'

[1] *Co. Litt.*, 9 b.   [2] *Ib.*, 16 b.   [3] *Ib.*
[4] *Ib.*   [5] 9 Rep. 97-98 (Reynel's case).

CHAP. XV.   This remark, not made in any case having relation to

It had no the peerage, made in a case having relation solely to
relation to offices, and made in illustration of the estate which could
Peers in
general, be acquired in an office, has been quoted again and again
but only to to show that the Crown has the power to create a peerage
Earls in an
official of any kind for life. The citation of the same case, genera-
capacity. tion after generation, has produced the appearance of
unanimous belief among the legal authorities who have
cited it during two centuries and a half. The opinions
founded upon it, however, cannot be of greater weight
than the report itself, and in the report there is practically
no decision at all upon the general question of life
peerages.

As has been shown elsewhere, an earldom was, in its
origin, an administrative, legal, and military office, which
only became strictly hereditary by degrees. The Judges
in Reynel's case brought into prominence the official
character of the early earldoms in order to use it in illustration of the points under consideration. They did not
say that the King could make any man a Peer of any rank
for his life alone, because he could not make a Marshal
of the Marshalsea for a term of years only, but they did
say that he could not make a Marshal of the Marshalsea
for a term of years, because he could not make other officers,
and among them Earls, for such a term. No point affecting
the peerage was touched in the report except that of the
earldoms in their official character, and even that point
was not discussed in relation to any particular earldom.
Since the time of the Conquest the Earls had commonly
been Barons, and the creation of an Earl, either for life
or otherwise, was not necessarily or even probably the
creation of a new Peer. The remark in Reynel's case had
thus no practical bearing on the question whether the
Crown could create a new Peer for the term of his life
alone.

Lords for When there is an express provision that a man having
life without
peerage. a grant of the name and title of Lord is to have no place
or voice in Parliament, it must be obvious that he has

no place in the history of the House of Lords. It is, Chap. XV.
therefore, unnecessary to say anything more of Lord
Hay, who was made a Lord of this kind in 1606 [1], or of
any similar case. They have practically no bearing upon
the power of the Crown to create a Peer for life only with
all the privileges of peerage.

Thus far all the supposed proofs of the creation of *No early instance of creation of a new peerage. for his life only, in the person of a man.* a life-peerage in the person of a man seem to fail. There
are, as we have seen, instances of promotions in the peerage
for life only. There are also many instances of the creation
of Peers for life, with remainders over to other persons and
their heirs [2]. These, however, are not true instances of the
creation of peerages for life, though the first holder, in
each case, enjoyed the peerage for his life only.

There is an important difference between the creation *Difference between creation of a Peer for life and creation of a peerage for life.* of a Peer for life and the creation of a life-peerage.
No one, whatever the form of creation, can enjoy his
peerage for a longer term than his life. If any one could
be created a Peer for his own life only, without any remainder, he would hold a life-peerage. If any one is
created a Peer for his own life with a remainder over,
though he becomes a Peer for life, the peerage is not a life-
peerage alone. An estate in the peerage vests in the
'remainder-man at the same time as in the Peer for life;
the remainder-man has a present interest in his future

[1] *Rot. Lit. Pat.*, 4 Jac. I, part 1. m. 36.

[2] Among these may be mentioned the creation in 1628 of Baptist
Hicks as Baron Hicks and Viscount Campden, for life, with remainder
to Edward, Baron Noel of Ridlington and the heirs male of his body
(*Rot. Lit. Pat.*, 4 Car. I, part 39. no. 7) ; that of Francis, Baron of Duns-
more, in 1644, as Earl of Chichester, for life, with remainders over (*Rot.
Lit. Pat.*, 20 Car. I, no. 12) ; that of Hugh, Duke of Northumberland,
in 1784, as Lord Lovaine, Baron of Alnwick, for life, with remainder to
a second son Algernon Percy, and the heirs male of his body (*Rot.
Lit. Pat.*, 24 Geo. III, part 4. no. 6) ; and that of George, Duke of
Montagu, in 1786, as Baron Montagu of Boughton, for life, with
remainder to the second and other sons of Elizabeth, Duchess of
Buccleuch, successively in tail male (*Rot. Lit. Pat.*, 26 Geo. III,
part 9. no. 18). The last creations, it will be observed, did not give
any new seat in the House of Lords until the remainders came into
operation.

CHAP. XV. peerage. The peerage differs from one in the more
ordinary form of creation only in the limitation affecting
the successors of the first holder. It is true that in such
cases the blood of the first holder is not ennobled, but it
will be found that where such cases have occurred the first
holder had no issue, or was already of noble blood and
acquired a new peerage, though nominally for his own life,
yet really, by force of the remainder, for some member
of his own family. Except in virtue of recent Statutes
there has, since the time when the expression ' Peer of the
Realm' first came into use, never, so far as is known, been
any creation for life alone, which has conferred a new
seat in the House of Lords.

Attempt to give a life-peerage only to Sir James Parke, as Baron Wensley-dale, in 1856.
The subject of life-peerages was never brought into
prominence and never underwent serious discussion before
the year 1856. It was at that time thought expedient to
strengthen the House of Lords in the judicial capacity,
and it was apparently believed that for this object Peers
might be created for life only. It was supposed that
the House might thus have valuable aid from men
whose means would be insufficient to support the dignity
of an hereditary peerage. Under the advice, as it would
seem, of Lord Cranworth, who was then Lord Chancellor,
Her Majesty directed the issue of Letters Patent purporting
to create Sir James Parke (who had been one of the Barons
of the Exchequer) Baron Wensleydale and a Peer ' for and
during the term of his natural life.'

Proceed-ings of the Lords : Resolution that the grantee could not sit and vote in Parlia-ment.
The Patent bore date January 16. On the following
February 7 there was a long debate in the House of Lords ;
and on the motion of Lord Lyndhurst, an ex-chancellor,
the Letters Patent were referred to the Committee for
Privileges by a majority of thirty-three. There was a long
discussion in the Committee for Privileges on February 12,
a further debate in the House on the same day, and
another discussion in the Committee for Privileges on
February 18. On February 22 a motion was made, in
the House, that the question should be referred to the
Judges, and this, after debate, was negatived. On the

same day Lord Lyndhurst moved, in the Committee for Privileges, a resolution 'that neither the said Letters Patent, nor the said Letters Patent with the usual writ of summons, enable the grantee to sit and vote in Parliament.' On a vote being taken there were Content ninety-two, Non-content fifty-seven, or a majority of thirty-five in favour of the motion. When the report of the Committee for Privileges was brought up on February 25, Lord Granville intimated that the Government would not oppose its confirmation. It was then 'resolved and adjudged by the Lords Spiritual and Temporal in Parliament assembled' in accordance with the terms of the report.

Although, however, there was no opposition on the part of the Government, there were several protests. They were in three different forms. The first was signed by Baron Cranworth, Baron Sundridge (the Duke of Argyle), Earl Granville, Baron Stanley of Alderley, the Marquess of Lansdowne, the Earl of Harrowby, Baron Panmure, Baron Glenelg, the Marquess of Breadalbane, and Viscount Sydney. The grounds of their dissent were, among others, that 'according to the uniform opinions of the highest legal authorities, for above two centuries and a half, the Crown has the prerogative of creating a Peer for life,' and that 'the creation of a peerage for life with a limitation in the patent to collateral relatives has been common even in modern times, and no such patent would have been valid if the prerogative contended for did not exist.'
Protest by dissentient Lords.

Except the Chancellor, none of the dissentient Peers, however eminent in other ways, were specially qualified to pronounce an authoritative opinion on the technical matters set forth in their protest. The Chancellor, having advised the grant of the Letters Patent, was bound to support it. Earl Granville and other supporters of the Government naturally took the same side.

Another protest was made by Earl Grey and the Earl of Devon partly on the same grounds as that of the Peers already mentioned, but partly on others, and more in detail.
Second protest.

CHAP. XV.   A third protest of great length was signed by Baron

Third   Monteagle of Brandon, Baron Glenelg, who had signed
protest,   the first protest, and the Earl of Devon who had signed
partly on
the ground   the second. This concluded with the final reason that
that the   the adoption of the report was dangerous as a precedent
Judges had
not been   'when it is considered that a motion has been made and
asked to   rejected requiring the attendance of the learned Judges
advise.
with the view of obtaining their opinion on the legal
import and just construction of the Letters Patent of the
Crown laid before the House, and referred to the Committee
for Privileges.'

This last was, perhaps, the best point made in any of
the protests. The Judges had without doubt been called in
on previous occasions when legal questions were involved—
and that long after the Judges had ceased to sit with the
King in his Council in his Parliament. The weak side
of the argument was that the Lords had not always
accepted the opinion of the Judges when given, and were
under no obligation either to ask it or to take it. In the
present instance, as the Lord Chancellor took one view,
and an ex-Lord Chancellor the opposite view, it is not
very probable that the Judges would have been in absolute
agreement, or that the House would have felt itself bound
by their decision even if unanimous.

Hereditary   For a short time Baron Wensleydale was in the position
peerage in
the end   of a Baron without a seat or a voice in Parliament, It was
given to   not denied that the Crown might confer upon a subject the
Lord Wens-
leydale.   title of Baron for his life, but it was not admitted that the
Crown could in this manner give him a place in the House
of Lords. The Lords had long taken all questions of their
own privileges into their own hands, and they regarded this
as a question of privilege. A few months later, however,
(July 23, 1856), 'Baron Wensleydale of Wensleydale in
the North Riding of the County of York,' for life, was ·
created by new Letters Patent 'Baron Wensleydale of
Walton in the County Palatine of Lancaster, unto him and
the heirs male of his body lawfully begotten and to be
begotten.' Having then acquired an hereditary peerage,

he was duly summoned to Parliament, and took his seat CHAP. XV. in the House of Lords[1].

Thus ended an important contest—whether rightly or wrongly it might, perhaps, be presumptuous to say, when the two great legal authorities engaged in the fray took different sides. The House of Lords, however, was at least theoretically competent to give a final decision, and the readers of these pages will have seen on what very strong reasons their judgement might have rested if the question was a question of privilege, and if it was to be determined by precedents subsequent to the time when the expression 'Peer of the Realm' first came into use.

Notwithstanding this decision, it was felt that, if the House of Lords was to retain its appellate jurisdiction, there was a need of skilled members, and that the most competent persons might not be able to make sufficient provision for the support of an hereditary dignity. A Bill was shortly afterwards introduced into the House of Lords, on the recommendation of a committee, in which it was proposed to give the Crown the power of conferring peerages for life upon two persons who had served for five years as Judges. They were to sit with the Lord Chancellor as Judges of Appeal and to be Deputy-Speakers. The project, however, though it passed a second reading, ultimately miscarried in the House of Commons[2]. *A subsequent life-peerage Bill miscarries.*

The question of life-peerages was now allowed to slumber for thirteen years. In 1869, however, Earl Russell again agitated the subject. He introduced into the House of Lords a Bill of far wider scope than that of 1856. The resolution of the House that Sir James Parke when created a Baron of the United Kingdom for life was not entitled to *Earl Russell's Bill for the creation of life-peerages in 1869.*

[1] The various documents, debates, and discussions relating to the Wensleydale Peerage are conveniently brought together in the '*Discussion and Judgement of the Lords on the Life Peerage Question.* Reports by John Fraser Macqueen. Under Appointment of the House.'

[2] Hansard's *Debates*, 3rd series, vol. cxlii. 780–797, 899–921, 1059–1084 ; vol. cxliii. 407–433, 568–613.

CHAP. XV. sit and vote in Parliament was recited in the preamble, in
which also it was declared to be 'expedient that Peers
created for life should, in limited number, and under
certain conditions, be entitled to sit and vote in the House
of Lords.' It was proposed that Peers created for life by
the Sovereign should be entitled to receive writs of summons
as Peers of Parliament, to sit, and to vote, and should have all
the rights and privileges of Peers of Parliament, during their
respective lives. They were to be selected by the Crown
from Peers of Scotland or Ireland, from persons who had
sat as members of the House of Commons more than ten
years, from officers of the army and navy eminent for
distinguished services, from persons who were or had been
Lord Chancellor, Lord Chief Justice of the Queen's Bench
or Common Pleas, or Lord Chief Baron in England or
Ireland, or Lord Justice General in Scotland, from persons
who had been for two years and had ceased to be Judges
of the principal Courts of Common Law at Westminster or
in Ireland, the Court of Chancery in England or Ireland,
the Court of Session in Scotland, the Court of Probate and
Divorce, or the High Court of Admiralty in England, from
persons who had been Attorney-General for England or
Ireland, Lord Advocate for Scotland, or Queen's Advocate-
General for England. They might also be selected from
persons distinguished for their attainments in science,
literature, or art, and from persons who had served in any
public office under the Crown with ability and fidelity for
not less than five years. It was, however, to be provided
that no more than twenty-eight peerages of this character
were to be in existence at the same time, and that no more
than four were to be created in any one year [1].

The
scheme as
amended
by Lord
Cairns.
    The principle of the Bill was well supported, though
there was much opposition on points of detail. Lord Cairns
proposed to amend it, in Committee, in a manner which
was practically a reconstruction. For Earl Russell's clause
in the preamble he wished to substitute one to the effect

[1] H. L., no. 49. Ordered to be printed April 9, 1869.

that 'it is expedient to afford, under certain restrictions, CHAP. XV. facilities for the introduction into the House of Lords of persons distinguished in the services of the State, or who, from their attainments or official position, are likely to add weight to the deliberations of the House, and who may not be. desirous to undertake the burden of an hereditary peerage.' He desired also to strike out all the clauses relating to the special qualifications of the persons to be selected, as well as those relating to the limitations of number, and to substitute for them a provision that only one life peerage should be created in any one year except in favour of the Lord High Chancellor of Great Britain, a Principal Secretary of State, the President of the Council, Board of Trade, or Poor Law Board, the Postmaster-General, or the Chancellor of the Duchy of Lancaster[1]. Earl Russell held to his total of twenty-eight in all. and four in any one year, but abandoned his clauses relating to the classes of persons from which the selection was to be made, suggesting in their place a clause in the preamble as to creation of Peers 'on account of their eminent merits or distinguished services to their country[2].' The Earl of Carnarvon moved, in Committee, to insert a clause that whenever a Peer created for life should be entitled under the proposed Act to sit and vote in the House of Lords, the grounds upon which the peerage should be conferred upon him should be stated in the patent of creation[3]. Amendments were also moved in Committee by Earl Stanhope[4] and Lord Penzance[5], which were not accepted either wholly or in part.

When the Bill emerged from Committee and was reported The Bill to the House, it partook of the character of Lord Cairns's rejected. amendments quite as much as of Earl Russell's original draft. All the clauses relating to special qualifications were omitted, the number of life peerages to be created in any one year had been restricted to two, and Lord Cairns's alteration of the preamble had been adopted with the

[1] H. L., no. 49 a, May 5, 1869. [2] H. L., no. 49 b, May 5, 1869.
[3] H. L., no. 49 c, May 13, 1869. [4] H. L., no. 49 d, May 21, 1869.
[5] H. L., no. 49 e, June 1, 1869.

CHAP. XV. exception only of the words relating to 'the burden of an hereditary peerage.' Earl Russell's original limitation of the total number of life-peerages to twenty-eight still remained [1]. The Bill, however, failed to pass its third reading. The question whether this result was fortunate or unfortunate is one of politics, but the desire expressed in the amended preamble, to introduce into the House of Lords persons likely to add weight to the deliberations of the House, appears a happy adaptation of the ancient reason for a Parliamentary summons to modern life and modern ideas.

Proposal of 1870 to exclude future Bishops from the House.

The action taken in the House of Commons in 1870 with regard to the Bishops ought not, perhaps, to be looked upon too seriously; but it was, like the projects of 1834, 1836, and 1837, an unsuccessful attempt from below to alter the composition of the House of Lords. Leave was asked to bring in a bill 'to relieve' the Lords Spiritual, who might in future be consecrated, from attendance in Parliament. The effect of such an Act would, of course, have been to remove the whole of the Spiritual Lords from the House by degrees, though no Bishop already consecrated would have been affected by it. Leave, however, was refused by a majority of fifty-six [2].

'Lords of Appeal in Ordinary' madeLords of Parliament during tenure of office, in 1876.

In 1876 another and more successful attempt was made in the Upper House to introduce Temporal Lords of Parliament without hereditary peerages. It was, however, on a very limited scale, and was intended, like those of 1856, solely for the purpose of adding to the judicial strength of the House. Power was given by Statute to the Crown to appoint two 'Lords of Appeal in Ordinary,' with further power to appoint a third Lord of Appeal in Ordinary upon the death or resignation of two paid Judges of the Judicial Committee of the Privy Council, and a fourth upon the death or resignation of the two remaining paid

[1] Bill as amended in Committee, H. L. 113. Ordered to be printed June 3, 1869.
[2] *Journals of the House of Commons*, June 21, 1870 (vol. cxxv. p. 169).

Judges. These Lords of Appeal in Ordinary were to hold CHAP. XV. office during good behaviour, but might be removed on the address of both Houses of Parliament. They were entitled to rank as Barons during their lives. They were entitled also to a writ of summons to attend, and to sit and vote in the House of Lords so long as they continued in office, but no longer, and their dignity as Lords of Parliament was not to descend to their heirs[1]. By these provisions an old principle was recognized, and a new principle introduced. The principle that the holder of a barony for life only (as in the case of Lord Hay) enjoyed the rank of Baron, and not the right of sitting and voting in Parliament, was, as it were, reasserted. The introduction of Lords with a right to be summoned, and to sit, and vote, not even for life, but only during the tenure of office, was quite new as applied to laymen, or was, at any rate, without precedent since the days of the earlier Chancellors.

This small innovation, designed for one particular legal The Earl of end, did not satisfy those who considered that a greater Rosebery's Motion change in the constitution of the House had become touching necessary. On June 20, 1884, Lord Rosebery moved, 'the efficiency' of 'that a Select Committee be appointed to consider the the House, best means of promoting the efficiency of this House.' in 1884. His Lordship argued that, as the House of Lords had existed about six centuries without reform, some alterations had become necessary in order to bring the institution into conformity with the changed institutions by which it was surrounded. He laid particular emphasis upon the development of the Colonial Empire and of the Newspaper Press, as well as upon the want of representation, in the House, of certain sections of the community. After a debate of some length, in which the subject of life-peerages was discussed, the motion was negatived by a majority of thirty-nine[2].

In the meantime those Barons for life who were Lords Lords of of Parliament only during tenure of the office of Lord of Appeal in Ordinary

[1] Appellate Jurisdiction Act, 1876, secs. 6, 14.
[2] Hansard, *Parl. Deb.*, 3rd series, vol. cclxxxix. 937-974.

CHAP. XV.

made Lords of Parliament for life, in 1887.

Appeal, had continued to exist, but were shortly to assume a different position. In 1887 an Act was passed which enabled a retired Lord of Appeal to sit and vote as a member of the House of Lords during his life [1]. The Lords of Appeal in Ordinary in this way became Lords of Parliament for life, but for life only, and without any dignity descendible to their heirs.

The Earl of Rosebery's Motion touching the constitution of the House in 1888.

Thus, twenty-one years after the memorable struggle over the Wensleydale peerage, the creation of Lords of Parliament for life was sanctioned by Statute. As, however, it had reference but to a few 'Law Lords,' a motion was again made by Lord Rosebery on March 19, 1888, 'that a Select Committee be appointed to enquire into the constitution of this House [2].' He referred to various political events which had occurred since his previous motion, and again urged the necessity of some reform of the House of Lords. Lord Wemyss moved, as an amendment, that 'it is not a safe thing to place the constitution of this House in the power of a Committee, nor consistent with its dignity to discuss before a committee the reason for its existence ; and, if any changes in the constitution of this House are wanted, they should be debated and made by the House itself on the motion of the responsible Ministers of the Crown.' After a debate, in which the Marquess of Salisbury and Lord Kenry (the Earl of Dunraven) took part, the amendment was carried. As a substantive motion, however, it was set aside by means of the 'previous question.'

The Earl of Dunraven's scheme of 1888.

The year 1888 was fruitful of other schemes for the reconstruction of the House of Lords. A very remarkable bill was introduced by Lord Kenry (the Earl of Dunraven). The rights and privileges of existing Lords of Parliament, whether Spiritual or Temporal, were not to be affected. The election of Peers to serve in Parliament for Scotland and Ireland, and the rights of the Peers elected, were to remain as before. The Prince of Wales, Princes of the

---

[1] Appellate Jurisdiction Act, 1887, sec. 2.

[2] Hansard, *Parl. Deb.*, 3rd series, vol. cccxxiii. 1548–1606.

Blood Royal being Peers of the United Kingdom, the
Lord Chancellor of Great Britain, the Archbishops of
Canterbury and York, and the Bishops of London, Durham,
and Winchester, the Lords of Appeal in Ordinary, whether
holding office, or after resignation, and Peers holding or
having held high judicial office, were in future to receive their
writs of summons to Parliament as before ; but, in other
respects, the House was to be completely remodelled.
There were to be one hundred and eighty Lords of Parliament elected by the Temporal Peers of the United
Kingdom ; and the effect of this provision would have been
that the legislative functions of the hereditary peerage
of the United Kingdom would have been delegated by
degrees to a body selected from their own number. There
were to be in addition Peers for life, not exceeding five in
number, ten Peers either for life or for a limited term to
represent the Colonies, two to represent the interests of
Roman Catholic subjects, two to represent the interests
of subjects who might be Protestant Dissenters, and two
to represent the interests of ' science, letters, and sound
learning generally.' Every County Council was to have
the power of recommending one person to the sovereign
to be appointed a Lord of Parliament. All Lords of Parliament elected by the Temporal Peers, or appointed on
nomination by County Councils, were to hold office for
nine years only, but to be capable of re-appointment or re-
election. No Bishop elected or translated to any see but
those of Canterbury, York, London, Durham, and Winchester
was, on that ground, to become entitled to receive a writ
of summons to Parliament. The number of Spiritual
Lords would thus have been gradually reduced to five.

It was also provided that Peers might resign their seats
and votes in the House of Lords, and that past Lords of
Parliament and Peers not entitled to vote in the House of
Lords should be capable of sitting in the House of Commons.

One of the proposed provisions was a modification of
an amendment suggested by Lord Cairns to Earl Russell's
Bill of 1869. This was that the First Lord of the Treasury,

C c

CHAP. XV. any of Her Majesty's Principal Secretaries of State, the President of the Council, of the Board of Trade, and of the Local Government Board, the Lord Privy Seal, the First Lord of the Admiralty, the Postmaster-General, and the Chancellor of the Duchy of Lancaster might be heard in the House of Lords (though not otherwise entitled to a seat or voice), when any matter touching his office should be under debate. He was not, however, to be entitled to vote [1].

The Marquess of Salisbury's scheme of 1888.

This very elaborate scheme, which was not accepted by the House of Lords, was very shortly followed by another, introduced by the Marquess of Salisbury on behalf of the Government of the day. His bill was of a far more simple character. The Crown was to have power to appoint persons with certain qualifications to be 'Peers of Parliament' for life. The total number of such Peers in existence at any one time was not to exceed fifty. No one was to be qualified for appointment unless he had been a Judge of a Superior Court in the United Kingdom for at least two years, had attained the rank of rear-admiral in the navy or major-general in the army, had been ambassador extraordinary and minister plenipotentiary, had become a privy councillor and been employed in the civil service of the Crown, or had been not less than five years Governor-General or Governor in any colony, or Lieutenant-Governor in India. No more than three persons so qualified were to be appointed in any one year. The Crown, however, was to have further power to appoint Peers for life on account of other special qualifications, but not more than two in any one year, nor any until the Sovereign had stated by message to the House of Lords the intention to appoint and the special qualifications for which the appointment was to be made [2]. This Bill passed a second reading in the Upper House, but was then immediately withdrawn [3].

---

[1] House of Lords (Constitution) Bill, 1888 (no. 51). Ordered to be printed March 23, 1888.

[2] House of Lords (Life Peers) Bill, 1888 (no. 161). Ordered to be printed June 18, 1888.

[3] Hansard's *Debates*, 3rd series, vol. cccxxviii. 471.

Thus, although various propositions have been made by CHAP. XV.
Peers of widely divergent political views, there have been
no changes in the principles which govern the composition The classes
of the House of Lords, since the Lords of Appeal in of which
Ordinary were made Lords of Parliament for life in 1887. of Lords
From that time the House has consisted of the following sists.
classes of members :—(1) the Lords Temporal holding hereditary peerages in virtue of the creation of a peerage of
England before the Union with Scotland, or of a peerage
of Great Britain after that Union and before the Union
with Ireland, or of a peerage of the United Kingdom at
a later date; (2) the sixteen representative Peers of
Scotland elected and sitting only during the term of each
particular Parliament; (3) the twenty-eight representative
Peers of Ireland, elected and sitting for their respective
lives; (4) those who are or have been ' Lords of Appeal in
Ordinary,' and are Lords of Parliament for life; (5) the
Lords Spiritual, or Archbishops and Bishops of English
sees, having seats in virtue of their respective provinces or
dioceses, or in virtue of their seniority over other Bishops
who are not entitled to be summoned.

When these pages were written the total number of The num-
Lords on the roll was 567 [1], there being one vacancy in class.
the representation of the Peers of Ireland. Of these,
sixteen were representative Peers of Scotland, twenty-seven
representative Peers of Ireland, four Lords of Appeal in
Ordinary, one retired Lord of Appeal in Ordinary, and
twenty-six Lords Spiritual, of whom two were the Archbishops of Canterbury and York, and the remaining twenty-
four were Bishops. The rest, 493 in number, were holders
of hereditary peerages, of whom a few only were minors and

---

[1] Roll of the Lords Spiritual and Temporal in the second session
of the twenty-fifth Parliament of the United Kingdom of Great Britain
and Ireland. Ordered to be printed Feb. 3, 1893. Since the above
was written the roll for the third session of the same Parliament
(ordered to be printed March 15, 1894) has appeared. It differs
slightly from its predecessor, but not in a manner to raise any new
question of principle.

CHAP. XV. disqualified for sitting ; and they thus outnumbered all the other classes in the proportion of nearly seven to one.

Conclusion : changes in the meaning of constitutional terms, and in particular of Parliament.

It would be difficult to find a better illustration than is afforded by the House of Lords of the transformations effected by time, on the one hand, and of the persistence, on the other hand, with which old names are used to designate changed institutions.   Trial by Jury, Parliament, the House of Lords, and the House of Commons have all lost the character which they had when the respective terms were first used to describe them.   Our English constitution was never in a condition of absolute stability, was hardly ever in any one century precisely what it had been in the century before.   The jury, of which in early times the chief qualification was that it should be acquainted with the facts before it came into Court, that it should consist of neighbours who knew the affairs of the neighbourhood, is now supposed to try an issue, without bias or prejudice, by evidence admitted only according to strict legal rules.   The Parliament which was at first only a meeting called by the Sovereign to discuss affairs of State, and varying in its constituent parts according to the subjects of discussion, is now in theory composed of the Sovereign, the Lords Spiritual, the Lords Temporal, and the representatives of the Commons.   At one time the word Parliament was often used in the sense of the Lords Spiritual and Temporal, or House of Lords with the Council.   At the end of the nineteenth century it is often used in current literature, in the sense of the House of Commons alone.   The House of Commons itself but little resembles that assembly of knights, citizens, and burgesses, which once represented persons of substance, and consented on their behalf to give the King a portion of their goods.   The House of Lords, however, is, perhaps, changed most of all.

Changes in the constitutional position of the Peers.

For some centuries the Lords were the pillars of the State in many senses of the term.   They not only put the greater part of the King's armies into the field, but also contributed largely to the revenue of the kingdom, both in

peace and in war. If laymen, they were the King's
generals, assisting him with their advice, and offering
their lives and the lives of their followers in his cause.
When foreign war was projected, their counsel was necessary in relation both to the plan of campaign and to the
means of carrying it on. When civil war broke out, the
King's reliance was on those tenants in chief who elected to
remain faithful to him ; and no rebellion could be successful
unless the rebellious tenants proved to be the stronger
party.

The members of the House of Lords, whether spiritual
or temporal, have now no longer any special burdens.
They are under no obligation to support an army, except
as tax-payers like any other subjects. They are not, as
Peers, necessarily able to put forces into the field in times
of emergency. As counsellors their occupation is gone, in
practice if not in theory, except when they may happen,
with commoners, to be members of the Privy Council or of
the Cabinet. They are not even consulted as a body when
the Sovereign is about to travel out of the realm ; and
many of their privileges are lost, simply as being no longer
possible in an altered state of society and law.

Yet, if two great events be left out of consideration—the Yet the
loss of the seats of the Abbots when the greater monasteries House of
Lords is
were dissolved, and the abolition of military tenure as the result
a consequence of the Great Rebellion—the House of Lords of a natu-
ral process
has become what it is by a gradual and natural process of of develop-
ment.
development.

It has lived the life of the nation, and grown with the Its ranks
nation's growth. It has, in the main, reflected the nation's have been
recruited
thoughts and manners, as additions have been made to its from repre-
numbers. If the descendants of some of the mistresses of sentative
men.
Charles II represent the profligacy of the Restoration, and
if the descendants of some Peers created since that time
represent political intrigues rather than the strictest political
integrity, it is because public opinion has not always been
cast in a puritanical mould, and because the nation has not
always been discriminating in its worship of heroes. The

Chap. XV. higher and nobler life of the nation, or that which the
nation has believed to be its higher and nobler life, has also
left a mark, and a clearer mark, upon the Upper House of
Parliament. The leaders of its armies and of its fleets,
who made its name respected in the world, and shed their
blood to build up its empire, have sat there and handed
down their seats to their posterity. The men whose
commercial genius contributed to render the nation the
richest in the world have been honoured in the same
manner as its great military and naval commanders—and
in recent times without distinction of party or creed. The
sages of the law, more irreproachable, as a body, than those
of any other land, have had their learning and their wisdom
recognized in the persons of those who were believed to be
most worthy.

The
national
habits
have
commonly
been re-
flected in
new crea-
tions of
Peers.

In one respect the House of Lords fails, and has always
failed, to reflect the powers of the nation. The new men
who have made their way into it have always been rather
the men of action than the men of thought. The inventors
and thinkers, who should, perhaps, be Britain's greatest
pride, and who have changed the face of the whole earth,
and the tone of all civilized thought, have never been
placed on the Roll of the Lords. No Newton, no
Hunter. no Arkwright, no Watts, no Stephenson is there.
Very few years have elapsed since a historian was, for
the first time, created a Peer; and he was a partisan.
Still fewer years have elapsed since a poet, as poet, was so
honoured for the first time. No painter, or sculptor, ever
gained a coronet. Yet even here the national habits are
faithfully reflected. The inventor and the thinker are
rarely appreciated by their contemporaries; and the man
of letters wins only in a later generation those spurs which
are never to be hacked off. The robes of the judge, the
wealth of the financier, the pomp and circumstance which
attend the victorious general strike more deeply into the
popular imagination than the untiring industry, the silent
meditation, and the unseen flash of intellect, which bring
into being things that the world has never seen before.

Thus, even in its defects, the House of Lords has, since
it ceased to be a house of feudal Peers, been a not unfaith-
ful mirror of the country—not, indeed, of all the country's
fleeting moods, but of the country's matured decisions and
accomplished deeds. It has always had, and, from the
nature of its composition, must have a deep-seated reverence
for the ages that have passed away, and a sympathy no less
deep with the men who constituted it in earlier generations.
Its roll is a register in brief of some things that Englishmen
would fain forget, of many things that every British subject
may be proud to remember. It links the history that has
been made with the history that is still in the making ; and
when matters of great moment are laid before it, the vote
which it records may be regarded not only as the opinion
of a particular body of living men, but also as the sentence
which is given upon the Present by the Past.

INDEX

D d

Oxford

HORACE HART, PRINTER TO THE UNIVERSITY

MACMILLAN & CO.'S HISTORICAL BOOKS.

By E. A. FREEMAN.

The Methods of Historical Study. Eight Lectures read in the University of Oxford in Michaelmas Term, 1884; with the Inaugural Lecture on the Office of the Historical Professor. 8vo, 10s. 6d.

Comparative Politics. Six Lectures read before the Royal Institution in January and February, 1873. With 'The Unity of History,' the Rede Lecture read before the University of Cambridge, May 29, 1872. 8vo, 14s.

Historical Essays. Fourth Edition. 8vo, 10s. 6d.

Historical Essays. Second Series. Third Edition. 8vo, 10s. 6d.

Historical Essays. Third Series. 8vo, 12s.

Historical Essays. Fourth Series. 8vo, 12s. 6d.

The Chief Periods of European History. Six Lectures read in the University of Oxford in Trinity Term, 1885; with an Essay on Greek Cities under Roman Rule. 8vo, 10s. 6d.

General Sketch of European History. Second Edition. Pot 8vo, 3s. 6d.   [*Historical Course for Schools.*

History of Europe. With Maps. Pot 8vo, 1s. [*History Primers.*

Four Oxford Lectures, 1887. Fifty Years of European History. Teutonic Conquest in Gaul and Britain. 8vo, 5s.

The Growth of the English Constitution from the Earliest Times. Fourth Edition. Crown 8vo, 5s.

Old English History for Children. With Maps. Globe 8vo, 6s.

English Towns and Districts. A Series of Addresses and Sketches. With Illustrations and Maps. 8vo, 14s.

Greater Greece and Greater Britain, and George Washington, the Expander of England. Two Lectures. With an Appendix. Crown 8vo, 3s. 6d.

History of Federal Government in Greece and Italy. With a General Introduction. Second Edition. Edited by J. B. BURY, M.A., Fellow of Trinity College, Dublin. Extra crown 8vo, 12s. 6d.

Sketches from the Subject and Neighbour Lands of Venice. With Illustrations. Crown 8vo, 10s. 6d.

History of the Cathedral Church of Wells, as illustrating the Cathedral Churches of the Old Foundation. Globe 8vo, 3s. 6d.

Macmillan & Co., London.

MACMILLAN & CO.'S HISTORICAL BOOKS.

By J. R. GREEN.

A Short History of the English People. By J. R. GREEN, M.A. With Maps and Tables. Crown 8vo, 8s. 6d.

A Short History of the English People. Illustrated Edition. Edited by Mrs. J. R. GREEN and Miss KATE NORGATE. In four vols. Super royal 8vo, 12s. net each vol.

History of the English People.

Vol. I. Early England—Foreign Kings—The Charter—The Parliament. With eight Maps. 16s.   '

Vol. II. The Monarchy, 1461-1540—The Reformation, 1540-1603. 8vo, 16s.

Vol. III. Puritan England, 1603-1660—The Revolution, 1660-1688. With four Maps. 8vo, 16s.

Vol. IV. The Revolution, 1683-1760—Modern England, 1760-1815. 8vo, 16s.

The Making of England. With Map. Third Edition. 8vo, 16s.

The Conquest of England. With Portrait and Maps. 8vo, 18s.

Readings from English History. Selected and Edited by JOHN RICHARD GREEN.

Part I. From Hengist to Cressy. Globe 8vo, 1s. 6d.
Part II. From Cressy to Cromwell. Globe 8vo, 1s. 6d.
Part III. From Cromwell to Balaklava. Globe 8vo, 1s. 6d.

By MRS. J. R. GREEN.

Town Life in the Fifteenth Century. By Mrs. J. R. GREEN. Two vols., 8vo, 32s.

By MISS KATE NORGATE.

England Under the Angevin Kings. By KATE NORGATE. In two vols. With Maps and Plans. 8vo, 32s.

Macmillan & Co., London.

www.ingramcontent.com/pod-product-compliance
Lightning Source LLC
Chambersburg PA
CBHW030941110726
47900CB00004B/1073